just for now

just for now

escape to new zealand book three

ROSALIND JAMES

ISBN: 0988761920
ISBN 13: 9780988761926

author's note

The Blues and the All Blacks are actual rugby teams. I have attempted to depict the illustrious history of the All Blacks in an accurate manner. Sadly, however, the characters in this book exist only in my own mind, and are not intended to resemble or represent any actual individuals, living or dead.

table of contents

new zealand map

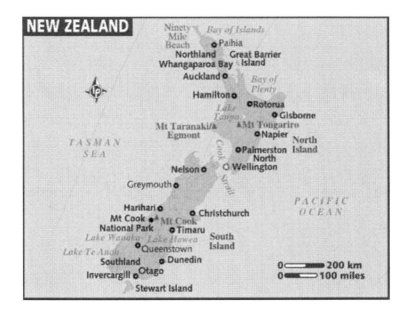

A New Zealand glossary appears at the end of this book.

prologue

♡

Well, that had been a waste of an hour.

Jenna switched her car off in the underground garage, then reached into the back seat to pull out the large messenger bag holding her student files. If she'd seen Richard's text before setting out, she'd have realized the meeting had been canceled and could have saved herself the trip. Oh, well. It was still only seven forty-five. Plenty of time to bake some cookies to take into the teachers' lounge tomorrow.

By the time she entered the black-and-white-tiled foyer of the modern flat overlooking Wellington Harbour, she had added a bread pudding to the list. That would give her a jump on tomorrow night's dinner. Jeremy wouldn't eat it, of course. He was watching his diet more carefully than ever these days, and spending more time in the gym, too. But it was one of her own favorites. And it was just bread, eggs, and milk, right? That was healthy, surely.

"I'm home!" she called. That was odd. Jeremy hadn't said he was going out. She dumped her purse and bag and made her way to the back of the flat. Maybe he'd gone to bed early. He'd seemed a little quiet earlier that evening, and she'd wondered if he were under the weather.

She got as far as the bedroom doorway. And froze. She saw the two figures on the bed, but her mind refused to acknowledge the truth of the scene unfolding so clearly before her. She stood rigid, mouth half-open in shock. Until Jeremy looked up and froze himself.

"Jenna. What…why are you home?" He scrambled to his feet, grabbed a shirt from the floor and held it pathetically, ridiculously, in front of himself.

Jenna held her hands out in front of her, backed away. "Sorry. Sorry. I'm just…I'll…I'm going."

She ran down the hall, back to the foyer. Grabbed up her bags again, looked around wildly for her keys. Why weren't they on the hook? She needed her keys. She needed to leave.

Jeremy hurried down the hall towards her. He'd managed to pull his pants on, was struggling to zip them as he ran. "Wait, Jenna. I can explain. Hang on."

Her keys were in her hand, she realized through her fog of panic. Purse. Bag. Keys. Out the door. She stood in the passage, punching the button for the lift. Jeremy was there with her now, still barechested, reaching for her arm.

"Don't leave. We need to talk about this. Jenna, come on. You must have known."

She stared at him. "No. No."

Finally, blessedly, the *ding* that announced the arriving lift. And the brushed steel doors sliding smoothly open, letting her in. Letting her escape.

the dog lover

♡

Twenty *months later*

"I like your dog."

Jenna looked down at the little boy, short blond hair rising in a comical double cowlick, blue eyes bright behind steel-framed glasses, who had come up to join her. "He's nice, isn't he?" she agreed. "Do you want to throw the ball for him?"

"Yeh," he breathed. "Will he chase it?"

"That's his very favorite thing," she assured him. "Oscar! Come!" The Golden Retriever bounded over from where he'd been distracted by a friendly Labrador.

"Sit," she told Oscar firmly, before handing the ball to the boy. "Here you go. It's a little slobbery. But if you don't mind that, give it a throw."

The boy laughed with delight as the dog twisted to catch the ball in mid-air, then bounded back with it, dropping it at his feet.

"Throw it again, if you like," Jenna urged. "He'll do it over and over. He loves it."

"That's because he's a retriever," the boy told her knowledgeably as he gave the ball another awkward toss. "That's his job."

"You're right. You know about dogs, huh? Do you have one yourself?"

"Nah," he said sadly. "Dad says Nyree has enough to do. And he says I'm not old enough to be responsible. I *am,* though. I'd be very responsible."

"So you're just here looking at the dogs today?"

He nodded, threw the ball again for an eager Oscar. "Nyree said a few minutes."

He looked up as a comfortably built Maori woman approached, together with a girl who looked to be seven or eight. "Can I stay a bit longer?" he pleaded. "I'm throwing the ball. And Oscar *likes* it. He wants me to throw it."

"Time to go," the woman said. "Sophie's not as keen on watching the dogs as you are. Not fair to keep her hanging about any longer. Besides, you want to climb to the top, don't you?"

"Yeh, I s'pose," he said reluctantly.

"Hi." Jenna put her hand out to the other woman. "I'm Jenna McKnight. You must be Nyree."

The older woman smiled. "Nyree Akara. Harry and Sophie's nanny."

"I'm guessing you're not Harry," Jenna said to the little girl, her brown hair touching her shoulders, large brown eyes serious in her heart-shaped face. "So that leaves Sophie."

"Hello," Sophie said, shaking Jenna's hand politely in her turn. "Harry's my brother."

"The dog lover. Oscar and I need to go too. We'll walk out with you."

She attached Oscar's lead and accompanied the others out of the fenced area. "He isn't actually my dog either," she told them. "I'm just like you, Harry. I'd love to have a dog, but I can't manage one right now. Your dad's right, it's a big responsibility. So I borrowed a friend's today. Thanks for helping me give him some exercise."

She smiled at the group and said her goodbyes, then began to jog down the road. It was a four-kilometer run back to Natalie's flat, and she'd told Nat's neighbor Eileen that she'd have Oscar back by five.

♡

"I've been thinking," Jenna said that evening over the quick dinner she'd prepared for her friend. "I was planning to look for another café job. But I don't know. I really miss working with kids."

"Hard to find a post in the middle of the school year," Natalie pointed out.

"I know. But I might at least check out possibilities in Auckland for next year. And maybe look into substitute positions for now, because I do like it here."

"What I told you," Natalie agreed. "Much warmer than Wellington. Less windy, too. You need a change anyway. More of a change. You've already done the physical bit. I was gobsmacked when I first saw you. I'd hardly have known you."

Jenna shrugged. "The Divorce Diet. That's what they call it. A decidedly mixed blessing."

"It wasn't just the dieting, though," Natalie said. "It was more the running, I'm thinking. What made you start with that? Last thing I would've expected from you."

"It was after you moved up here," Jenna explained. "After the separation. It wasn't part of any grand life plan. More running away, really. Literally. I'd leave school and I'd think, go home and sit watching telly with my flatmate, or get out? And I had to get out. The worse my life looked, the more I ran. And the more I ran, the more I liked it. It made it easier to eat better. And then I started to look different, and…" She shrugged. "It was like there was this one thing that was actually improving. My life was a mess, but hey, something was working."

"Maybe I should give it a go, d'you reckon?"

"What, running? Or getting your heart broken?" Jenna smiled wryly. "I recommend the first. But I can't say much for the heartbreak thing."

♡

"Jenna!"

She turned, Oscar on the lead this time, to see Harry running up the final bit of the path to the observation area at the edge of the enormous volcanic crater that was Mt. Eden. Nyree puffed up the slope after him with Sophie following behind, dribbling a soccer ball.

"Hi, Oscar!" Harry thumped a willing Oscar vigorously on the shoulder, then laughed as the dog swiped a tongue over his cheek in welcome. "He remembers me!"

"He sure does. You're his friend for life, now that you've thrown the ball for him. You guys are playing soccer today, huh?"

"Just Sophie," Harry said dismissively. "Nyree kicks it with her, not me."

"I see that," Jenna watched Sophie execute an intricate dribble, followed by an accurate kick to Nyree, who trapped it neatly with a foot and sent it cleanly back to the little girl. "You don't like soccer?"

"Nah. It's boring. I like animals best. D'you like animals too? Besides dogs?"

"I do. All kinds. Even extinct ones. How do you feel about dinosaurs? They're some of my favorites."

Harry stared at her, awestruck. "I *love* dinosaurs," he breathed. "But there are hardly any dinosaur fossils in New Zealand, did you know that?" He sighed. "I saw a bit of a foot in the museum once. But that was all."

"That *is* a little disappointing. On the other hand, New Zealand was the only place that had moa. And moa were very cool. It's hard to imagine a bird that big, isn't it? Twice as tall as an emu. Have you seen emu?"

"Yeh," he brightened. "Dad took us to Aussie, and we saw heaps. Sweet as. I wish the moa hadn't all died off, though. I wish I could see one."

"You've seen the models they have in the Auckland Museum, I'll bet," Jenna guessed. "I like to imagine walking around here when it was still native bush and meeting one. That would've been a bit of a surprise, wouldn't it? You wouldn't even have come up past the top of its legs."

"Yeh! And imagine if you saw a Haast's Eagle attacking a moa!"

"I'd want to hide, if I saw that," Jenna said. "That would be pretty scary. I'd be worried it would carry *me* away."

She stopped to greet Sophie and Nyree as they approached. "You're a pretty good soccer player," she told Nyree admiringly. "You must have played at school."

"And practiced with my own kids, when they were growing up," Nyree said. "I'm too old and fat to run anymore, but as long as Sophie kicks it to me, I can send it back to her."

"That's good," Sophie told Jenna seriously. "I have to practice my accuracy. And Nyree helps."

"Sophie practices *all* the *time*," Harry complained. "We have a goal set up in the garden at home. All she ever wants to do is practice kicking, and read. Bor-ring."

"I'll bet when you learn to read, you'll be doing it a fair bit yourself," Jenna suggested. "There's so much cool stuff to find out about. Are you Year One?"

Harry nodded. "I haven't learnt to read yet, though." He gave another gusty sigh. "I thought we were meant to learn in Year One. But all I can read are little words. And baby books."

"You have to keep trying," Sophie said. "I told you that. It's just like soccer and footy. Like Dad says. You have to practice hard to get better." She did a little more dribbling with the ball, clearly itching to get started. "Can you play soccer?" she asked Jenna. "Because you can run. I saw. Can you practice with me?"

"I can try," Jenna said doubtfully. "Do you and Harry mind holding Oscar?" she asked Nyree.

"We'll take him to the dog area, let Harry throw his ball," Nyree said. "There's a bit of an open area near there where you can kick the ball till you've worn this girl out, if you really don't mind. Then come find us."

Jenna did her best, but her inaccurate kicks kept Sophie running, while her inept stops had her scrambling after the ball herself. She called a laughing halt after fifteen sweaty minutes.

"I don't think this is my game," she apologized to Sophie. "I'm afraid you're the one wearing *me* out. Let's go rescue Nyree from the dog park, all right?"

"You tried hard, though," Sophie said encouragingly, finally displaying her seven-year-old gap-toothed smile.

Jenna laughed. "That's very nice of you. But I think you'd better stick to practicing with Nyree."

"Jenna! Oscar comes when I call him!" Harry told her excitedly when they joined the others inside the dog park. "Watch this!"

"You're a Dog Whisperer, that's for sure," Jenna told him approvingly as Oscar came running at Harry's enthusiastic shout. "Someday you're going to be a really good dog owner. What kind of dog do you want, have you thought? A retriever, like this?"

"Nah," Harry said confidently. "I want a plain dog. Loads of dogs get killed, did you know that? Because there aren't enough homes for all of them. I think that's sad, don't you?"

"I think it's very sad," Jenna agreed. "And it's wonderful to adopt a dog from a shelter."

"Maybe when I get it, I can walk it with you and Oscar," Harry suggested.

"Hmm. We'll see. For right now, though, why don't you give Oscar's ball one more good toss? Then I need to be getting him back to his owner."

no prize

♡

Jenna put a hand up to her auburn hair and verified her suspicions. Her carefully blow-dried waves had become corkscrew curls, even under the shelter of her umbrella. So much for a polished, professional appearance. Giving herself a time cushion had meant walking in the rain for twenty minutes before the appointment, but she hadn't wanted to risk a late arrival.

She looked up at the imposing villa set against the hillside of the Mt. Eden Domain, squared her shoulders, and made her way through the wooden gate set into the stone wall and up the front steps to the polished wood door. She reminded herself that the job was a long shot, but she couldn't help being excited all the same. When she'd seen the ad, it had seemed tailor-made for her. The six-month post as a nanny and housekeeper would end in mid-December, giving her a chance to get settled before the new school year started at the end of January. It was live-in, which meant she wouldn't have to find a place here in Auckland right away, and could save most of her salary as well. She'd enjoyed staying with Natalie for the past couple weeks and catching up on their friendship, but she needed to move on before she wore out her welcome.

"Hello," she smiled up at the tall man who answered the door at her ring. "Mr. Douglas? I'm Jenna McKnight. I think you're expecting me."

"Come in. And call me Finn, please." He took her umbrella from her with a raised brow. "You got pretty wet. Couldn't you find a parking space?"

"No car. Shoes off?" she asked, glancing at his stockinged feet.

"If you don't mind," he agreed, and watched as she bent to pull off her boots. "You've learnt Kiwi ways, obviously."

"I'm a permanent resident, actually. I may not sound like it, but I *am* pretty much a Kiwi at this point."

"You do know that this job involves driving," he commented as he led the way into a spacious lounge, its original rimu flooring polished to a high russet gloss and covered by a large Oriental carpet.

"I can drive," she assured him. "And I have a clean record."

"Yeh," he said absently, gesturing her to a seat on the big leather couch and picking up her CV with a frown. "You have good qualifications. Six years teaching Year One. You're not... exactly what I was hoping for, though. This is a temporary job, but it's a serious one. You'd have a couple days off each week, but otherwise you'd be here with the kids. Twenty-four hours a day some of the time, though there's additional help you could call in. I travel a fair bit, as I'm sure you know."

"Did you say that on the phone? I don't recall that. But of course it's a serious job. It's taking care of your children, after all, and that's serious business. I wouldn't have applied if I hadn't been prepared to do that."

He didn't seem to be warming to her. Was it the hair? She put her hand up to it again, then pulled it away quickly and tried to project more calm than she was feeling.

"You don't know who I am," he said. It was a statement, accompanied by a piercing stare from his light blue eyes.

"Should I know? Are you an actor or something?" She looked at him doubtfully. He was certainly striking, with his height and powerful build, but his features were much too rough-hewn to be called handsome. And that gravelly voice—he could play villains, she supposed. He must have some kind of lucrative career, anyway, to be able to afford this house, in its exclusive neighborhood. He looked young to be a successful businessperson—early thirties, maybe.

"I'm a rugby player," he answered briefly, still looking at her. "You didn't know that?"

"No. I don't follow sport."

"You didn't look me up online, before the interview? That isn't why you're here?"

"What?" She was staring at him now. "I don't understand what you're talking about."

"Look." He sighed and set her CV down. "I've tried to do this discreetly, but somehow, most of the candidates have turned out to be attractive young women. I advertised because I needed a temporary nanny and housekeeper. Not a girlfriend, and definitely not a wife."

Jenna sat with her mouth open for a moment, then shut it with a snap. "And astonishingly enough, I came here today, on the bus, in the pouring *rain,* to interview for a job as a temporary nanny and housekeeper. Not to…what? Audition to be your girlfriend? Sleep with you? Maybe you should look in the mirror. You aren't that good-looking."

She forced herself to stop before she said anything even ruder, and stood up to leave. All she'd lost was her time and some bus fare, she reminded herself, taking a couple calming breaths to prepare for a dignified exit.

As Finn rose to join her, those eyes even harder now, the front door banged and excited voices rose in the hallway.

"Daddy! We got so *wet!*"

Jenna turned in surprise as two familiar little figures rushed into the room, then skidded to a stop, staring at her.

"Jenna!" Harry rushed forward and gave her a hug that Jenna reflexively returned. "Why are you here? Did you come to visit us? Where's Oscar?"

She smiled down at him and reached out to smooth his hair. "No Oscar today. I came to see your dad, but I was just leaving, buddy."

"Hi, Jenna!" Sophie came forward for her own hug. "Did you come to talk to Dad about being our nanny?" she guessed. "He said he was going to talk to some ladies while we were gone. Are you going to stay with us? That would be so cool."

"Afraid not," Jenna told her. "Your dad and I were just realizing that it wouldn't work out. See you soon, though, OK?"

"Wait," Finn protested. "What's going on here? How do you know my kids? I thought you weren't working as a teacher now."

Jenna turned to him. "I see them quite a bit at the Domain, when they're there with Nyree."

"Jenna knows all about birds, and dogs, and extinct animals, and *everything,* Dad," Harry told him. "She's very, very good at discussing."

Finn looked down at his earnest son with a smile. "I know how much you like to discuss animals. Why don't you two say goodbye to Jenna and run back with Nyree now, though?"

"But why aren't you going to be our nanny?" Sophie asked with disappointment. "We'd like you best."

"It's not going to work," Finn told her firmly. "Say goodbye, now."

Both children looked mutinous, but obeyed at last. After they had left the room, Finn turned back to Jenna, his expression even more skeptical. "You got to know my kids. But you don't know who I am."

"No. And frankly, I find myself caring less and less. Good luck finding your elderly nanny."

"Look." He followed her out of the room and watched as she pulled on her boots and retrieved her raincoat and umbrella from the hooks that lined the entryway. "If that's true, I'm sorry I insulted you. It's just..." He ran a hand through his close-cropped brown hair. "It's awkward, you know. Because the person has to live in the house with me. I know what I look like, and that I'm no prize. But for some reason, whether you believe me or not, I've met a fair few young women this past week who seem to be looking for more than a job."

Jenna nodded stiffly. "No point in my telling you I'm not interested. You can't prove a negative. But you have great kids. So, really, good luck with the nanny." She reached out a hand to shake his.

"Let me ring for a taxi," he suggested, looking a bit shame-faced now.

"No worries. I'm already wet." She gave him a brief smile and left the house.

Finn shut the door behind her. Sighed and ran his hand through his hair again. Why did Nyree have to leave, anyway? That was selfish, though. Her mum needed her. Hip replacements were no picnic. But this was too hard. He must have sounded like an arrogant prat just now. Jenna really hadn't known who he was. He looked at himself in the hall mirror and grimaced. She was right. No prize.

♡

"Daddy, can we talk to you for a minute?"

Finn looked up with a frown. "Isn't it bedtime?"

"Yes." Sophie picked up the TV remote and turned the set off.

"Oi," Finn protested mildly.

"This is serious," she told him as she and Harry came to join him on the couch, one on either side of him.

"Right, then," he said. "What?"

"We don't like Mrs. Donaldson," Harry burst out. "She's mean."

"Mean? She's been here less than a week," Finn said. "What has she done?"

"She smacks," Sophie told him.

"Smacks? Smacks what?"

"*Daddy. Us,*" Sophie explained in exasperation. "Well, me mostly. But Harry once too."

"*What?* She smacked you?" He had a hard time believing it. "When? How?"

"When Harry wasn't ready for school. When I wouldn't eat that smelly fish she made last night. She gets a really mean face, and she smacks."

"Like this," Harry explained. He stood up, pushed up his glasses, and frowned menacingly at Finn. "Then she smacks on the bottom." He illustrated on himself. "And we don't like it. Nyree never smacks."

"No," Finn agreed grimly. "Right, then. I'll put you to bed, then I'll talk to Mrs. Donaldson. She won't be your nanny anymore."

It was a good thing there was no training the next day, he thought worriedly. But then what was he going to do?

"We have something else to say," Sophie told him. Clearly, she was the spokesperson tonight.

"We want Jenna!" Harry burst out.

"*Harry,*" Sophie frowned him down. "I was supposed to explain."

She looked up at her father, determination written all over her little face. "We want Jenna to be our nanny," she told him. "For these reasons." She opened the notebook she was carrying and turned to the latest page. "Reason One: Jenna is nice. Reason Two: Jenna knows all about animals."

"Yeh," Harry interjected again, impatient with his sister's list. "And the other reason, Jenna smells very nice. And we like her. We want her to be the nanny, please, Dad."

"She can't kick a ball very well," Sophie pointed out fairly. "I don't think she can help me with soccer practice, not like Nyree does. But maybe you could help me instead."

"Right. Your points are noted," Finn said. "But you know, Jenna may have another job now. Or she may not want this one. I'm not sure she likes me as much as she likes you."

"That's because you made the Scary Face when she was here," Harry said. "You just have to smile, Dad. Then she'll know you're nice, and she'll want to stay with us. Please?"

"Please, Dad," Sophie added. "Please ask her."

Finn exhaled. "I'll think about it, all right? Now let's get you to bed."

Talking to Mrs. Donaldson was easy. She started out hostile, but when he reminded her of the legal ban on smacking, most of the wind went out of her sails. A week's severance and a taxi waiting while she packed took care of the rest. Calling Jenna the next day, though, proved a much tougher proposition.

"Look, I know I got offside with you," he told her at last. "But I'd like to try again. I talked to the head of your school in Wellington and she gave you a glowing recommendation. Rang your other references too, with the same result. You were right, and I was wrong. Can't say fairer than that. So could you come back and talk to me again? I'll send a taxi for you," he went on hurriedly. "Have a heart. I'm in a right mess here."

"I'll come talk to you again," Jenna said warily. "As long as all that other business is over."

"My being irresistible. Done and dusted. You told me, and I got it."

She laughed. "I suspect we both find each other resistible. But I'll come talk to you. For the kids' sake."

♡

"You're a teacher, eh," he asked when Jenna was once again sitting across from him in the lounge. "Why aren't you teaching now?"

"Taking a year off," she explained. "I've been living in Wellington, as you saw, for some years now. I decided after last year, though, that I wanted to find someplace new to live. I've been traveling and working for the past six months."

"Working where? That's not on your CV," he pointed out.

"Cafés. I can give you references, if you like, but they're not really to the point. Short stints, anyway, with a bit of travel in between. It's been a nice change, but I've decided I want to settle in Auckland and get another teaching post for the new year. And this could be a good interim position before I start that again."

"Not too glamorous," he said dubiously. "Kids, cooking, washing, shopping. Not much cleaning, at least. I have a firm that comes in every week to do that. But still."

She noticed his assessing look. She could say with fair confidence that he wasn't seeing anything glamorous enough to give him pause. At least the weather, and her hair, had cooperated. But she was afraid the plaid skirt and loose jumper didn't do much for her. She'd wanted to appear serious, but she suspected she might have crossed the line into dowdy territory. That was probably good, though. She didn't want him to think she was trying to appeal to him, or stalking him.

Because she *had* looked him up by now, of course. Not a movie star after all, but New Zealand's closest equivalent. A star player for the Auckland Blues and a senior All Black, a member of the country's international rugby team. No wonder he had women applying to live in his house. He would be a major matrimonial prize, even with two kids.

"Believe me, being a Year One teacher isn't very glamorous either," she assured him now. "And I actually like to do those things, odd as it may seem. I do have a few questions, though. Where is Sophie and Harry's mum, if you don't mind my asking? Would I be handling visits with her?"

"Nah. She passed away a few years ago. It's just me."

"Oh," she replied, taken aback. "I'm so sorry."

"You'd have respite help, though," he hastened to point out. "Because I'll be gone a fair bit, as I said. Aussie, South Africa, as well as traveling in En Zed. Argentina and Europe as well, later in the year. The last trip, the Northern Tour, that's a full five weeks. There'd be extra pay, of course, when you were with the kids all the time, and we'd make sure you got your days off. Nyree's cousin helps out with that."

"That sounds fine. About cleaning, though, I did want to tell you that I believe in kids doing some chores. Not to make my life easier," she smiled. "It's always easier and quicker to do it yourself, as I'm sure you can imagine. But I don't think it's good for children to have someone picking up after them. I'd be expecting them to keep their own rooms tidy, and to help with clearing the table, taking out the rubbish, those sorts of things."

"Fair enough. Because I do worry about that, them becoming spoilt. I didn't grow up with all this." He gestured around him at the historic villa, restored to gleaming, if comfortable, perfection. "I can't pretend we're short of a dollar, but I try to make sure they appreciate what they have, and that they know how to work. And as I'm gone so much, I'd need your help with that. I don't think Nyree's had them doing much for themselves."

"I'd say that you've both done pretty well, though," she said, "based on what I've seen of them. It sounds like you and I are on the same page there. What about cooking? Anything special I should know, or any questions you have? I'm a pretty reasonable home cook, I think, but not a gourmet one."

He laughed. "Don't think any of us would appreciate gourmet cooking. I take a fair bit of feeding, I should tell you, when I'm home."

"That works for me. I like my cooking to be appreciated."

"Does this mean you'll take the job?"

"I'd love to," she decided. "When do you want me to start?"

He looked a bit harassed. "Today, if you can. You don't have a car, is that right?"

"That's right. I've been traveling light. Just me and a couple bags. And yes, I can start today. I'll just go back and pack up."

He exhaled in relief, then stood up and shook her hand. "Take a taxi back here, and I'll reimburse you. I'll be home the next couple days, at least. That'll give you some time to settle in, before you're on your own with the kids. And Jenna. Thanks."

brontosaurus in the water

♡

"This is your room," he told her a couple hours later, setting her bags down inside the bedroom door. "Sorry there isn't an ensuite. You'll have to share a bath with the kids, I'm afraid."

"No worries. I've lived in New Zealand for seven years now, remember? I know about sharing the bath."

He smiled. "I confess I've never understood the American fascination with bathrooms, why everybody in the family needs their own."

"I agree with you, actually. This will suit me fine."

Jenna looked around the comfortable room. A queen bed with nightstand sat against one long wall, while French doors opened onto one of the villa's many brick patios, the garden showing green beyond. Closet and drawer space wasn't overly abundant, but she didn't have many clothes anyway. And a desk and chair, she saw with pleasure, would provide her with her own workspace.

Finn scratched his cheek thoughtfully. "Nyree doesn't live in all the time. So this is all a bit new to us, too. We'll have to work it out as we go along, I reckon."

"She just stays over when you have games?" Jenna guessed.

He nodded. "But as we're into the All Black part of the season now, more travel, this way seemed better. Let me show you the rest of the house."

He began to conduct her through the grand old villa, and she saw with relief that the ground floor contained a small powder room as well as the large full bathroom with its original, massive clawfoot tub and separate shower. That was the one part of sharing bathrooms that could be a problem with young children, she suspected.

"Sophie's room." He opened the door to the bedroom across the hallway from her own. It was decorated in a pleasant mint green, with accents of yellow and white. "Nyree helped us choose the colors a year or so ago, when Sophie wanted something more grown-up."

"You did a good job," she said admiringly. "And it's easy to see where Sophie's interests lie. Besides the obvious clue of the bookshelf. Soccer posters, and the All Blacks." She looked more closely at the framed poster of the team doing the haka, the pre-match Maori challenge so strongly associated with New Zealand rugby. "Where are you?"

She looked where he pointed at his image, taller than most of the players, near the middle of the front row. "Wow. Prominent. And I have to say, you look pretty mad. Scary, too."

He smiled. "My game face. I try not to show that around the house too much, scare the kids." He led her out of the room, opened the next door. "Harry, obviously."

Jenna laughed. Harry's room was painted a light blue. But the walls were nearly obscured by maps and posters of animals taken from wildlife magazines and the *National Geographic*, and low shelves held collections of large and small animal figurines. She saw a farm set, a jungle set, and plenty of dinosaurs. Another set of shelves held Legos, she was glad to see. So Harry had more than one interest, after all.

"And finally," Finn told her, opening the door of the room next to her own. "Guest room."

"Do you have a lot of company?" she asked. "Entertain a lot? I should have asked that sooner. I don't have much party planning experience, but I could try."

He smiled ruefully. "Other than the occasional birthday party for the kids, or my family coming up for a visit, I'm not much for that. One of the benefits of being a single dad, I reckon. Nobody expects anything."

He gestured towards the end of the passage. "I should say, I'm up the stairs here." He led the way up a carpeted set of stairs that led to a large bedroom and ensuite bath that took up the top of the house, its large windows offering views over the neighboring houses and trees. "Not that you'll need to do anything with this. The cleaners come on Fridays, and they keep it from getting too disgraceful."

"I'd say you're very neat," she told him. "Hard to imagine this ever getting disgraceful." Other than a book on the bedside table, the room was almost painfully orderly.

"I don't like clutter," he admitted. "I can live with the kids' things," he went on hastily. "Toys, and that. Not rigid about it, I hope. But I like my own space to be clear."

She nodded. Help the kids straighten up before he got home, check. She wasn't worried about the kitchen. She knew she'd be keeping that clean.

"Kitchen and laundry?" she asked now. "And we should talk about what you like to eat."

"Had this all redone ages ago, the first year we lived here," he told her when they were standing in the huge, sunny kitchen, with a large rectangular table set into the windowed nook at one end. "Nyree consulted." He smiled. "I should say, Nyree *planned.*"

"Well, Nyree did a great job," Jenna said. "Anyone could cook well in this kitchen."

Nyree planned? she wondered. Not his wife? She viewed the modern appliances and granite countertops with approval. "Now. Favorite foods? Likes and dislikes?"

"I like pretty much everything. Not too fond of Brussels sprouts and cauliflower, but that's about it as far as vegies. And any kind of meat. I eat heaps of that, I should warn you."

"I can imagine. OK. I can work with that. What about the kids?"

"They'll eat most things. Except what I cook." He made a wry face. "They're not keen on my efforts. I'm not either, tell you the truth. We end up at the pub a fair bit, when Nyree hasn't cooked. Or eating leftovers."

"Cook extra the night before my day off," she nodded. "Got it."

"If you don't mind. They'd thank you."

"All right, then," she decided. "Now go do whatever it is you need to do, and leave me to get on with it. Because it's already one-thirty, and I need to unpack, and then get started here. Tell me where the primary school is, and when the kids get out, and I'll pick them up."

"I'd appreciate it. I have some film from Saturday's game I'd like to look over before practice tomorrow. And I've got a bit behind, being on my own with the kids. It's five or six blocks away, is all." He went to the computer set up on a desk in the kitchen and pulled up a map of the area. "Here. You can drive the Toyota." He showed her where the keys hung on the hook. "I usually take the Range Rover. School's out at three."

"I'll walk. Now, really. Go watch your film. Because I'm going to need to open every cupboard here, and find my way around. And figure out what I'm going to fix you for dinner, so you don't sack me my first night."

"No chance of that. Just so grateful you took the post, and that you're here. And that I can go to training tomorrow, and on to Hamilton on Friday, without worrying about what's happening at home."

♡

21

"Go get your dad, OK?" Jenna asked Harry that evening. "Tell him it's dinnertime. And you and Sophie go wash your hands, please."

"OK." Harry bounced off.

"Sophie," Jenna said more sharply, seeing the little girl still sitting at the table she and Harry had just finished setting, once again engrossed in her book.

When she still got no response, Jenna went over and closed the book gently. "Dinnertime," she said when Sophie looked up. "Go wash your hands, please."

Sophie got up with a sigh, still holding the book.

"I'll take this for now," Jenna told her firmly. "Till after dinner."

"Nyree lets me read at the table when Daddy isn't home," Sophie objected.

"Well, first," Jenna told her cheerfully, "he's home tonight. And second, I'm not Nyree. Even when he isn't home, I'm going to be talking to you at dinnertime, and I require my dinner partners to answer me."

Sophie gave another martyred sigh, but set off toward the bathroom to wash her hands. Jenna smiled and put the book on the corner of the bench. She understood the fascination. She'd been known to read at the table a fair bit herself.

"Why are there only three places?" Finn asked in surprise when he came into the kitchen with Harry. "Aren't you eating?"

"I thought you'd want family time," Jenna explained. "On the nights you were home."

"So you'd eat, when?" he asked.

She shrugged. "Afterwards, I suppose."

"This is one of those things I should've thought of," he realized. "It didn't come up with Nyree, because she only stayed for dinner on nights I was gone. But we're not Poms, and I'm not comfortable with that. Unless you'd really rather not, I'd prefer that you eat with us. Please."

"Please, Jenna," Harry put in.

"That's fine with me." Jenna pulled together another place setting, then turned back to the stove where she'd been keeping the meat warm. "I didn't have a chance to go to the store today, but luckily you had meat in the freezer."

"Steak," Finn said with pleasure.

"Easy dinner," Jenna agreed.

"What's this?" he asked, picking up the bowl of sauce she'd set down between the platter of steak and the bowl of roasted winter vegetables.

"Mustard butter. Try it on your steak and vegies. It's quite tasty. Next time, I'll buy some mushrooms and sauté them to go on top of it all. That's the best."

"Quite nice as it is," he said after sampling it. "So, Harry, how was school today, mate?"

"Bad. It wasn't *fair,*" Harry complained. "Mrs. McMinn was *wrong.* But she wouldn't even listen!"

Finn looked at his son with surprise. "What happened? Did you get yourself in trouble?"

"She was talking about dinosaurs," Harry told him indignantly. "And she said Brontosaurus stayed in the water most of the time because it supported his weight. And that's *wrong!*"

"Ah. Dinosaurs. What's the strength of that? He wasn't in the water, then, after all?"

"First," Harry explained, "it's *Apatosaurus* now. Everyone knows that. And they *didn't* need to be in the water. People used to think so, but not anymore. But when I tried to explain, she said not to con...con..."

"Contradict?" Jenna asked.

He nodded emphatically. "She went crook at me. But she was *wrong,* Dad."

Finn looked at Jenna. "Teacher's advice, please."

"How old is Mrs. McMinn?" Jenna asked.

"*Old*," Harry said. "And mean. Everyone calls her Mrs. McMean."

"Harry," Finn said sharply. "We don't call her that." He told Jenna, "She's an older teacher. Sixty or thereabouts, I reckon."

Jenna nodded. "A different generation. And she was right, when she learned her dinosaur facts," she explained to Harry. "Apatosaurus used to be named Brontosaurus. But you knew that. And they *did* think, before, that his tail would have dragged on the ground, and that he stayed in swamps because the water supported his weight. All that changed some years ago with new discoveries, and now we know how Apatosaurus really lived. But Mrs. McMinn probably isn't as interested in dinosaurs as you are. She learned those facts when she was younger, and she didn't hear about the new information afterwards."

"But I should say, if it's wrong," Harry argued. "That's science."

"It is," Jenna agreed. "When new facts come up, scientists have to be able to change their minds. You're right about that. But let's think about Mrs. McMinn. She doesn't like someone to tell her she's wrong, during class. That makes her feel embarrassed. How else could you have explained it to her, do you think, that wouldn't have embarrassed her?"

Sophie spoke up. "You could've told her afterwards, maybe?"

Jenna smiled at her. "That's a good idea. Think how you feel, if your teacher tells you that you did something wrong in front of all the other kids. Isn't that embarrassing?"

Harry and Sophie nodded.

"Teachers don't get embarrassed, though." Harry wasn't ready to concede yet. "They're grownups."

"Grownups get embarrassed too," Jenna explained. "It's much nicer if somebody tells you what you did wrong when you're by yourself, isn't it? So nobody else hears? Even for teachers."

"Even for footy players," Finn put in. "A good coach tells a player the really bad stuff on his own. Nobody likes to be yelled at in front of his mates."

"Do you have a book that talks about Apatosaurus?" Jenna asked.

Harry nodded. "That's how I know. About Brontosaurus, and everything."

"Then," she suggested, "maybe you can take it to school tomorrow. And when you get a chance, you can show Mrs. McMinn what you were talking about. We can look at it tonight, find the place and mark the page for you."

"What if she's still angry, though, when I tell her?" Harry asked doubtfully.

"Then that's her problem," Finn decided. "If you explain politely, and in private, you've done all you can. Because you're right, I reckon. If you're studying science, it's important to get the facts right. Even if the facts change."

He turned his attention to his daughter. "What about you, Sophie? Did you get into a stoush with your teacher today, too? Let's hear all the bad news."

"Nah," Sophie shrugged. "It was boring."

"What's your favorite subject?" Jenna asked. "Reading?"

"Lunch," Sophie said firmly.

Jenna couldn't help smiling. "Well, help me clear the table, you two, and we'll have pudding. On that note."

"You made pudding?" Finn asked. "What is it?"

"Wait and see," Jenna told him.

When she set the apple crumble and homemade custard on the table, Finn smiled with appreciation.

"Choice," he said as he dug in.

"Daddy loves pudding," Sophie informed Jenna.

"So I gather. Good to know. And now I need to know what you all like for breakfast. And when."

"We usually have Weet-Bix and toast," Sophie said.

"All right," Jenna nodded. "Easy. Is that what you like best, too?"

"Waffles!" Harry piped up.

"We like lots of things," Sophie told her. "But on school days, it's usually Weet-Bix."

"We'll try something special on Saturday, then," Jenna decided. "What about you, Finn?"

"You don't have to fix mine if you don't have time," he said. "I have as much as I can manage to make."

"Eggs, bacon, toast, potatoes, tomatoes," she guessed. "And maybe sausage as well."

"If I can get all that," he agreed. "But otherwise, just eggs and toast."

"I'll see what I can do," she smiled. "And what you have in the fridge just now. I'll go to the store tomorrow."

"I'll shift money into your account for groceries and gas," he promised. "You can keep track, and tell me how we're going, if you need more. That work for you?"

"It does. I'll save the receipts and give you an accounting at the end of every week."

"Very businesslike."

"That's the best way," she told him. "In our situation."

barbie and cricket

♡

"Sure you're comfortable being alone with the kids again tonight?" Finn asked, coming into the kitchen where Jenna was preparing dinner on Sunday afternoon. "I may be out pretty late. I'll have my mobile, of course."

"Yeah." She smiled at him. "We're good, got the routine down. I'll get them to bed on time, as they were up late last night watching you. Check with them too, though, if you like. See how they feel about it."

He snorted. "Yeh, right. All I've heard lately is 'Jenna says.' Starting to give me a bit of a complex."

"Don't worry. They're crazy about you. Nobody's going to be taking over that spot in their hearts."

The doorbell rang when Jenna and the kids were in the middle of a Balloon Lagoon game. She'd bought the board game the day before, and the kids had been clamoring to play it ever since, with the wet weather keeping them indoors.

"Two frogs in!" Harry announced proudly as the carousel music ceased. He worked carefully to stuff two balloons into his basket.

"Good work, buddy," Jenna told him.

"My turn!" Sophie was already reaching for the carousel to spin it.

"Hang on," Jenna admonished. "Your dad's guest is here. Let's say hello." She got up from the floor where they'd been sitting to greet Finn's date, stunning in a deep blue wrap dress whose neckline dipped in a low V, the short skirt showing off long, shapely legs. As the blonde looked her over coolly at Finn's introduction, Jenna wished she were wearing something more flattering than a T-shirt and jeans. Too bad the humidity had made her hair curl up again, too.

"I recognize you, don't I?" she asked Ashley. "Aren't you a presenter on TV3?"

"I am," Ashley answered, becoming a bit more animated. "That's how Finn and I met. I was doing interviews when the All Black training squad was first named, talking to some of the new caps as well as the veterans. And, well..." She shrugged modestly, put a proprietary arm through Finn's and smiled up at him warmly.

"Ashley came by before we went to dinner tonight because she has something for you," Finn told Sophie and Harry, already dressed for bed in warm pajamas.

"That's right!" Ashley said in a too-bright, syrupy voice that set Jenna's teeth on edge.

Some people didn't know how to talk to children, she reminded herself. No need to be judgmental.

"I brought you each a pressie," Ashley said, handing each child a gaily wrapped parcel. "Go on and open them," she urged. "I know it's hard to wait."

"Oh." Sophie finished ripping off the paper and looked at the Barbie Fashionista doll, complete with necklace and flower-bedecked purse, in its plastic box.

"She's poseable, see?" Ashley told her, pointing out the jointed limbs. "And look, here are more outfits for her too. Won't that be fun, to dress her up?"

"What do you say, Sophie?" Jenna prompted.

Sophie looked up, pasted a too-polite smile onto her face. "Thank you, Ashley. She's very pretty."

"What did you get, Harry?" Jenna asked, anxious to shift the attention from Sophie's less-than-genuine response.

"A cricket ball," he said, holding it out to her.

"Lovely," Jenna approved. She gave Harry a gentle nudge.

He blinked behind his glasses and said, "Thank you very much, Ashley."

"I thought you could probably use another cricket ball," Ashley told him. "My brothers were always losing them."

"That was very kind of you," Finn said, looking a bit embarrassed. "We'd better get on now, though. I booked a table for eight."

He bent to give his children a good-bye kiss. "All right?" he asked Jenna.

"Of course," she assured him. "We're playing a bit more, then off to bed. Have a nice dinner, both of you. It was a pleasure to meet you," she told Ashley.

The slender blonde smiled, but there was little warmth now in the blue eyes that looked back at Jenna. "Likewise." She took Finn's arm again and left the room with him, tanned legs making a spectacular show in the high heels.

As she heard the front door close behind the pair, Jenna turned back to Sophie and Harry. "Pick up the wrapping paper and throw it away, please. Then take your presents into your rooms, unless you want to play with your doll instead of doing our game, Sophie."

"I don't want to play with this," Sophie told her, gathering up the wrapping paper and setting the doll and clothes onto the coffee table. "I don't like Barbie."

"I noticed you didn't have many dolls," Jenna said.

"Except Martha," Sophie reminded her, referring to the baby doll who held pride of place on her dresser. "But Martha's different. She's like a real baby. I don't play with her much any-more. I'm too old now. But I still like to look at her and change her clothes sometimes."

"Not interested in changing Barbie's clothes, huh?" Jenna asked sympathetically.

Sophie shook her head. "Barbie's boring. All she does is go shopping and get dressed."

"Jenna?" Harry tugged at her hand, having deposited his wrapping paper in the kitchen rubbish. "I don't like cricket. Do I have to play with this?"

She laughed. "Poor Ashley. I guess she doesn't know you two very well, huh?"

"She's talked to us heaps," Sophie countered. "But I don't think she really listens. She just wants Daddy to think she likes us."

"It was still nice of her to bring you presents," Jenna admonished.

"Nah, it wasn't," Sophie insisted. "Ladies always bring us pressies. They do it so Daddy will like them."

"What?"

"They want him to kiss them," Harry explained. "Ladies like kissing. But they never discuss like you do. They just smile like this"—he stretched his mouth into a horrible grimace—"and ask us if we like school."

"Lame as," Sophie offered.

"That's not very kind," Jenna admonished her. "And Harry, I hope they don't look like that. That would be pretty shocking. If you don't want these presents, we'll take them to the hospital Op Shop next week and donate them, how's that? That way, kids who *do* love Barbie and cricket, but can't afford nice things like this, can have something brand-new."

"OK," Sophie agreed, and Harry nodded.

"Now," Jenna said, "let's get back to our game. We can manage a few more turns before bedtime."

♡

She looked up, startled, when she heard the front door open, closed her book, and was getting up to leave the lounge when Finn stepped in.

"Sorry," she told him. "I thought you'd be home later. I'll go on to my room."

"Nah." He sank into one of the big leather chairs with a sigh. "Stay out here and talk to me for a bit. Is there any of that cake left?"

"You saw that, huh?" She smiled. "Plenty left. Want me to get you a piece?"

He shook his head. "I'll get it. D'you want one?"

"No thanks. I don't eat that stuff anymore. My glass of wine is my treat."

He nodded and left the room, coming back a few minutes later with a huge slab of chocolate cake and a tall glass of milk.

"Breakfast of champions," she remarked.

He laughed. "They don't feed you enough at those flash restaurants Ashley likes. I'm starved."

He took a bite, then opened his eyes wide. "This is bloody marvelous."

"Thanks," she said with pleasure. "American style. I like to remind myself of my roots sometimes."

"Going to have to watch my figure," he said.

"Seems to me you burn a lot of calories," she objected. "It must be hard to keep the kilos on, in fact, training as hard as you do."

"I try to keep the weight consistent, not gain during the time off, not lose during the season. Too hard on the body otherwise, easier to get injured if you're unfit starting out. But you're right, it takes a lot of eating, specially for an AB."

"An All Black?"

"Yeh. Long season," he explained, stretching his legs out in front of him and taking another bite. "They break up the Super 15 season for these three test matches we've just finished up against England, then it's back for three more rounds and, hopefully, the Super 15 playoffs. And then on to the Rugby Championship with the ABs again. Not to mention the Northern Tour. All the way from January till early December, without much layoff in there."

He shrugged, dug into the cake again. "Have to stay fit to make it all the way through, specially at my age. Loads of protein. And the occasional chocolate cake doesn't go amiss either."

"Anything special you want, just ask," she assured him.

"Can you cook salmon? I had it at Kermadec tonight, and it was pretty good. But such a mingy wee bit, just left me wanting more."

"Of course I can. I'll get some from the fish market tomorrow," she promised. "Enough so you can eat as much as you like. I have a good way to cook it. You sear it, and serve it with a glaze of balsamic vinegar, honey, and orange juice. Pretty tasty. If you really want it two days in a row."

"I would. Sounds delicious. Not sure how much the kids like salmon, though."

"Plenty of leftovers from tonight, since you weren't here," she said. "They can have those if they'd rather."

"Cheers for that. Anyway. What are you reading?" He glanced at the book she'd laid on the couch next to her.

"Guilty pleasure. *Jane Eyre*." She showed him the cover. "One of the few books I haul around with me."

"Not much of a guilty pleasure." He looked her over. "Pretty tame evening, I'd say."

"Glass of wine, *Jane Eyre,* in my dressing gown," she agreed. "That's about the size of it."

"May have been more entertaining than mine, at that," he told her, starting to laugh. "Couldn't quite get over those naff pressies."

Jenna couldn't resist a chuckle of her own. "I thought the kids did all right, after the initial shock. But yeah, she couldn't have chosen much worse. Poor Ashley. She must not know them very well."

"I've talked to her about them, though," he said thoughtfully. "I'm sure I've told her that Harry doesn't care for sport, and Sophie does."

"Adults without kids can make assumptions," she said. "Sometimes even adults *with* kids. They tend to think that kids will like whatever they themselves liked when they were young. They don't realize that children are individuals, just as much as adults are."

"You realize it, though. And you don't have any."

Jenna flushed, felt the familiar stab of pain. "No. But I've been a teacher for six years. When you have a classroom full of five-year-olds, believe me, you understand pretty quickly that they're all different. You can say, for example, that boys in general are more active and noisier. But even there, you're just generalizing. Look at Harry and Sophie. Harry doesn't care about sport, and Sophie loves it. When we watched your game last night, Sophie was explaining the penalties and the tactics to me. I hate to tell you, but Harry was back to looking at the new dinosaur book we got from the library well before the break."

He smiled. "My son isn't my biggest fan."

"You're wrong," she corrected gently. "He *is* your biggest fan. One of the two, anyway. Just not your biggest rugby fan. That would be Sophie."

"Why *do* you like kids so much, though, and understand them so well?" he asked her. "Even before you took this job, you'd got to know the kids. Why? It wasn't to meet me. I've been put right on that. And most people don't pay any attention to other people's kids."

"I don't know." She shrugged, a little embarrassed. "I like kids better than adults, to tell you the truth. I relate to them better, I suppose. Kids are honest. You know what they're really thinking. They're going to tell you the truth."

He looked at her more sharply. "As opposed to who? Your ex-husband?"

"What? Why do you think I was married?"

"Pretty obvious. You listed another name on your CV. You either got married since you stopped teaching, which doesn't seem likely, or you were married before. He lied, eh."

"Yeah. But hey, if we're going to tell sad marriage stories, we could be here all night. And it's past my bedtime." She stood and picked up her empty wine glass, gathered up his dishes. "See you in the morning."

He watched her go, sorry he'd brought it up. That had cleared the room in a hurry. Pity. Chatting with her had been the most fun he'd had all evening.

wombat bottom

♡

"Wanted to tell you, you can start your time off earlier than I originally said, this week," Finn said over a late breakfast the following Saturday.

"Oh?" Jenna turned from the stove to slide another tall stack of pancakes onto his plate. Good thing she'd doubled the recipe. She averted her eyes to avoid a closeup view of the line of stitches along his eyebrow and the bruise that had formed around them. "When do you mean?"

"Ashley's coming by to cook dinner tonight," he told her, pouring syrup liberally over the multigrain pancakes and topping the stack with a heaping spoonful of chopped oranges and kiwifruit and a dollop of vanilla yoghurt. "So you're free to go out."

"What will we do?" Sophie asked. "Do we get to go with Jenna?"

"Nah," he frowned at her. "That's the point, eh. Ashley wants to make dinner for all of us."

"Jenna too?" Harry piped up.

"No," Jenna put in, as she saw Finn looking uncomfortable. "Just you two and your dad. That's nice of her, isn't it? It's nice for me too. I'll get to go out on Saturday night. Do you need another pancake, Sophie? And Finn, want another egg or two to go with those?"

"No, thanks," Sophie said. Finn nodded, though, and Jenna cracked a final three eggs onto the griddle together with her own pancakes.

"What time does this cooking extravaganza begin?" she asked. "So I can make sure everything's ready. Does she need anything special? Groceries?"

"No groceries. She's bringing them. And she said five. But you don't have to leave straight away," he hastened to assure her.

Jenna laughed. "Somehow, I think Ashley'd prefer it, though. That's fine. Do you need an icepack for your face, while I'm up?"

"Thanks."

"Daddy, I thought that was a deliberate sprig," Sophie said with concern as Finn put the cold pack to his eye, continuing to eat bacon and pancakes with the other hand. "Why wasn't Nick Holmes sent off?"

"What's a sprig?" Jenna asked curiously, serving Finn his final eggs and bringing over her own plate of breakfast.

"Aw, got to expect a few sprig marks now and then at the bottom of the ruck," Finn shrugged. "No worries. And the sprigs are the spikes in rugby boots," he explained to Jenna. "My protective daughter thinks Nick sprigged me deliberately last night."

"I still think he did," Sophie argued.

"If the refs started citing us all for a bit of carelessness with our boots, I'd be in as much trouble as anyone," he told her. "Got to have a bit of mongrel in your game when you're a loosie. Sorry, darling."

"You're not a dirty player, Dad," Sophie said, shocked. "You're a hard man. That's different."

He smiled. "Reckon that depends on who you talk to. But I hope not."

"What's a loosie?" Jenna asked. "Sophie, Harry, if you're finished, please put your dishes in the dishwasher."

"Loose forward. Six, seven, eight," he explained.

"You're eight, I know that," Jenna said. "Have you always played that position?"

"Yeh," Sophie broke in. "Dad's been the best No. 8 in New Zealand for ages. Loads of people think he's the best in the world," she announced proudly. "That's why he's always selected for the All Blacks, since before I was born."

"Aw, you'll make me blush," Finn told her, reaching over to pull her close to him and give her a kiss. "Some of the young boys are nipping at my heels now. Hoping to hang onto that starting spot for another couple years, though. One more World Cup, anyway, next year. It'd be choice to repeat as world champions. Specially since nobody's done it yet."

"Nobody's won two in a row?" Jenna asked in surprise.

He looked at her, amused. "You didn't happen to hear that, last time around? It was only three years ago, and I know you were here then. You may recall that we won. It made a wee bit of a splash at the time."

"Sorry. My rugby indoctrination's been minimal. My hu— My friends were never interested in rugby, and it barely exists in the U.S. Good thing I have Sophie to educate me now." Jenna smiled affectionately at the little girl as she got up to clear her plate and Finn's own, moved to the sink to start the dishes.

"I'll help you, Jenna." Harry picked up the syrup carefully and brought it to the kitchen island.

"Thanks, buddy. How about if we go to the library after this, guys, let your dad rest?"

"Need a little time in the spa," Finn admitted.

"Can we come in with you?" Harry asked.

"For a bit," he agreed. "Help Jenna first, both of you, then get your togs on. Jenna, you go on and do your run once you're done here, if you like, before the library. I'll be around anyway."

"Thanks. I've missed a couple days."

"Thought so. School holidays make it tough. You need to ring Nyree's cousin, set something up for next week. She can come in and help out a couple days, give you a break."

"Miriam's nice," Harry said, carefully putting the carton of eggs back into the fridge. "Not as nice as you, though, Jenna."

"Don't tell Miriam that, when she comes," Finn admonished his son. "You'll hurt her feelings."

♡

"Well. Wasn't that fun?" Ashley asked brightly as Finn finished the last bite and set his napkin on the table. "I enjoy cooking so much."

Finn couldn't suppress a little smile. Ashley's cooking was definitely on the low-calorie side, which his children had been decidedly unenthusiastic about. Almost as unenthusiastic, he admitted, as he was himself. Skinless, boneless chicken breasts, a green salad, and steamed broccoli had obviously done yeoman service in maintaining Ashley's slim figure, but he found himself hoping that there was still some of Jenna's lamb and roasted vegies in the fridge for a late-night snack. And maybe the vanilla slice she'd made the other day for pudding. He thought there was a bit of that left.

"Thank you, Ashley. That was delicious," he told her. He fixed his children with his best reminding stare until they echoed his thanks. "Let's all help clean up. Get it done quicker," he suggested.

"Can't we leave it for...Jane?" Ashley asked. "Isn't she the housekeeper?"

"Jenna," Finn corrected with a frown. "And it's her day off tomorrow."

"Right." Ashley sighed. "Though I don't understand the point of hiring help if they won't, you know, *help* you. Surely she could do a bit of washing-up before she started her day off."

"Jenna helps all the time," Harry said, outraged. "She cooks, and she washes up, and she washes our clothes."

"And she takes us to school, and drives us," Sophie added, springing to Jenna's defense in her turn. "And helps with homework, and everything."

"Well, since Jenna helps us so much," Finn pointed out, anxious to placate an increasingly ruffled-looking Ashley, "Let's help her by doing the washing-up, eh."

He looked around in shock upon entering the kitchen. The family normally ate at the table set at one end of the big room, but Ashley had insisted on setting an elegant dining room table, including tablecloth and candles. And had excluded him from the kitchen while she "worked her magic." If "magic" meant "destruction," she'd worked it, right enough. Every utensil and pan she had used was scattered around, and the stovetop and benches were a sticky mess. How had she managed all this, with her limited menu?

"Right," he decided. "If you kids can clear the plates, we'll get started here."

♡

Jenna shivered as she ran the last couple blocks from the bus stop. She'd enjoyed her evening out with Natalie, but the rain had started in earnest after the movie had let out. She hadn't wanted to come back in the middle of the evening, try to steal off to her own room without the kids seeing her. It was after eleven now, though. She was tired and wet, and ready to be home.

She used her key to enter the quiet house, slipped off her soaked boots and coat in the entryway. Finn appeared in the doorway to the lounge, frowning at the sight of her dripping hair.

His eyes traveled down to the wet jersey clinging to her body, lingered there for a moment before he brought them hurriedly back up to her face again.

"Forget your umbrella?"

"Blew inside out in the middle of Queen Street," she told him ruefully. She was surprised to see Ashley appear and slip an arm through Finn's.

"Don't let me disturb you," Jenna told the two of them. "I'm headed to bed anyway, once I wring myself out."

"I was a bit concerned about you when it started raining so hard," Finn said. "Next time, you should take a car."

"I was fine," she assured him, seeing the impatience on Ashley's face. "Off to bed now, though. Nice to see you again, Ashley."

The other woman nodded briefly. "Come on, darling," she urged, taking Finn's hand to pull him back into the lounge.

He gave one last look over his shoulder at Jenna, then let Ashley lead him off.

♡

"Jenna!" Harry called out, coming in the front door late the following morning. "Are you home?"

"Jenna's day off." Finn pulled his son back when he would have dashed ahead. "If she's here, we need to leave her alone. You can say hello. But then we're having Dad Time."

"Jenna!" Harry called out as he ran. "We went to the museum! We saw the moa again! And cockroaches! They were really alive!"

Finn caught up with Harry at the kitchen doorway, then stopped at the sight of Jenna on her knees, halfway inside the oven, the racks leaning against the wall next to her. "What are you doing?"

"Oh." She shrugged, backing out and pushing her hair back with one rubber-gloved hand. "Just taking care of a spill."

"The oven." Finn exchanged a glance with Sophie. "We didn't think of that."

"Ashley's messy," Sophie explained. "We tried to clean up. But we forgot about the oven."

"Why are you cleaning it, though?" Finn asked.

"I didn't want to leave it till tomorrow," Jenna explained. "As soon as anyone turned the oven on, that spill would've become even harder to get off. I wish New Zealand had entered the Age of the Self-Cleaning Oven, but I've never even seen one here."

"Why didn't you wait for me, or leave a note?" Finn demanded. "I'd have cleaned it. Would've cleaned it last night, except I didn't realize Ashley'd managed to...that there'd been a spill."

"All right," Jenna said, surprised but agreeable. "I'm letting you know now. Finn, there's a bad spill in the oven." She stripped off her rubber gloves and slapped them into his palm with a smile. "Be my guest."

He laughed. "That's told me."

"Since I'm a lady of leisure, then," Jenna said to Harry, "I'm going to make a cup of tea and ask about the museum. You guys saw live cockroaches? That sounds very interesting."

"Very disgusting, is what it was," Finn said. "A whole colony of them. These gloves are useless. I can't even get them on."

Jenna looked over and laughed at the sight of him trying to force the gloves over his huge hands. "I don't think they make them in Rugby Forward Size. And that cleaner is caustic. Let me finish wiping it out, then you can do the rest, once I've got rid of the bad stuff." She took the gloves from him again, put them on, and dove into the oven once more.

"Jenna, you know what?" Harry said from behind her. "You have a bottom like a wombat!"

Jenna nearly hit her head on the oven ceiling as she pulled it out and sat back on her heels. "What?" she asked, staring at Harry.

"Harry!" Finn barked at his son. "That was dead rude. Apologize to Jenna."

"Sorry, Jenna," Harry said, his lip trembling at his father's tone. "I didn't know I shouldn't say."

"I forgive you," Jenna told him. "But it isn't polite to talk to ladies about their bottoms. It isn't polite to say things about how people look anyway, unless you're saying something very nice, like, 'Your dress is pretty.'"

"But I *am* saying something very nice," Harry argued, anxious to explain himself. "Wombats have special bottoms. Their bottoms are their superpowers! Remember, Sophie?" he appealed to his sister. "When Dad took us to Aussie, and we saw them?"

"Hmm? Yeh," Sophie agreed, looking up from her book. "They looked funny, I thought."

"You see, Jenna," Harry went on earnestly, "wombats dig tunnels. They have very powerful legs for digging. And if a dingo comes to try to get into the tunnel, the wombat can back up. It blocks the tunnel with its bottom. The dingo tries to get its face around the wombat. Then the wombat squeezes with its bottom, and it squishes the dingo!"

"Ah," Jenna said, trying not to laugh. "Superpower bottoms. I see."

"Even though wombat bottoms may be nice," Finn put in, a smile attempting to escape his own stern expression, "we still don't talk about ladies' bottoms. Not ever."

"Sorry, Jenna," Harry said again, looking worried. "Are you angry?"

Jenna reached out to give him a hug, then remembered the rubber gloves. "No. Of course not. Your dad told you, and now you know." She turned back to the oven again, then stopped. It *had* been kind of funny, but she wasn't about to offer Finn another view of her Wombat Bottom.

"Ah…" she looked around. "Why don't you let me finish up in here? The fumes," she realized with relief. "I'll come tell you, Finn, when I've got most of the oven cleaner wiped out and you can get in there with the elbow grease."

"Course. Let's go," he told the kids. "Leave Jenna to get on with it."

He didn't know much about wombats, Finn thought as he shepherded Harry and Sophie out of the kitchen. He knew a thing or two about ladies' bottoms, though. Jenna's may or may not have been able to squish a dingo's face. But it definitely had some superpowers.

an elephant never forgets

♡

"Explain this loose forward thing to me," Jenna told Sophie as they watched the telecast of the Blues' game against the Brumbies in Canberra on Saturday evening. "Why are they loose?"

"We have to wait for a scrum," Sophie said. "Then I'll explain."

A few minutes later, she got her chance. "OK," she said. "The Brumbies just knocked on, and now our team gets a scrum. Look at how the forwards are lined up. The tight five, the first rowers and the ones just behind them, see how they're hanging on to each other? That's why they're tight. The six and seven in the second row, they're pushing too, but they're at the edges. That's why they're loosies."

"I get it. And your dad's at the back. He's pushing too. But he's not...attached. So he's loose too."

"Right. He's a forward, but he kind of works between the forwards and the backs. He works in the scrum and the ruck, and he jumps during the lineouts too. Because he's so tall," Sophie said proudly. "But he carries the ball as well. And he'll help get it to the backs so they can run with it. Daddy has to be strong *and* fast. He has to understand the game plan, too, and what the other team's likely to do. He has to study heaps."

44

Sophie leaned forward as Finn delivered the ball and the group of backs began to run and pass, working toward the Brumbies try line. "Come *on*," she urged. *"Go."* She leaped up as the ball carrier went to the ground. "High tackle!" she shouted angrily. "Get him, Dad!"

She was jumping up and down now in her excitement, and Harry looked up from the puzzle he was working on. Jenna watched in confusion as Finn waded through the ruck to grab a Brumbies player by the jersey, pull him roughly to his feet. She could see Finn's mouth working as he held on, shoving the other man, pushing him back. Several other Blues pulled Finn off, held him as the trainer ran onto the field with his medical bag.

"Wait, wait. What's going on?" Jenna asked. She watched with relief as the injured player got up with the trainer's help and walked to the sideline, and the referee held up a yellow card.

"Sent off," Sophie said with satisfaction as play resumed and Harry went back to his puzzle, unimpressed. "Did you see how that player wrapped his arm around Koti James's neck when he tackled him? That's a high tackle. It can be really dangerous. That's why the ref sinbinned him."

"But what was your dad doing in there?" Jenna asked.

"I told you," Sophie replied matter-of-factly. "He's the hard man."

"He fights?" Jenna asked, appalled.

"Not *fights*," Sophie said. "He didn't punch him. Then *he* would've been sent off. But if somebody needs sorting, Daddy'll do it."

"He doesn't need to do that, surely," Jenna protested. "That guy got sent off anyway. He got penalized for what he did."

Sophie looked at her pityingly. "The ref doesn't always *see*. But Daddy always does."

"Oh. Wow," Jenna said blankly. "Hard man. Got it."

"Wish we didn't have to go back to school tomorrow," Sophie sighed the next morning over breakfast. "This holidays was too short."

"Sounds like we'd better do something fun today, then," Jenna said. "We're not going to mope around all day thinking about it."

"Dad's coming home from Aussie, though," Sophie said dubiously.

"Not till later this afternoon," Jenna reminded her. "I know. We'll go to Parakai Springs. I've been wanting to take you two there anyway. Today sounds like the perfect time."

"What's that?" Harry asked.

"A great big thermal pool," Jenna explained. "Thermal means that the water's heated by geothermal forces under the earth. The same kind of forces that produce volcanoes. What we saw in the museum, remember?"

"Yeh. Because the lava comes up between the plates," Harry said.

"That's it. You know how hot lava is, so you can see why it warms up the water. And it isn't only warm water. They have water slides and a fountain, too, that you can play in. Your dad said that you two swim pretty well. I'd like to see that for myself."

"Isn't it too cold for swimming?" Sophie wondered.

"Nope. It's just right. The warm water is going to feel so good. Go on and find your togs and jandals, and I'll get some towels and snacks for us."

"What if Daddy comes home and we aren't here, though?" Sophie worried again when she came back into the kitchen holding her swimming costume and flip-flops.

"I've written him a note," Jenna promised. "Telling him where we are, and that we'll be back soon."

"Swim to me," Jenna encouraged Harry as Sophie watched. "You're doing great."

"Dad!" Sophie cried, launching herself through the water. Harry reached Jenna, looked up, and was hard on his sister's heels.

Jenna turned in surprise to see Finn wading across the pool, picking up a child in each arm along the way.

Wow. That was the only word that came to mind. Despite their close quarters, she'd never seen him this closely without his shirt before. There was a lot of chest and shoulder there. A whole lot. He held both children easily, biceps and forearms bulging with their weight, thighs flexing beneath his swim trunks as he moved through the water. Once he reached her, though, her attention shifted to the liberal pattern of bruises and scrapes showing clearly even through the light furring of hair on arms and chest.

"Hi." He set the kids down, watched them heading for the side of the pool and hopping out again. "Thought I'd join you. Bit cold for swimming, isn't it?"

"Maybe for you and me," she said. "But the kids are moving around so much, they're fine. They needed to get out, and I thought you'd be home later. Were you upset not to find us there when you got in?"

"Nah. I got an earlier flight. No worries."

"Watch me, Dad!" Harry called from the top of a slide.

"Watching," Finn called back. He glanced at Jenna again, then looked away and cleared his throat. "Are you sure that costume is…right for you? For here, I mean."

"What?" Jenna stared at him, then turned back hastily to check on the kids. "Sophie! Walk walk walk."

Even as she called out, she felt the slow burn starting. "Sorry I don't look like Ashley," she snapped, anger and humiliation warring for pride of place within her. She pushed the humiliation aside, focused on the anger. "This is how a real woman looks, one who actually eats and has a normal body type. You don't have any right to criticize my costume, or my body. I don't get paid enough to put up with that."

She moved away from him. "Come on, Harry. Show me your crawl. Swim to me."

"Hang on," Finn protested. "That wasn't what I meant."

"Did you see me, Dad?" Harry asked eagerly. "Were you watching me swim?"

"Well done, mate," Finn told him. "Can you swim back?"

He waited a moment, watched Harry make his way back to the edge of the pool. "Aw, geez," he told Jenna. "Did you think I was saying you were fat?"

"Of course I did. Because that's exactly what you were saying."

"Nah. It wasn't. Not at all."

"What, then?" Her eyes narrowed as she looked at him suspiciously.

He gestured at her bikini top and the boy short-style bottoms. "It's a bit sexy, isn't it?"

She looked down at herself. "This? Next to all these teenage girls in their tiny bikinis? I don't think so. Nobody's looking at me."

"You're joking. It's…the way you fill it out. You must know that. Look at that poor bloke." He gestured in the direction of the teenage lifeguard. "Hope nobody drowns anytime soon, because he's bloody useless, the way he's staring at you. If he has to get down off that stand, he's going to embarrass himself."

"Really?" She turned to look, gave the boy a wave, watched him turn hastily away. "Wow. Cool. Although actually, you know, he's probably a rugby fan, looking at you."

Finn laughed. "Trust me. He wasn't looking at me. I don't have what he likes. And you do. So much of it, too."

"Again, inappropriate. Not as bad as I originally thought," she admitted. "But still. And I'm not going to wear some matronly one-piece with a skirt, just because you think I have too much..." She broke off.

"Too much going on," he said helpfully. "No, not too much," he corrected. "Just...*so* much. You're right, though. Stupid thing to say, and I shouldn't be talking to you about it anyway. I never realized, that's all. You wear your clothes so loose."

"I do? Are my clothes too big?"

He smiled. "Well, yeh, a bit. Unless you really are trying to hide how you look."

"Thanks for telling me. I was heavier," she said self-consciously. "I lost about fifteen kilos a year or two ago. And transformed my body some, I guess."

"All the running," he guessed.

"Yeah. And strength training too. But I'm not used to thinking I look OK. Buying this costume was a big step. I wasn't sure. And then when you said..."

"Sorry," he said hastily. "But trust me, you look OK. More than OK."

"You, on the other hand, look battered," she told him, eager to change the subject. "It did look like a tough game. Sorry you lost."

He grimaced. "Yeh, nah, we were pretty gutted. We weren't the form team last night, that was clear. Couldn't do the business in the end, even with that yellow card."

"I saw. Sophie explained the penalty to me, luckily, or I'd have been completely confused about what was going on. But do you always get that beat up? All those bruises?"

"That's the job, eh. My possie too. My position," he explained. "Offense and defense. Tackling, and getting tackled. I hit the ground a fair few times in eighty minutes."

"Then you should go sit in the spa pool," she suggested. "Soak some of that out. Wouldn't that feel better than standing here in the cold air?"

But the cold air was doing so much for her, he thought, keeping his eyes on her face with an effort. *Quit perving,* he scolded himself. Hard not to, though. When he'd first seen her with the kids, he'd been gobsmacked. The way her backside filled out those little purple shorts, their low rise showing off the curve of her hips. And when she'd turned around and he'd had a squiz at the front view, it had fair taken his breath away. Maybe she shouldn't wear her clothes any tighter, he decided. Because he had to live in the same house with her. That was going to be a bit of a challenge, now that he had the full picture.

"Why don't we all go over there?" he asked. "You must be getting cold yourself."

"It's probably time. Harry! Sophie!" she called. "Come on."

"Wow," Harry breathed, watching from the spa pool as a teen-aged boy dove from the higher of the pool's two diving boards. "Cool."

"Would you like to be able to do that?" Jenna asked him. She was stretched out on the top step of the spa with Harry and Sophie while Finn sat further down, enjoying the warmth on his bruised body.

He nodded vigorously. "It looks hard, though."

"Not really," Jenna said. "You have to learn, of course, and then practice. Just like everything else. I could teach you, if you like."

"OK!" He jumped up.

"Not right now," she laughed. "But once it gets closer to summer, and more pools are open, we can work on swimming and diving some more."

"Book them in for more lessons, d'you reckon?" Finn asked lazily.

"I can do it for now," she told him. "I taught kids to swim and dive every summer during high school. You have me anyway, might as well take advantage of it."

He turned his head to look at her. That had been a bit provocative. She clearly hadn't meant it that way, though. Pity.

"Can I learn, too?" Sophie asked.

"Of course," Jenna said. "You're both pretty good swimmers already. By the time I leave, we'll have you swimming like fish, and diving too."

"Do I have to dive off the high board?" Harry asked dubiously. "It's a bit scary."

"Not if you don't want to," Jenna assured him. "We'll do a little at a time. If you dive off the high board someday, that'll be wonderful. And if you don't, that'll be just fine too."

"Can you do it?" Sophie asked.

"Sure. I wouldn't be much of a teacher if I didn't know how, would I?"

"Would you show us?" Harry begged, and Sophie immediately added her entreaty.

"OK to leave them with you?" Jenna asked Finn.

"Good as gold."

"OK, then. I haven't done this in a couple years, but you know what they say. An elephant never forgets." She winked at the kids, then stepped out of the hot pool and walked to the diving area.

Not so much of an elephant, Finn thought, watching her sway across the pool deck in those tiny shorts. More of a...His mind blanked. What was a sexy animal? He couldn't think of one. Except for Jenna. She was a sexy animal, and no mistake. He watched as she climbed to the higher board, walked to the end and looked down, then turned back.

"Isn't she going to do it?" Sophie asked in disappointment.

"Watch," Finn commanded.

Jenna ran to the end of the board, bounced once, sprang from her toes and dove off, executing a perfect jackknife in the air and hitting the water dead straight.

"Yay!" Harry and Sophie applauded as Jenna approached them again, one hand going up to slick her wet hair back from her face.

She laughed as she slid back into the warm water to join them. "That was great," she said with a satisfied sigh. "I'd forgotten how much fun it was to do that."

"Very impressive," Finn said approvingly. "Reckon you'll be able to teach these two to dive, at that."

"Reckon I will," she teased. She winked again, slid down to the next step, and leaned back in the warm water.

Bloody hell. This was turning out to be so much more than he'd bargained for.

lean cuisine

♡

"And that's another term begun," Finn said the next morning as he came back into the kitchen after walking Sophie and Harry to school.

"Much to Sophie's disgust." Jenna fixed herself a cup of tea, then picked up some papers from the computer desk set into one end of the kitchen bench and went to sit with him. "It's interesting that she's so unexcited about it, despite being such an avid reader."

"I was never keen either," he admitted. "How about you?"

"The opposite," she said wryly. "School was the best part of my life. I spent summer vacation longing to get back. If they'd said I could go all year, believe me, I would have. I remember what a disappointment it was when I figured out that the teachers didn't actually live at school. I think I was hoping to live there with them."

"Home life that good, eh."

She smiled. "Yep. But my loss is your gain. Because that's why I'm so big on providing structure. Life's hard enough. Kids need a calm, orderly place where they can recharge."

"Reckon everyone needs that, but they don't always know how to do it. You make it look so easy."

"Well, to be fair, it's a whole lot easier when there's plenty of money to hire somebody like Nyree or me to help provide it, not to mention the housecleaners. If you were a single dad trying to do this on a limited budget, and on your own…"

"Still. You *are* good at it, and I appreciate it."

"Thanks. And on that note, do you have a few minutes to go over the schedule for the next few weeks, before I leave for the day?"

He nodded, and she pulled forward the calendar printout. All his games and the children's activities were on there, he saw, as well as her own days off. He went through it with her, answered her questions about his travel schedule, watched her taking notes in her neat schoolteacher's hand.

"Any evenings you're planning to be out, that you know of?" she asked, prepared to note them down.

"None. No plans, anyway."

She shot him a glance, and he added, "Ashley and I broke up last week. After that dinner she cooked." He chuckled. "Sounds wrong. Not because of the dinner. Though it didn't help."

"Sounds like condolences aren't in order."

"Nah. Mutual, I reckon. We weren't suited after all. Turns out I wasn't the glamorous international sportsman she was expecting. Story of my life. I'm a country boy, and a family man. Not too exciting for someone like Ashley. And she…" He stopped. "I didn't share her values, put it that way. And she didn't share mine."

"Good to find that out sooner rather than later," Jenna offered. "I'm glad you're not hurting about it."

"Not hurting, trust me."

He sat for a minute, took a sip of tea. "Oh, about the swim lessons," he remembered, "since we're talking about schedules. Meant to tell you that I appreciate that, but you're not obligated. If it's too much, just book them in somewhere."

"I'd like to do it," she assured him. "And I think it would be especially good for Harry. He isn't as physically confident as Sophie, and I'd hate to see somebody pushing him too fast and scaring him. He actually swims very well for a five-year-old. I think it might be a sport he could get good at."

"He's not very sporty, in case you haven't noticed," Finn said doubtfully.

"Team sports, and spectator sports, you're right. But sometimes kids like him enjoy individual sports much more. You don't have to be aggressive as a swimmer. You don't even have to compete, unless you want to."

"Unless you're a water polo player," he pointed out.

She laughed. "I think we can safely rule that out as a career for Harry. It'd be good for him to get the exercise, though. And to know that he can excel at something athletic, even if it's not what you do."

He looked at her in surprise. "Does that matter? I don't care if he does what I do. I love footy, always have. I'd play even if they didn't pay me. But I don't expect him to."

"You might want to make sure he knows that," she suggested, her gentle tone taking any sting out of the words. "You're a lot to live up to, you know. Especially in New Zealand, where everyone's so focused on rugby, and being an All Black is the ultimate goal. And also because Sophie *is* such a good athlete."

"Reckon she'll end up as a Football Fern, as much as she loves soccer."

"And as good as she is at it," Jenna agreed. "I've seen how you encourage her. Not all dads care so much about their daughters' athletic success. That's great. But it could also leave Harry out in the cold. If he had his own sport, it would help."

"So, swimming lessons. With the best teacher." He grinned. "You."

"Me," she agreed, smiling back at him.

"Can I ask you a question?" she went on hesitatingly.

He lifted his eyebrows inquiringly.

"When Sophie said you were the…hard man," she began. "I wasn't sure what that meant. But the other night, when you went after that guy, I figured it out. You're the one the other team's a little nervous about going up against. Because they might get hurt."

"I reckon. One of them, anyway. Why?"

"Well," she said slowly. "It just seems…odd. I mean, you're, like you said. A family man. I'd think somebody like that, the hard man, would be more of a hothead. A jerk, frankly. But I don't see that."

"Glad of that, anyway. I have a bit of a temper, it's true. You have to have it under control, though. Use your fists, and you'll be suspended. That doesn't do you or the team any good. And yeh, I tackle hard. Not always too careful with my hands and feet in the ruck, either. I may look a little scary out there. But I'll have a laugh with the boys on the other team after the game. I leave it on the paddock. Don't need to bash my kids to prove I'm a man, if that's what you mean."

"No, I wouldn't say you have a lot to prove in that department," she agreed. "I think it's fairly clear." She smiled at him, saw the answering smile start in his eyes, spread over his face.

She blushed as she replayed her words in her mind. "Time for me to get going," she decided, rising and carrying her mug to the dishwasher.

Finn's praise of her abilities gave her a glow of satisfaction that stayed with her as she began the long run that would take her through two domains, then on to the Central Business District and back. It was true that her own childhood hadn't featured much order or warmth. Which was, she knew, why it gave her so much pleasure to provide those things for these children. For this family.

In fact, living here was just about as complete a change as possible from the mobile home park where she'd grown up. The trees, ferns, and flowering plants of the lush gardens in the Mt. Eden neighborhood were a stark contrast to the few oleander bushes that had provided a touch of color here and there in the park, not to mention the border of white gravel surrounding the modest mobile home she'd shared with her mother. Nothing survived in the Las Vegas heat without care and water, and her mother had never been a gardener. Or a housekeeper. And Sherri McKnight had had only contempt for Jenna's housewifely impulses and attention to her schoolwork.

"If you'd spend half the time on your appearance that you do on all that crap, you might be able to get a boyfriend," her mother had snapped one Saturday morning. Sherri had come home from her overnight "date" to find Jenna vacuuming, ponytail hanging down her back, baggy shorts and T-shirt concealing the puppy fat that hadn't melted away, even though she had ceased to be a puppy some time ago. "Look at you. You're a mess."

"I'm only sixteen, Mom," Jenna answered defensively. "Lots of girls in my class don't have boyfriends."

"You've never even been on a date, though, have you?" Sherri pointed out. "I had boys asking me out from the time I was thirteen. You aren't even trying. You need to go on a diet. I can give you some pills."

"Those pills aren't healthy," Jenna told her. "And I am trying. I'm doing my best to eat right." Except when she was feeling bad, she thought guiltily, and bought bags of cookies or candy bars with the money she'd earned babysitting for the other families in the park. Food that she hid in her underwear drawer to escape her mother's criticism.

"Joe told me last night that I had the body of a twenty-five-year-old," Sherri told her daughter complacently, turning sideways to look at herself in the full-length mirror on the wall of the tiny living room. "I look ten years younger than my age, and you look ten years older."

Her mother was thirty-nine, not thirty-five, Jenna knew, but she didn't correct her. "Remember, Mom, I'm teaching swim lessons this morning, so I need to borrow the car. I got an extra class added, the three-year-olds. That'll be fun. But it means I won't be back till one or so."

"Mm-hm," her mother answered, picking up the remote and turning the TV on before sitting down on the couch and beginning to flip channels. "I'll be in bed. I need a nap before work. Be quiet when you come in."

"I was going to make a chicken salad for dinner tonight before I babysit for the Rosses," Jenna offered. "Do you want me to leave you some for after work?"

"No. I'll have a Lean Cuisine," her mother told her, lighting a cigarette. "You should have one of those instead too. Less than three hundred calories in the chicken stir-fry, and you don't have to go to all that trouble. Heat it up and you're done."

It was good to know, Jenna thought now, that nobody here was ever going to suggest that a frozen dinner would be preferable to her own efforts. And it was gratifying to feel that her hard work was appreciated, and that she was helping to make this home a warm, happy place. Even if wasn't actually her home. Or her place.

daddy's ladies

♡

"I need to find something else to do," she told Natalie that evening over a dinner of boneless, skinless chicken breasts she'd first pounded, then dredged in beaten egg and dukkah, the Turkish mix of finely chopped nuts, herbs, and spices, and finally pan-fried. She'd sliced carrots into matchsticks and cooked them with dill, and served a baby spinach and microgreens salad and seeded Turkish flatbread as an accompaniment. The result had been a quick winter meal that, she thought, she'd be trying out soon on Finn and the kids.

She'd been going to Nat's flat every Monday since she'd started the job to fix supper for the two of them. A bit of a busman's holiday, but she hadn't been able to face the prospect of going out to dinner alone every week. Instead, she'd begun trying new recipes on Natalie, who was more than willing to accept the personal chef service at the start of her workweek.

"You don't like the job?" Natalie asked now in surprise. "I thought it was working out."

"Besides the job," Jenna clarified.

"Besides taking care of Finn and the kids, not to mention me," Natalie said dubiously. "Why?"

"Because it's not enough. What am I supposed to do with a day and a half off every week? Hide in my room? OK, I do my long run. I come over here and cook for you. I hang out a little bit. That's maybe one day, all together. *If* I stretch it out."

"I see what you mean," Natalie said. "It'd be different if it were your own house."

"Exactly. That's their family time. And Finn's quiet time to recover after the game. Plus, you know, if he wanted to have anyone over, I'd be in the way. It feels awkward to be there, so I stay away. But it's pretty hard to find somewhere to be all that time. And it feels a little pathetic, you know. Wandering the streets." She tried to make a joke of it, but felt forlorn all the same. "I hadn't anticipated how hard it would be not to have my own place to go to."

"You could always come here," Natalie offered. "More than you do. My flatmate wouldn't mind, I'm sure."

"Thanks. I appreciate that. But I was actually thinking of volunteering. Finding a Year One classroom where they could use my help. If I'm going to go back to teaching in the new year, it'd be good to spend a little time in the classroom, see how they do things in Auckland."

"Not that differently to how they do them in Wellington," Natalie laughed. "Not like it's very far away."

"I was thinking about one of the schools with more Maori and Islander kids. That'd be a change, and a challenge. South Auckland, maybe."

"Don't want to get too far away, without a car. You don't want to spend half your Monday on a bus, going all the way down to Manukau or wherever. You could try Onehunga or Mangere, though. They'd be chuffed to have you, I know that."

"Good ideas. I'll make some calls tomorrow, see what would work," Jenna decided. "You want any more of this?"

"Nah. Thanks, as always."

"No worries." Jenna got up to wrap the leftovers and put them into the fridge for Nat's dinner the following night. "Thank you for the company. And the suggestion."

♡

"I appreciate you coming with me today," she told Natalie the next weekend as they left Smith & Caughey's and made their way down the road toward Glassons. "It's lucky that Finn's game was at home this week, so I could get you to help me. I'm not that confident picking out clothes by myself. And I'm going to feel much more secure tomorrow if I know I look good. Kind of silly, I know. It's not like the kids will care. But it'll help anyway."

"I've decided I'm glad you have something else to focus on," Natalie said. "And something to remind you that this post is temporary. Because I'm worried about you."

"Why? I'm doing great."

"Yeh. Too great, I'm thinking."

"What does *that* mean?"

"Do you realize how many times you've mentioned Finn and the kids today? And every time I've seen you? How involved you are?"

"Well, of course I am. I'm living there. That's my life right now, taking care of them."

"But it *isn't* your life. Not really," Natalie said bluntly. "It's a job. They're not your family. You do realize that, don't you? D'you think it's a good idea to get so attached?"

"You can't help but get attached. You know that. It seems like you get one or two kids every year who are special, who worm their way into that spot in your heart."

"Yeh, but you don't adopt them. And you don't go live with them—or their fit All Black dads either."

"What, Finn? Come on. I'm smarter than that."

"Yeh, right. Why are we shopping today, again?"

"Because I need new clothes for volunteering. I told you."

"Uh-huh. Then why did you just buy three pairs of jeans that make your bum look good, instead of those Mum jeans you were wearing? And why have you suddenly decided to stop hiding your tits? Mind you, I'm not saying that's a bad thing. If mine looked like that, I'd be showing them off left, right, and center."

"You're awful," Jenna laughed. "Yeah, OK, I realized I was wearing my clothes too big. *All* my clothes. I'm not overweight any more, and I should be enjoying that. I've worked hard enough for it."

"Yeh, you have. But, I forget now, who pointed that out to you?"

"You, for one. I know you said something like that, the first week I was here."

"And it made such an impact that you bought, let's see, *no* new clothes in response. But Finn Douglas tells you you're hot, and suddenly you're out with me, buying a new wardrobe."

"He didn't say I was hot," Jenna protested.

"Yeh, he did," Natalie said. "Told you your togs were too sexy, right?"

"Just because he was concerned about, you know, my image or something, out with his kids."

"Nah. Because he liked what he saw, and that made him uncomfortable."

"Even if he does think I look...nice," Jenna said, "it doesn't mean he has a thing for me. You didn't see his girlfriend. I don't even come close."

"I could debate that too. Anyway, he's a sportsman. I think we can take it as read that he has a thing for you. I'm not concerned about that. I'm worried about how much of a thing *you* have for *him*. He's not your man, and they aren't your kids." Natalie was serious again now. "I have a feeling that you wish they were. And I'm worried that you won't be guarding your heart."

Jenna stopped walking and turned to look at her friend. "Nat. I told you, I'm smarter than that. I know who and what I am. And that it isn't what Finn's looking for. I like him. I like him a lot. He's a really decent guy, and a good dad. And yes, I like how he looks. How big and strong he is."

"But you don't fancy him," Natalie said dubiously.

"Come on. I can appreciate him—*and* how he looks—without climbing into bed with him. You think he's hot too. Admit it."

"Oh, I admit it. I'd be all over that, given the chance. You can invite me to come by anytime, not that I think you will. He may not be a looker, but he's got that craggy, manly thing going on. Great physique. But it's dangerous, living with someone you fancy. I'm not so worried about you jumping him. I don't really see that happening. What about when he makes a move on you, though? What are you going to do then? Tell him you're not that kind of girl? I reckon it's going to be more like, 'Kiss me again, big boy.'"

"Let's hope my strength of character isn't put to the test," Jenna said ruefully. "I'm afraid you could be right. *If* that happened. But I don't think it would, because Finn's realistic too. He needs me too much. As a nanny," she clarified hastily. "And he's not short of girlfriend options, I'm sure."

"But he isn't dating anyone now, is he?" Natalie asked.

"It's only been a couple weeks since he broke up with the personality-impaired Ashley," Jenna pointed out. "And that's another thing. All right, she was gorgeous. But she wasn't exactly warm and fuzzy. Cool to cold, I'd say. So, I'm clearly not his type. I can look, but I'm not fooling myself there's going to be any touching going on. Don't worry about me."

"Just watch yourself," Natalie warned. "That's all I'm saying."

♡

Jenna studied herself critically. The outfit had looked good in the shop yesterday, and Natalie had assured her that it was flattering.

But now, in her own bedroom mirror where she was used to viewing herself in decidedly looser clothing, she wondered. Was it a bit much? She wanted to make a good impression, and it *was* a classroom. And her first day. Better to err on the conservative side. She debated changing back into one of her familiar, comfortable outfits. But both Finn and Nat had said she wore her clothes too loose. And she did look better this way, she could tell.

Everything she'd bought yesterday had passed muster with both Natalie and the saleswoman, Jenna reminded herself. The black knit skirt wasn't really short, after all, just a few inches above the knee. Her Kiwi-style black tights meant that she wasn't even showing any skin. And the long-sleeved top was pretty. She stroked a hand down the side of the knit fabric with its richly saturated purple and green paisley print. The cut, although trim, couldn't be called tight, while the high keyhole neckline added a bit of flair without being in the least revealing.

She couldn't stand here dithering. If she didn't get going, she wasn't going to have a chance to eat anything before catching the bus.

All the same, when she entered the kitchen and found Sophie and Harry finishing their cereal and toast, she couldn't resist the question.

"What do you think of my new outfit, Sophie? Does it look OK?"

Great. Now she was asking fashion advice of a seven-year-old.

Sophie paused with her spoon halfway to her mouth and looked her over critically. "I like the shirt," she pronounced. "It's pretty. You look nice."

Jenna exhaled. "Thanks. I bought new clothes yesterday when I went shopping with my friend, and I'm a little nervous about them."

"Let's ask Daddy," Sophie suggested as Finn came into the kitchen. "Don't you think Jenna's new clothes are pretty?" she demanded of her father.

Finn looked Jenna over. "Very pretty, I agree."

"Daddy sees heaps of ladies," Sophie told Jenna helpfully. "And they always wear lovely dresses. So he knows."

"Jenna's prettier than Daddy's ladies, though," Harry argued. "Jenna's the most beautiful woman in the world."

"Thanks, buddy," Jenna laughed. "My target demographic," she explained wryly to Finn. "I profile extremely well with five-year-old boys."

"I reckon you can aim a wee bit higher than that." Finn's answering smile was warm, his eyes appreciative. "You did some shopping, eh."

"Yeah. You said my clothes were too big," Jenna said self-consciously. "And my friend agreed. I'm not used to looking like this, though. You don't think everything's a bit...a bit tight? Like I'm trying to be..." Her voice trailed off.

"Sexy?" he asked bluntly. "Nah. I wouldn't say you look like you're trying. I'd say you just can't help it."

"I knew it. OK. I'm changing." Forget breakfast, she decided. Better to go hungry than to show up looking like she was headed to a nightclub.

"Aw, geez. Don't change," Finn said hastily, putting out a hand to stop her as she turned to go. "I shouldn't have said that. Nothing's too tight. There's nothing wrong with looking pretty, wherever it is you're going. Unless you're volunteering at Pare, that is. Then I'd consider a nun's habit. Anyplace short of that, you're gold."

"At where?" So this outfit *was* wrong for volunteering. She'd known it.

"Paremoremo. The prison," Finn explained. "Sorry. Stupid joke. You look good. Don't change."

He was sweating a bit now. How had he got himself into this? At least she hadn't asked if the skirt made her bum look big. But there was still no right answer. He certainly couldn't tell her that the skirt made her bum look choice. Or that his hands itched to untie the little bow at the top of that hole in her shirt.

Inappropriate, he reminded himself again. Inappropriate and dangerous.

"Done with brekkie?" he asked the kids instead. "Hit your straps, then, and let's get on to school. Give Jenna some peace."

He looked back at Jenna as the three of them left the kitchen. "Don't change," he ordered her again. "You look good. Trust me."

friendship bracelets

♡

Jenna smiled a hello at the group of mums waiting for their kids outside the gates of Mt. Eden Primary on Thursday. She stood a bit apart, as always. Everyone was pleasant, but she was a nanny, not a mum, and she'd felt the distinction being made from the beginning.

"Jenna!" Sophie burst out of the gate with her friend Caitlin beside her. "Can Caitlin come over?"

Jenna blinked in surprise. Sophie'd been weepy this morning as she'd said goodbye to Finn, and she'd expected more tears this afternoon. It was good to see her so cheerful.

"I think so," she said cautiously. "If she asks her mum."

"Hi." Caitlin's mum moved to join them, her small son with her. "Siobhan," she reminded Jenna. "And this is Ethan."

"Jenna McKnight." Jenna reached out to shake hands, then braced herself for Harry's exuberant arrival. He'd been the last to arrive, as always. Somehow, it always seemed to take him longer to get out the door than anyone else. His mind was on more important things, no doubt.

"Sophie'd like Caitlin to come to the house today," she told the other woman as she disentangled herself. "Would that work for you?"

"Don't see why not, for an hour or so," Siobhan agreed. "She's been there before. I know where you are."

"Let me give you my mobile number." Jenna dictated it as Siobhan typed it into her phone. "Till four-thirty? Does that work for you?"

"Course. We're just a few streets away. Ethan and I will walk part of the way with you, in fact."

♡

"Muuumm!!" Caitlin wailed when Siobhan arrived at the house later that afternoon. "We aren't finished yet!"

"They're making friendship bracelets," Jenna explained. "Sophie got a kit for her last birthday, but for some reason she's only now become interested. Now, of course, it's the new obsession. Can you stay a few minutes while they finish up, have a cup of tea?"

"Always the way," Siobhan agreed. "And I'd love a cuppa."

"Harry, why don't you take Ethan to your room?" Jenna suggested. "Show him your collections. I'll bet he'd like to see them."

"OK," Harry said agreeably. "C'mon, Ethan. Come see my animals."

"I really appreciate your letting Caitlin come today," Jenna told Siobhan once they were seated at the kitchen table, their cups of tea in front of them. "Sophie always has a hard time on the day Finn leaves."

"Where is he this week?"

"Wellington. The Hurricanes, for the quarterfinal. So not a long trip. He'll be back Sunday morning. But with Nyree gone as well, it's hard for her right now."

Siobhan nodded. "I heard about Sophie's mum. She's attached to her dad, eh."

"You could say that." Jenna smiled ruefully. "They both are. But Sophie especially."

"I know a fair bit about it, as you see, even though I'm a newcomer myself," Siobhan said with a smile of her own. "Finn's the subject of a good bit of gossip amongst the mums. Always causes a stir when he delivers the kids at school."

"Everyone loves an All Black," Jenna agreed. "You're a newcomer too? You're a Kiwi, though, aren't you?"

"Cantabrian," Siobhan explained. "We moved from Christchurch at the beginning of the school year. The earthquakes finally got to be too much for us." At Jenna's sympathetic murmur, she continued, "It was one thing when the kids were littlies, when I had them with me all the time. But when Caitlin started Year One, every time one hit, especially if it was a big one, I'd be thinking about how to get to her. And thinking about Ethan getting ready to start kindy too…She sighed. "My family's always lived in Christchurch. It was hard to leave. We felt like traitors. But the kids were scared, too. Crying whenever there was a good shake. It just got to be too much."

"I can imagine," Jenna said. "Or rather, I can't really imagine what it must be like to live with so many earthquakes, not being able to trust the ground under your feet."

"Every day, sometimes," Siobhan said. "And then, of course, the big ones. Those really do get to you. Worrying about my hubby, too. Declan worked in the CBD. He wasn't in one of the badly damaged buildings, thank God. But it was awful, that day. Horrible, waiting to hear, knowing what was happening down there. And after that, even though his firm relocated, it was scary having him so far away from me and the kids. And all the firms that closed, not being able to go to the café, no real city life…"

She paused, looking into space. "It hasn't felt the same place. We resisted for a long time. But last year, Declan began looking up here, and we made the decision to move."

"It must have been so hard," Jenna said. "After so long."

"Reckon you know what it's like to move far from home," Siobhan said, a smile lighting her plump, freshly pretty face. "From the States, aren't you? Here on a working holiday visa, or for longer?"

"Longer. I've been here since I was twenty-two."

"Really." Siobhan's eyebrows rose. "We don't get many immigrants from the States. Came here on a visit and decided to stay, eh."

"Not exactly. I followed a man. Classic story."

Siobhan nodded. "Man's gone, I take it."

"*I'm* gone," Jenna corrected. "Or rather, I'm still here, in New Zealand. But not with him, if you see what I mean. But," she went on briskly, "it's all good. I'm in Auckland now, I have a good job, I'm enjoying myself."

"It's hard, though, in a new place," Siobhan said. "At least for me. The mums are friendly enough, but..." She shrugged. "It takes a bit. They have their friendships. Their kids went to kindy, Year One together. It can be tough to be the new one."

"Especially if you're a nanny," Jenna said.

"Even harder. And now," Siobhan sighed as she stood up, "much as I'd prefer to sit here and keep chatting, I reckon I'd better collect the kids and get home, get a start on tea, or we're not going to eat tonight."

"Did they say when you'd have it back?" Jenna asked as Finn hopped into the Toyota at the mechanic's where he'd just dropped off the Range Rover on the following Tuesday afternoon.

"A few days. I'll get Ben Thompson to collect me, next couple days. Won't worry about getting it back till I'm home from Canberra. No point, as long as you and the kids'll give me a lift from the airport on Sunday."

"Of course. I could drive you to training too, if you'd rather," she offered. "And pick you up afterwards as well."

"Nah. No worries. Ben'll be chuffed."

"Why would he be that pleased to drive you? Are you his hero or something?"

He laughed. "Not a hope. But he's looking for that starting spot. He'll be taking the opportunity to pick my brain."

"And that's OK with you?"

"Well, to be dead honest, not so much. But it's part of the job to mentor the younger boys. And to make sure there's a fit replacement ready to go if I'm injured in the next game, or when I retire. Or, God forbid, when he overtakes me and I'm the one riding the pine."

"Tough, then," Jenna said sympathetically. "To have to teach him all your special tricks. Those boots in the ruck, and everything."

Finn chuckled. "Nah, Ben's never going to be the hard man. Not enough edge to him. You'll see."

Jenna dashed the last few yards through the rain that had done a good job of drenching her during the run home. She reached the gate and opened it as a tall man in his early twenties hopped out of a sports car that had pulled up to the curb.

"Morning," he called, pulling his Blues beanie down over his mop of blond hair and jumping up the step to join her. "I'm Ben. Here for Finn."

"Come on out of the rain, then." Jenna ran up the stone steps with Ben close behind. Once they were under the shelter of the villa's broad front porch, she pulled out her house key and opened the door. He reached for it and held it for her, shutting it after them.

"Phew. That blew up fast," she laughed as she hung her rain jacket on the hook, toed off her shoes and pulled off her soaked socks. "Hang on a second. I'll get Finn for you."

Before she had a chance to go looking for him, Finn came out of the kitchen, still munching a slice of toast and taking a final mouthful of tea. "Morning. You're early."

"Didn't want to be late," Ben answered with a cheeky grin, "and have you going crook at me."

"Too right. And Jenna, you should've driven the kids." Finn frowned at her.

"No worries. They didn't get wet. The rain started on my way back."

"That's what I meant," he said. "You should've driven them."

"I didn't melt. Just a bit bedraggled, that's all." She took the empty mug from him. "Have a good day. Nice to meet you, Ben." She gave him a smile and headed for the kitchen. No point in changing out of her running capris. She'd towel them off as best she could, then clean the kitchen and start the washing before she went on her real run. It was likely to rain on her again anyway.

♡

"Right. Let's go, then. Thanks for the lift." Finn finished tying his shoes and picked up his duffel from its spot beside the door.

"That's the nanny, eh," Ben said bemusedly as they headed down the steps. "Bloody hell, she's fit. You should've warned me. I'd've combed my hair. Good thing you aren't married, though. The missus would never go for that."

Finn stared balefully at him through the rain, but didn't comment until they were in the car.

"Jenna's a professional," he said at last. "She's a trained teacher. Bloody good cook, too. I'm lucky to have her."

♡

"Mind if I come in for a minute?" Ben asked when they approached the house again that afternoon. "Haven't seen your kids for a while. I could say hello."

"My kids. Right. Didn't know you were so fond of them."
But Finn led Ben up the steps to the front door again.

The house was quiet as Finn dumped his duffel by the door.
"Jenna!" he called, then shrugged. "Maybe she's out getting the
kids now. Come on into the kitchen, have a cuppa."

They walked into the warm room and saw Jenna, her back to
them, hips swinging back and forth, body bopping to an invis-
ible beat while she worked at the kitchen bench. Finn stepped up
behind her and tapped her gently on the shoulder. She whirled in
alarm, an icing-covered spatula still in her hand, and the implement landed squarely on his warmup jacket, leaving a messy
smear of white.

She pulled the headphones from her ears, laughing in dismay. "Oh, no! What a mess. That's what you get for sneaking up
on me, though."

She reached for her hip and turned off her iPod. "Hi, Ben.
You guys caught me dancing. How embarrassing. Here, Finn, let
me clean you up." She wet a paper towel at the sink and moved
close to wipe the white icing off his chest, then stopped abruptly,
flushing, and handed him the towel. "Maybe you'd better do it.
Or, better yet, throw it in the basket, and I'll wash it. Because
that's going to leave a mark."

"No worries," Finn told her with a smile, giving a cursory
wipe to the spot and tossing the towel in the bin. "Nice show you
put on for us there. What're you making?"

"Carrot cake. Would you guys like some?"

Finn raised an eyebrow at Ben. "I would," the younger man
agreed. "Please."

"Couple cups of tea, too, then. This cake requires that."
Jenna pushed the button on the electric jug and got out three
mugs, putting a teabag into each and pouring in the water that
had boiled within seconds.

"Where're the kids?" Finn asked.

"Sophie has soccer, and Harry has kapa haka. New Wednesday schedule, remember? I'm leaving to get them in about twenty minutes. How was training?"

"Gym day, mostly," Finn told her. "As it was so wet. Did a bit of work outdoors as well, though. It's good to practice in the wet sometimes. We play in it often enough."

"That must have been unpleasant." She cut two generous slices of cake and put them on plates, adding a fork to each. "Milk and sugar, Ben?"

"Both, please," he said. She added them to his mug, poured a splash of milk into Finn's tea, and handed them their tea and cake, fixed her own mug, and sat down with them at the big table.

"This is yum," Ben told her after his first bite of cake. "What's in the icing?"

"Fresh ginger," she said. "That's the secret. What did you guys work on today?"

She listened, drank her tea as Finn and Ben began to fill her in.

"Ben was having trouble with his boots," Finn told her with a smile. "Least that's what he told us. He came a real greaser, fell bang on his face during a running drill. While the newsies were out there, too, doing a piece about our being the form team. Cameras and all."

"Oh, no," Jenna commiserated in laughing sympathy. "Poor you. I'm sure they won't show that, though. You must have got good and muddy, Ben."

"And I don't have anyone to do my washing," he sighed piteously. "Have to go home and put it in the machine myself. Nobody to fix my tea, either. My work day's just beginning."

"Rough," she agreed, a smile quirking the corner of her mouth. "You may have to get a takeaway. The horror. And you may want to work on your story as well. I know the team takes care of your kit for you, remember? But speaking of work, I need to go get the kids."

"I'll walk you, or drive you if you'd rather." Ben bounded up and went with her to the entryway. "That's why I came in, to say hi to the kids. Didn't know I'd be getting cake too. That was choice. Thanks."

♡

"So you're a nanny, eh," he said to her as they crossed the main road on their way to the primary school.

She nodded. "Just for now. I'm a teacher, normally."

"Yeh, Finn said. And a cook, obviously. Is it hard work?"

She laughed. "No. Finn isn't a very exacting employer."

"He gives you days off, then?"

She looked at him in surprise. "Of course he does. Once the game's over, and he's back from wherever."

"So your days off are the same as ours, more or less," he said. "Sunday, I reckon."

"Unless you're in South Africa or Perth, slow getting back."

"Maybe you'd like to have dinner with me this Sunday, then," he suggested. "Have somebody else do the cooking."

She thought about offering an excuse, decided to keep it simple. "Sorry, but I can't."

"Monday?" he persisted.

"Sorry." She smiled up at him apologetically. "I'm not available. For dating, I mean."

She saw with relief that Harry and Sophie were waiting outside the school gates. Harry ran to her with his usual enthusiastic hug, Sophie following behind.

"You guys know Ben, right?" Jenna asked them. "He's keeping me company today."

Sophie looked at him suspiciously. "Why?"

"Sophie!" Jenna exclaimed, shocked. "That isn't very nice."

"He's the backup No. 8," Sophie explained. "He's trying to get Daddy's job. You shouldn't be nice to him."

"Oi," Ben said plaintively. "I just do what I'm told. I have to earn a crust somehow. Have a heart, Sophie. After I gave your dad a lift today, and all."

"Apologize, Sophie," Jenna said sternly. "Ben hasn't done anything wrong, and that wasn't at all polite."

"Sorry," Sophie muttered.

"Did practice go badly, or something else go wrong?" Jenna guessed. "You seem a bit out of sorts."

"I missed four goals, and didn't make any at all," Sophie told her glumly. "I was rubbish."

"Sometimes that happens," Ben put in. "I fell on my face today, myself. Fell on my ar—my bum a few times too, in the rain."

"Really?" Sophie brightened.

He nodded. "Looks like that starting job's eluded me again." He sighed theatrically. "Your dad's just too good for me. Tell me more about what happened, though. You were a bit off pace, eh."

"Jenna," Harry was tugging at her sleeve, impatient with the conversation as Sophie and Ben continued to chat during the walk back. "We learnt a new waiata today in kapa haka. *E Te Iwi E.* It's one that men sing, did you know that?"

"I know that one," Jenna said with pleasure. "Will you sing it to me tonight?"

"If I remember," he said dubiously.

"I think I do," she said. "I can look up the lyrics. After dinner, we'll have a bit of a practice, all right?"

"I'll be off, then," Ben announced as they arrived back at the house. "See you, kids. And Jenna. Cheers for the cake. If you change your mind at all, Finn has my mobile number."

"Thanks." She smiled at him apologetically. "But I don't think so."

♡

"Jenna has a boyfriend, eh," Ben asked Finn the following day on the way to the team's Eden Park training facility.

"Not that I know of," Finn said in surprise. "Turned you down, did she? Is that what she said?"

"Not exactly. Said she was 'unavailable.' Whatever that means. Pity. That cake was choice, and she isn't bad herself. Some other reason, d'you reckon? Not a lesbian, is she? That'd be a bloody waste."

"None of your business. Or mine. But I doubt it. Maybe she just didn't like you, did you think of that? Or could be she thought you were a cheeky kid, and she's looking for a man."

"Like you?" Ben asked slyly.

Finn looked across at him. "No. Watch what you're saying."

"Come on. It hasn't occurred to you? You can't tell me that. Because I thought I saw something there, looking back."

"Did you pay any attention at all to that sexual harassment training at the start of the season?" Finn asked. "About unwelcome attention? There's a reason you boys need to watch those vids."

"How d'you know it'd be unwelcome?" Ben argued.

"I'm her employer," Finn said irritably. "That's the definition of unwelcome. Because she's not in a position to say no, not while she's working for me. Well, she is, of course," he amended. "But she may not think so. It's not a good position to put her into," he finished in exasperation. "Bad idea."

"I can think of a few positions I'd like to put her into," Ben said with a grin.

"Shut up," Finn said sharply.

"What? Just a bit of fun."

"Not funny. You asked her, and she said no. Drop it."

consolation prize

♡

" Come *on,* Dad. Come *on,*" Sophie urged from her spot on the lounge floor, her little hands gripping the edges of the coffee table.

Conditions in Canberra were dreadful, the winter wind and rain lashing not only the players, but also the spectators in the open stadium. Fans huddled miserably under raincoats and ponchos, but nobody in the capacity crowd of twenty-five thousand seemed to be interested in leaving with the score standing at 23-21 with only ten minutes to play in this semifinal match. Ominously, the Blues' first-five had been forced out of the game fifteen minutes earlier with a knee injury, and his replacement had already missed a post-try conversion that would have tied the game.

Even Harry was watching now. "If they don't win, what happens?" he asked Sophie. "Do they still get to play next week?"

"*No,*" Sophie said in exasperation, watching anxiously as the Brumbies mounted another attack on the Blues' try line. "It's the *semifinal,* Harry. The Brumbies would go to the final, not the Blues. Dad *told* you."

She exclaimed in relief as the Blues' captain, Drew Callahan, stole the ball and the Auckland team took possession. Over and over, the Blues charged ahead, to be met every time by fierce

resistance from the Brumbies' forwards. One particularly ferocious collision, a commotion on the field, and the camera panned
to a player in a blue jersey lying motionless on the turf.

"Who is it?" Jenna asked, eyes straining to sort out the figures in the ruck. "Can you see, Sophie?" She looked down, realized Sophie was sitting rigid, hands over her mouth.

"Hey, now." Jenna dropped to the floor herself, put her arm
around the little girl, saw the tears beginning. "Look," she said as
her eyes searched the screen. "It's not your dad. See him, there?"

"It's the No. 11," she added, just as the announcers told the
viewing audience that the injured player was Kevin McNicholl,
the right wing, and the trainer signaled for the gurney. The three
of them watched as McNicholl was loaded onto the contraption
and wheeled off to a round of applause from the spectators.

"He's moving," Jenna told Sophie. "That's good. Look at the
replay. I'd say a concussion, wouldn't you?" She saw that Sophie's
tears hadn't abated, hugged her more tightly. "Come on, now.
He's going to be all right. And they're starting to play again. You
want to watch this, don't you?"

"I thought it was Dad," Sophie said in a small voice, her eyes
still streaming.

"It wasn't, though," Jenna told her gently. "Look at your
Dad. Look how hard he's working. He's fine."

"What if it is, though?" Sophie sobbed. "What if something
really bad happens to Daddy?"

"Well, something does happen, lots of times," Jenna pointed
out practically. "But he seems pretty tough to me. He's been
playing a lot of years, right? And he's still out there, not missing
many games at all, from what I've seen. He wouldn't want you to
be crying now. He'd want you to watch him, don't you think?"

Sophie nodded, her sobs turning to sniffs as the Blues continued to play with a replacement who had come off the bench for
the missing No. 11. She groaned when the substitute first-five

missed a penalty kick that would have won the game for the Blues in the final few minutes, and she and Harry both cried out in dismay when the final hooter sounded leaving the score unchanged, signaling an abrupt ending to the Blues' season.

Jenna felt dejected as well. In the short time she'd been watching, she had come to expect the Blues to win their games, and knowing that the team wouldn't be going to the final caused her own heart to sink. Watching Finn as he congratulated the Brumbies players and put a consoling arm around the replacement first-five, she could see the disappointment and pain he couldn't quite hide behind his stoical mask.

"Well," she said to a drooping Sophie and Harry, "they did their best. You know that. It's too bad, but you know what your dad says. Losing's part of the game too. You can tell that they hate it, but they couldn't do any more than they did. They got unlucky with the injuries, didn't they?"

Sophie nodded, her face somber.

Jenna gave her another hug. "Let's get you into bed, both of you. Sophie, do you want to come to Harry's room with me? It's late, but I think we could use a chapter from *Charlotte's Web* tonight, don't you?"

Harry bounced up, his mood, as always, shifting quickly. "What do you think will happen to Wilbur?" he asked. "Will they sell him?"

"Once you go to the toilet and get in bed, we'll find out, won't we?" Jenna asked. "Come on, Sophie," she urged. "You'll feel better once you've washed your face. And tomorrow, we'll go pick your dad up at the airport. You can tell him how much you love him. That'll make him feel better too, don't you think? Because I'll bet he's pretty sad himself, right now."

♡

"What's this?" Finn asked gently the next day, dropping to a crouch to hug his children in the International Arrivals area of the Auckland airport. "Those tears aren't for me, are they, Sophie Bee?"

"I'm sorry, Daddy," Sophie sobbed. "I'm so sorry you lost. I wanted you to win *so much.*"

"Yeh. We wanted that too," Finn told her. "But you know you can't always win."

Jenna could see the evidence of the hard-fought match in the cuts and bruises on his face, the stiff way he and his teammates carried themselves. She thought she'd have been able to tell that they'd lost, even if she hadn't known it already, just from their body language.

"Were you very sad, Daddy?" Harry asked.

"We were all very sad," he admitted. "We'll have to barrack for the Crusaders now, though, won't we? We'll watch together next Saturday night, eh. Send them our good thoughts."

"And you know what this means," he added, hefting his duffel and taking a child's hand in each of his to lead the way out to the carpark. "Means I get to start training with the All Blacks this week instead of next. Give me that much more time with the squad before we meet the Wallabies. I'll get to see some of those Brumbies boys again. We'll see how they do against the ABs."

"Yeh," Sophie agreed, brightening a little now. "They'll be sorry then, won't they, Dad?"

"Hope so," he grinned at her.

"How are the injured players doing?" Jenna asked him once they were back in the car again. Finn had raised no objection to her driving, seeming content to stretch out and relax in the passenger seat. "That concussion didn't look good."

He grimaced. "Yeh, that was a fair knock. He was only out for a bit, but you hate to see that. They'll keep a pretty close eye on him for the next couple weeks. May rest him for the first game or two with the ABs. Kevvie's played some hard footy anyway, this season."

"Just like you," Jenna pointed out. "At least it looks that way to me. Will they rest you?"

"I hope not," he said with alarm. "I'm in good nick. Least I will be by the time we start practicing again. Bit sore today."

"We'll take care of you, Daddy," Sophie promised. "Jenna made a chocolate cake for you for tonight."

"Lucky me," he said seriously. "I'll be looking forward to that."

"Not sure that's much of a consolation prize," Jenna told him with a smile. "But it was the only thing I could think of."

It would do, Finn thought. But it wasn't the only thing he could've come up with. He shifted wearily. The loss still gnawed at him, and the couple of beers he'd had the night before hadn't done much to drown his sorrows. Sinking into a willing woman would definitely have helped, though. He needed to find a new girlfriend. And Jenna, unfortunately, wasn't giving him any go-ahead signals. Anyway, it would make his life too complicated. She was doing a proper job with the kids, and that was the important thing. He didn't want to risk mucking that up.

"Sophie seemed pretty upset about the loss," he remarked to her later that afternoon, sitting in the kitchen over a cup of tea and watching her marinate chicken for that night's dinner. "Did you have a hard time with her last night?"

Jenna nodded as she squeezed a lemon into the ziplock bag and squeezed the bag shut, shaking it to mix the marinade. "It was tough on her. Especially the concussion. She thought it was you, at first. It terrified her. Then the loss too. But mostly, I think it was the injuries. She worries about you."

He frowned. "I know she does. Not much I can do about it, though. If you start worrying about being injured, holding back, you're useless. That's the beginning of the end."

"I can see that. But…" He could see her hesitate as she looked at him, before turning her attention back to the chicken pieces she was sliding into the bag. "I do need to ask you. Can you tell me more about what happened to your wife? Because I think that's what worries Sophie so much. That she could lose you too."

"I reckon you're right. I told you that Nicole died a few years ago, eh."

"Yes, but not how. "Was she ill for a long time? Is that what was so traumatic?"

"Nah. The opposite. It was sudden. And pretty awful. It was a car smash. She crossed the center line on Highway One, up in Northland. Nobody knows why."

"Oh, no," Jenna said with obvious distress. "Was anyone else hurt?"

"Nah. She clipped another car. Overcorrected, ended up rolling the car. No seatbelt. Nicole was always a bit careless about things like that. I've been so thankful she didn't have the kids with her. I never trusted her with the car seats. It was bad enough as it was, but I still have nightmares about that."

"I'm sure. How horrible. But if she was alone…were you off playing somewhere?"

"Safa. Pretoria. It took ages for them to tell me, and then for me to get back. About thirty-six hours. Luckily, Nicole had arranged for Nyree to stay with the kids. And both Nicole's parents and mine came pretty quickly. But as you can imagine, it was a rotten time. Lots of high emotion. And Sophie…" He sighed. "Sophie was four. By the time I got back, she'd gone quiet. Harry was little, not even two yet. Don't think it had as much of an impact on him. But even though she'll tell you she doesn't remember, I reckon it did something to Sophie."

"It's a hard thing to measure," Jenna told him. "People tend to think that, because kids don't remember them, traumatic events in their early years don't register, somehow. But we're finding, more and more, that that isn't true. And for a sensitive child like Sophie, I can imagine it would have had a big effect."

"Jenna!" Harry burst into the kitchen. "I'm *starved.* When's tea?"

"Can you say excuse me?" Jenna asked. "I'm talking to your Dad right now."

"Sorry," Harry said. "Excuse me. Jenna, I'm starved. When's tea?"

He had to smile, and so did Jenna. "OK," she said, "but next time, say it first. Look at the clock. What time is it now? Where's the little hand?"

"On the four," Harry said, disappointed. "That means four o'clock, right?"

"Four-fifteen, because the big hand is on the three," she agreed. "More than two hours to go, buddy. How about an apple? And look in the snack compartment. I think you'll find some cubes of cheese in there. That should hold you until tea."

"OK." Harry opened the fridge and removed two cubes of cheese from the low compartment, then went to check the fruit bowl. "I'll have a kiwifruit. And could Trevor come over to play, d'you reckon? Since it's so long till tea?"

"Up to your Dad," Jenna said. "He may need some quiet time today."

"We'll be very quiet," Harry pleaded. "Please, Dad?"

"You can't make any more noise than the young boys on the team bus," Finn told him with a smile. "And I've put up with them for days now. Course Trevor can come over."

"If his mum says yes," Jenna pointed out as she picked up her phone.

She spoke a few minutes, then rang off. "He's on his way," she told Harry. "A few minutes."

"Sweet as," Harry said with satisfaction. "I want to show him my new animals. I got a cheetah, and an otter, and a meerkat, Dad. At the museum yesterday. Jenna took us."

"Hope you didn't ask Jenna for them," he said.

"*Dad.* I spent my own money, of course. I've been saving up. D'you want to see them?"

"I do," Finn said. "After Trevor leaves, you can show me. What's your sister doing?"

"Reading," Harry said with disgust. "We were playing, but she stopped. That's why I need Trevor. I'm going to go wait for him by the door," he announced.

"Bye." Finn smiled as Harry rushed to the door again. "Yeh. They're a bit different, Harry and Sophie," he said to Jenna. "People don't always notice Sophie, or her feelings. You think she's sensitive, eh."

"Of course I do," Jenna responded with surprise. "She isn't expressive, like Harry. But she feels things deeply, and doesn't get over them as quickly. Harry's more volatile. But Sophie runs deep."

"She does. I'm glad you can see that. Most people can't."

"Because she's quiet," Jenna suggested. "Quiet children, especially girls, tend to get passed over. People think, 'Oh, she's fine,' and pay attention to the kids who are acting out."

"It's true. And I probably didn't do enough for her in that first year or so. I was having a bit of a hard time myself. Luckily, Nyree was there. She's been the real constant in their lives."

"I wouldn't say that. You're Sophie's shining star. It's because you matter so much to her that she worries about you. Nyree's important too," she hastened to add. "To both of them. But you're the one Sophie looks to."

"Wish I'd done better, then," he mumbled.

"Oh, I don't know. I'd say you've done a pretty terrific job. She knows how much you love her, and she trusts you to be there for her, no matter what. I'd say she's a lucky girl."

"Really." He felt more cheerful. "I've never known what I was doing," he confessed. "I've tried my best, but I've always wondered if it was enough. Specially being gone so much."

"It's a big burden, being a single parent," she said. "Of course, you've had Nyree, but in the end, you're the parent. And all parents—all *good* parents—wonder if they've done well enough. They worry about the things they've got wrong, because kids don't come with an instruction manual. You're learning all the time, right along with them. But the important things—you've got those right, it seems to me. You have great kids, and they didn't happen by accident."

"Thanks," he said gruffly. "It's good to hear." He shifted in his chair and winced at the soreness.

"But it seems to me you've earned a rest now," she went on. "Why don't you go spend some time in the spa? I'll keep an eye on the Wild Bunch. I'll bet you're as starved as Harry, too. How about a sandwich out there?"

"You don't have to do that. I can make it. Or I can check the snack compartment myself."

"I don't think a couple cubes of cheese are going to do it," she smiled. "Not as hard as you worked last night. I'm still on duty till tomorrow morning, with not much to do besides making dinner. It'll take me five minutes to fix you a snack. Go on. Get out of here."

He laughed and got up gratefully. Ten minutes later, she stepped out onto the huge wooden deck and handed him down the melamine plate. A generous handful of crisps was piled high beside a huge BLAT, the bacon freshly fried, avocado and tomato plump between the slices of toast.

He took the plate from her with a "Cheers" that turned to a grin when she handed him the bottle of beer she'd been holding behind her back.

"How'd you know?" he sighed, stretching out in the warm water, the jets pulsing against his lower back, and taking a swallow of cold beer.

"Psychic," she told him with a smile. "Enjoy."

He watched her opening the ranch sliders that led back into the house and stepping inside. He'd have enjoyed it more with a bit of female company in here. But for now, a fat sandwich and a beer weren't too bad.

school days

♡

"Have a good day." Jenna gave Harry and Sophie each a discreet squeeze around the shoulders and watched them walk through the school gates.

"Jenna!" She saw Siobhan beckoning from the group of mums chatting nearby, hesitated a moment, then went to join her.

"Hello, love," Siobhan greeted her. "Missed you yesterday."

"My day off." Jenna smiled at her gratefully, acknowledged the nods of the other mums.

"We noticed," Siobhan said. "Finn looked a bit done for."

"But choice," one of the other mums put in. A general laugh greeted the comment.

"We all enjoy Mondays," Siobhan grinned. "Do you know everyone, though?" She introduced Jenna to the four or five women around her. "Jenna's a Year One teacher, normally, did you know?" she told them. "I've taken shameful advantage of her expertise, palming my kids off on her."

"No, you haven't," Jenna protested. "You took Sophie and Harry last week."

"Only out of shame," Siobhan declared. "I couldn't live with myself."

"Pity the Blues lost this weekend," a woman named Clarice offered. She was the mum of a boy in Sophie's class, Jenna remembered. Danny, she thought. "We were hoping to see them in the final."

"We were hoping to see *Finn,*" Monique, a pretty brunette, corrected. "Our local celebrity."

"Speak for yourself," Clarice offered tartly. "I was watching the footy."

The other women scoffed in disbelief. "I didn't notice you running away when he brought the kids yesterday," Monique said.

"I wanted to congratulate him on a good game," Clarice said stiffly.

"He did play well, didn't he?" Jenna put in hastily. "I know they were all so disappointed to lose. But it does give him a rest. It'll be hard on the Crusaders on the All Black squad. Playing in the final next weekend and then going into training straightaway."

"I never thought of that," Clarice said.

"Though I know he'd rather be tired, and play," Jenna said with a smile. "Any of them would. Guess that's the way it goes."

"Must be an interesting job, yours," Monique said.

Jenna laughed. "Well, not so much. Cooking, housework, looking after kids."

"Exactly like my life," Monique agreed. "Except that you get a day off, and no questions asked, eh. That'd be nice."

"None of the real responsibilities of kids," Clarice put in. "And you get paid for what you do. Lucky you. Want to trade places?"

Jenna flushed and shifted, unable to think of a retort.

"I need to get Ethan to kindy," Siobhan broke in. "Come on, Jenna. Walk me."

She pulled Jenna away from the group, set a brisk pace that had Ethan complaining.

"Sorry, darling," she told him, slowing down after they'd crossed the road. "She didn't mean it, you know," she said to Jenna. "Not thinking, that's all."

"What?" Jenna asked, startled.

"When she said you were lucky. She can be a bit tactless. And she's jealous."

"Was it obvious?" Jenna faltered.

"I hope you haven't been considering a career shift, becoming a poker player," Siobhan smiled. "Because you'd be rubbish. No worries, though. It's just because I know you."

"Jealous, though," Jenna said. "That's a laugh. Being a nanny isn't exactly a glamour job."

"You haven't seen her husband." Siobhan shuddered theatrically. "Nightmare. Belly out to there. But come on," she urged. "Walk Ethan to kindy with me, go for a coffee. I need a treat."

♡

"Thank goodness you're here," Maggie, the Year One teacher Jenna had been assisting, said with relief when Jenna joined her in the teachers' lounge of Mangere Primary during lunch the following Monday. "I can really use your help today. The school's having a visit from a few of the All Blacks, and I've got a room full of wound-up five-year-olds. I'm not looking forward to this afternoon."

"What's involved? And how can I help?" Jenna asked.

"They'll be having a chat with the students first, then going out to the field for a bit of rugby practice. We've got it pretty well organized, but I could do with another supervisor."

The children were every bit as excited as Maggie had predicted, and when she announced that it was time to go, their anticipation became even more intense.

Jenna walked at the tail of the queue of Year One students as they made their way to the auditorium and arranged themselves cross-legged on the floor directly in front of the stage. Once they were settled, she stood against the wall to one side and watched the big room fill up with the older pupils.

"Quite a day."

She turned at the words, smiling a welcome at Ian Foster, one of the Year Five teachers. "It is," she agreed. "Who exactly are they sending, have you heard?"

"Not sure. Three or four of them, anyway."

Somehow, Jenna wasn't surprised when the doors to the auditorium opened and Finn led the procession of four players who leaped up the steps to the stage to thunderous applause from the students and a welcoming speech from the head of the school. It made sense that the Auckland-based players would be making this local appearance, and she knew what a soft spot Finn had for children. She was proud to know him as she witnessed his easy rapport with the kids, his joking good humor that had both students and teachers laughing.

She saw the moment he became aware of her, his eyes meeting hers in surprised recognition before he turned back to answer a question about a teammate's pinup status.

"Yeh, I know the girls are rapt to have Koti here. Me," he sighed regretfully, "I'm a bit bashed about by now. The old beak's been broken a fair few times. But if any of you kids need help with your tackling, you'll want to see me for that, because everyone knows the forwards do all the real work."

When the athletes filed off the stage to head outside, Finn muttered a quick word to one of the other players, then made his way toward Jenna as the head began to explain the second half of the day's program to her eager audience.

"Moonlighting?" he asked quietly. "Doesn't your employer pay you enough?"

"Volunteering," she corrected. "My employer pays just fine. Oh, this is Ian Foster, one of the teachers here. Ian, Finn Douglas."

"Gidday," Finn said, giving the other man a firm handshake and a quick once-over. "See you outside, Jenna?"

She nodded. "With the little ones."

"I'll take care to get myself assigned there, then," he told her before he left to catch up with his teammates.

Jenna saw Maggie beginning to get the class up. "Here we go," she said to Ian. "See you later."

During the session that followed, Jenna could see all the years of working with Sophie in Finn's encouraging instruction as he ran lines with the Year Ones, offloading the ball gently, reaching to catch their own wobbly passes in one big hand. She had to laugh to witness their version of touch rugby, Finn matching himself against five eager students, the excitement when he deliberately missed his mark and a little girl danced past him to score a try.

"How do you know him?" Ian asked, coming up to join her again and following the direction of her gaze.

"Hmm? Finn?" she asked, still smiling. "I'm his nanny and housekeeper. His kids' nanny, I mean. Just for now, the rest of the year."

"Huh." Ian frowned as Finn accepted the help of several children to get to his feet from where he lay sprawled on the grass after his failed "tackle" and made his way toward Jenna again.

"Disappointing," she told him severely, watching him brush grass from his black Adidas track pants. "I hope your defense is going to be stronger than that in Perth, or I'm not watching."

He laughed, his eyes sliding towards the man on her left. "Think you'll find I rise to the occasion. Looks like we're finishing up here, so I'll say goodbye. See you at home. Good to meet you, Ian."

Jenna watched him trot off, then turned to Ian with a smile. "He's a really good guy. You wouldn't know it from watching him play, though, would you?"

"I wouldn't know," he said stiffly. "I don't watch much rugby."

"I never did either, before," she confessed. "But I've learned a lot about it recently, and it's surprisingly enjoyable. I need to go on and help Maggie, though. See you next week?"

"Yeh," he said. "See you."

♡

"What a surprise to have you turn up today," she told Finn after they had put the kids to bed that evening and were chatting comfortably in the kitchen. "I had no idea you were doing that."

"Community relations. I like the school visits, tend to volunteer for those. We're all expected to do our bit, but we do get a choice. Talking of surprises, though, I had no idea you were doing that either, going into the school to help out. Isn't it a bit much after working all week?"

"This job isn't exactly onerous," she said, "especially when the kids are in school. The volunteering's been fun, and it gets me out, gives me a chance to meet some new people."

"I noticed the new people. Specially that bloke Ian. He fancies you, eh."

"He does not! He's just being friendly."

Finn laughed. "Yeh, right. He's never invited you for a coffee?" He interpreted her expression correctly. "He has. Ha. I knew it."

"A couple times," she said defensively. "Just for a chat. Just friends."

"Uh-huh. Friends."

"He'd have asked me out for more than coffee, if he were interested."

"Nah. He's too weedy to make a move that fast," Finn said. "It's been...what? Two coffees?" At her reluctant nod, he went on. "Next week, he'll ask you out. Not for dinner, though. Too scary. For lunch, maybe. Over another coffee."

"That isn't fair. Anyone would seem weedy next to you. Most men don't have your self-assurance, either. Anyway, just because he enjoys chatting with me, that doesn't mean he wants to take me out."

"What time is it? Gone nine? He's thinking about you right now. I saw. I know," he insisted at her shake of the head. "Give me credit for that much, anyway. I know what blokes think about. He's imagining you naked." He took a sip of his beer and nodded in satisfied certainty.

"Finn! Completely inappropriate."

He held up his hands. "Sorry. But somebody has to look out for you. You're like a baby out there. Though I don't think you're in too much danger from that fella. Bet he lives with his mum."

"No," she admitted. "His sister."

He pointed his beer bottle at her in triumph as they both burst into laughter.

"You realize you've now eliminated any chance of my saying yes," she complained. "If that ever does happen."

"What a pity," he intoned with his best sincere expression, then grinned at her again.

♡

"So how was school today?" Finn asked her the following Monday evening. "Volunteer day, right?"

"Right. It was good. Looks like they'll have a vacancy for a Year One teacher in the new year. I'm thinking of applying."

"Bit of a challenge, Mangere," he said. "Quite a mix of kids they have out there. New arrivals, limited English. All the Islander kids, too. Not like Mt. Eden."

"I can handle it. I'm a pretty good teacher, you know."

"I believe it. Third coffee date too, eh," he added slyly.

"Yes. And you were right." She laughed. "Sunday lunch, just as you predicted."

"I'm good," he admitted modestly. "Not really, though. I could see that one coming well down the track. What did you say?"

"I said yes. Then I took him into the supply cupboard and we had passionate sex. None of your business, and you know it."

"True. But I'm glad you said no."

She scowled at him. "It's really your fault. You shouldn't have said the weedy thing. Because I couldn't help noticing that his arms were kind of..." She trailed off.

"Spindly," he offered helpfully. "Nah. He wasn't your type anyway."

Jenna tried not to look at the size of his own arms as he sat with his elbows on the table, picking at the label of his beer bottle. The comparison wasn't really fair, after all. Ian hadn't thought so, anyway.

"I know I'm not an All Black," he had said in frustration when Jenna had declined his invitation, as gently as she knew how. "But I do have something to offer, all the same."

"What does that have to do with it?" she asked in surprise.

"I saw how you looked at Finn Douglas last week. I was hoping I was wrong, but it's clear to me now that I wasn't."

"Finn's my employer," she told him sharply. "I'm looking after his kids. And I take that responsibility very seriously."

"I know what I saw," he said stubbornly. "And a sportsman like that isn't a good bet, not for someone like you. You don't know what you're getting into."

"Ian. I'm not going to have this conversation, or to try to convince you that you're wrong. And I'm sorry to say no. It's not you. It's just that I'm not in a position to be doing that right now. Dating."

"It's not you, it's me." He smiled bitterly. "I've heard that one before. Never mind." He shrugged into his jacket and rose to leave the cafe. "Whatever you're telling me, or yourself for that matter, I have a pretty fair idea of what you're after. And I'll just say, good luck with that. Because you're going to need it."

♡

"I'm not sure what my type is anymore," Jenna confessed to Finn now. "But I'm pretty sure the guy has to weigh more than me."

He laughed. "I don't think Ian had any complaints. In fact, I can tell you with fair certainty that he liked the way you look."

"It's not really fair of you to criticize my potential partners anyway," she complained. "I never said anything about your choice, even though I may have been tempted."

"True. You didn't. Go on, though. Tell me how I can choose better next time."

"Well, you did fairly well in the looks department," she was forced to admit. "I can't really say much there."

"I dunno. I'd like to find someone who eats. I'm tired of watching women push a lettuce leaf round their plate while I scoff down my tea."

"I should point out, in all fairness, that there aren't many models or TV presenters who eat a lot," she told him. "Unless they're bulimic, of course. And that doesn't seem real attractive, at least not to me."

"You're probably right," he conceded. "But I reckon someone who ate a bit more might be a better cook as well."

"Yeah, the kids told me about Ashley's dinner party," she said with a smile.

"That's another one. Somebody who actually likes my kids would be good. Who could at least have a conversation with them. I don't much enjoy the uneasy feeling that they're researching boarding schools."

nurturing and peace

♡

Jenna grabbed for her phone as she gently folded the scrambled eggs in the pan. "Hello? Oh, hi, Nat."

She cradled the phone between neck and shoulder, brought the pan over to the table, and dished up three servings: two small, and one extra-large, then smiled apologetically at Finn and went back to the kitchen bench to butter toast as she continued her conversation.

"Thanks," she said. "I'm fixing breakfast right now, but I appreciate you taking the time to call, especially while you're away.... Yeah, it's the big one. Thirty. Oh, well. Beats the alternative, right? Talk to you soon. And thanks again."

She delivered the toast to the table. "Sorry about that. My friend Natalie is on holiday in Aussie, and she wanted to catch me while she could."

"No worries," Finn said. "Sorry to eavesdrop, but is it your birthday, by any chance?"

"It isn't eavesdropping when the person's talking right in front of you. And yeah, it's my birthday. Thirty. Zero on the end and everything."

"Daddy says it's not polite to ask grownups how old they are," Sophie told her.

"He's right," Jenna said. "But I just told you, and there's nothing wrong with you knowing. I'm thirty years old today."

"Happy birthday," Finn said. "What are you going to do to celebrate?"

She smiled ruefully. "No plans. It's not my day off anyway. But, yeah. No plans."

"That's not right," he objected. "At least you shouldn't have to cook dinner. You can go out if you like. I'll fix something." He ignored the groans of dismay from Sophie and Harry. "Or better yet, we'll all go out to the pub."

"That's a good plan, Dad," Sophie said. "We like the pub."

"And we don't like your cooking," Harry pointed out unnecessarily.

"Not polite," Jenna told him. "But if you mean it, Finn, then, yes, I'd like to go to the pub."

"Sure you wouldn't rather go out without us? You may not do Harry's taste buds any favors, but you won't hurt our feelings," Finn assured her.

"Unfortunately, with Natalie gone, I wouldn't have much to do," Jenna admitted. "Sad, but there you go. I haven't been in Auckland long enough to make many friends."

This would be her second birthday on her own, without Jeremy. Last year, it had been hard, but she'd got through it with the help of a couple girlfriends. She hadn't been looking forward to this one. What was it about birthdays? Maybe that it was supposed to be your own special day. But if there was nobody around to tell you that you were special…it just seemed to spell that out for you.

"The pub it is," Finn pronounced. "And I'll take the kids for a bit beforehand. Give you some time to yourself, at any rate. I should be home around three. Short practice day, Captain's Run. We'll leave at six, if that suits you."

"That's fine," Jenna said. She'd have a bath, she decided. And dress up just a bit. It was her birthday, after all. She began to feel much more cheerful about the whole thing.

♡

"No cake, even on your birthday?" Finn asked as they placed their dessert orders.

"Phew. No, thanks. I've had plenty to eat. I'll take a decaf trim flat white, though," she told their server.

"Whoa. Living large," Finn said.

"Hey. Works for me," she laughed. "Maybe I'll be really decadent and have a second glass of wine at home, after we put the kids to bed. And you can help me toast turning thirty."

"It's a date," he promised. "Have to be a nonalcoholic toast for me, night before the game. But it's the thought that counts."

"Is it time now?" Harry asked eagerly.

"*Harry,*" Sophie hissed. "Not *yet.* Wait till pudding comes."

"Ooh, a surprise?" Jenna asked. "How exciting."

"You have to wait," Sophie said severely. "That's the rule."

"All right," Jenna sighed. "I'll try to be patient." She winked at Finn and saw his answering grin.

"*Now* it's time," Sophie announced, when their desserts and Jenna's coffee arrived at the table.

Harry dove underneath and produced the small bag he'd brought with him, pulled out two heavily decorated homemade cards, and knelt on his chair to put them in front of Jenna.

"Oh," Jenna said helplessly. Harry's card showed a curly-haired stick figure with a triangle for a skirt, beneath a laboriously printed "Happy Birthday Jenna." The "J" was backwards, and Jenna's heart twisted with love. She opened the card to find a hugely printed, "I Love You. From Harry."

"It's beautiful," she told him. "Thank you, Harry."

"Mine next," Sophie urged her.

Sophie's card was an explosion of color, featuring flowers and stars and heavily embellished with shiny stickers of hearts, rainbows, and more flowers. Jenna read aloud, "I hope you have a very nice birthday. Thank you for taking care of us. Love, Sophie."

"Thank you," she told the little girl. "It's lovely. I'm going to put both of these next to my bed when we get home, so I can look at them every day."

"That's not all, though," Harry said. "We have a really, really big surprise." He pulled a gift-wrapped box out of the bag and reached again to place it ceremoniously in front of Jenna. "It's your birthday pressie!" he announced, wriggling with excitement. "We all bought it. Daddy took us, but Sophie and I helped choose it. It's really, really pretty. It's for you to wear."

"*Harry,*" Sophie hissed. "Don't give it away. Wait till she opens it."

"I didn't say it was a *necklace,*" Harry protested. "I just said it was pretty."

Sophie groaned and slapped her palm to her forehead as Finn and Jenna laughed.

"Never mind," Jenna consoled a mortified Harry. "I'm opening it now anyway, see? I'm *very* surprised that you bought me a present. And so happy."

She *was* happy, she realized, opening the white box and peeling back the tissue paper. In fact, she was in danger of crying, right here and now. Her mouth opened in genuine shock as she pulled back the final layer of paper and took out the greenstone pendant.

"You can't be a real Kiwi if you don't have a pendant," Finn told her with a smile. "We reckoned you needed one."

"It's a koru!" Harry was bouncing in his seat now. "And it's real pounamu, Jenna! It's green, like your eyes! D'you like it?"

"I love it," Jenna said fervently, holding the jade ornament in her hand, tracing the delicately carved spiral shape with her thumb. "It's so beautiful. Thank you."

She really was crying now, she realized. She picked up her napkin and wiped the tears away with an apologetic laugh, then put the black cord around her head, adjusting its length so the deep green spiral sat just beneath her collarbones, cool against her skin.

"Are you sad?" Sophie asked anxiously. "We thought you'd be happy. We thought it was pretty. We thought you'd like it."

"It's so beautiful," Jenna told them through her tears. "Thank you." She got up and went around to the other side of the table to give each of them a hug and kiss. Then looked across, her eyes meeting Finn's. "Thank you," she told him quietly. "This means a lot to me."

"No worries," He smiled back at her. "We did think it would match your eyes. And that the symbol was right, because the koru's all about nurturing and peace, and I'd say that's what you're all about, too. It's the symbol for new beginnings as well, and unless I've guessed wrong, I reckon that works. Your first thirty years may not have been everything you could've wished for, but the next thirty are a whole new story."

"Why are you still crying?" Sophie asked as Jenna reached for another napkin. "Aren't you happy?"

"Sometimes people cry when they're happy too," Jenna told her, pulling herself back under control and returning to her seat. "And right now, I'm very, very happy. Thanks to all of you."

"Cheers." Finn reached across the coffee table with his mug of tea and clinked it against her wine glass. "Happy thirtieth."

"Thanks." Jenna took a sip and set her glass down on the coaster. "And thank you for dinner, and my present." She touched the pendant at her throat, traced the design with her finger. "I wasn't expecting anything like this. You really did surprise me. I'm so touched."

"We all wanted to do something. Did you have a good day, though? Hear from your family, and all?"

"Ah. That would be somebody else's thirtieth birthday."

"Not even your mum?" he asked in surprise. "Sorry. Has she passed away?"

Jenna shook her head, took another sip of wine. "Not dead. Let's just say I don't really have any family. But hey, that's why I could come to New Zealand and reinvent myself. Which people have been doing for a long time now, right?"

"Well, I'd say you've done a good job of it." He smiled across at her and lifted his mug again in salute. "Here's to new beginnings."

Jenna sat on her bed in her nightgown. She adjusted the black cord to lengthen it, then pulled the pendant over her head and sat fingering the koru, her fingers sliding once again over its pleasing coolness, the smooth, polished curves. She looked at the two cards, sitting as promised on her bedside table, and felt the lump rising in her throat again.

They're not your family. She felt the truth of Natalie's words like a blow to her chest. It had felt so much like it, though. Sitting in the pub, opening her birthday cards and reading their sweet messages. Knowing that Finn had gone to the trouble to take the kids shopping and, she knew, urge them to make those cards. And that he'd chosen something with such significance to her.

The koru's all about nurturing and peace. And I'd say that's what you're all about, too. She'd spent her entire life wishing to be part of a family like this, trying to find the kind of connection she'd felt tonight. First with her mother, then with Jeremy. And had never even come close, until now.

But Jeremy had got her here, she reminded herself again. Her life with him hadn't worked out the way she had imagined it would, but he'd been a good friend once. Whatever she could say about this birthday, she was light years away from where she'd been ten years ago. She'd had her very first chance, that year, to get away from Las Vegas. And what a revelation it had been, even though it was only the first small step in the journey that had led her here.

"I got the job!" She had put her phone down that late spring day and given Jeremy an exuberant hug.

"Awesome," he congratulated her. "Pity you can't come back to En Zed with me, though. Mum told me we're doing a trip to Queenstown for the skiing."

"Winter does sound good," she said, looking out her dorm window at the heat-baked sidewalks of the UNLV campus, the sprinklers arcing over green lawns. The mercury was regularly hitting ninety already, and it was only May. "Or just some-place cooler. I wasn't looking forward to staying here. But New Zealand—I can't ski. And I need to earn money for next year, you know that." And most importantly, she wouldn't even have been able to afford the plane fare.

"Two good reasons," Jeremy admitted. "One, anyway. You could learn to ski. But being a counselor at a summer camp? Are you sure this is what you want? Kids, all the time?"

"If I'm going to be a teacher, it had better be," she said. "And don't start with that. You, the guidance counselor, my high school teachers, even some of my professors. Everybody."

"Maybe the fact that everybody's saying that should be telling you something. Teaching pays sod all, and business courses aren't really any harder. You're the one helping me with the maths."

"It's not what I want to do," she reminded him as patiently as she could. "It isn't what you want to do either, and you know it. At least I'm studying what I like."

He grimaced. "Mum and Dad're so keen for me to enter the firm, though. And I can always write on the side, like I'm doing now."

"Yeah," she sighed. "You're doing what your family approves of, but it's not what you want. And I'm doing what I want, and *nobody* approves of it. Neither of us is exactly matched up, are we? I thought college was supposed to be this carefree time when you explored all your options."

"You'd have to work a bit less for that to be true, in your case," Jeremy pointed out. "Unless you really wanted to explore the option of working in the dining hall. Did you mention the job to your Mum yet?"

"No," Jenna admitted. "I can't tell which I'm dreading more, that she'll be upset that I'll be gone all summer, or that she won't be."

She got her answer soon after Jeremy left.

"Oh. Hi." Sherri answered the phone unenthusiastically. "I'm on my way out. What's going on?"

That wasn't a very promising beginning. "Just wanted to tell you, Mom, I got a summer job, a good one, as a camp counselor in Colorado. It pays pretty well, because some of the kids have special needs. But it means I'll be gone all summer. Starting in early June, as soon as school lets out."

"Uh-huh." Jenna heard her mother inhale, then blow the smoke out again. "I don't know why you'd want to work with a bunch of retarded kids. It sounds disgusting. But I was going to call you anyway. Can you come get the rest of your stuff? Because I think Dwight's going to ask me to move in with him, and I don't want to store all your shit."

"Uh...sure." Jenna wondered why she had even considered the possibility of her mother's being upset at her absence. She certainly hadn't seemed to be pining at the loss of her company so far.

"Call before you come by, though," Sherri continued. "Because I haven't exactly told him about you. He thinks I'm thirty-three. It'd be a little hard to explain you. He's not going to believe I had a baby when I was thirteen."

"All right." Jenna felt the familiar disappointment seeping through her. She shouldn't expect any more, after all these years. But being asked to disappear herself from her mother's life… surely that was a new low. "Which one is Dwight again?" she asked.

Sherri sighed impatiently. "The dealer. He deals twenty-one at Caesar's. He makes plenty, and he's not shy about spreading it around, especially to people he likes. And believe me, I've made sure he likes me. I don't want to screw it up now. I'm thinking that if I handle this right, he just might propose."

"That's great, Mom."

"How's your boyfriend, anyway?" Sherri asked without much interest. "That what's his name? You still hanging onto him?"

"Jeremy," Jenna reminded her. "And yes, we're still together. He's going back to New Zealand for the break, though."

"And you couldn't get him to take you with him?" her mother asked.

"He did ask, actually. But I can't afford it, you know that. The fare, and not working."

"Don't say that like it's my fault," Sherri told her sharply. "I've sacrificed plenty for you. I raised you, didn't I? And if you think it was easy, you're kidding yourself. I had dreams once too, you know."

"I wasn't saying that, Mom," Jenna sighed. "Just that I can't afford to go."

"His family's loaded, though," her mother complained. "Why didn't you hint around, get him to pay for it? Sometimes I can't even believe that you're my daughter. It's like they switched babies on me. I could've got that trip out of any man by the time I was sixteen."

"Yeah." Jenna wished she had a snappy comeback, but, as usual, she couldn't think of anything to say, anything that would make her feel stronger, more powerful, let alone impress her mother. "Anyway. I just wanted to tell you."

"Come get that stuff," Sherri reminded her. "But call first. I gotta go."

"Bye." Jenna put the phone down. Good thing she did have that job. Because it looked like whatever had remained of her childhood had just ended.

Someday, she promised herself, feeling hollow inside. Someday she'd have her own family. And when she did, she was going to do it differently. She was going to do it right.

finding nemo

♡

"Can Caitlin spend the night tomorrow?" Sophie asked when Jenna arrived at school on Thursday afternoon. "Please, Jenna? We want to make more jewelry."

Jenna looked at the beseeching little faces. "It's all right with me," she said. "We'll have to ask Caitlin's mum, though."

"It'll be OK with my mum," Caitlin said confidently. "She loves me to have sleepovers. She says it gets me out of her hair." Seeing her mother approaching with Ethan by the hand, she called out, "Mum! Can I sleep over with Sophie tomorrow night?"

"You need to wait to be invited," Siobhan chided. "Sorry, Jenna," she apologized. "My offspring have no manners, I'm afraid."

"It's all right," Jenna smiled. "I was just inviting her. We request the favor of Caitlin's company tomorrow night. And Ethan's as well," she decided, "if you think he's old enough. He and Harry have been getting on so famously, and I know Harry'd enjoy it."

"Yeh," Harry agreed. "We could make a jungle scene, Ethan!"

"What do you think?" Jenna asked. "Date night?"

"Date night sounds choice," Siobhan said. "If I remember how. I'll probably start cutting Declan's meat for him. Are you sure it won't be too much, though, to have both of them?"

"You'd be doing me a favor," Jenna assured her. "Giving them both some company. Finn's gone for twelve days, and I'm going to get a little nuts."

"And the solution for that is two *more* kids?" Siobhan asked dubiously.

"Variety," Jenna said. "And it'll keep them entertained too. Keep me from having to play Candyland."

"You can't put a price on that," Siobhan agreed.

"There is a catch, though," Jenna warned. "You have to have a cup of tea and a chat with me when you come to get them Saturday morning, give me some adult companionship."

"Think I could fit that in," Siobhan said. "Help me recover from my big night out. Wait till I tell Declan. He's going to be chuffed."

♡

"Mum! We made cookies!" Ethan ran to his mother on Saturday morning and gave her a hug.

"How'd he do?" Siobhan asked Jenna as they went into the kitchen after promising Ethan and Harry that they could finish building their jungle.

"Great. We watched *Finding Nemo* last night, and we made cookies this morning." Jenna handed Siobhan a container of still-warm peanut butter cookies laced with chocolate chunks. "Some to take home."

"Just what my waistline doesn't need," Siobhan said ruefully. "Declan'll be rapt, though. *Finding Nemo,* eh."

"Sophie's favorite, for obvious reasons. She has a bit of a Daddy thing."

"Understandable, with no mum." Siobhan watched Jenna pour tea into her cup, added milk and sugar, and took a peanut butter cookie without too much coaxing.

"Yeah," Jenna sighed. "Makes this long road trip tough for her. Having Caitlin over helped a lot. And we'll watch him play tonight. That always makes her feel better. As long as he doesn't get injured, that is."

"I can't imagine," Siobhan said. "Seeing your dad on TV every week. A bit weird."

"It's what they've grown up with," Jenna pointed out. "It's normal to them. He calls, too, almost every night. He's really good about that. But seeing him play is the best. Gives Sophie something to discuss with him, too. You should hear her," she chuckled. "I don't even know what she's talking about, half the time."

"I wouldn't know, either," Siobhan said. "Declan tries to explain all the rules to me, but I'm not that interested. Just like watching the boys in their little shorts." They laughed together. "There're some fit fellas on the All Blacks. Finn amongst them."

"Mmm," Jenna agreed.

"Does he have a girlfriend now?" Siobhan asked curiously.

"Sorry," Jenna said with a smile. "My employer, you know. I can't really talk about that."

"Course," Siobhan said with disappointment. "No rules about the other blokes, though, are there? You could give me a bit of gossip about somebody else. That'd do me."

"Finn doesn't tell me anything interesting that way, alas. If you want to know who's got a separated shoulder, I'm your woman. But as to who's separated from his wife..." Jenna shrugged. "Can't help you."

"Oh, well," Siobhan said. "Nothing quite as interesting anyway, since Drew Callahan got married and Koti James got himself engaged. Wedding day coming up, I hear. That'll be a national day of mourning for the female population."

"Why is that, though?" Jenna wondered. "Why do we feel disappointed when somebody like that gets married? I mean, did you or I really think we were going to sleep with Koti James in this lifetime? Have we really lost anything?"

"Lost the dream," Siobhan sighed. "Now I'll have to kill off his wife in my mind before I get horizontal with him. So much work."

"Homicide does take the edge off that sexual fantasy," Jenna laughed.

"I don't really want to do it," Siobhan said. "Shag him, I mean. I love Declan. I just…" She sighed again. "It'd just be nice to touch a body like that, once. Sad to think I'll never have the chance. Think Finn would let me come over and feel his chest for a bit? Purely in the spirit of scientific inquiry?"

"No," Jenna said through her giggles. "I don't think that'd go over well. It'd make the school drop-off so awkward afterwards, too."

"He could auction it off," Siobhan said. "At the next school fundraiser. That'd raise a fair sum amongst the mums."

"Also never happening. I guarantee it."

"Pity. Have to keep dreaming," Siobhan decided.

"So what does all this mean?" Jenna asked, wiping her eyes. "Good date last night? Or bad date?"

"Good date," Siobhan smiled. "Definitely. Makes me saucy."

"I guess that means you'll be up for the kids coming over again. I wouldn't mind having them next Friday as well, since Finn won't be back till that Sunday. And Sophie's soccer game will be in the afternoon again, next Saturday."

"If you're sure," Siobhan said doubtfully. "Can't I reciprocate, next time? Wouldn't you like a night off yourself?"

"Nyree's cousin Miriam will come on Monday, give me my day," Jenna assured her. "That's all I need. With the kids in school and without Finn here to cook for, there really isn't that much to do. But we could all use some company. And I'll take a rain check on the sleepover at your house. Who knows, some other road trip, I might need it."

"Let's make it a date, then," Siobhan decided. "Friday night sleepover. And let's have coffee one morning next week too. Tuesday suit you?"

"I'd love to," Jenna said with pleasure. "On both counts."

Well, look at that, she thought as she and the kids waved goodbye fifteen minutes later. Nanny or not, she'd made a new friend. The best kind, one who made her laugh. Who would have guessed?

♡

Jenna juggled the pile of clothes, pushed the door open with her backside. Sophie looked up fast from her cross-legged position on the bed, then slammed shut the pink, bejeweled notebook she'd been writing in and shoved it under her pillow together with her pen.

"Sorry," Jenna said calmly, taking the armload of clothes across to Sophie's dresser and setting it down on top. "I didn't realize you were in here, or I'd have knocked. Somehow." She smiled. "Maybe I wouldn't have. I need to grow another hand. Can you help me put these away, please?"

Sophie got off her bed reluctantly and came across to lend a hand. Jenna saw her cast a glance back at her notebook, one corner still showing under the pillow.

"You know," she told the little girl, opening the top drawer and handing Sophie her neatly folded underwear, "I think it's a wonderful thing to have a private book, a place to write your private thoughts."

She saw Sophie's eyes fly to hers, continued in a conversational tone. "Of course, private means that nobody else is allowed to read what you write. Unless you invite them to, of course."

She opened the next drawer, gave Sophie a stack of shirts. "Which is why," she finished, "I'd never *read* anybody's private notebook."

"You wouldn't?" Sophie asked her doubtfully.

"Nope. I sure wouldn't. I wish I'd had the good idea of getting a notebook like that, when I was seven or eight, say. It would have helped when I was mad at my mum, that's for sure, to have a place to write it down."

She put away Sophie's socks, refolded a pair of jeans and added them to the bottom drawer, giving a quick tidy to the contents while she was at it.

"You were mad at your mum? Really?"

"I sure was," Jenna leaned back against the dresser to look down at Sophie. "Lots of times. When she hurt my feelings, or I thought she wasn't paying enough attention to me."

"Even though she cooked you dinner, and washed your clothes, and everything?" Sophie asked. "You were still mad sometimes?"

Ah. "Even though. I don't think that was really so ungrateful, do you? I mean, I did know that she did those things. And I helped as much as I could. At least I hope so. But I couldn't help my feelings, could I? It would have been nice to have a notebook, a safe place to talk about it. Like you. When did you start writing in yours?"

"My birthday. Last year. I always made lists. When I was little, I mean."

Jenna fought back the smile that tried to creep out at that, listened as Sophie went on. "Once I learnt to write, in Year One. That's why Daddy gave me the notebook. He said it would be a place for my lists. And my drawings, and anything I wanted to put in it. He said it was special, just for me."

"That was a very thoughtful present," Jenna told her. "Your dad's pretty special himself, isn't he?"

Sophie nodded emphatically. "He's not like other dads. Nobody else's dad is an All Black. Nobody at my school."

"That's a big honor, I know," Jenna agreed. "But it must be lonesome sometimes for you too."

"He *has* to go, though," Sophie argued. "That's his job."

"It is. But it can still be hard, can't it? I'll bet it's hard for him too, to leave you and Harry."

"He says he misses us," Sophie said in a small voice.

"I know he does," Jenna said. "He calls you just about every night, I know that. I'll bet he needs to hear your voice as much as you need to hear his."

"D'you really think so?"

"I really do. You can ask him on Sunday, when he comes home. But I'll bet he says yes. And," she said briskly, straightening up again, "you've been in your room since you got home from school. I could use a hand with dinner. Do you think you could come set the table for me? I could use the company, to tell you the truth."

"OK. I can help."

"Thanks." Jenna smiled down at her, rested a hand briefly on the top of her head. "Let's go get to it, then. We can plan what we'll do, tomorrow night when Caitlin and Ethan come over. You can help me make a menu. We'll make a list."

♡

"So good to be back." Finn stretched his long legs out under the kitchen table on Sunday evening and sighed. "Long time. Long journey."

"Your internal clock must be completely out of whack," Jenna said. "More than twelve hours' difference. Does it feel like breakfast time?"

"It does. And strangely enough, I'm hungry."

"I kind of anticipated that. I made a Greek lasagna for tonight. Not exactly breakfast food, but I thought it might be satisfying for the day after a game. Give me forty-five minutes, OK?"

"Choice," he said.

"Sorry you lost, Dad," Sophie said, coming up to stand next to him.

He put his arm around her and pulled her close. "Even the ABs lose now and then, darling. We did our best, but some days even that isn't enough. The Springboks were in form, and we weren't quite clicking."

"I thought the ref robbed you," Sophie said stoutly. "He totally missed that knock-on by Franck. They shouldn't've had that last try."

"Nah. Can't go blaming the ref. It goes one way as often as it goes the other. Just have to chuck it into the loss column and let it motivate you for next time."

Jenna paused in her salad preparations at the sound of a phone ringing. Hers, she realized. She wiped her hands on a tea towel and picked it up. Jeremy's number leapt out at her from the screen. It had been more than a year since she'd seen those digits, but there was no way of mistaking them.

"Hello?" She moved out of the room as she spoke. She had a feeling that this wasn't going to be short.

"Jenna." Jeremy's familiar voice, once so dear to her, sounded strained. "How're you going?"

"I'm fine. What can I do for you?"

He sighed. "You still haven't forgiven me. Wish we could move past this."

"I'm working on it. But it's not easy. I'm assuming there's a reason you called. Is it to do with the dissolution?"

"Yeh. The two years are up on the tenth of September."

"Yes," she couldn't help pointing out. "I do recall that date."

"Yeh. Anyway. I'd like to speed up the process a bit. Which we can do, if we appear in Family Court instead of applying through the post. Would you be able to do that? I'll schedule it at your convenience, of course, and my lawyer will prepare all the paperwork."

"And the difference is, what? I'd assumed we'd just send in our petition in the normal way."

"If you do it in court, it takes effect immediately. We'd be done. Walk out with our marriage dissolved, able to move on."

"Ah. Move on to what?"

"Marriage," he explained, sounding a little shamefaced. "But it'd be better for you too," he hastened to point out. "You can't have enjoyed these past years either, waiting to make it official. Wouldn't it be good to have it done and get on with your life?"

"Yes," she admitted. "It would."

"I'll pay for your return ticket to Welly," he assured her. "I realize it's an inconvenience. I don't even know where you're living now. Just that you left."

"Auckland," she said. "And I'll take you up on that, since you're the one who wants this. What date are we talking about?"

"As soon after the tenth as you can do it."

She consulted the calendar on her desk. "The fourteenth is a Monday. That'd work for me. If not then, the following Monday."

"The fourteenth should work. I'll be in touch, let you know. And Jenna. Thanks. You're awesome, as always. I really appreciate this."

Yeah. Awesome. She ended the call and sat for a minute holding her phone, made a note on her calendar. So awesome that here she was, alone. And about to become unmarried as well.

♡

Finn looked up as she came back into the kitchen. "Everything all right?"

"Sure." She busied herself with sliding the pan of lasagna into the preheated oven, then went back to her salad. Her hands were trembling as she sliced the carrots, she realized with surprise. She swore under her breath as a vegetable skittered out from under her knife. Not a good sign. She set the sharp implement down and took a deep breath.

Finn moved Harry from his lap, where he'd been reading him his dinosaur book. "Look at the pictures for a minute, mate, while I talk to Jenna," he told his son.

"What's happening?" he asked her in a low voice, coming up beside her at the kitchen island. "Anything I can do?"

She blinked the tears back. "Sorry. I'm all right. Something I wasn't expecting, that's all."

"Need a hand?"

She began to refuse, then looked down at her hands, still gripping the edge of the island. "Would you mind slicing some vegetables for me? I'm not doing too well right now. I may need a little help to get this dinner on the table."

"Course. Just tell me what to do."

She began to relax, his solid presence nearby comforting her as she moved around the kitchen, warming the loaf of Turkish bread and setting the table.

Luckily, she wasn't required to make much conversation during dinner. Sophie and Harry had plenty of news for their father, and he was clearly happy to be back amongst his family again, laughing at their stories and asking questions. The bedtime routine went more quickly than usual as well with Finn chipping in, to her relief.

"Sit with me for a bit, if you don't mind," he offered. She'd come out of Harry's room just as he was closing Sophie's bedroom door. "I'm not going to be able to sleep for hours yet. I'd like the company."

"Actually, I think I need some quiet time. Thanks for all your help tonight, though."

"Anything I can do," he promised. "Just ask."

my android

♡

"Do you have time for a schedule check, before I take off?" Jenna asked Finn the next morning when he came back in after walking the kids to school.

"Course." He watched with amusement as she made them each a fresh cup of tea and picked up the pages she'd set ready. "You are the most orderly person I've ever known."

"Except you," she said. "I've never seen you set anything out of place yet."

"Yeh, I pick up after myself. But you pick up after everyone."

"No, I don't. I make sure everyone picks up. There's a difference."

"Whatever it is, I like it," he decided. "Now. Schedule?"

"You leave for Buenos Aires when?"

"Sunday afternoon. Can you and the kids give me a lift to the airport? Around eleven. And d'you mind collecting me again, Tuesday week?"

"Of course." She made a note of the times. "What else this week?"

"Barbecue at Drew and Hannah's on Friday night, as we won't have training that day."

"Just you? Or you and the kids?"

"Just me. So you'll be on your own with them."

"I'm pretty used to that by now," she assured him. "Anything else?"

"I thought I'd take the kids out to the pub on Saturday night before I leave. We've missed a fair few Dad Times here, and we'll be missing a couple more. Thought it'd give you another night off, too, before you're stuck again, ten more days."

"OK. Friday and Saturday night out, Sunday afternoon to the airport. Check. Otherwise, you're home?"

"Otherwise I'm home. Putting the oven's capacity to the test."

"I think I can handle that. But you tell me."

♡

"Oh, sorry," Nat said regretfully that evening over a rainy-evening dinner of mulligatawny soup and salad. "I made weekend plans already."

"OK. I'll find something else to do. Good plans? Date?"

"Yeh," Nat said with satisfaction. "One of my students' dads, can you believe it? Came in for a parent-teacher conference, and…" She shrugged. "Sparks flew."

"Guess you weren't telling him his child was out of control, then," Jenna said dryly. "That's the only time sparks ever flew during my parent-teacher conferences."

"Fortunately, he has a well-behaved daughter, so it was all good. And amidst all the mutual complimenting, he managed to ask me out for a coffee, 'to get my advice.'"

"And you gave him your advice," Jenna guessed.

"Gave him more than that," Nat said, a satisfied smile growing.

"How long has it been going on?" Jenna asked. "You haven't said anything."

"Well." Natalie shrugged. "You know how it is. Or, you don't. But trust me, when you've been single as long as I have, you want to be sure before you start getting chuffed about it. It's been a couple months now, though. Not a long time, but feeling more…more solid every week. He's dead nice," she sighed. "And I know that sounds boring, but it isn't. He's an engineer. His wife went off with somebody else, year or so ago. More fool her, I say."

"Long enough ago that he's not in the rebound stage," Jenna said. "He can't get his dissolution yet, but he isn't reeling through those first months, either. That's great news, Nat. I'm really pleased for you. And if my coming over on Mondays gets inconvenient, say the word."

"Nah. We're just doing the weekends, so far. Specially when his ex has the kids."

"More than one, then."

"Yeh. The boy's older, Year Four. We're keeping it low-key for now, going slowly."

"Not too slowly, I take it."

"Well…" Natalie laughed. "A girl's got to have a shag now and then, after all."

♡

"How about a free babysitter, Saturday night?" Jenna asked Siobhan the next morning.

"Why?" Siobhan asked, looking up to thank their server as their coffees were delivered to the café table. "Are you volunteering?"

"Yeah. Finn's taking the kids out before the Argentina trip, so I suddenly have a free evening, and nothing to do. Don't make me hide in my room. Please. Let me come over and watch *Cinderella* with Caitlin instead."

"Nah. We can do better than that," Siobhan decided. "Come out with us. We'll get an actual babysitter."

"With you and Declan?" Jenna stared at her. "That's not exactly a date for you."

"Nah. With us and Declan's mate. Richard Evans. He's separated from his wife, just starting to go out again. I think you might like him. He's a pretty good bloke. Declan's accountant."

"My heart's going pitter-pat already," Jenna said gloomily. "I don't know. I've never even met the guy."

"Hence. The date," Siobhan enunciated.

"I should tell you, I'm still married," Jenna admitted. "Technically, anyway. For a few more weeks."

"And so is he," Siobhan pointed out. "You don't have to shag the bloke, just have a bit of a laugh, some adult conversation, let somebody else pay for dinner. You've been babysitting so much, Declan and I've run out of topics for discussion. Come on, give us something to gossip about on the way home."

"All right," Jenna smiled reluctantly. "But we're all going together. I don't want someone I don't know coming to the house to pick me up."

"Done. Let me check with Declan, and I'll get back to you. Assuming we can get it all sorted, we'll be by to collect you. I'm thinking around eight."

♡

"So, you two, how're you going with the wedding plans?"

Finn turned his head to look at the speaker, Hemi Ranapia's wife Reka. The group of players and their partners were all relaxed now, sitting over the remains of their Friday dinner on Drew and Hannah's spacious deck. The sparkling waters of Waitemata Harbour were no longer visible now that night had fallen, but the lights of the City and the Harbour Bridge, not to mention a brightly lit cruise ship coming in to dock at Princes Wharf, provided their own spectacular view.

"Pretty well," Kate Lamonica, a pretty, petite brunette, answered. "Not that Koti has any idea. Let's hope he remembers the date. December twelfth," she reminded her fiancé. "Just in case."

"Been traveling a bit here, you know," Koti protested. "Besides, nobody wants my opinion. Between my mum and all my sisters, Kate's hardly able to get a word in edgewise, never mind me."

"Where are you having it?" Reka asked. "I never heard the final decision."

"At the marae," Koti said. "We thought about doing it the way Drew and Hannah did, flying everyone to Tonga to get away from the media. But my mum said it had to be the marae, or it wouldn't be a real Maori wedding. 'What about all the cousins?'" He imitated his mother's wail of despair. "You know how it is. And in the end, we realized that no journo's going to want to try to get past the boys in my whanau. Plus we hired a security firm," he added practically.

"Coals to Newcastle," Drew said. "Can't imagine the security firm that's going to outperform a marae full of Maori boys."

"I take it you didn't sign with *Woman's World,* then," Hemi put in for the first time. "I was half expecting to hear the announcement, knowing what a show pony you are."

Koti sighed theatrically. "Yeh, nah, Kate wouldn't go for it. I told her she could have a really flash car if we did, but no joy."

"Oddly enough," Kate said tartly. "Thank you very much, but I have no desire to have every woman in New Zealand looking at photos of me in my wedding dress, telling each other I'm not really that good-looking and that Koti could have done better. Guess I'll have to keep driving the Yaris." But she smiled at Koti as she said it, and Finn could see the love behind their teasing ways.

"Think we can do better than that," Koti smiled back. "I do have something in mind. Wedding present."

"Oh, goody," Kate said happily. "I can't wait."

"What about you, Finn?" Reka asked. "Can't help but notice you're here alone again tonight. When are we going to see you with somebody special? Somebody I get to meet more than once?"

"I'm looking," he protested. "Not that easy with two kids. Maybe you can put out the word, vet them for me."

"Nobody you're even interested in?" Reka probed. "Nothing on the horizon?"

"Maybe," he admitted. "But it's a bit complicated."

"Ah." Reka sat back with a smile. "By the way, how's Jenna working out? Your new nanny? We met her while we were all waiting for you boys after the semifinal," she explained at his startled look. "We were surprised that she was American."

"Not entirely," Finn said. "She's applied for citizenship."

"So she's planning to stay," Reka said with satisfaction. "I'm glad. We liked her. Very pretty, too. Didn't you think so?" she asked her husband.

"Dunno," Hemi answered. "I didn't notice. I was looking at you."

All the men laughed at that. "Good one," Koti said appreciatively. "I'm writing that down."

"Been married eight years," Hemi told him. "Watch and learn, cuz. Watch and learn."

"Well, we thought so, anyway," Reka said to Finn. "Nice, too. And the kids certainly seem to love her."

"Yeh. They do," Finn said. "She's awesome with them, you're right." He cast a hunted look at Hemi. "Help."

"Dessert." Hannah stood with a smile, began to pick up plates with the tact that made her such a graceful partner to the Skipper. The other women rose with her, to Finn's relief.

"I'll do it." Drew moved to get up, but Hannah waved him back down.

"Save your strength for the washing-up," she told him. "Maybe you could get Finn another beer instead. I think he needs one."

"Too right," Finn said gratefully as the women moved into the house and he took the bottle of Mac's from Drew. "I'm knackered. Meant to know a wee bit about defense, aren't I. Not sure I came off best there."

"Never mind," Hemi said consolingly. "You were up against a force of nature this time."

"We've all been there," Koti grinned. "What Reka can't winkle out of you isn't worth knowing. No shame in that."

Finn got up at the sound of the front door opening the following night. He'd been sitting in the lounge, sipping a beer, his mind wandering over the previous evening's conversation, the kids, and the upcoming match against the Pumas. Not waiting up for Jenna, he'd told himself. Just thinking.

He went into the entryway to find her slipping inside. She took off her jacket, hung it on the hook. "Hi," she told him. "Still up, huh?"

"Geez," he said blankly, barely hearing her. "You look beautiful."

"Huh. Thanks." She reached down to pull off one high heel. He saw her wobble a bit, put out a hand to steady her. Her cheeks were flushed, he noticed, the waves of her hair mussed. But there was nothing at all wrong with the collarless, deep purple blouse or the flirty black tulip skirt that made the most of her curvy shape.

"Is there any more of that wine?" she asked, holding onto his shoulder while she took off the other shoe, settled back down to her normal height. "I need it."

"Think so," he said, a grin beginning to form. "Go sit, and I'll check."

"Brought the bottle too," he said as he returned to find her slouched on the couch, arms folded, bare toes curled around the edge of the coffee table. He took his usual spot in the chair across from her, poured wine into both glasses. "Emergency supplies. Hot date, I take it."

"Huh," she snorted again. "Total waste of makeup. 'It'll be fun,' Siobhan said. 'Some adult conversation,' she said. 'You don't have to shag the bloke.' Somebody should have told *him* that."

"That good, eh," he sympathized.

"And I know I've drunk too much. I needed some help, to get through the evening. It just went *on* and *on*." She glared across at him. "He's an *accountant*. How is that a glamour occupation? What gives him the right to judge me?"

"Nothing," he agreed. "He didn't think a teacher was up to standard?"

"We didn't even get that far. I told him I was a nanny. Watched his eyes glaze over, and I got stubborn. I didn't tell him I was a teacher. If a nanny wasn't good enough for him…" She shrugged, took another gulp of wine. "Tough. I could actually see the moment," she continued. "When he said to himself, 'Great rack. Kinda hot. Embarrassing job. I'll just do her, and not tell my mates about it.'"

He choked on his wine. "You could, eh," he got out when he'd finished coughing.

She finished her glass, poured another one. "He wasn't interested in my views on Labour's chances in the next election, put it that way."

"I said you were a baby out there. Reckon I was wrong."

"I went to high school," she told him in exasperation. "I know when someone's staring at my chest. When their brain has switched off and they're thinking with…" She flushed. "Well,

I do know. I'm not that stupid. It was one thing with Ian. You can't blame me for not being able to tell there. He was so respectful, it was almost insulting. And Ben, all right, he's young. But he at least *pretended* to look at my face when he talked to me."

Finn held up his hands. "I stand corrected. *In vino veritas.* Didn't know you were so…perceptive."

"Yeah. Well, I am," she muttered. "Now I know what my single friends have been talking about, all these years. Men are jerks."

He registered that, moved on. "Want me to hunt this fella down? Do him over for you? I have time. My plane doesn't leave till one-thirty."

"No," she said grudgingly. "He didn't do much, other than the emergency tonsillectomy. I didn't give him a chance."

He frowned, suddenly not finding it all quite so funny. "That's all?"

"Yeah. Oh, he tried," she admitted. "But I got my shoulder in there." She demonstrated the twist, shoving her elbow up.

"You have hidden depths," he said appreciatively.

"I did go to high school," she repeated. "Is there any more of this wine?"

"You've killed it." He picked up the empty bottle to show her. "And I reckon it's going to be getting its revenge tomorrow morning."

"OK," she sighed. "I'm going to bed."

He got up with her, steadied her as she swayed a bit. She leaned into him, pulled his head down and gave him a soft kiss that he couldn't help returning.

"You're nice," she murmured against him. "If he'd kissed like that, I wouldn't have used my shoulder."

He set her away from him with an effort. "Time for bed," he said firmly. "Or you're going to be very, very sorry tomorrow."

♡

"Ah." Finn looked up as Jenna appeared in her dressing gown, one hand going out to grasp the kitchen doorway. "Sleeping Beauty awakes."

"Morning," she got out. "Cup of tea?"

He handed his own across to her, moved to the jug to make another.

"Morning, Jenna!" Harry called.

She winced, took a sip from Finn's mug and sat down at the table, holding the back of the chair as she levered herself into it. "Morning," she said to Harry and Sophie, still in their PJ's. "I have a bit of a headache this morning. Could you talk softly, please?"

"Will you make us brekkie?" Harry whispered. "We haven't had any yet."

"Oh." Jenna stared blankly at him. "No Weet-Bix?"

"I want bacon!" Harry said enthusiastically, forgetting his quiet voice in his excitement.

Finn smiled, seeing Jenna's face go green. "Reckon Jenna needs coffee this morning, Harry. And I don't think she's feeling like cooking. We'll go to the café. We have time. Don't have to leave for the airport till eleven."

He pulled the bottle of ibuprofen from the kitchen cabinet, shook out two tablets. "Here." He set them in front of Jenna with a tall glass of water. "Take these, drink all the water. Go get your gear on, and we'll walk to the café. Some fresh air, one *very* large flat white, a couple pieces of toast and some orange juice, and you'll be yourself again."

"Promise?" she asked, squinting up at him.

"I promise."

"I have a bad feeling," she said cautiously as they made their way toward the café, Harry and Sophie dashing ahead. "That I may have...said some things last night."

He smiled. "You may have, at that. Fortunately, I have a shocking memory."

"I didn't…*do* anything, did I?" She looked up at him. "I have a *really* bad feeling that I kissed you."

"Could be. In a purely sisterly way," he assured her. "Which is also receding quickly from the memory banks."

"I was that good, huh," she said gloomily. "I figured."

He laughed aloud, then apologized as he saw her wince at the sound. "Sorry. Forgot. You do realize you've put me in the classic no-win situation here, though. If I say, yeh, completely unmemorable, you're offended. And if I say, too right, I had all I could do not to take you to bed, you're even more offended. And you quit, just when I'm off to Argentina for ten days. What's a fella to do?"

She smiled painfully. "We'll just leave it at that, I guess. But please remind me, next time, that there's a reason I only drink one glass of wine."

"Never had a hangover before, eh," he said sympathetically.

"No," she sighed. "Not like this. Sorry. You must be wondering who you've entrusted your kids to."

"Nah," he decided. "I like it. Makes you human. I was beginning to wonder if you were an android." He grinned down at her startled look. "Not like you went on the piss while you were watching the kids. And you'll be apples by the time you drive me to the airport. If a bit tender, still."

"I will," she promised. "If there's any doubt of it, I'll call you a taxi. I wouldn't endanger your kids, Finn. You know that."

"I do," he agreed. "And once I get a coffee into you, you'll be back to your perfect self." He gave her another grin. "My android."

in the cake tin

♡

"But I want to go!" Sophie wailed, sitting up in bed. "You said we could! You *promised,* Daddy!"

"Be sensible, Sophie," Finn told her. "You and your brother've had the bot ever since I got home, and Jenna's been run ragged looking after you. Even if you're feeling better by tomorrow, Harry's still not too flash. I'm not having you up late tomorrow night, all that excitement. Or letting Jenna wear herself out getting you to the park."

"She could just take me," Sophie argued. "You could get Miriam to look after Harry."

"Sophie! That's dead selfish," he rapped out. "I just told you how knackered Jenna was. You're sounding so spoilt, I don't even want to tell you the plan we've nutted out."

"I'm sorry, Daddy," she said, beginning to cry. "I didn't mean to be selfish. I just want to see you play so *much.* I've been thinking and thinking about it."

"Aw, geez," he said helplessly, sitting down on her bed and pulling her into his lap. "I know it's disappointing, darling. I wanted you both to come too. But things happen sometimes. You know that. Do you want to hear our plan?"

She nodded, still tearful, and he handed her a tissue. "Blow."

Once he'd cleaned her up, he went on. "You know that we're playing the Boks in Wellington next week. Jenna's offered to take you both down for the match. So you see, you'll have your chance to watch your old Dad run round the paddock in the black jersey after all."

"Do we get to stay with you?" Sophie demanded.

"I'll come stay with all of you, afterwards," he promised. "And we'll have a wee holiday on the Sunday, come back Monday morning."

"We have school Monday," she reminded him.

"So you do. Think you can stand to miss a few hours?" he asked seriously.

Her broad smile left no doubt of her approval. "I think it's a brilliant plan, Dad."

"No more whingeing about tomorrow night, then," he reminded her. "No pestering Jenna to take you."

"I promise."

"You won't forget to watch me on the telly, barrack for me, will you?" he asked in mock alarm. "Not going to boycott me? You know you're my good-luck charm."

Sophie threw her arms around him. "You know I'll watch you, Dad. I'll even make Harry watch," she promised extravagantly.

He laughed. "Nah. Harry isn't a rugger bugger like you. No worries. You just send me those winning thoughts."

He put his finger on her forehead, and she reciprocated with her own. "Bzzzzz," they said together.

He gave her a hug and kiss, tucked her into bed again. "Night, Sophie Bee."

"Night, Daddy. I love you."

"Love you too, darling. Sleep tight."

He turned out the light, left the door open a crack. Met Jenna coming out of Harry's room.

"Did you tell her?" she asked.

"Yeh. She was disappointed about tomorrow, right enough. But surprisingly, she's willing to miss out on a bit of school to come see me play next week."

She laughed. "What a shock."

"Harry OK?" he asked, serious again now.

"Better," she nodded. "I gave him some cough syrup. Hopefully he'll have a better night."

"I'll go say goodnight, then."

How had he got so lucky? he wondered as he closed Harry's door again and made his way back to the lounge for a last bit of quiet time before game day. He might not have had an award-winning marriage, and Heaven knew he'd stuffed up enough as a dad, hadn't had a clue what he was doing most of the time. But somehow, with enough help and plenty of good luck, he'd wound up with the best kids a man could ask for.

Jenna felt as if she were dragging herself up the stone steps to the big villa on Monday night. She'd cried quietly throughout the bus ride to the Wellington Airport, then the hour-long flight home, had sat numb, finally drained of tears and emotion, on the Airporter bus back to Mt. Eden. She hoped Finn had got the kids to bed on time. She couldn't face them tonight.

She let herself in quietly, but not quietly enough. Finn came to the door of the lounge while she was taking off her jacket and shoes, began to greet her, then stopped short as she turned and he saw her face.

"What's wrong? What's happened?" he asked sharply. "Are you ill?"

"No. Just a hard day. I'm all right." She took a deep breath. "Did the kids get to bed OK? Harry still doing all right?"

"Course." He looked at the way she was hugging herself. "You're freezing." He pulled his sweatshirt from its hook and handed it to her. "Put this on and come sit with me a minute, warm up. I've got the heat pump on in there. If there's a problem, maybe I can help. Call someone."

She laughed tiredly, but went with him into the lounge and sank onto the couch and pulled the sweatshirt around her, grateful for its comforting size and warmth. "I don't think your connections are going to help with this one. I don't even know why I'm so upset about it. I should be relieved. I thought I would be."

"Sounds like this problem requires alcohol. I'll get you a glass of wine, and you can tell me. I was having a beer anyway."

He disappeared, came back with a generously poured glass. "Pinot Noir. Your favorite. Where did you get off to today, anyway? Didn't realize you'd be gone by the time we got up." He picked up his own beer bottle and sat in the easy chair across from her, propping his stockinged feet on the coffee table.

"Wellington. For my dissolution hearing." She might as well tell him. She didn't have anyone else to talk to about it right now. The thought made tears of self-pity well in her eyes again, and she dashed them away impatiently.

He raised his eyebrows. "In person, eh. So it's done?" At her nod, he added, "Most people just apply once the two years're up, wait for the order to come in the post. What made you decide to go to the trouble? Oh," he realized at the look on her face. "Somebody has a new partner, wants to get married again straightaway. And we know that isn't you."

"Not exactly new," she said, unable to keep the bitterness out of her voice. "But yeah, they want to go ahead. And I was just as glad to get it over with. I thought I was, anyway." The tears threatened again. "I don't know why I'm reacting like this. It's a long time to be in limbo, and now that's over. I'm free. So why do I feel so sad?"

"Because it isn't what you expected, when you got married," he told her gently. "When you see it in writing like that, you remember all the dreams you had. The way you thought it would be. And you know that dream's gone."

She couldn't hold back the tears this time. She groped for the tissue box on the end table, wiped her eyes, got herself back under control. "You sound like you know. But your wife died. Is that the same thing? Does it feel like that?"

"Reckon it doesn't, not if she died loving you," he said. "But she didn't. So I've had those same feelings. You tell yourself, while you're married, that it's all right. That nobody's marriage is perfect. You lie to yourself, eh. And then, when it happens..." He shrugged. "You can't do that anymore, can you."

"Some things you can't close your eyes to," she agreed. "No matter how the person's tried to explain it away."

"I was right, then. He lied," Finn guessed.

"Yeah. And then some."

"He had someone else, and you found out. How?"

"The hard way," she admitted. "Classic. An evening meeting that got canceled, so I came home. And there they were, in our bed. You wish you could walk away, forget what you saw. But you can't. I realized that I'd known all along, but I didn't want to see. I wanted to believe that I had a marriage."

He nodded. "I know all about that."

"It happened to you too? And you found them?"

"Nah. Thank God. Who knows what I'd've done. But after Nicole died, I found out why she was on that road. Who she'd been going to meet. And that it had been going on for a while. She'd probably have left us, in the end. Well, she did at that, didn't she? But it was all such a shock, I was just...numb for a long time. Would have gone round the bend if it hadn't been for the kids. Even so, I drank too much, did some things I regret. It took a long time to get myself right. To see that we weren't suited. It wasn't about him. It was about the two of us, who we were. What she wanted that I couldn't give her."

"But you're so great," Jenna protested. "I mean," she went on at his surprised glance, "such a good dad. And such a strong man. A good man. Why wouldn't she want that?"

"I could say the same thing," he pointed out. "I can't see why your husband didn't want you, either."

"That's different," she assured him. "I wasn't his type, trust me."

"Well, I wasn't Nicole's either, as it turned out. And she wasn't mine. She was Aussie, and a model, you remember. Very beautiful. A bit spoilt, I realize now. We met over there, when I was playing, had a long-distance romance for a few months before we got married. But she wasn't prepared for what my life really was. She just saw the publicity, the travel. She thought it'd be some kind of glamorous existence. Turned out she didn't like anything about it. She hated living in Dunedin," he went on. "I was playing for the Highlanders at the time. It was too cold for her, too small, too quiet, after Sydney. She was used to the bright lights, and God knows Dunedin doesn't have much of that on offer. Then, being married, being a mum. She'd always had heaps of attention, men being after her all the time, telling her how beautiful she was, taking her out. Even leaving out that I was gone so much, I'm not the best at that. Pretty simple bloke. I'd rather stay home, most of the time."

"Of course you would," Jenna said, outraged for him. "As hard as you work."

"That was the other thing. She resented giving up her career, the modeling. She was starting to have some pretty fair success when we got married. She didn't like what having kids did to her body. And she couldn't do much from Dunedin anyway, not with a baby at home. When Harry came along, it made it that much worse. I signed with the Blues, moved to Auckland so she could have a bit of city life, hired Nyree. I thought she might be happier here. But it wasn't enough."

"She must not have realized how much she'd need all that," Jenna mused, "if she said yes in the first place. You must not have, either."

He looked at her wryly. "Three guesses why we jumped into it so fast."

"Oh," she realized. "Sophie."

He nodded. "We were careless. Stupid. But I wouldn't have given up Sophie, not for anything. Harry either. So," he shrugged. "Reckon I'm an expert on marrying the wrong person. And on how bad it feels when you find out. You look at the wedding photos, your wedding ring, after you take it off that last time, remember all your high hopes. It's like all that, all your feelings, were a lie. When you find out she was seeing someone else, and lying to you about it."

"You really do know," Jenna told him. The combination of fatigue and emotion had made the wine go straight to her head, and she had to concentrate to set the empty glass back on the coffee table. "That's exactly how it feels. It's all…" She made an expansive gesture. "Gone. Wiped out. And I don't know how to fill that space now. What my life is going to look like, when it… starts up again."

"It's going to look better," he promised. "It's hard now. Got to expect that, when you see the paperwork signed. Or in my case, when you face life without your wife in the house. When you're Dad, and you're all there is. But it gets better. Because you aren't living that lie anymore. Not spending all that energy trying to convince yourself it's going to work out, when you know deep down it isn't. That whatever was there once is gone."

"Shoot." She was crying again. "Sorry." She reached for another tissue. "I hope you're right. Thank you for talking to me, sharing that with me. It helps."

"No worries." He smiled ruefully. "If hearing my sad story helped you, I'm glad. All I can tell you is, you wouldn't be normal if you weren't sad. Because it hurts."

"Yeah." She wiped her eyes again, got up with a watery smile. "I need to take a shower and go to bed. And figure I'll feel just a little bit better in the morning."

He rose with her, bent down to kiss her cheek. "Reckon you will." He gathered up her glass, his own beer bottle. "See you then. Sleep well."

♡

"Still OK with bringing the kids down to Welly this weekend?" Finn asked the following afternoon. He'd been gone to training by the time she'd come back from walking the kids to school, and although she'd fixed him breakfast as usual, this was the first time they'd had to talk alone since their conversation of the evening before. But now the kids were in the lounge working on their homework and Finn was keeping her company in the kitchen, filching bits of apple as she prepared a crumble for tonight's pudding.

"Of course. That's the plan. Unless you've changed your mind."

"Nah. I'd like it. But I thought, bad memories. Didn't realize when we set it up."

"I'd like to go, actually. Heaven knows I never went to a rugby game when I lived there. I'd like to take the kids to Te Papa too. And the Botanic Garden. It'd be kind of nice to have some different experiences there," she tried to explain. "Other associations."

He nodded. "I can understand that. Wait for Te Papa till Sunday, if you don't mind, so I can go too. I'll have to educate myself anyway. You know how Harry likes to discuss. Can't have him thinking his dad's ignorant."

"We'd both better be taking notes," she said with a smile. "There's a lot to learn. It's a wonderful museum. Have you been?"

"I'm ashamed to admit that I haven't. This'll be my chance, eh. And your chance to experience the Cake Tin."

"I'm not so interested in the stadium. I'm much more excited about seeing you playing with the All Blacks. Since I've never seen the team play in person. I hadn't seen any All Blacks games at all, for that matter, until these past weeks."

"Those were the first test matches you'd ever seen?" he asked in surprise. "After all this time in En Zed?"

"It seems astonishing now," she agreed. "But my husband didn't care about rugby, and neither did his friends, so we never had it on at home. And I didn't grow up with it either, of course. I didn't know what I was missing."

"Not even the World Cup?"

"Nope. I did realize you'd won," she hastened to assure him. "I could hardly miss that. And I'd catch glimpses of rugby games at the pub, restaurants. But since I didn't have Sophie to explain the game to me, I never knew what I was looking at, so I wasn't very interested."

"She's a good teacher, eh."

"She certainly is. And she'll have another chance to instruct me on Saturday."

"The paper says the Springboks could win tonight," Jenna said to Sophie as they found their seats in Wellington's circular stadium, so aptly nicknamed for the metal-walled cake tin it resembled.

Sophie scoffed. "Just because we lost last time against them, and we've had some injuries. We have a deep side, though, you'll see. The Boks think they can win again with that boring kick-and-chase footy, but they're wrong about that too. Where they kick the ball downfield, then chase after it, race for it," she explained at Jenna's bewildered look. "Watch, and I'll show you."

Despite Sophie's confident words, Jenna knew the little girl was nervous. Harry was more keyed up than usual, too. Clearly, watching a game in person was different from seeing it on television.

"Here they come!" Harry shouted. The crowd was on its feet, roaring its approval as the team took the field behind their captain, and again when they lined up facing the Springboks to perform the haka. When the Maori player pacing between the rows called out the first words of instruction for the traditional challenge and the players dropped into their squats, hands beginning to slap their thighs, the noise grew to almost overwhelming proportions, stayed that way throughout the ferocious movements and shouted chant. The team finished as a staring, intimidating mass of black, and the stadium erupted.

Harry was still jumping up and down with excitement as the crowd took its seats to await the kickoff. "Did you see that, Jenna? Did you see Daddy doing the haka?"

"I did," Jenna smiled, pulling him down to sit next to her. "He looked fierce, didn't he?"

"Because he's feeling that way inside too," Sophie explained. "He told me," she went on as Jenna looked at her in surprise. "He has to get himself right to go hard all night. Most of the boys listen to music once they get on the bus, and in the sheds before the game. But Daddy just concentrates. He thinks about what he's going to do, till he feels dead fierce and strong."

"Daddy isn't really fierce, though," Harry protested. "He's nice."

"Not when he's *playing*," Sophie told him patiently. "He has to be able to hurt people. He can't do that if he's feeling nice."

Sophie was right, Jenna decided. She'd never have recognized her thoughtful companion of a few nights ago in the warrior she saw attacking the ball carrier, or carrying the ball himself like a battering ram through a line of South African defenders.

Whether he was pushing from the back of the scrum, leaping for the ball in a lineout, or racing to the breakdown, Finn emanated focus and determination. She marveled at the strength and stamina it took to work that hard for forty minutes straight, then back for another forty after a brief break.

Midway through the second half, the All Blacks captain, Drew Callahan, made a sudden turn to tackle an opposing player, pulled up short, and went down on the turf. The crowd seemed to hold its breath until he limped off, supported by the trainer and a huge round of relieved applause from the crowd, as a substitute ran from the bench to take his place.

"That's bad, right? He seems like an important player," Jenna said to Sophie.

Sophie looked at her in mild exasperation. "Yeh. He's the blindside flanker, remember? He does heaps of tackling, and the Boks are strong. But Matt Ropata is pretty good too. We can still win."

She seemed to be trying to convince herself, and Jenna reached for her hand. "We'll just have to see. What happens when the captain's gone, though? Who does...whatever it is that he does?"

"Daddy," Sophie said in surprise. "He's the vice captain. Didn't you know?"

"No. Really?"

"Yeh. Daddy's been on the squad almost as long as Drew. He's been vice captain for ages."

"So what's he doing now that's different?" Jenna asked, watching Finn arriving at the breakdown, where the ball carrier had just been tackled, to help get the ball to the backline.

"Talking to people more," Sophie explained. "Especially the No. 10. About what they're going to do. But it's hard to see from here."

The lead shifted back and forth twice more in the final fifteen minutes, the most gripping of a tense match, with the All Blacks scoring a drop goal after the final buzzer had sounded to win by a single point. By the time it was all over, Harry was asleep with his head in Jenna's lap, his enthusiasm no match for the day's excitement and the late hour. But Sophie was even more wound up than before, leaping and cheering the All Blacks' narrow margin of victory.

"I *told* you, Jenna!" she exulted as Jenna picked up a drowsy Harry, settling him on her hip for the slow exit from the stadium. "I *told* you they could do it!"

"And you were right," Jenna agreed. "They did great, didn't they? Stay close to me, now. Hold onto the strap of my purse. I don't want to lose you in this crowd."

"Is Daddy coming back to the hotel tonight?" Sophie asked, still bright-eyed and overexcited on the way to the carpark. She let go of Jenna to dance ahead of her, facing backwards. "Can I stay up and wait for him? I want to tell him well done."

"No, he said he'd be going back to the team hotel. We'll see him in the morning, though," Jenna promised. "And we'll all go to the museum together after that. Once he's had a good sleep, and a nice big breakfast." She could tell he was going to need both.

game face

♡

"The Colossal Squid was actually found very close to New Zealand, did you know that, Jenna?" Harry asked the following afternoon. "It's from Antarctica. That's not very far away, did you know that?"

"That's true," Jenna told him. "We can look at the world map when we get home and figure out how many kilometers it is."

Harry bounced happily along next to her on their way across the expansive pedestrian bridge and plaza beside Wellington Harbour, clutching her hand and still talking about the huge squid that had so taken his fancy in the museum, but Jenna had stopped listening. Her heart sank at the sight of the two men approaching, recognition dawning on their faces as they drew closer. She found her steps slowing until she came to a stop. Harry stopped too, his face turned up to her questioningly. Finn, noticing, turned back with Sophie as well.

"Jeremy." Her mouth had gone dry. "And Alan." She took a breath and continued. "Finn, I'd like to introduce you to Jeremy Davies, my former husband. And his partner, Alan Green. This is Finn Douglas, my employer, and his children." She went on to introduce Sophie and Harry as well, and Finn reached out to shake both men's hands. He had his game face on, Jenna saw. His stone face.

"What are you doing back in Wellington?" Jeremy asked her curiously, his eyes darting from her to Finn.

"I brought the kids down to see their dad play. Finn's an All Black," she explained as Jeremy and Alan still looked blank. "They played the Springboks last night."

"Right." Alan nodded, looked at Finn with renewed interest. "I heard about that."

"You'll want to catch up, Jenna," Finn told her. "I'll take the kids back to the hotel, get them into the bath. Take your time."

"I'll just be a few minutes," she hastened to assure him. He nodded again at Jeremy and Alan, then took both children's hands and continued across the bridge.

"*Major* hotness," Alan told Jenna approvingly. "And an All Black too. New boyfriend?"

"No," Jenna frowned at him. "My employer, like I said. I'm the nanny."

"Whatever," he shrugged. "Though I'd have a go, if I were you. Because you look good. Jeremy told me, but I didn't realize. We've all come out of this better in the end, haven't we?"

"Uh…" Jeremy had the grace to look a bit ashamed as he saw Jenna stiffen. "Anyway. I'm glad we ran into you. I was about to email you an invite to the wedding. We're doing it in two weeks, down here, and I'd like you to be there. *We'd* like you to be there," he corrected hastily, with a glance at Alan. "We were always good friends, weren't we? I thought we could get some of that back, now that all this is behind us. Will you come?"

Jenna flushed, hating being put on the spot. She couldn't think of an excuse, settled on the truth instead. "I'm sorry, Jeremy. I do wish you well. But I can't do that."

"Oh. Right." He chewed his lip, then nodded. "Whatever you think."

"What about your family?" she asked. "Are they coming?"

He gave a bitter laugh. "You're joking. Clarissa and Elaine both told me they'd like to, but they're not going to go against Mum to do it. And Dad does what Mum says. You know that by now."

"I'm sorry to hear that," she told him sincerely. "What about your family, Alan?"

He nodded. "They're coming. Reckon they're our family now. And we'll have heaps of friends there too, of course."

She smiled a little painfully. "I know you'll have those. But I need to get back now, give the kids their tea."

She saw Jeremy reach for her, then hesitate.

"I guess it's time," she decided. She leaned forward and gave each man a hug. "I'm not ready to dance at your wedding, but I'm trying to be happy for you." She blinked the tears away and made her way across the bridge, walking quickly now, just wanting to get away.

This bridge was bad luck for her. This wasn't the first difficult encounter she'd had here. She remembered the Saturday afternoon she'd run into her mother-in-law, Victoria, a few months after she'd left Jeremy. Kiwis might be known for their friendly, down-to-earth nature, but Victoria had never let that stop her.

♡

"Jenna." Victoria had looked her over with her usual critical gaze. Her own attire, as always, was impeccable: black slacks and an apricot silk blouse that emphasized her stick-thin figure, her stylish blonde bob and flawless makeup making her look younger than her fifty-six years.

"Victoria." Jenna didn't have to pretend anymore. She'd tried her best to be a good daughter-in-law, had bent over backwards to get along. And what had it got her? Nothing. She was done.

"You've lost weight," Victoria said grudgingly.

"I've lost my appetite," Jenna told her. "Being unhappy can do that, I hear."

Victoria stiffened. "And whose fault is that?"

"I don't know. Whose?" What could possibly be coming now?

Victoria didn't leave her in suspense. "Men don't stray if they're satisfied at home. You've started losing those extra kilos at last, I'll grant you that. But maybe you should have thought of dieting a few years ago. Because if you'd worked harder to make yourself attractive, Jeremy wouldn't have had to look elsewhere. William's always been faithful, because *I've* never let myself go. Even though I've had three children."

"Excuse me?" Jenna asked blankly. "Aren't you forgetting something? Do you really think there's anything I could have done to make myself sexually attractive to your son?" And as for her father-in-law, she thought privately, she'd bet he had somebody tucked away somewhere. She couldn't help hoping he did, anyway.

Victoria waved a hand. "So Jeremy has other...urges. He married you, didn't he? He could have gone the other way, if there'd been anything to hold him there. He had girlfriends while he was growing up. And you should have had children. I always said so."

The words hit Jenna like a slap in the face. She'd thought it would be better to face up to Victoria this time, better than smiling and biting her tongue. But there was nothing more to be gained from this.

"Ask him why we didn't," she got out. "I need to go."

"Don't think you're getting anything from him," Victoria said warningly. "You signed an agreement, remember. I looked it over myself. It's ironclad."

"Goodbye, Victoria." Jenna walked away, shaken to the core. Why did Victoria dislike her so much? How was this her fault? It must have been easier to blame her than to accept the truth about her son. But that didn't make it any easier to hear. She'd never been able to please the woman anyway. It was a wonder, given his mother, that Jeremy was as kind a person as he was.

♡

Not kind enough, or strong enough, she thought now, to have lived his life honestly, until he'd been forced into it. She found herself hoping, for his sake, that he could do that now. Jeremy had inherited his father's softer nature, his easy charm. But he'd inherited his weakness as well.

♡

"Right," she said as brightly as she could manage, walking into the hotel suite twenty minutes later. She'd stopped in the ladies' toilet in the lobby to dash some water over her face and compose herself. "Who's had a bath?"

"We both have." Harry jumped off the couch to greet her, pulling his attention away from Animal Planet. "Daddy gave me mine. We're hungry, though. Is it tea soon?"

"Very soon," she assured him, dropping her purse and moving into the kitchen. "Finn, are you eating with us, or going out?"

"Not enough energy to go out, even if I wanted to," he admitted from his own spot on the couch, muting the wildlife documentary he'd been watching with Harry. "Think I'll sit with this ice on my knee and watch you cook, if you have enough for me. Or we could order a takeaway if you'd rather. Easy as."

He looked searchingly at her, and she felt her chin wobble a bit as she turned hastily away.

"No, I'm good," she told him briskly after a moment. "Venison stir-fry. Very simple. Do you want a beer?"

"I could murder a beer," he said gratefully.

She felt better once she'd busied herself preparing quinoa and a simple meal of cubed venison and vegetables. By the time they sat down to eat, she had herself under control again.

"Can we watch a movie?" Sophie asked after dinner was over.

"*May* we," Jenna corrected automatically.

"*May* we watch a movie? Please?"

"Your brother's looking pretty tired," Jenna decided. "We'll put on a cartoon. If you're still awake after that, you can read a bit. OK with you?" she belatedly asked Finn.

"No worries," he said. "Sounds good to me. I'll get them settled."

Harry was looking decidedly droopy by the time teeth were brushed and the children tucked up in bed. "Are you sleeping in here with us, Daddy?" Sophie asked. "Or is Jenna?"

"Me," he told her. "Reckon Jenna deserves the night to herself, anyway."

"Want some help with the washing-up?" he asked Jenna as he shut the door on their bedroom, the sound of the cartoon fading to a murmur.

"No, thanks. Be done in a second." She was already wiping down the benches after loading the dishwasher. "Here." She reached into the freezer, handed him the icepack again.

"Cheers." He sank onto the couch and put the cold pack back on his knee with a sigh. "Come have a glass of wine. You look like you need it."

"You saw my purchase, huh?" she asked him with a wry smile. "Didn't realize just how useful it'd be, when I bought it. Do you want some too?"

"Wouldn't say no."

"So now you know," she told him as she handed him his glass of Marlborough Sauvignon Blanc and settled on the other end of the couch with her own, determined to address the scene she knew must be uppermost in his mind. "Why my marriage didn't work."

"That would do it," he agreed. "You didn't know?"

"Of course I didn't know. I wouldn't have stayed if I had. I just thought…" She flushed. "That he had, you know, a low sex drive. Or just wasn't that attracted to me. Stupid, I realize that now. But at the time, it made sense."

"Why would it make sense? You're a very attractive woman."

"I weighed more then, for one thing," she reminded him. "I told you that. And the longer it went on, the more weight I gained. What you see now is the result of a lot of hard work. But I never felt very attractive, so it didn't seem that strange to me, even at the beginning. 'Low self-esteem.'" She made air quotes with her fingers, made a face. "Classic."

"He was the same at the beginning?" he asked with surprise. "And you married him anyway?"

"He was my friend," she tried to explain. "We had such a good time together. He was so funny, and when I was with him, I could laugh about things. All the messy stuff in my life. When I shared it with him, he made it all seem funny instead of, you know, kind of sad and sordid. We had a lot in common. Messed-up family backgrounds, being different, wanting another path for our lives. And the physical part…" She shrugged. "I never expected a man to be crazy about me that way, so I wasn't surprised that things never…heated up. Never got much beyond snuggling. I've heard women say they like that better. I don't know, though. It didn't do much for me."

"Never?" he frowned. "He isn't bisexual, then?"

"Don't hold back. Go right ahead and ask."

"Sorry. You don't have to tell me if you don't want to. It was a shock to me too, though, seeing them. I'm glad I did. It explains things. Because I couldn't imagine any man lucky enough to be married to you not wanting you."

She turned her head in surprise to look at him more fully. "Really? You really think that?"

"Course I do. You're sexy as hell, you love kids, you can cook...what more is there?"

She couldn't help laughing. "I didn't realize the list was so short. Sexy as hell, though? That's a new one."

"It is? Think any man—any straight man—would say that."

"Well, I guess that's the answer," she said. "Turns out I haven't hung out with any straight men."

"None?" He looked startled. "Not even since you separated?"

She flushed. "No. At least, you've seen the extent of it. I was still married until last week, remember? OK, separated, I know. But it's still married, isn't it? At least it was to me. I wasn't feeling very desirable anyway, for a long time. Having your husband not want you can do that."

"OK. Going to ask again. Not at all?"

"I think he told himself he was bisexual, like you said. He deceived himself as much as he deceived me, in the beginning. Almost," she corrected. "He knew he was attracted to men, obviously. And he didn't share that tidbit. I think he persuaded himself that he could be interested in me. But, as it turned out, not so much."

"Are you telling me you never had sex with him?" he asked bluntly. "You were married for, what? Five years?"

"Three and a half, not counting these last two years. And no. Even I would have figured that one out. But it was never very much. In any sense. Less and less as time went on. I just wish I'd known why. It would have saved me a lot of pain."

The tears came to the surface again. "They invited me to their wedding," she burst out. "And I wish I could go. I really do. Whatever else he was, Jeremy was a good friend, at a time when I needed one. He got me out of Las Vegas and over here, which was the best thing that's ever happened to me. But when they told me that today…" She stopped, swallowed. "I'm still mad. I can't help it. Because I wasted all those years. I wanted kids. That's what I've wanted most in my life. The one thing. It doesn't seem like too much to want, does it? And now I'm thirty. If he'd had the guts to tell me, I could have got out, tried again. But now…" She shrugged helplessly, the tears starting to spill over now. "Shoot." She got up, grabbed a paper towel and wiped them away. "I need to go check the kids."

She returned a few minutes later, shutting the door quietly. "Fell asleep watching," she told him with a determined calm. "They were up late last night, and they love being with you so much, today was a lot of excitement."

She picked up her glass of wine. "And now I'm going to go to my room to read my book," she told him. "I'll let you relax. Quit telling you my sad story."

"Jenna." Finn reached for her hand, pulled her down to sit beside him. "Don't. I'm glad you told me. And I have something to say too." He reached for the wine bottle and topped up both glasses. "I told you any man would be lucky. I meant that. Matter of fact, I've been wishing I'd be that lucky."

"You?" she faltered.

"Yeh. Me. Didn't you know?"

"Sort of. Something," she admitted. "But I'm not even close to your type, I know. You date women like Ashley."

"Not for a while now, if you've noticed." He set down his wine glass, took hers from her hand, moved closer to her on the couch, raised a hand to her face and cupped it in his palm. "Because I've wanted to do this for a long time."

She leaned into him as he came closer. Then his mouth was on hers, kissing her in a way Jeremy never had. Hungrily, his hand at the back of her head now, his other arm going around her, pulling her closer to him.

"Open your mouth for me," he murmured. She sighed and did as he asked, and his tongue was inside her mouth, diving and exploring as she melted into him.

He pulled back at last, leaned his forehead against hers. "You have a great mouth. I've been waiting so long to do that. But it's all of you. All of this."

His hand was moving down her side to her waist, making her shiver. He outlined her lips with his tongue, slipped it inside her mouth again to taste her. She found herself falling back against the couch, lost in the feeling of his mouth on hers, his hands holding her so close. His mouth moved to her ear, kissing her there, taking the earlobe between his teeth to nip it, then moving down her neck to her throat.

"Finn," she groaned as he she felt his mouth on her neck, his teeth grazing her, his hand moving over her. "I can't...we shouldn't..."

"I know," he told her, his mouth on the sensitive spot where her neck met her collarbone, biting gently there, making her shiver and shift beneath him. "Bad idea. I know. Just a few minutes more. Just want to kiss you a little more, touch you. Then we'll stop."

He went back to her mouth, his lips moving over hers until she was limp against him. His hand stroked her waist, moved up her side, closed at last on one round breast.

"We shouldn't," she protested weakly. But his hand was exploring now, and she'd never felt anything like this, the heat of it. She held his shoulders, moved her hands down his arms. He felt so solid, so firm under her palms. She reached around to his back, felt the shifting planes of muscle there, tentatively moved her own tongue to touch his own. He groaned and reached under her sweater, touching her skin at last, and she jumped at the feeling of his big hand against her bare skin, shivered as he slid it up to her breast, his hand moving inside her bra to hold her there, stroke her.

She surrendered to the pleasure he was giving her for long minutes, then pulled her mouth from his, put her hand on his arm, made a supreme effort and pushed him away.

"Finn." She wrenched herself up next to him. "We can't. The kids are right there. And it's a bad idea anyway. We can't."

He let go of her with an effort of his own, leaned his head back against the couch cushions. "You're right. Thought I could just kiss you, see what it felt like, finally. But geez. It's like I'm fifteen again. On the couch and everything. And wanting you so much I can't stand it."

"Me too," she admitted shakily. "But not here. Not now."

"Right," he groaned. "I know you're right. But go to bed now, because I can't sit here with you anymore. We'll be good in the morning. If you stay out here tonight, though, I'm going to touch you again. And if we go any further, it's going to be even harder to stop."

neanderthal brain

♡

"I may never want to travel by myself again," Jenna told Finn the next morning over breakfast in Air New Zealand's luxurious Koru Lounge in the Wellington Airport before their flight. "I'm going to miss this when I'm on my own again, down amongst the Regular People."

He laughed. "There are a few perks. Good thing, as much time as I spend in airports."

"Stop reading for a bit so you can finish your breakfast, Sophie," Jenna admonished. "We're going to be getting on the plane in a few minutes."

Sophie sighed as she reluctantly set *Fantastic Mr. Fox* aside and went back to her Weet-Bix, soggy now. "I'm just at the good part," she complained.

"You can look forward to finishing it on the plane, then," Jenna told her firmly. "And in the queue, too. I know you. Stay close, OK? I don't want to lose you because you're walking and reading."

Harry looked up from his *Zoobooks* magazine, featuring sharks this time. "Will you read my magazine to me on the plane, Jenna?"

"Sure. Stick with me, buddy." She smiled back at him, then reached over to push up his glasses. "We need to get these specs adjusted before we go to Dunedin. They keep falling down. And you'll want to look your handsome best for your grandparents and all the rest of your relatives."

"Talking of that," Finn told her, "my mum called this morning. She and Dad want to take the kids back to Motueka after the wedding, keep them there for the first week of the school holidays. My sister said she and Kieran—her husband—can bring them back up to Auckland. Give them a chance to take a couple days off as well. They run a holiday park, won't have much opportunity to get away once we're into spring. You'll still need to fly down with the kids, but you could have a week's holiday yourself. Stay in the South Island, if you want. A bit cold down there this time of year, but if you don't mind that, you may enjoy it. I could help you work out places to stay. Or you can go back to the house, of course."

"Ah…" she looked at him, then down at her coffee cup. "We should talk about it."

He raised his eyebrows. "OK. I'll still pay you, if that's what you're worried about."

"That helps a lot," she told him gratefully. "And that's nice of you."

"Not really. I should've built in holiday pay anyway, just didn't think of it."

Jenna nodded and began to help Sophie and Harry gather their belongings as the plane was called, while Finn shouldered the bags for the short trip to the gate.

"I wish we didn't have to go to school today," Sophie complained as they climbed into the Range Rover in the Auckland Airport carpark after the brief flight.

"You left early Friday, and you're going in late today," Jenna pointed out. "You're going to be missing this Friday as well, and then it's going to be all fun. You have to learn something before that happens."

"We went to the museum yesterday, though," Sophie reminded her. "That was educational."

Jenna laughed. "That's why I don't feel bad about your missing the morning. And after dinner tonight, remember, we're starting our new book, since we finished *The Hobbit*."

"What are you reading us next?" Harry asked with his usual enthusiasm.

"I thought, since Sophie enjoyed *Fantastic Mr. Fox* so much, I'd read *Matilda* to you. I'm going to see if I can get it from the library this afternoon. If you both help me clean up after dinner, we can get started early."

"We'll help," Sophie promised.

"Do I get to listen too?" Finn asked. "I like the way you read."

"Of course you do, if you flatter me like that, and if that's the way you want to spend the last bit of your time off. Be warned, I might make you help clean up too."

"Think I could run to that," he agreed. "As this is meant to be your own day off."

"You're right. But this is actually pretty selfish. I've been wanting to read it again myself. It's one of my favorites."

She remembered what a revelation it had been the first time she had read the book. Her own third-grade teacher had recommended the Roald Dahl story, seeing something of Matilda in Jenna's quiet, bright eight-year-old self. TV dinners. Literally and figuratively. They'd made Jenna, like Matilda, a reader and a cook in self-defense, which was why the book had always resonated so powerfully with her. Too bad she'd never had superpowers. She'd magically flown from her chaotic upbringing into this life, though, and that was something in itself.

"Well," she said as Finn pulled the car to a stop outside the villa after dropping Sophie and Harry at school.

"Well," he grinned back at her. "Here we are."

He hopped out, began pulling bags from the back of the Range Rover, and she went to help him.

"Reckon we've got a choice here," he said, making his laden way up the villa's front steps. "You could start your time off. Or you could go upstairs with me."

There was nothing she wanted more right now. She wrestled with herself as she pulled out her key to open the front door, preceded him inside.

"I'm really tempted," she admitted at last, pulling Harry and Sophie's bags from the pile he tossed into the middle of the entryway floor. "But I was right, last night. Bad idea. So I'm going to get the kids unpacked, start the washing, and then I'm going to go for a run. And I must regretfully decline your kind invitation."

He sighed. "I was afraid that was going to be the answer."

"Remember, I have my volunteer day tomorrow." Time to move on. "Rescheduled. Miriam's coming in the morning. She'll take the kids to school, but I'll be back to fix dinner."

"I'm remembering. Can I ask you for a lift to the airport Wednesday morning, though?"

"Oh. Right. Because you'll be driving the Toyota back again after the wedding," she realized. "Sure. I can do that."

"Thanks." He watched her heading down the hallway with a sigh of regret. She was probably right. It was probably a bad idea. But it felt like such a good one.

♡

"How was the volunteer day?" he asked her the following evening. She had at least joined him as usual for her glass of wine, he'd been glad to see. *No jumping her,* he reminded himself sternly, or he was going to lose any chance he had, and find himself minus a nanny as well.

"Good. We worked on maths. And I had a great moment. There's this one little girl, Fa'alele. Samoan, obviously. Very quiet, very overwhelmed, new arrival. I've been working with her on her reading, before this. She's been struggling. So today, like I said, was maths. And she sailed straight through it. She did all the addition and subtraction, so I tried her on multiplication. And she got that, too!"

"Multiplication? How d'you do multiplication in Year One?"

"It's all more concrete," she explained. "You don't use the abstract numbers. You use picture cards, and counters. 'Tane has three kete. If there are four kumara in each kete, how many kumara does he have?' Rather than three times four."

"And she got that?" he asked, impressed.

"Yes!" He watched her face light up as she recalled the moment. "I tried her with a bunch of them. She has a real mathematical mind. It was so exciting."

"I can see that. Think Harry'd have a hard time with that problem."

"He's more verbal," she said. "Bright at maths, too, but it's not his strongest point."

"And how's my mate Ian?" he asked with a smile.

"Stiff," she admitted. "Still a bit offended, I'm afraid. He asked about you today. Sarcastically. He blames you."

"Me?" he asked, touching his chest and opening his eyes wide in mock alarm. "What'd I do?"

"Exist," she said with a sigh. "He thinks I have...other interests. That he can't measure up." She smiled. "Probably true."

"Could be that trip to Dunedin's going to be a good thing after all, then," he said. "Four weeks off before AB training starts up again. And the kids with their grandparents for a week. Fancy a bit of company on your holiday?"

She smiled ruefully. "Always a mistake for me to sit with you and drink wine. I keep getting myself into trouble. In a couple months, when we're done with this…Ask me out, and I'm not going to be saying no. If you still want to."

"I'll want to," he assured her. "No worries. I want to so much right now. Can't tell you."

"Time for me to go to bed, then." She got up, scooped up his beer bottle together with her wine glass. "Before I change my mind."

♡

"Got all the info you need?" he asked her from the passenger seat the next morning. "About packing the kids up, and all?"

"If not, I have your sister's number. I'll figure it out."

"Right. Glad you're staying for the game, anyway. Should be quite a contest. Everything at once, eh. Final game of the Rugby Championship, and if we win it, we'll have the trophy as well. And I get to play it in Dunedin, in front of all my rellies. Always a treat when your family's there."

"And even better when you win, I'm guessing." Jenna glanced over her shoulder as she merged onto the motorway.

"Too right. We're ready to get stuck in, though. We've had some pretty good intensity this week. Everyone knows they need to step up another level with Drew out. Course, we'll have to see how we go on the night."

"I'm confident," she told him. "If you have anything to do with it."

They drove in silence for a few miles. "It's really not right," she mused at last.

"What isn't?"

"Violence shouldn't be attractive. Right? It must be my Neanderthal brain or something. Why am I looking forward to watching you so much?"

"Well, that's good news. Another reason to win, eh."

"Sadly," she told him with a sigh, "it doesn't even seem to matter. It's just the effort, and the sweat. And the hits," she admitted. "I'm not proud of it, but there you are."

His grin grew as he watched her steer the car into the Departures lane, pull up to let him out.

"Have a good game," she said. "Play hard. And I guess maybe I'll see you Saturday before I leave. Or after my holiday, if not."

He unfastened his seatbelt, leaned across the center console, and put a hand behind her head. "Saturday morning," he promised. He pulled her more closely to him and closed his mouth over hers, felt himself falling into the sweetness of her mouth, the taste of her.

He broke away at last, smiled into her eyes. "I'll do my best to appeal to your Neanderthal brain."

"You do that." She smiled mistily back at him. "I'll be watching."

He got out of the car reluctantly, grabbed his duffel from the back seat. He slammed the door shut, then leaned in through the open passenger window for a final word.

"We're not going to be waiting till December," he informed her. "Fair warning."

bringing the goods

♡

"Auntie Sarah!" Sophie called out as they came through the gate into the unassuming Dunedin Airport on Friday afternoon. She ran to the tall, rangy woman and gave her an enthusiastic hug. Harry wasn't far behind to add his own greeting. "Where's Uncle Kieran?"

"Back at home," Sarah told her, laughing as she pulled both children close. "We didn't have enough people to work, in the end, and one of us had to stay."

She straightened up as Jenna approached, held out a hand. "You must be Jenna. Thanks for bringing these two down to see us."

Jenna wasn't used to feeling short, but Sarah topped her by a good three inches. It was easy to see that Finn's height was a family trait. "No worries," she assured the other woman. "I was glad to do it. And I get to stay over tonight, go to the game as well. I'm looking forward to that. I want to see the results of all that extra time Finn's been putting in this week."

"Heard about that. That Drew's ankle's still crook," Sarah said. "I'm sorry to hear it for his sake, and the team's. But I'll admit that, as a sister, it gives me a good thrill—and a fair dose of the collywobbles for his sake—when Finn's the skipper. And being able to see it live tonight will be pretty special."

"I'm looking forward to it," Jenna said again. "Though I may have to ask you to take Sophie's place as my rugby tutor."

"I've been teaching Jenna all about footy," Sophie told her aunt. "She didn't know much about it before."

"That's putting it charitably," Jenna laughed. "But Sophie's an excellent teacher." She rested her hand on Sophie's head as the little girl beamed with pride.

"We don't get to go to the game tonight with you, though," Sophie told her aunt with disappointment. "Too late, Dad said. We have to stay at the hotel with Nana instead."

"The weekend will be busy enough, with the wedding on Sunday," Jenna told her. "And you can watch the game on TV with your Nana."

"It's not the same, though," Sophie scowled. "It's not fair. Just because Harry's too little. *I'm* not. *I* didn't fall asleep last week."

"I know it's disappointing, but your dad said no," Jenna reminded her. "And I agreed with him. Can you give me a hand with this luggage, please?"

Sophie still looked mutinous, but didn't protest further, grabbing a wheeled case and moving toward the carpark with the others.

"Thanks for the lift," Jenna told Sarah as she climbed into the front seat of the Toyota people mover. "I hope it isn't putting you out. I could have hired a car as well. Then Finn could have used it after tonight."

"Dunedin's not what you'd call a sprawling metropolis," Sarah said. "We can walk nearly everywhere we'll want to go from the hotel. Finn knows that. Besides, I couldn't wait to see my favorite niece and nephew."

"We're your *only* niece and nephew, Auntie Sarah," Harry piped up from the back seat. "So that's silly."

"Like I said. My favorites."

"Are Nana and Grandpa here yet?" Sophie asked. Jenna was grateful that she seemed to have put aside her disappointment over missing the game, at least for the time being.

"At the hotel, waiting for you," Sarah promised. "And they asked me to invite you to join us for dinner," she told Jenna. "They're quite keen to meet you."

"Me?" Jenna asked in surprise.

"Seems they've heard a fair bit about you from their grandchildren, these past months. And from Finn, I gather." She cast a quick glance at Jenna. "You've made an impression."

"That's nice to hear. I'd enjoy having dinner with all of you."

"You may change your mind once you know how many that is," Sarah grinned. "Most of the family's here for the wedding, as well as all Ella's family and friends. And everyone who could manage it got here early to go to the game tonight. It'll be a bit of an open slather, I'm afraid."

"Sounds fun," Jenna said determinedly.

"We'll meet at six, then, in the lobby," Sarah told her as she pulled into the hotel carpark. "Don't say I didn't warn you."

♡

"How ya goin'?" Sarah asked as they began the trek to Forsyth Barr Stadium that evening after dinner, their large family group just part of the happy throng headed that way, many wearing All Blacks apparel or carrying the distinctive black flag with its silver fern, some even having decorated themselves with white and black face paint in honor of the occasion.

"You were right," Jenna admitted. "Fun, but a little overwhelming. I'm going to have a job remembering everyone's name."

"Finn said you'd been a teacher. You must have had some practice remembering names."

"True. More challenging in the pub, though, than in a nice orderly classroom."

"Why *are* you doing this now? Being a nanny, I mean," Sarah clarified. "Bit overqualified, aren't you?"

"I'm taking a year off," Jenna explained. "I'd been living in Wellington since I moved to New Zealand, and never even got around that much. I knew I wanted to live someplace else, but I wasn't sure where. So I traveled around the North Island for a while, working in cafés, staying in backpackers' hostels, looking for somewhere to settle. I tried New Plymouth, Rotorua, a few other places. I ended up in Auckland, because…" She shrugged. "Because everyone ends up in Auckland, right? I was visiting a friend there when I saw Finn's advert. I was missing working with kids, and the timing was right. It seemed like a fun thing to do, just for now. I like to cook, and Finn's an appreciative audience, let me tell you. I've never cooked for anyone who ate that much, or enjoyed it as much as he does. I love that."

"How've you found it, other than that?" Sarah asked. "Sounds like a dead bore to me. How does my baby brother rate as an employer? Besides eating so much. Didn't realize that was such an attractive trait."

"I realize it may not be everyone's cup of tea," Jenna laughed, "but I do like it. I was born with an extra domesticity gene, I guess. And it's hard for me to imagine Finn as anyone's baby brother. It sounds so funny."

"Well, I'm seven years older," Sarah conceded with a grin. "So I *do* remember when he was a baby. He didn't come into the world wearing those size fifteen boots. But come on now, tell me. How're you going with him?"

"Great. Although we didn't start off too well, when I first interviewed. He thought I was after his money. Or maybe it was his body." Jenna giggled, then slapped a hand over her mouth. "Sorry. Getting a little too relaxed here, I'm afraid."

"Thought you were having a go, did he?" asked an amused Sarah. "Not really that surprising. He may not be much in the looks department, but he doesn't actually break the looking glass. I know he's had more than his fair share of girls interested. It's being an All Black, I reckon."

"I didn't mean...I wasn't saying he wasn't good-looking," Jenna said, horrified. "He's very attractive. I mean," she stumbled, "I'm sure he does. That he has. Oh, dear." She gave up. "I'm just digging myself in deeper, aren't I?"

Sarah laughed. "Yeh. You are. No worries."

Interesting, Sarah thought as they entered the stadium. She'd been suspicious when her mother had told her how often Finn had mentioned Jenna's name during his phone calls. And now that she'd met her, she was definitely wondering.

♡

"Nice," Jenna told her as they found their seats in the rapidly filling stands of the modern covered stadium. Sold out this evening, she'd read, despite Dunedin's small population. "Very comfortable, isn't it?"

"It is now," Sarah agreed. "But it used to be known as the House of Pain, before the new stadium was built a few years ago. Because the ground was so shocking to play on. And because the Highlanders, including Finn then, were famous for dealing out a good hiding to teams unfortunate enough to come down here to play. Still hoping for a good hiding tonight, of course."

"I noticed that the crowd's pretty lopsided," Jenna agreed.

"Nothing Kiwis like better than dealing to the Convicts," Sarah agreed with satisfaction. "Not even beating the Poms."

They stood and cheered with the rest of the crowd as the All Blacks ran out onto the field behind Finn. Jenna's heart swelled to see him on the field and projected on the large screen overhead, features set in the hard, determined lines he assumed for every game, big body rock-solid under the skintight black jersey.

"Phew." Jenna sat back down again as the crowd subsided following the national anthems and the emotional haka. "It's only my second time seeing that in person. But even on TV, it gets me every time."

"Me too," Sarah admitted. "And I've watched them do it for years. Don't think it does the Aussie boys any good either."

Jenna thought back to the way the Wallabies had lined up, hands on each others' shoulders in their gold and green jerseys to face the aggressive black wall. "Do you think it actually scares them?"

"It should do," Sarah told her. "As the ABs have won about seventy percent of the test matches they've played against them, from the beginning of time."

"There's that much difference?" Jenna asked in surprise.

"Where did you say you've been living recently?" Sarah wondered.

"It's true," Jenna admitted. "I've been here more than seven years now, and I'm a permanent resident. You'd think I'd know more about rugby."

"I'd think, yeh. If you ever plan to apply for citizenship, reckon you'd better educate yourself. The ABs rank first in the world nearly every year, by a fair margin."

"I know much more than I used to," Jenna assured her as the Australian team lined up to kick off. "Thanks to Sophie."

And Finn? Sarah wondered. They didn't talk much during the continuous action that followed, except when Sarah was forced to explain a penalty or point of strategy that had eluded Jenna. She couldn't tell for sure, but Sarah was reasonably certain that Jenna's eyes were mostly on Finn, whatever else was happening on the field, and suspicion began to grow into certainty.

"Want a beer?" she offered at the halftime break.

Jenna smiled. "I think I've done my drinking for tonight, thanks. I have to get up and catch my plane tomorrow. That's going to be hard enough as it is."

"Why don't you stay over till Monday, come to the wedding Sunday?" Sarah asked. "Unless you have special plans. Finn said you'd be on holiday anyway. I can change my room for one with two beds. You'd give me some company. Be my date, eh. You wouldn't need to be fussed about the kids, either. Mum's already booked a babysitter for them for the reception."

"Dan and Ella won't want somebody added to the guest list at the last minute like this, though," Jenna protested.

"Let's find out," Sarah suggested. She turned in her seat. "Oi, Dan! Can I bring Jenna to your wedding, take Kieran's spot?"

"Good as gold," he called back from his spot two rows up.

"Sorted." Sarah turned back to Jenna with satisfaction.

"Pretty formal," Jenna laughed. "Just about as formal as going to a rugby game two days before your wedding."

"Not just any rugby game," Sarah pointed out. "A test match in Dunedin doesn't happen that often. Having a chance to see Finn play—that's not something Dan's going to pass up."

"Is Ella all right with that too?"

"Course," Sarah answered in surprise. "She'd be here too if she didn't have so much to do."

"All right," Jenna said. "I'm accepting this as a major cultural event. And thank you for the invitation to stay with you. I'd like that very much. I don't have anything to wear, though. I only brought clothes for a couple days. Certainly nothing appropriate for a wedding."

"Excuse to go shopping," Sarah decided. "Sweet as. I'll take you to the Meridian Mall tomorrow. We'll get you sorted."

"I don't want to put you out," Jenna began.

"How much shopping d'you think there is in Motueka?" Sarah demanded. "Or Nelson, for that matter? I'll tell you. Bugger all. I'm going with you, and that's that."

♡

"I don't know," Jenna said dubiously, tugging upward on the scoop neckline of the metallic copper-and-black print dress, then turning to see how the skirt looked from behind. "I like it, but isn't it too low in front?"

"Nah," Sarah said confidently. "It's perfect. If I'd ever looked like that, believe me, I'd've taken advantage of it."

"For a wedding, though," Jenna protested.

"Your girls aren't having a song and dance," Sarah told her. "Just peeking out a bit to wave a wee hello. We'll find a black shawl for the church. Good as gold."

The shop assistant chimed in. "It's lovely on you. Like your friend says, just a hint of cleavage. The skirt's not far above the knee, and not too tight, so you're not showing too much down below. Cleavage or leg, one or the other. That's the rule."

"Does it make my bum look big, though?" Jenna asked.

"You're balanced," the assistant smiled. "That's obvious, in that dress. Here." She dove into a neighboring carousel. "See if you fit this."

Jenna took the wide black patent belt with its double row of buckles and fastened it around her waist. The assistant nodded. "Even better. Makes your waist look tiny on top of that skirt. You have a beautiful figure. No reason not to show it. Add some heels, and the boys'll be sitting up to take notice, I guarantee it."

Jenna hesitated. "Excuse us a moment." She took Sarah's arm and walked a bit apart.

"What is it?" the other woman asked.

"It's Finn," Jenna explained. "He told me once that my swimsuit was too…revealing. I'm a little concerned about what he's going to think of this."

Sarah stared at her in astonishment. "Your togs. The ones you wore in the spa last night?"

"Yeah. I know, ridiculous, right? You'll notice I'm still wearing it these days. But still. I *am* the nanny. Maybe I should be more conservative."

"Not tomorrow, you're not the nanny. Tomorrow you're my date," Sarah told her firmly. "And I demand that my dates be dead sexy. Finn can go stuff himself."

"Here we are. Undies," Sarah told Jenna, pulling her into a lingerie boutique adjacent to the shoe shop where they'd just found the perfect pair of black heels.

"I have underwear, though," Jenna told her. "At least, I do once I wash some."

"Huh," Sarah snorted. "I saw your undies. Not nearly good enough."

"How do you look?" she called a few minutes later from outside the dressing room. "Bloody hell," she said when Jenna pulled open the door to allow her inside. "Those are the goods, all right. And I have another idea too."

"Why do I need all this?" Jenna protested. "It's expensive. Why can't I just wear what I have? Nobody but me is going to see it."

"That's when you need it most of all," Sarah explained. "You need to feel sexy to look sexy. Which is why we're doing hair and nails next, and having our legs waxed. And maybe a bit more," she smiled mischievously. "My shout. Girls' day out. I don't get them very often, and I'm taking full advantage of this one. I already booked us in, so don't argue. Because looking good where everyone can see it isn't enough. You need to know what's under there, imagine how gobsmacked all those boys would be if they could see what you've got. That's your secret weapon."

If Finn had thought Jenna's cossie was too sexy, Sarah thought with satisfaction, wait till he got a squiz at her in that dress. She hadn't missed the way his eyes had tracked Jenna when she'd moved around the room at breakfast that morning, or that he'd laughed and smiled more than she'd seen in ages. And she didn't think it was all down to winning the Championship.

She hadn't liked Nicole above half. From what she'd heard and seen, none of the women Finn had dated since her death had been much chop either. But Jenna was different. She was exactly the kind of woman he needed in his life, if only he had the sense to see it.

She'd give that a bit of a nudge. Then it'd be up to him.

quite a nice dress

♡

"Hi, Jenna!" Harry bounced in the pew of the church the following afternoon. "Come sit by me!"

"Shhh," Jenna cautioned him as she slid in beside him. "Use your quietest voice, please."

"Your dress is very pretty," he said in a stage whisper.

"Thank you. You look very handsome yourself," she told him. "You too, Sophie. That outfit looks even nicer than I remember."

"Nana helped me with my hair," Sophie explained, touching a hand to the pink headband that matched her dress. "I couldn't make the headband go right, and Daddy couldn't either. I wanted to ask you to help, but he said no."

Jenna smiled. "Your Nana did a good job. You look lovely."

"Thanks for taking them shopping," Maureen Douglas told her above the children's heads. "I was a bit worried, with Nyree gone. And Finn's hopeless." Her blue eyes looked Jenna over warmly. "You look lovely yourself. That dress is stunning with your hair."

"I thought, maybe a bit much with the red tones," Jenna confessed. "But Sarah convinced me."

"And I was right, wasn't I, Mum?" Sarah asked, sliding in beside her. "Don't I have a gorgeous date, Dad? Kieran's been well and truly replaced."

John Douglas smiled wryly. "You have a cheek, Sarah Bee. But yeh, both you girls look very pretty. I'm glad you could join us today, Jenna."

"Thank you for including me," Jenna said. "Everyone's been so kind."

"We're grateful to you for everything you've done for the kids," Maureen told her. "We've heard heaps about Jenna, haven't we, John? It's nice to have the chance to get to know you a bit ourselves. since our grandchildren are pretty special to us."

They turned towards the front, quiet now, as the music changed and the groom and his groomsmen came out from the side door at the front of the church.

"There's Daddy," Harry whispered excitedly. Jenna squeezed his hand and shot him a reminding glance, and he subsided.

Finn did look handsome, though, she thought, the severe lines of the black dinner jacket and white shirt setting off his powerful physique. He was the tallest of the four men standing together near the altar, and by far the most imposing, though none of them were small.

Finn saw her looking at him, and a corner of his mouth quirked up in a smile. He wiggled his fingers at his kids, seeing them unable to resist the temptation to wave at him, even under their grandmother's and Jenna's admonitory influence on either side. Then his eyes returned to Jenna. She'd done something with her hair, and it fell in soft, shining auburn waves onto her shoulders. He couldn't see much else from here, except that she looked pretty.

His attention was diverted by the swelling music, the sight of the two bridesmaids beginning their slow walk down the aisle, followed by the maid of honor and the bride. His cousin had done well for himself, Finn thought as he watched the procession. Ella was down-to-earth and warm, like Dan himself. They seemed well suited. He'd give this one a good chance of lasting. Not like his own marriage. He couldn't help thinking about it, whenever he went to a wedding these days. And there'd been heaps of those.

Lately, seemed like everyone he knew had been getting married. Pity he couldn't always feel happy about it. He hated that he'd become such a cynic. But when he saw one of his teammates marrying a woman who reminded him of Nicole…well, he couldn't help wondering how long it'd be before she'd realize that being married to a professional sportsman meant days and weeks apart, and a husband who came home from a game wanting nothing more than to lie in the spa and have a bit of quiet for a day or two, before heading back into training to do it all again the following week. And how long it would take her to get bored, start looking for excitement someplace else.

♡

Jenna sighed as the bride and groom kissed, husband and wife now. They both looked lit from within, and she envied them their obvious belief in their future happiness. She found herself praying their marriage would work, that they'd find the kind of partnership she'd always dreamed of. She had to blink a tear or two away as they walked up the aisle to the swelling music, followed by the bridesmaids and groomsmen. Finn grinned at his waving kids as he passed, a pretty bridesmaid on his arm, and Jenna felt a pang of jealousy. She'd like to have been the woman by his side.

She pushed the errant thought aside. She was going to a party, and thanks to Sarah, she looked better than she ever had. She was going to enjoy feeling like an attractive single woman tonight. Maybe even dancing a bit.

Harry and Sophie weren't as thrilled, though, when they were reminded of the program for the evening.

"Why do we need a babysitter?" Harry asked. "Why can't Jenna stay with us?"

"Jenna isn't working now," John chided. "She's having her holiday, and she doesn't need to be bothered with you tonight. Don't be a nuisance, Harry."

"Don't you like taking care of us, Jenna?" Harry asked, his lip quivering. "I thought you liked us. I didn't mean to be a nuisance."

The excitement of the day had been too much for him, Jenna saw. She crouched down as best she could in her heels and gathered him in for a hug. "Hey, now. Of course I like taking care of you. I love being with you both, you know that." She gave Sophie a squeeze as well. "I need some grownup time, that's all. I'll see you both in the morning before I leave, OK?"

"OK," Harry sniffed, Sophie adding her own sober nod. Jenna rose to her feet again, and Maureen offered her a grateful smile as she left with the children to meet the babysitter in the lobby.

"Sorry," John said, abashed. "I didn't put that right."

"He's a bit overtired," Jenna told him reassuringly. "They both are. It's been a busy weekend. It was a good idea of yours and Maureen's to give them this quiet evening."

"What's going to happen when this job's over, d'you reckon?" Sarah asked as the two of them made a stop in the ladies' toilets before heading to the ballroom for the reception dinner. "Seems like the kids have got awfully attached to you. Harry in particular. Does that concern you?"

"A little," Jenna admitted. "They're both sensitive children. Sophie doesn't wear her heart on her sleeve like Harry does, but it's tender all the same. And on some level, kids know that a nanny isn't the same as a mum. That she's working, and she can leave. Harry and Sophie are lucky, though. They've had Nyree with them since they were small. And Finn doesn't seem to have brought women in and out of their lives. Nobody they've been attached to, anyway."

"Nah," Sarah agreed. "Don't think he's had anyone that serious, not since Nicole died. But that brings me back to it. What about you?"

"I'll still see them," Jenna said, surprised at the question. "As long as that's all right with Finn, and I don't know why it wouldn't be. I'm planning on teaching in Auckland in the new year. I hope to be spending some time with them at the weekends. I guess I'd better discuss it with Finn, though."

"He doesn't seem keen on losing you himself," Sarah said.

Jenna shot her a quick glance and picked up her purse to leave. "I hope not. I think the job's been working out well for both of us."

"Huh," was Sarah's only response.

♡

"Auntie Hetty's pissed already." Finn's cousin Stewart, the groom's brother and best man, nodded across the ballroom to where an improbably red-haired woman was shrieking with laughter.

"Hmm?" Finn brought his attention back with a start from Jenna, sitting several tables away with his sister, mum, and dad. And several young men from the bride's side, all of whom seemed fascinated by her. The reason was plain to see. Sarah had told him she'd taken Jenna shopping for the wedding, and that she'd found her "quite a nice dress." He'd have been happier with his sister's choice if he'd been able to join them, instead of being marooned here at the head table. As it was, he was having a hard time keeping his eyes off her. "Pardon?"

"Auntie Hetty," Stewart repeated patiently. "And Sean isn't much better. Like mum, like son, eh."

Finn looked with disgust at his cousin Sean, now weaving his way across the tables towards him, even though dinner was still in progress. "Aw, geez. Going to have this again."

"Price of success, cuz," Stewart grinned.

Sean wobbled to a stop in front of Finn. "Enjoying the party, mate?" he sneered. "At the best table as usual, I see. Not down the back with the peasants."

"Reckon you could've been a groomsman yourself," Finn said levelly. "If Dan'd been able to count on you not getting cut before the evening's even got well underway."

"Yeh, right," Sean scoffed. "Like I'd ever be chosen over the *famous* Finn Douglas. The Golden Boy. The fucking *All Black*."

"Watch your mouth," Finn said sharply. "You're at a wedding. And there're ladies here."

"Yeh, noticed there're ladies here," Sean retorted. "Even your bloody nanny's special, isn't she? Blow that for a joke. Why the hell isn't she upstairs looking after the kids?"

"Jenna's a guest here tonight," Finn told him, eyes hard. He stood up, deliberately looming over his smaller cousin, and took a menacing step towards him. "And that's enough. Rack off." He stared Sean down until the younger man's eyes shifted under his own and he turned to leave, still cursing Finn under his breath.

"Wanker," Finn muttered, sitting down again but keeping a careful eye on Sean as he made his way back to his own table.

"He's always been rough as guts," Stewart agreed.

"He's always been a dickhead," Finn corrected him.

"That too. Worse than ever these days. You don't have to see much of him. Lucky you."

♡

Finn looked over the maid of honor's head at Jenna, dancing with yet another of his young cousins. So far, in addition to his current partner, he'd danced with one bridesmaid, the bride's mother,

and the groom's mother. One more bridesmaid to go, he reckoned, and he'd be free. Unless his mother and sister thought he
should ask them. He groaned inwardly. Surely not.

The song ended at last, and he returned Isabel to the table
and turned to Zara, about to sit down again herself. "Would you
like to dance?" he asked, as politely as he could manage.

His cousin laughed. "Normally, I'd say yes. But I'm not too
keen on dancing with someone who's looking over my shoulder
at somebody else the entire time."

He gave her a rueful grin. "Has it been that obvious?"

"Well...yeh. To me, anyway. You're off the hook. Go get her."

"Thanks." He leaned down and kissed her cheek. "You're a
great girl."

"Yeh, yeh." She waved him away. "Someday my prince will
come. Bugger off."

He began to make his way to Jenna, being claimed now by
yet another partner, one he didn't recognize. Another of Ella's
relatives, he guessed. Who was clearly looking down her dress.
He started towards them, veered off in another direction as an
idea struck him. He made his way around the dancers to the
corner of the big room, where a DJ sat with his laptop in front of
him, monitoring the playlist.

"Mate." Finn stopped in front of the white-clad table. "Can
I ask a bit of a favor?"

The young man looked up, recognition clear in his face.
"Reckon you can. What can I do?"

"You must have a fair few slow songs in there," Finn guessed.
"How about playing, say, four of them for me, starting now? The
best you have."

The DJ nodded. "Four songs, guaranteed to pull. I could do
that."

"Don't shock any grannies," Finn warned. "But...far as you
can go, short of that."

"Done," the other man promised. "Best of luck, mate."

That was Step One sorted. As long as he was the one dancing with Jenna while those songs were playing, instead of that bloke who was perving at her now.

The song ended, but Jenna's partner showed no sign of releasing her, and the slow notes of a saxophone were coming over the speakers. His song. His dance.

He moved up behind the other man, tapped him on the shoulder. The young man's protest died on his lips as he turned and looked up into Finn's face, set into its best Hard Man glare.

"Time for you to find another partner," Finn told him. "This one's mine."

"Right. Sorry." The man released Jenna without saying goodbye and hastened back to his table.

"Hey!" Jenna protested. "I was dancing with that guy. And he was nice. What was that all about?"

Finn stepped up, took her in his arms. "What I said. My turn now."

She looked at him suspiciously even as she began to move with him, swaying to the slow, insistent beat. "Did you come over here to tell me I was doing something wrong? I know I've been dancing a lot, but everyone's been so great about asking me, and I'm not working now."

"Yeh. I've noticed how they've been asking you. Because you look beautiful." He couldn't resist a peek down the front of her dress himself. He wasn't surprised that fella had been so mesmerized. It was quite a sight from above, the swell of her breasts just visible above the neckline, and that enticing shadow in the middle. A man could put his hand right down that, get lost there.

"Really? You think that's why?" She sounded so pleased, he couldn't help but smile. "Your sister helped me pick out this dress. Do you like it?"

"I like it so much," he assured her. "But it's not the dress. It's you *in* the dress. You're gorgeous."

"We're getting inappropriate again," she warned him. "Do you think this is a good idea? Dancing?"

"I'm past caring," he admitted. "I'm beginning to think it's inevitable. Feels like a freight train coming down the track. And like I'm standing in front of it, just waiting to be hit. Maybe, just for tonight, we could forget about everything else. About the kids, and all the complications of it. Pretend we've just met."

"Dangerous," she cautioned, looking up at him.

"Like I said. That freight train. My name's Finn Douglas, and I've been watching you all night. Because you're beautiful."

Those full pink lips stretched into her generous smile, and he felt his heart rate kick up a notch. "Jenna McKnight. I'm glad to meet you. Because you're quite something yourself."

He felt her move a little further into his arms as the music shifted to a smooth, romantic Michael Bublé song. Her hand felt right in his, her body warm as he pulled her against him, moved her around the floor. He sensed the moment when she melted against him, her head coming to rest against his chest, felt her snuggle in closer, run her hand over his shoulder.

Norah Jones over the speakers next, her smoky voice crooning as the two of them danced, barely swaying together now.

"I like this music," Jenna sighed against him, and Finn smiled a bit above her head. As the song ended, he let go of her hand, raised his own to stroke her cheek. He heard the opening strains of *Unchained Melody,* but he wasn't waiting for the fourth song. He didn't think he could. But he couldn't kiss her here, either. And he needed to kiss her, so badly now.

"Come on," he urged. "Let's take a walk." He took her hand and moved to the door, then into the wide passage.

Jenna went with him willingly. This wasn't a good idea, but she didn't care anymore. She hadn't drunk enough tonight to blame it on the wine. It was Finn. She'd been thinking about touching him again ever since that night in the hotel. Thinking about the way he had touched her, how he had kissed her. She needed him to kiss her like that again.

He was trying doors now, moving faster. "Finn," she protested as she stumbled, her heels sinking into the carpet. "Slow down. Please."

He looked down at her in surprise.

"High heels," she explained. "I can't walk this fast."

He exhaled in relief. "Thought you were saying something else." He tried the next door, and the handle shifted. He looked inside, shot a quick glance at the passage behind them and pulled her through the doorway.

"Where are we?" she asked.

He reached for her, the darkness complete around them. "Storeroom," he got out. Then his mouth was on hers, his arms around her.

She felt him walking her backwards, up against the door they had come in. His mouth was insistent now, greedy and feverish on hers, his hands pulling her to him. She felt the length of him hard against her, and a thrill shot all the way through her body.

One hand continued to hold her to him while the other moved to a breast. "Aw, Jenna," he groaned into her mouth. "I've wanted to touch you here all night."

She felt his mouth on her neck, his lips and teeth moving against her skin, and shivered with it. Then jumped at the shock as his hand slipped inside the neckline of her dress, cupped her warm flesh, held her there. She moaned as his palm moved over her, as she felt the sensation going straight to her center.

His big body pressed her back against the door, and he shifted the other hand from behind her, lifted the edge of her skirt to grip a thigh. She felt his hand moving upward, the size and heat of it. She was kissing him back hard now, clutching at his shoulders, lost in his hands, his mouth on her. Then a new sensation, the shock as the hand on her leg found bare skin. And stopped there.

He broke the kiss, kept his hold on her, his thumb above the lace top of the stocking, warm against her inner thigh. She could hear his labored breathing, and her own, in the darkness.

"Jenna." His voice was strained. "Are you wearing stockings?"

She felt herself blushing. "Yes."

He groaned. "I need to see you. And we can't do this here. But I'm in a room with the kids."

"And I'm in one with your sister," she reminded him.

"Right. Getting a room. Wait here for me." He pulled his hands away reluctantly, then leaned against the wall next to her. "Give me a moment."

"Are you all right?" she asked tentatively.

He laughed a little. "Burning up for you. Only so much a dinner jacket can conceal. Saying my twelve times tables here."

"Right," he said after a minute. He lifted her gently away from the door. "Stay here. Back in a few minutes." He bent to kiss her again, lingered there as her mouth opened under his, broke it off at last. "Wait for me."

Alone in the dark, Jenna wrapped her arms around herself, reality slowly returning like a cold spigot running into a warm bathtub. What was she doing? This was a really, really bad idea. Never mind the future. Tonight was frightening enough.

She had worked herself into full anxiety by the time Finn gave a quiet knock and slipped through the door again.

"Jenna?" he called softly. "Still in here?"

"Yes," she said tentatively, moved towards him in the darkness. "But...are you sure?"

He reached for her, pulled her into him. "I'm so sure. I need to do this. But if you don't...you can say no. Praying you won't, though." He found her mouth, kissed her again. "What do you think?"

"I want to," she said honestly. "But...what I told you. I'm not good at this. What if you're disappointed?"

"Do you want me?" he demanded.

"Yes," she admitted. "So much."

He exhaled in relief. "Then here's what we're going to do. I'm going to take you upstairs. I'm going to get you naked, and then I'm going to put you on your back and do some things to you that I've been thinking about for a long, long time. Trust me, I'm not going to be disappointed. I'm going to be feeling like the luckiest man in the world."

stockings

♡

Finn opened the door with the keycard, allowed Jenna to precede him into the room. He'd kept his hands off her during the walk to the lift, the ride up with a family whose young son had been awestruck at the bit of chat he'd offered. But now he had her here, and he was done. He bent down to pull off his shoes and socks, saw her beginning to kick off her own high heels.

"No," he said sharply. "No," he added more gently. "Please. Leave them on for me."

He saw her uncertainty. "Jenna. Come here." He folded her in his arms, gave her a long, slow kiss. "I'm going to tell you what to do," he said when he had her warm and soft again, melting against him. "And I'm going to find out what you like. It's all good. No worries."

"You'll tell me?" she asked, looking up at him. "Because I want to please you."

He took his arms from around her to pull off his dinner jacket and throw it across a chair. "You please me so much. Just looking at you is pleasing me. But if you want to help, why don't you unfasten this tie?"

She stepped in close, untied the bow tie from around his neck, and he saw her breath coming faster at the contact.

"Could you take these cufflinks off for me too?" He lifted his wrists and watched as she carefully removed the black onyx links and set them on the desk. "And can you do the shirt studs as well? They're a bit fiddly."

His shirt fell further open with every black ornament she removed and placed on the desk with the cufflinks, and her hands slowed.

"I want to touch you." She looked up at him. "While I do this."

He smiled. "Funny, that's what I was just going to suggest."

He took a breath as she set her palms on his chest, moved them slowly over him. She removed another stud, ran her hands down his abdomen, slid her arms around him beneath the shirt, reached up to kiss the spot above his collarbone, then the place where his neck met his shoulder.

"You're so strong," she breathed against his skin. "I love how big you are. How you feel."

He bent to kiss her again as her hands continued to move on his back. "Better take care of the rest of those," he told her. "Touch me a bit more while you're there, too."

She pulled out the last stud, looked up at him questioningly as she pulled the shirttail from his black trousers. "Can I take it off?"

"Hoping you will." His breath was coming faster now.

She pulled the white shirt from his shoulders, set it on the chair next to the jacket, then turned back to look at him, explore him with her hands again. Over his shoulders and chest, down his forearms with their shifting ropes of muscle, then, more daringly, down his defined abdomen, following the trail of hair that ran from his navel, dipped into his waistband.

He closed his hands over hers as they moved to the button of his black trousers. "I'm taking that dress off first," he said. "I need to see you."

She reached for her belt, but he brushed her hands aside again. "Oh, no," he told her.

"I'm doing this. Been planning it all night." He unfastened the wide belt, set it aside, then reached around to pull down the long zipper that ran the length of her back. The sleeveless dress gapped as the zipper parted, revealing more of her breasts, the top of her bra. Black, he realized, his pulse giving another kick. He pulled the dress up over her head, dropped it on the chair. Then stood back and just looked.

Auburn waves fell over her white shoulders, and that was good. A black lace demibra left the upper curves of her full breasts exposed, and matching black lace bikini panties began at the wide curve of her hips, dipped in a V that pointed where he wanted to go. And that was better, but it wasn't all. He'd felt the top of a stocking as he'd kissed her in the dark, but that hadn't prepared him for the sight of the wide band of black lace encircling each white thigh, changing beneath to sheer black nylon that ended in the high heels.

"Shit," he breathed.

"Is it all right?" she asked him tentatively. "Too much?"

"Oh, yeh," he groaned. "Too much." He pulled her to him, began to kiss her as he covered a breast with one hand, brought her hips against him with the other. Dove beneath the waistband of the lace panties, rubbed his hand over her backside, felt her response, her hips rocking into him, her mouth opening wider under his own as his hands moved on her. Her own hands sliding over his shoulders, his back, coming down to his waist now. Then she was stepping back, reaching for his button again. Unzipping him, pulling his pants down his legs.

"Condom in my pocket," he muttered. He grabbed for it, then hesitated, not sure what to do with it.

She took it from him, tucked it into the front of her bra. "Ladies' pocket," she smiled.

He watched her face grow serious again as she hooked her fingers into the waistband of his boxer briefs. "I want to take these off," she told him. "I need to see you, too. All of you."

He nodded, dry-mouthed, as she pulled them down. He stepped out of them and his pants and kicked them aside.

"Oh." She reached out to hold him. "So much here, too." She ran her hand over him, and he closed his eyes. Then opened them again, because the sight of her, dressed like that, doing that, was something he didn't want to miss.

"Time for you to lie down for me," he told her. He walked her backward until her thighs hit the bed behind them, came down with her onto it, reached down to pull off first one black high heel, then the other. He moved over her again, kissing her harder now, a hand going to her breast, thumb tracing the edge of the lace. Down to kiss her neck, her throat. And then the flesh rising above that lace bra. Dipping into the space between her breasts, that shadow she'd been showing all night. All his, now. He pulled the condom packet out, set it aside. Then reached around at last, unfastened the bra and pulled it off, exposed her to his gaze.

She moved her hands towards her breasts to cover them, uncomfortable with his silence. "Big."

He pulled her hands away. "Perfect."

His hand closed over one breast, stroking and teasing, while his mouth moved on the other, found the nipple and took it between his teeth, and the shock of it went through her, straight to her core. Her breath was coming fast now, and a moan escaped her at the feeling of his mouth and hands on her. She felt her thighs falling open, the electric moment when his hand moved down from a breast to cover her, his hands moving to pull the lace panties off.

Then he wasn't touching her anymore. He was sitting up and staring down at her as she lay on the white duvet cover, wearing only the black stockings.

"Bloody hell," he said, breathing hard now himself. "You're like Disneyland. Everything I like best, all there for me. And I want to go on every ride."

He ran a hand from her breast down her stomach, then lower, looked into her eyes as he began to stroke her, and she knew he was seeing her eyes glaze over as he continued to touch her. "You're so gorgeous," he said. "All I want to do is play here all night. Do everything to you."

"Finn," she breathed. "Please. Please." Her hips moved towards him, her entire body calling to him. He kissed her breasts again, moved lower, and her legs were parting, because she couldn't help it. He pulled a pillow from the head of the bed and shoved it under her hips, then put a hand on each thigh and opened her to him.

"Wait," she gasped as he began to kiss her. "No. Don't." She tried to close her thighs, struggled against him.

He looked up. "What's wrong?"

"You don't...you can't want to do that." She was blushing furiously now, could tell that the color was staining her chest and her face as she struggled onto her elbows.

He came up to hold her, kiss her mouth again. "Jenna. I want to do that so much. You're gorgeous, and I want to kiss you, and please you."

"You do?"

"Trust me. If you don't like it, I'll stop. I promise." His mouth went to her breast again, his hand stroking her, and her breath hitched. "Now lie back and let me love you."

♡

He could tell that she still felt shy, at first. And he could sense the moment when the feelings became too much for her, the pleasure too intense. When she forgot to be shy and was rising into him, calling out now, hands clutching his hair as he took her higher, then higher still. When she felt her entire being centered there, where he was touching her, kissing her. He drove her up until she shattered with a long cry, her back arching as she rose into his mouth again and again.

She was still trembling with the aftershocks as he grabbed for the condom packet. Her hands went to the stockings. "I should…"

"Oh, no." His hands closed over hers, stilled them. "We're not taking those off. Ever since I saw them, I've been wanting to feel them against me." Still holding her hands, he moved over her, looked down to watch as he slid inside, then up again to see her eyes glaze as he filled her. The heat of it, the sight of her mouth opening, her breath coming hard now. Her hands still in his, her hips rising to meet him. He kept it slow, a smooth rock, watched her, listened to her responding to him.

"Wrap your legs around me," he told her at last. He felt the lace tops of her stockings against his back, and his pleasure ratcheted up another notch as the ride continued, higher and higher now.

"Harder. Please. Finn. Do it harder. Do that to me." She was crying out at every stroke, moving against him, and he was lost, no control now, taking all of her. He felt her convulsing around him again, the contractions pulling at him. The sensation was too much, and he felt himself going up and over, calling out hoarsely as he emptied into her.

He rolled to his back, pulled her on top of him, both of them fighting for breath. "Worth waiting for," he told her at last. "My God. So worth waiting for."

She buried her face in his neck as his hand moved over her, stroking her. "Me too. I never knew it could feel that way. That was…it was amazing. Thank you."

He smiled lazily. "My pleasure. As you're a bit amazing your-self. Happy to help you out that way anytime."

The next thing he knew, he was waking from a doze he hadn't realized he was falling into to hear her say, "Finn. We need to get back. We've been gone so long."

"Mmm." He ran his hand over her hair. "And we can't slip out tonight. Pity. What do you think about coming back to the house with me tomorrow, staying with me there for the week? We're going to have to do this a fair few times to get through everything I've thought of. Unless you had plans you don't want to change."

"Nothing that sounds better than that," she sighed. "But do you think that's a good idea?"

"Do you mean, will we jump each other if we're alone together? That's what I'm counting on. At least, I plan to jump you. Whether you reciprocate…well, that's up to you. But that's my game plan. Since we're sharing."

"I'm working for you, though," she said. "This time was one thing, and I'm not sorry. But we shouldn't do this again."

"Why not? You're on holiday. Nothing to do with working for me. We can go away, if that helps. Because I bloody well need to do it again. And I think you do, too."

"And what about after that? I don't want the kids to know. It wouldn't be fair to confuse them. It wouldn't be right, or doing my job. Anyway, sleeping with your kids' nanny? Isn't that kind of a classic? And not in a good way."

He pulled her down to him to kiss her. "If you're mar-ried to the kids' mum. Which I'm not. Or looking for a bit extra on the side. That's not me. We can't help that this is how we got to know each other. And if you want to stop, you can tell me. We just have to keep the two things separate in our minds. There's the job, and there's us. The kids, and me. Separate. Easy as."

She laughed reluctantly. "You're very persuasive. But nothing in front of the kids. Not while I'm staying in the house."

"Done," he agreed. "Now let's get dressed, get back to this party. You've got a just-been-done look about you, and I want to dance with you and watch you, and know I did that. And that I'll be doing it again tomorrow."

"Finn!" she laughed. "If I really look like that, I'm not going down there."

"No worries." He kissed her again, then gave her a slap on the bum. "Long as you only dance with me."

♡

They stepped off the lift, sedate again now. If Jenna's hair wasn't quite as smooth as it had been an hour or two earlier, that was understandable. And if his own shirt was a bit wrinkled, well, that was what the jacket was for, wasn't it?

Finn saw a group of his younger cousins standing in the hallway near the ballroom, Sean amongst them, and groaned inwardly.

"Go on ahead of me," he told Jenna. "I'll follow along in a minute or two. Less conspicuous."

She nodded, said a pleasant hello as she passed the men, and disappeared into the ballroom. Finn strolled up to his cousins, saw that Sean was even further gone than he'd been at dinner. No surprise.

"Evening, boys. Enjoying yourselves?"

"You're already having a bit of that, eh," Sean challenged, jerking his head in the direction Jenna had gone. "Should've guessed you'd be in there before the rest of us could have a go."

Sean never even saw the hand that shot out, pinned him to the wall. "Shut yer gate, ya little scunge," Finn snarled as his cousin choked beneath his hand.

"Finn." Liam had his own hands on Finn now, pulling him off, voice urgent. "Don't be bloody stupid. It's not worth it. He's full as a tick anyway. Pull your head in, mate."

Jesse weighed in. "Hurt him, and you'll be suspended. Not good for your kids."

Finn loosened his grip, continued to glare as Sean gulped in lungsful of air. "And that's the only reason I'm letting you go. That, and because Jenna doesn't need the publicity either. But I've had a gutsful of you. If I hear you saying anything like that again—if I even hear that you said it to somebody else—I'll be doing you over, and no beg pardons. Suspension or no."

Sean nodded, staggering a bit, raised his hands in a placating gesture. "Not saying anything," he agreed hoarsely.

"Get this arsehole out of here if you want to keep me out of trouble," Finn told Jesse and Liam with disgust. "I don't want to see him again tonight."

He could stop Sean from saying anything, he realized as he stalked into the ballroom. But he couldn't stop what other people would be thinking if they saw him with Jenna the way his family had tonight. They were going to have to be more discreet from here on out. For her sake.

no livestock involved

♡

"Got everything you need?" Finn asked his mother the following morning. "I'll have my mobile on. You can call me anytime."

"No worries," Maureen said. "We're going to have heaps of adventures, aren't we, kids? Go on, now." She reached up and pulled her son down from his considerable height for a hug and kiss. "It was good to meet you too, Jenna," she added, giving Jenna her own kiss. "Have a safe trip, and a good holiday."

"Sure you don't want me to give you a lift to the airport, Jenna?" Sarah asked helpfully, watching with interest from one of the lobby's big chairs as Finn gave each child a final kiss goodbye. "I thought your flight was leaving after Finn's. Do you really want to hang about in the airport all that time?"

"Ah…" Jenna looked to Finn in confusion.

He straightened up and looked at his sister. "I need to have a bit of a talk with Jenna. This past week was pretty busy. Plans to make."

"I see." Sarah was smiling now. "Plans." She got up to give Jenna a warm hug. "Enjoy your holiday. Hope you have heaps of adventures yourself. See you next week."

Finally, the taxi was pulling away from the hotel. Jenna gave one last wave at the kids out the rear window, then settled back with a sigh. "I have a feeling Sarah knows."

"She's not a gossip," Finn said. "She'll tell Kieran, that's all. But I don't want to think about my sister just now. I have some other things in mind. Those plans we need to talk about." She made a face at him, indicating the taxi driver with her head, and Finn laughed. "For now, though, I'll hold your hand. How would that be? Discreet enough for you?"

They had to forego even that simple contact when they reached the airport. As always, Finn spent a few minutes having his picture taken with fans of all ages, signing autographs, and generally showing his most pleasant face. Finally, though, they were sitting at a table in another Koru Lounge, having a coffee while they awaited their flight.

"Now I see why these lounges are necessary," Jenna said, "after a couple trips with you. It's not just about the VIP treatment. Does all that happen every time?"

He shrugged. "I'll wear a hat and sunnies sometimes. That helps a bit. But I'm tall enough that I'm usually recognized eventually. With me, it's mostly the young kids, the rugby-mad ones. I don't get the mob scene that some of the boys do, specially the backs. Reckon forwards aren't flash enough. And I'm not one of the lookers." He smiled at her protest. "No worries. Just as glad not to draw the crowds."

"But if they recognize you, you have to pose with them, sign autographs?" she asked. "Believe me, no U.S. athlete would do half as much of that as you do. They charge for autographs, you know. If they sign them at all."

He laughed. "Like to see the response to that idea here. You can't be a tall poppy, specially as a senior player, setting an example for the younger boys. You're an All Black 24/7, on and off the field. If you aren't willing to live that way, you aren't worthy of putting on the black jersey. Because it's not really about us. It's all about the jersey."

"Except that you're the one doing all that work," she pointed out. "It's not the jersey signing those autographs."

"Which I'm well compensated for. You won't hear me whingeing about my hard luck," he told her firmly. "Anybody'd want to be where I am. Specially where I am just now."

He took her hand again under the table, threaded his fingers through hers. "Not to mention where I'm going to be in a few hours."

♡

Jenna woke, confused for a moment by the sloping shape of the ceiling overhead. She was in Finn's bed, she realized as she came to full consciousness, pulled herself up against the massive headboard. Naked. And alone.

She got out of bed, looked for her clothes. Nothing.

Downstairs, she remembered at last. They'd finally got up the evening before to go out to the pub for dinner. And he'd started undressing her again at the front door. She flushed at the recollection.

She was in the passage, headed for her room, when Finn appeared, fully dressed in T-shirt and jeans, at the kitchen doorway. He looked her up and down with a smile. "Wearing my favorite outfit, I see. That's the thing I appreciate most about you, I've decided. How you give me exactly what I want."

"Somebody took off my clothes last night," she reminded him. "And failed to collect them for me this morning when he got up."

"Oi. I've been busy."

"Doing what?" She shivered. "Sorry, but I'm freezing. I need my dressing gown."

He wrapped his arms around her, pulled her up on tiptoes to kiss her, his hands reaching under her bottom to hold her against him. "Let me warm you up," he suggested.

"Mmm." She snuggled against him. "You are warm."

"I'd warm you up some more," he said, reluctantly letting her go, "but I really have been busy. And I want to tell you about it. Go put your dressing gown on, come have a cup of tea."

♥

"OK," she told him, pulling her sash tight as she came into the kitchen, took the mug of tea he held out. "What's this mysterious activity?" She sank into a chair at the kitchen table. "I know I slept in, but I was up late last night, for some reason. Did you go somewhere already?"

"Did a bit of research, made some bookings," he told her, taking his own seat. "Decided I'm taking you away for the rest of the week. I don't want you thinking about anything you have to do. Other than pleasing me."

Another rush of heat filled her at his words. "Where are we going?"

"The Far North. Warmest I can get, with just a few days for it. I've booked a bach outside Mangonui, on Doubtless Bay. A few days with the dolphins, a bit of time on the beach. Not many people there, this time of year. We'll have it to ourselves."

"Sounds great. I've never been."

"You've never been a fair few places," he pointed out. "For someone who's lived in En Zed all these years. Never been to Doubtless Bay, or to Dunedin. Or much of the South Island at all, from what I can tell."

"You're right. Jeremy was more...urban. He liked to travel to Sydney, Thailand. Places like that. And he didn't always want me to go with him."

He snorted. "Three guesses why not. Well, I'm not urban, and I do want you with me."

"Both things I'm thrilled about, trust me," she assured him. "I just want to spend time with you. But if I can do it at the beach, hey, bonus."

"The water's a bit warmer there, but we'll stop by the surf shop in Takapuna all the same, get you a wetsuit and a snorkel. Since I have a bad feeling I won't be able to keep you in bed the entire time."

"Most of the time, though." She took another sip of tea and smiled at him, reached out to run a hand over his bicep, feeling it flex at her touch. "I have a lot of catching up to do, I've decided. A lot to learn. And you're an amazingly good teacher."

He stood up. "Get your skates on, then. Pack your togs, a few clothes, and we'll go. We'll have brekkie at the café on the way. Because if you keep saying those things, we aren't going to be leaving this morning after all."

"I have to say," she sighed two evenings later as they lay in the spa pool on the deck of their bach, the Southern Cross and the rest of the Southern Hemisphere constellations in a dizzying array overhead, stars bright against the black night. "This has to be the most…physical period of time I've ever spent in my life. Nothing but eating, sleeping, swimming, and…"

"And making love," he agreed. "Welcome to my physical world. You've slipped up and done a bit of reading, though. I've noticed."

"Otherwise, I'm going to turn into some kind of mindless zombie," she said.

"Hmm." She could see his teeth flash in the darkness as he moved to pull her closer. "I've always wanted my own zombie."

"You said I was your android before," she reminded him, sighing as he ran warm hands over her body, his hands lingering on her breasts. "Make up your mind."

"Reckon you're mine, whatever it is you are," he decided, pulling her onto him.

"I'm so crazy about you," she said breathlessly, feeling his hands guiding her, the warm water bubbling around them, "I'm afraid I am becoming one of those things."

"Keep moving like that," he instructed. "That's really good." He moved his hand between them. "I'm going to touch you here. Tell me what you want. Harder, softer. Tell me. Move my hand, show me."

"You don't mind?" she got out, breathing hard now at the feeling of him inside her, his big hand on her. She leaned back, allowing him better access, felt the excitement begin to build.

"Tell me," he commanded. "Or show me."

She reached down, laid her hand over his, showed him what she needed. "There," she sighed. "Oh, Finn."

She was barely managing to move now as he found the perfect spot. She felt him taking her up as he stayed there for long minutes, kissing her, murmuring words of encouragement, his hand stroking, the heat building higher and higher within her. Her breath came in panting gasps as she forgot to worry about him, about whether he was enjoying himself enough. The bands within twisted tighter and tighter until, at last, they released in a series of convulsions that had her sobbing against him.

He held her hard now, moved her limp body over him, drove into her as she clung to him, called out as he found his own release. Held her afterwards while she curled against him, languid and boneless, stretching her neck to allow him better access as he kissed her there. She shivered as he ran his hand over a breast.

"That really didn't bother you?" she murmured.

He chuckled softly against her hair. "Did I seem bothered?"

"I mean, my...showing you?"

"Aw, Jenna." He bent down to kiss her, long and sweet. "Do you know how good it feels to me when you're that excited? When you're coming, and I'm inside you?"

"It does?"

"It does," he assured her. "Whatever gets you there, that's what I'm going to do. And I need to know what that is, so I can do it. I'm always going to want to know. And if that's my hand, or your hand..." He shrugged. "Doesn't matter. It's all good."

"Mine?" she faltered. "Really?"

He laughed aloud. "Do you have any idea how hot that is? How much I'd like to stand there, watch you do that? Especially if you didn't know I was there. Making me hot again just thinking about it. You may have to put on a show for me, now I've thought of it. Because after that..." he sighed. "After that, I'll be turning you up, down, every way there is. Oh yeh. That'll work."

He kissed her again, lingering over it. "You turn me on," he told her. "You always have, and it just keeps getting stronger. Your gorgeous body. The sounds you make, the way your eyes glaze over when I come inside you. Thinking about what I'm going to do next time, how it's going to feel. Wondering how far I can go, how much I can push you before you tell me no. That's the only mental exercise I've been getting this week. And it's keeping me occupied."

"The answer is," she said against his chest. "The answer is, as far as you want. Anything you want to do, I'm willing to try. As long as you don't hurt me. And there's no livestock involved. Or other people."

"No livestock. And nobody else. The last thing I'd do is to share you, or to hurt you. But cheers for the green light. You've just given me something to think about, the whole drive home tomorrow."

She sighed. "Yeah. Going back. I'll be glad to see the kids. But so sorry to leave this place."

"We can come back," he promised. "Another time. And now..." He got up, pulled her out behind him, handed her a towel. "We're going to go inside, take a shower to wash off this chlorine, sleep for a bit. Until I wake you up because I need to do it again."

discretion

♡

"Dad!"

Finn received the full force of Harry's hug as the boy charged through the security gate and into his arms. Finn gathered Sophie in as well, then kissed Sarah hello, shook hands with Kieran.

"Good to see you both. Thanks for bringing them up. Flight OK?" he asked as they waited for their luggage.

Kieran laughed. "Hour and a half. Can't complain. Nothing to what you do, bro." He pulled a suitcase off the belt with a stocky arm. Years of working outdoors had tanned and seamed his face, making him look older than his forty-three years. But the lines around his eyes and mouth were good-humored ones, and Finn counted himself lucky in his brother-in-law.

"Those two behaved themselves, eh," Finn asked, pulling off Harry's and Sophie's suitcases as well.

"*Daddy,*" Sophie sighed. "We aren't *babies.*"

"Where's Jenna?" Harry asked as they made their way to the car park. "Isn't she back from her holiday yet?"

"Nah, she's home. Not enough seats in the car, see?" Finn said. "And she's taking the chance to get her run in before everyone arrives."

"Heard a lot about Jenna," Kieran remarked from the back seat where he was wrestling with seatbelts. "From multiple sources. Can't wait to see for myself."

"Oh?" Finn glanced across at his sister, who smiled back at him. "This'll be your chance, then."

Harry was out of the car as soon as Finn had pulled to a stop and turned off the car, pounding up the steps ahead of the rest of them.

"Reckon he's in love," Kieran commented dryly. "She must be pretty special."

Jenna was at the front door, then, pulling Harry in for a hug, reaching for Sophie as well, laughing in delight. "Oh, how glad I am to see you two," she exclaimed. "And Sarah. I'm so glad you're here." She embraced the other woman, then greeted Kieran with a warm smile and a handshake. "Thanks for lending me your wife to be my date last week. I had a great time with her. I hope I can return the favor by making you comfortable for a couple days."

She showed them to the guest room next. "I understand this is your holiday," she said. "You've been here before, of course. So you know your way around."

"Never had flowers in our room before," Sarah commented.

"Lunch in an hour or so," Jenna promised. She looked out the French doors, saw Finn already in the garden, dribbling the soccer ball with Sophie, and smiled. Physical again.

"Did you have a good holiday?" Kieran asked Jenna after finishing off the first half of his ham and cheese panini in a few juicy bites. "Sounds like you've earned it."

"I don't know about that. But, yes, I had a very good holiday."

"Where'd you go? Finn said you were staying on the South Island," Sarah said.

"Ah. Changed my mind, in the end." Jenna felt the treacherous color rising, did her best to sound casual. "I went up to the Far North, to Doubtless Bay. Pretended it was summer. I saw lots of dolphins," she remembered, turning to Harry with relief. "And orca, even. That was very cool."

Harry's eyes gleamed behind his specs. "Wow," he breathed. "A whole pod?"

"We counted four," she said.

"We?" Sarah asked.

"Oh. I did a cruise, one day," Jenna said. "Yeah. We saw them."

"Fancy that. Have you seen orca yourself, Finn?" Sarah asked innocently. "Ever?"

"A few times," he said blandly. "Always a treat, eh. Unless I'm kayaking. Then I'm not too keen."

"But I want to hear about what you kids did," Jenna said, watching Sarah and Kieran exchange knowing glances. "How was the farm?"

"It was so cool," Harry said. "Nana and Grandpa have barn cats, did you know that, Jenna? And one of them had kittens. They were tiny, like this." He held his hands out to show her. "And their eyes were still closed! You can't pet them, though," he sighed. "That was sad."

"And they have chickens," Sophie put in. "Heaps of chickens. They're really silly. They have *beards.*"

"Araucana," Sarah explained. "They *are* silly, but Mum loves them. They do lay the most beautiful blue eggs, but they have these ridiculous tufts of feathers on their faces."

"We collected the eggs for Nana!" Harry told Jenna proudly. "Every day. It was our job."

"What kind of farm is it?" Jenna asked. "I've never heard."

"Pears," Finn said. "It's a pear orchard."

"Really. Isn't that a lot of work?"

"It is," Sarah said. "Dad has some help managing it, though. And they've been using a new scheme that's going surprisingly well, having young people working for him. From all over the world, on working holiday visas. They come and do anything from a week to a month or two. Four hours a day in exchange for a place to sleep, and one big meal that Mum cooks. No pay, unless they want to work a full day."

"And that works?" Jenna asked in surprise. "Without any training?"

"Yeh, it does, surprisingly. Dad says it's the best workforce he's ever had. None of the problems he used to have with casual labor. They're all bright, all keen. Finishing Uni, or taking a year out from it. And those kids from Germany and Norway speak better English than the Kiwis."

"I can believe that," Jenna said. "Wow. I wouldn't have thought."

"They're really nice," Sophie assured her. "I learnt how to say Good Morning in different languages. D'you want to hear?" She rattled off greetings in French, German, and something that Jenna decided must be a Scandinavian language. "Ohayou gozaimasu," she finished.

"What's that?" Finn asked.

"Japanese." She smiled triumphantly. "There was a Japanese girl there, Yuki. She taught me."

"So when I go play in Japan, one of these years, you'll be one step ahead of the rest of us," Finn said.

"Is that likely to happen?" Jenna asked.

"That's where the money is."

"In *Japan?* They play rugby? Successfully?"

"Surprisingly. Can't match up to the top sides, but heaps of ticker. And more to the point, they're willing to pay big bikkies for All Blacks to come and play for a season. We call it the AB Superannuity Scheme."

"Well." Jenna got up, began to clear the table. "I guess you're right, then. Sophie's got a head start."

Japan, she thought with a pang. *Too far away.*

♡

"Hmm?" Jenna murmured at the feeling of Finn's body against her, his hand moving over her breast. "Finn?"

"Hope so," he murmured behind her as he pulled her closer. "Unless you were expecting somebody else."

"Everybody's here, though," she protested, keeping her voice low. "We shouldn't."

"We'll be quiet. Least I will be. May be a bit of a challenge for you." He rolled her, moved over her to kiss her, and stayed there a while, enjoying the way she wrapped her arms around his neck to pull him closer, the feeling of her hands in his hair, her generous mouth moving under his.

"I may have to kiss you the whole time tonight, keep you from making all that noise," he said at last, propping himself on one elbow and reaching down to pull off her nightgown. "Course, it'll be a sacrifice. But I'm willing to make it."

"Is the door locked?" she asked. For all her concern, he noticed, her hands were making short work of his T-shirt, and reaching now for his underwear.

"Locked," he agreed, moving to take her lower lip in his mouth, give her a little nip there, his hand wandering again. "Any more questions I can answer before I get started here?"

"Oh," she sighed. "You've already started. And you know I can't think when you're doing that."

She was shaking by the time he laced his fingers through hers and moved over her. He could tell that forcing herself to stay quiet had been hard for her, and as erotic as he'd found it himself. Now, as he pushed inside, he sought out her mouth again, smothering the moan she couldn't help.

"You make me want you so much," he told her softly, moving slowly, listening to her sigh against him. "I tried to sleep without you tonight, but I couldn't."

"I should say no sometime, I know," she answered breathlessly. "But I can't. Every time, I want it more. You make me feel so good."

He bent to kiss her, took her up again, so slowly this time, feeling her respond, the moment when she needed more. He kept her there a bit longer, until she was moving hard against him, savored the sighs and moans he took into his mouth, the urgency she couldn't hold back now. Finally gave her what she needed, felt her convulsing around him in response, the sweetness and power of it, and found his own release, his mouth still locked over hers, stifling both their voices as they cried out together.

Afterwards, he held her close to him, heard her breathing change as she fell asleep again. Dropped off himself before waking, chilled, to pull the duvet around them both. He remembered where he was, then, and that he couldn't spend the night in her bed. He searched for his clothes, pulled them on in the dark as she stirred into wakefulness.

"Nightgown," she said sleepily, feeling around the floor for it.

"Here." He moved to her side of the bed, helped pull it over her head, and leaned down to give her a kiss. "Thanks. Better than warm milk."

"I could say the same," she sighed. "Except you woke me up. But it was worth it."

"Mmm. Good night." One last kiss, then he got up to leave.

"Be quiet," she urged him as he made his way to the bedroom door.

"No worries. See you in the morning." He unlocked the bedroom door and left the room, easing the door quietly shut behind him. He took a few steps toward the stairs, swore inwardly as the bathroom door opened and he made out his sister's form.

She jumped with surprise, eyes not yet accustomed to the dark. "Who is it?" she hissed, keeping her voice low.

"It's me. Finn," he sighed. "Just...ah...checking on the kids."

"Checking on the kids," she said dubiously as he came up to join her. "At two-thirty in the morning."

"Thought I heard something," he improvised. "Nightmare, I thought."

He could almost hear her disbelief coming across the space between them. "Yeh, right. Going to bed now, though? Your *own* bed?"

"Course. See you in the morning. Jenna's fixing something special, I think."

"Already did, I reckon," he heard her say behind him as he made his escape to the stairs and the privacy of his own room. He loved his sister, but she really was the nosiest woman in the Southern Hemisphere.

♡

"This is choice." Kieran reached for another slice of the pear- and dried-cherry-filled coffee cake, only to have Sarah slap his hand. "What?" he protested.

"You'll get fat," she admonished him. "Two was enough."

"Oi," he complained. "Finn's had three already. I saw. Bet he's not done, either."

"Yeh, and when you're playing rugby instead of spending the day cutting the grass and unblocking toilets, you can have three too," his wife told him firmly.

"Would you like some more eggs, Kieran?" Jenna asked him. "They'll be ready in a second here, along with another pan of bacon."

"Am I allowed to have more eggs?" Kieran asked Sarah with exaggerated concern. "Would that fit into my dietary program?"

"Eggs are allowed," she pronounced.

"Thank you *so* much," he said sarcastically. "And thank you," he told Jenna with genuine warmth as she brought the pan of scrambled eggs and vegetables over to him. "Great tucker."

"Thanks." She smiled back at him. "Finn, what can I give you?"

Kieran gave him an elbow in the side when he didn't answer. "Eyes glazing over, bro," he muttered.

"Sorry," Finn said hastily. "What did you say?"

"Can I get you something else?" Jenna asked him patiently. "Eggs? Bacon?"

"Both, please. And then come sit," he told her, pulling out the chair next to him.

"May we be excused?" Sophie asked.

"Yeh. Go ahead," Finn told his children.

He thanked Jenna as she refilled his plate, then watched her as she dished up her own meal and sat down at last. She shouldn't look so good dressed in gray yoga pants and a white T-shirt. But the knit fabric clung in all the right places, the V-neck was almost tight and just a bit low, her feet were bare, and the whole thing made him want to take her back to bed right now. Well, maybe he would've let her finish breakfast first, if there'd been a hope of sneaking her away. Which there wasn't, not with his sister looking knowingly at the two of them from across the table and his brother-in-law using his napkin to hide a smile.

Jenna wouldn't agree to it anyway, he thought with an inward sigh. Even if it were fast. In the bathroom, maybe. His mind began to explore possibilities as he sat, absently chewing a strip of bacon, and watched her eat.

"Right. Washing-up." Sarah got up and nudged Kieran. "Come give me a hand."

"I'll do it," Jenna offered. "As soon as I finish. My job."

"Nah," Sarah said. "You didn't sign on to look after us. And I'm not used to anyone waiting on me. Brekkie was a treat, though. Why does food always taste better when someone else makes it?"

"One of the mysteries of life," Jenna agreed. "Fish tonight, OK? Salmon. Finn's favorite." She smiled at him. "Cooked the way you like."

"I'm a lucky man," Finn told the others. "As you see."

"Yeh, mate," Kieran said, standing up and beginning to gather plates from the loaded table. "We're getting the picture."

"What d'you reckon today?" Finn asked Jenna. "Kieran and I were planning to take the kids to Mission Bay, give them a bit more beach time. Want to come with us? You could have a swim, wouldn't have to worry about them. Water's still a bit cold, but you don't seem to mind."

"In my inappropriate costume? Are you sure Kieran's ready for the sight?"

"Oi. I already apologized for that. And you know why I said it."

"Heard about that," Sarah remarked, scooping up jam and butter containers. "You're a fool, Finn."

"Cheers," he said, lifting his mug to her. "You wouldn't understand. It's a man thing."

Sarah snorted. "Reckon I understand better than you think. But Jenna, let's leave this boy's mind in the gutter and move on to more important things. I'm going to take my chance to do some shopping on High Street. Want to come with me, keep me company?"

"Wow, two good options," Jenna sighed. "Both sounding really attractive. But no, thanks. I don't want to tempt myself. I've bought a lot of new clothes lately, thanks to somebody telling me my wardrobe needed an overhaul. Anyway, I want to go for a run, as soon as I've digested all this food. And I need to do some grocery shopping, finish the kids' washing, start on tonight's pudding. I think I'd better hang around here today. I was thinking gingerbread, with an apple-pear sauce and home-made custard," she mused. "That would go well. Everyone all right with that? Anybody hate molasses?"

"I don't think I've had it," Sarah said, looking at Kieran, who shook his head as well. "Gingerbread, I mean. Or even molasses, that I can think."

"It's more American, I suppose," Jenna said. "Spicy and dark. I've made it for people here, though, and they seem to like it."

"We'll give it a go," Sarah promised. "You know these boys'll eat it. How do you make all this, Jenna, without gaining weight? That's what I've been wondering."

"She never eats it herself. Didn't you notice?" Finn put in.

"How can you do that?" Sarah asked. "I couldn't."

"Easy," Jenna said, standing up and carrying her dishes to the dishwasher. "I can't stop once I start. I know that about myself, so I don't eat sweets, period. That's my amazing diet plan, and it works for me. But I confess, I still love to make them."

"And as I love to eat them, it's working out well for me too," Finn said. "Though I do try to restrain myself. Luckily, she feeds me pretty well with the healthier stuff, as you've seen. But she lets me indulge my sweet tooth, too."

Jenna laughed. "All this flattery is going to my head. But if I don't get busy, it's going to be McDonald's tonight, and my reputation will be ruined. I'm going to say thanks for doing the washing-up, and get on with it."

Finn's eyes followed her as she left the kitchen, and Kieran looked at him in exasperation. "Get your A into G, boy." Kieran snapped a tea towel at his brother-in-law. "If we're taking the kids to Mission Bay, better get them sorted, because I'm not hanging around here all day watching you look at that girl. It's a bit sick-making, tell you the truth."

"Kieran!" Sarah scolded.

"Nah, that's OK." Finn got up and cleared his place. Somehow, he realized, he'd managed to finish off his eggs and bacon. He grabbed a final slice of coffee cake, to the accompaniment of another caustic comment from Kieran, before heading off to round up the kids.

He'd better have a swim himself, he decided. And a trip to the gym later. Because with another couple weeks off before All Blacks training started up again, and Jenna cooking like this, he really *was* going to turn up unfit if he didn't get his workouts. And he had a feeling that sex in the bathroom wasn't going to happen today.

dad time

♡

"So," Sarah said that evening, loading the dishwasher as Jenna dished leftover roasted potatoes and kumara into a plastic container, ready to become home fries the next morning. "Where are you going after this? I know you said you were teaching in the new year, but you'll be done here soon after Finn's back from the Northern Tour, eh. Before Christmas, he said. What happens in between? Back to the States?"

"No. I haven't gone back for a long time," Jenna told her. "I'm not sure what I'm going to do. Something new, hopefully. I haven't spent nearly enough time in the South Island, considering how long I've been down here. That trip to Dunedin made me realize what I've been missing. I was considering looking for an interim job over the holidays. Someplace where I could get away, though, enjoy the summer. Do you have any suggestions?"

"I have a perfect suggestion," Sarah said. "Come to me. To us. We always need extra help at the holiday park during the summer holidays, specially those two weeks starting on Boxing Day, but before that as well. It won't be glamorous, but seems like you don't require that."

"Motueka, right?" Jenna asked. "Is it nice?"

"Best weather in En Zed," Sarah pronounced. "Nah, really. It's gorgeous. That's why I've never left. People come from all over the world to visit. Farewell Point, the Marlborough Sounds, Abel Tasman. You can put in a day's work, then be off to the beach. Borrow my car, when I don't need it. Sweet as. I can use you over Christmas especially, if you're free."

"I'm free. Nobody freer. And that'd be great."

"Housekeeping OK?" Sarah asked. "Don't want to deceive you when I say it's not glamorous. Doing the washing, cleaning the toilets and the kitchen."

Jenna laughed. "In other words, exactly what I'm doing now, minus the cooking. Will there be someplace for me to stay?"

"Staff cabin. You're sure? Should I mark you down?"

"Please," Jenna decided. "It sounds perfect."

Sarah opened her mouth to mention that Finn and the kids would probably be visiting over Christmas as usual, then shut it again. No matter what Kieran thought, she was capable of some discretion. Whatever was going on between those two now, who knew where it would be by December? But she liked Jenna in any case. And, she thought practically, she really *did* need good help, especially over the summer holidays. Jenna would be a Godsend.

"Thanks again," Finn said the next day as the Land Rover neared the Auckland Airport. "I appreciate you helping with the kids, and bringing them up to me."

"No worries," Sarah said. "Good excuse to get away for a couple days. Short as it was, that's the last holiday we'll have before March."

"Good thing it wasn't longer," Kieran said. "Because Sarah spent enough yesterday. Give her another day, and she'd've been really dangerous."

"You'll be at Mum and Dad's for Christmas this year, right?" Sarah asked Finn, choosing to ignore her husband's remark. "No other plans?"

"Nah. No plans."

♡

"So he's not making any plans that include Jenna, at Christmas,"
Sarah frowned as she and Kieran walked through the automatic
doors into the small domestic terminal. "Which is what she said,
too."

Kieran looked at her in surprise. "Were you expecting him
to?"

She shrugged. "I suppose not. It's early days yet. But they
seem so right together. You didn't see them at the wedding. I was
sure I'd done right, then. I hope I have."

"Don't think you had much to do with it," Kieran scoffed.
"They're living in the same house, and she's bloody fit. I doubt it
would've taken him much longer to make that move, whatever
you did or didn't do."

"You don't think that's all it is, though, do you?"

Kieran shrugged. "He wouldn't be the first bloke. But nah.
Because remember, he likes her cooking, too."

♡

"What d'you reckon we should do tonight?" Finn asked on arriving home again. "Anyone want to walk over to Civic and choose
a DVD with me?"

"The pub first!" Harry said. "And then a DVD."

"What do you think?" Finn asked Jenna. "Do you fancy the
pub tonight?"

"Jenna isn't going, though!" Sophie protested. "It's Monday.
It's Dad Time. Jenna doesn't get to come."

"Sophie!" Finn barked, his face thunderous.

"No," Jenna put in quickly. "Sophie's right. It's Dad Time.
And my day off." She got up from where she'd been sitting on the
floor, helping Harry with his puzzle at the coffee table. "What am

I doing here? I'm going to have words with my employer about unfair working conditions. I completely forgot it was Monday."

She was buttoning her blouse in her bedroom when she heard a knock at the door.

"Just a moment," she called as she zipped her skirt, then added, "Come in."

Finn stepped inside, shutting the door behind him, and stood leaning against it.

"Sorry," he said. "I don't know where that came from. Are you OK?"

"I'm fine," she said with a determined smile. "And Sophie's right." She sat on the end of bed, patted the duvet beside her until he sat down. "I should have seen this coming, so we could have talked about it before. I blame you for distracting me, keeping me from thinking it through more clearly."

"What?" he asked.

"You're Sophie's world," Jenna said gently. "And she's been the most important female in yours for years. That's precious to her. And she isn't used to sharing you."

"That's rubbish. I've dated heaps. Sorry," he added hastily. "Shouldn't say that to you. But I've been out with a fair few women these past years, and we've never had this before."

"And did you bring any of those women along during your special times with the kids?" she asked. "Any of them go to the pub with you on Monday nights?"

"Nah," he said, running his hand through his hair in frustration. "I've always been careful about that. Specially as I'm gone so much. I've tried to preserve that time with them."

"And that's a good thing," she said. "That the kids have had their Dad Time, and that you haven't had them get...intimately involved with everyone you've dated. Because getting attached, then having the person suddenly be gone...that would have been difficult for them. Especially if it had happened over and over."

"What about Nyree, though? Sophie's never said anything like this about her. And Nyree's been with us more than four years now."

"And did she go along during Dad Time?"

"Nah," he sighed. "She didn't. Her day off."

"Right. The boundaries were clearer. Besides, Sophie's sensitive. We've talked about that. She wouldn't be able to tell you what she's sensing, but I'll bet you something's coming in over her radar. And she's reacting by trying to hold you closer, hold you to her."

"What's the answer, then? I don't form any attachments till she's out of the house? That's not going to work for me."

"You don't have to do that. But we need to go slowly here. For now, she needs to be reassured that she's still important to you. Especially right now, when she and Harry have been gone. She needs her special time to reconnect to you. It's all right, Finn," she went on as she saw him still looking troubled. "I understand. She isn't rejecting me. She just needs to know that her world's still intact."

"Not Harry, though," he said. "He doesn't seem to be having any problem at all with you."

"He's a boy. Girls and their dads...that's different. There's bound to be some jealousy there. It's completely natural," she hastened to assure him as he frowned, "even if there's a mum in the picture. You've heard of Oedipus and Electra, right? There's a reason behind those myths. There usually is."

"Right," he said grudgingly. "If you think this is right. How do you know this stuff, though?"

"What?"

He made an expansive gesture. "You know. Kids. *My* kids. All that, that you just said. I reckon you're right about Sophie. But how did you know?"

"I don't know," she shrugged. "I just do. Why are you so good at rugby? Plenty of people play it. But almost nobody else is as good at it as you. Why is that?"

"Training. Luck."

"Talent," she agreed. "And a whole lot of hard work. This is what *I* do. What I'm good at. Too bad it doesn't pay as well as rugby, huh?"

"It should," he said. "It matters more. Anyway. What will you do tonight? Go to your friend's?"

"No. She's gone to Northland for the school holidays, with her boyfriend and his family. I'll find a movie of my own, I guess. A pub of my own, too. Someplace to have dinner first."

"No pulling," he warned, reaching out to pull her close.

"I don't need to pull, do I?" she asked, looping her arms around his neck and smiling into his eyes. "With any luck, I can wander into the wrong bedroom tonight and talk some big, strong man into groping me a little. What do you think?"

"I reckon you can, at that," he grinned, then bent to give her a lingering kiss. "Take the car, though, if you're going into the CBD," he added practically as he got up to go.

"Nope. I want my glass of wine. Plus, I don't like to park down there. I'll take the Link bus. And I'll be back before eleven."

"I'll be waiting," he promised. "Ready to do some of that groping you're so keen on."

unbirthday present

♡

"You can do it," Jenna encouraged from her spot a few meters out from the side of the pool. "Come on. I've got you."

Harry stood, knees bent, hands together above his head, at the edge of the deck. Jenna could see him taking a deep breath, gathering his courage. The first dive of the day was always the hardest, she knew. He pushed off at last, landed in the water with a splash.

"Swim to me," Jenna urged him as he bobbed up. "Come on."

When he reached her, she swept him into her waiting arms. "You did great!" she congratulated him.

His grin was huge. "I did it!"

"I'm going now," Sophie called out from the deck. She performed her own dive, swam to join the two of them.

"Excellent," Jenna approved. "You both tucked your heads so well. Let's try it again, and this time, think about keeping your legs together as you jump off."

This was the fourth day of their swim lessons. After enjoying her own ocean swims so much the previous week, Jenna had determined to use these final few days of the spring holidays to get a start on the instruction she'd promised. Both children seemed to be getting something out of them, and the pool wasn't as crowded as it would become during the summer months.

She was watching Sophie practice her crawl when she heard the familiar deep voice from behind her.

"Can anybody join this party?"

"Dad!" Harry swam to his father, laughed as Finn swept him up overhead. "Toss me!"

Finn tossed him a couple meters, smiled with obvious pride to see Harry swim back to him. Sophie demanded her own toss, shrieked as she sailed through the air.

"Didn't get enough training at the gym, huh?" Jenna asked, coming to stand next to him. "You needed to add some more weight lifting?"

"Decided I needed to see the progress," he told her. "Let's see this diving you've been telling me about," he said to the kids. "Show me what you've learnt."

He watched the two of them take off with the increased assurance they'd begun to show. "Very impressive," he said. "You've done a lot in four days."

"That's the best way," Jenna agreed. "Daily lessons. It gives them confidence, making that rapid progress. And your body remembers better, if it's going through the same motions every day."

He grinned at her, and she blushed. "Sorry," he apologized. "Can't help it. It's seeing you in your togs. Gets my mind on that track. But you're right, that's how we train, too."

"Yeah, well. This'll give them a good start. They can work on it more during the summer holidays, now that they have the basics down."

The kids swam to join them. "Time to get out," she told them. "We're all becoming prunes." She held out her wrinkled fingers for inspection. "Let's see yours. Yep," she decided, looking at the little hands. "Definitely prunes. Time to hit the showers."

"I get to take a shower with you, right, Dad?" Harry asked excitedly. "I don't have to go in the ladies' with Jenna, right?"

"Too right," Finn said. "We men'll meet you girls out front in a few minutes." He helped Jenna gather towels to wrap around the shivering children. "Need to talk to you at home," he told her in an undertone. "An idea I have."

♡

"Jenna." She heard the knock, the low voice at her door, opened it to let him in as she finished tightening the drawstring on her running shorts.

"Ah." He looked at the sturdy athletic bra. "Exactly what I came to talk to you about."

"What? My chest?" She went to the drawer for her running top, pulled it over her head. "I've noticed you like it, but I'm not sure how much it has to offer as a discussion topic."

"Your limited lingerie selection, I mean. I went out for a coffee with a couple of the boys after the gym. And we walked by a boutique on High Street. The Pajama Company, it's called. Made me have some thoughts about that. Not sure what you have planned for this afternoon, but I'm thinking you might do a bit of shopping for me."

"You want to wear ladies' lingerie?" she asked, opening her eyes wide. "Why, Finn. This opens up a whole new dimension in our relationship."

He laughed. "Getting pretty saucy, aren't you? Nah, you know what I mean. I'd like you to buy a couple things. I saw a bra and thong in the window. Lacy. An aubergine color that I quite liked. I thought you might get that, maybe another set as well. Looked like they had some pretty nighties, too."

"I know the shop you mean," she said. "But their things are a little pricey for me. My employer pays me pretty well, but French lingerie isn't in my budget."

"Which is why I went by the bank," he told her, pulling out his wallet and extracting a sheaf of hundred-dollar bills. "Call it my birthday present."

"Is it your birthday?" she asked with shock. "You should have told me."

"Nah. Months away. Call it my Unbirthday present, then."

"I don't know." She hesitated. "It seems a little…mistressy, doesn't it?"

He sighed. "You have a beautiful character. I admire and respect you. You're an awesome swim teacher. And I want to watch you walk round my bedroom tonight in a thong. Can't help it. It's my own Neanderthal brain, I reckon. You want to watch me tackle, and I want to take lacy undies off you."

"Well, if you put it like that…" She smiled up at him, took the money he held out. "You've got me."

"That's what I'm hoping."

"Could make me late fixing dinner," she warned, putting the cash safely away in her wallet. "It's going to take me a while to do that shopping. You'd be surprised how long it takes to find bras that fit."

"That's what they make pizza for." He opened the bedroom door, stepped into the hallway. "Oi! Kids! Who wants pizza tonight?"

"Me! Sophie cried, shooting out of her room.

"Pizza!" Harry shouted. "Yay!"

"All right," Jenna laughed, coming to join him. "*And* salad, though."

"Go do your run," Finn said. "And this afternoon, you can take yourself out to lunch, do your shopping. I'll give these hungry beasts their lunch."

"*Dad,*" Harry complained.

"I can make sammies," he protested. "One of my few talents."

♡

216

She took some extra time in the shower that evening, then used some of the Manuka honey body butter she'd bought to complement her new lingerie, massaging it in until her skin was soft and glistening. Then she dressed in the bra and thong set he'd requested, inspected herself critically in her bedroom mirror, twisting to look at the rear view. She wouldn't have chosen, personally, to display that much of her backside, but he seemed to like it. As long as he didn't have too many lights on, she supposed it was all right.

It looked good from the front, anyway, and he did have fair taste. The blue lace overlay on the deep purple background was striking, and the balconet bra made the most of her considerable assets. She smiled at herself in the mirror. She knew he'd appreciate that.

She gave herself one last look to make sure everything was adjusted properly, then slipped on her dressing gown and made her quiet way upstairs to his room. She found him lying propped against the headboard, fully dressed, an open binder in his lap.

Locking the door behind her, she leaned back against it and looked at him. "Studying, huh? All Black stuff?"

He closed the binder, set it on his nightstand. "Yeh. A bit."

"Still want to do this tonight?" She suddenly felt a little shy. He'd obviously imagined how she'd look in this outfit. She hoped the reality would measure up. "If you have work to do...."

He laughed. "Nah. Just trying to distract myself."

He swung his legs off the bed, came across to her, slid his hands under her hair and took her mouth in a long kiss. "You took your time, eh." He smiled down at her. "Making me wait for it."

It was going to be all right. She had this. She reached down and untied the sash of her dressing gown, lifted her shoulders and slowly shrugged the garment off so it fell to the ground near her feet, then stepped out of it. "Was this what you had in mind?" she asked him.

"Shit, yeh," he breathed, standing back to look. "That's it."

"Want me to take it off, then?" she teased. She raised her hands to the hooks at her back, hesitated there. "Oh, wait, that's right. I forgot." She came to him, wrapped her arms around his neck, pulled his head down for a kiss. "You said you wanted to be the one to do that, didn't you?"

"Bloody hell. Going to do more than that." He took her hand and pulled her across the floor, not to the bed, but to a spot near his mirrored closet door. He kissed her again, and she opened her eyes to see him watching her reflection in the mirror. She'd been right. The amount of backside on display seemed to work for him.

"Going to ask you to do something," he told her, his hand moving to a breast. "Can I say that bit again first? About respecting your many fine qualities, and that?"

"Oh, boy. I can tell this is going to be good," she sighed, tilting her head to allow him access to her neck, feeling herself melting as he kissed her there, his hand inside the lacy bra now. "You know you can ask. I told you. Anything."

"Right, then. Want you to get on your knees for me. I want to watch in the mirror while you take me in your mouth."

"Ah. That's your fantasy, huh?" She smiled slowly. "I can do that for you. Oh, yeah. I can do that."

She reached under his T-shirt, ran her hands over his abdomen, then slowly pulled the shirt up, kissed his chest as she uncovered it, ran her tongue over one flat nipple, heard him suck in his breath.

"Yeh," he got out. "That's one I've thought about a fair bit."

"Mmm," she said, pulling the shirt over his head. She spent a bit more time on him, her hands and mouth working on his neck, his chest. Only when she could see the sweat beginning to glisten there, hear his breath coming hard, did she reach for his belt buckle, then his zipper. She pulled his jeans down his hips, together with his underwear.

"Step out," she breathed against his chest. "Give me some room to work here."

He groaned, did as she asked, kicked the discarded garments aside. She took him in her hands then, ran a palm down the length of him.

"Sure you want this?" she asked, closing her mouth over his neck again, using her teeth as her hand continued to stroke. "Last chance to back out."

"Oh, God," he moaned. "Please."

She smiled again as she dropped first to one knee, then the other. "Is this what you had in mind? Good enough view?"

His only answer was to wrap his hands around her head, fingers threaded through her hair. "Trying not to shove you here," he gritted out. "But I need this."

"And you're going to get it," she promised, then bent her head and gave him what he wanted. Slowly, taking her time. Letting it build for him.

♡

Finn fought the urge to close his eyes. Because looking down at her working on him, watching her reflection in the mirror, was almost as good as what she was doing. He lost himself in the feel of her mouth, her tongue, her hands on him, the sight of her.

He was almost too far gone when he forced himself back. This wasn't all he wanted to do right now, while he had her in front of the mirror.

"Jenna. Stop." He pulled her head gently back, almost changed his mind as she let go of him, sat back on her heels and looked up at him, her hair disheveled, mouth soft, eyes huge. He made his decision, dropped to his knees, reached for the strap of that aubergine bra.

"This has been working so hard," he said, unfastening the hooks and pulling it off her. "Time to give it a rest." He took a breast in each hand, heard the hitch in her breath as he caressed her. "Feels good, eh." He looked into her eyes, pupils dilated with passion. "I think you got something out of that, too. But you need something else now, don't you?"

"Yes," she told him. "Yes. Please."

He smiled, reached down to pull off the thong. "Let's get this off you, then, so I can give it to you."

She wriggled out of the lacy strip. "Tell me what you want from me."

"I love it when you say that." He bent his head to kiss her, reached down to touch her. "You're so wet. So ready for me. Get on your hands and knees, then."

He moved behind her. Another perfect view, he realized. From where he knelt, and in the mirror. He looked down, froze.

"Shit. Condom. Stay there," he commanded. "Exactly like that." He raced across to the bed, pulled out the nightstand drawer, grabbed the packet and came back to her.

"Bloody hell," he said. "You're so gorgeous. Waiting for me, just like I asked you to." He pushed inside slowly, felt her respond, watched as her head dropped, looked at her hands supporting her, his hands on her hips as he moved in her.

"Reach your hand back here," he gasped. "Touch yourself. Because I need to feel you come while I'm doing this to you."

She moaned, did as he asked. He watched in the mirror as she began to caress herself, and felt the change in her, the shift at the added stimulation. She was panting now, and he could sense her spiraling up, feel her tightening around him.

"That's right," he told her, his breath exploding from him. "Come on, Jenna. Give it up. Give it to me."

She was pushing back into him, crying out, and he was over the edge. He grabbed her harder, thrusting into her so forcefully he was moving her across the floor. He felt her going over, the contractions surrounding him, pulling at him as she sobbed out her release, and he lost control, joined her in sensation, tumbled with her into a long, powerful orgasm that seemed to draw everything from his body.

"Aw, geez," he gasped at last. "I'm squashing you." He rolled to his side, pulled her against him. "All right?"

He felt her sigh against him, a long, drawn-out sound. "Yeah. Good."

He ran a hand over her, felt the goosebumps form. "Go get in bed. Give me a sec." He got up, went into the bathroom to get rid of the condom, looked at himself in the mirror. He was wrecked. Shattered.

He came back to bed to find her nestled under the duvet. She pulled an edge back, invited him to slide in next to her.

"Was that what you had in mind?" she asked with a little smile. "For your Unbirthday present?"

He pulled her to him, gave her a long, slow kiss. "That was," he promised. "It was brilliant. Absolutely the best Unbirthday present anyone's ever given me."

"I'm so glad. We aim to please."

"And you do," he assured her. "You do please. So bloody much."

He went on, running his hand down her back. "I've spent a fair amount of time thinking back on how you looked that first night, in those black stockings. But I know which picture I'm going to be taking on tour with me."

♡

She froze for a long moment. "What?" She shoved herself away from him, pulled herself up to sit, the shock like a dose of ice water. "What did you say?"

"Just now. In the mirror. What? You couldn't tell how much I liked it?"

"But you...you took a picture? Finn. You can't take my picture, doing that." She realized that her voice was rising, lowered it with an effort. "That's not OK," she hissed furiously. "You have to erase that. Where is it?"

"What?" he asked blankly.

"Where *is* it?" she demanded. "It's not...it's not a tape, is it? Oh, no. Please tell me you didn't do that."

"What are you *talking* about?" He sat up, stared across at her. "What tape?"

"What you just said!" she snapped. She got up, grabbed her dressing gown and pulled it on, clumsy in her haste. "Give it to me."

"Whoa. Whoa. Hang on. You've got the wrong end of the stick. I was talking about the picture in my *mind*. Course I didn't take a picture of you. Much less a tape. Bloody hell."

"Oh. Thank God." She sat down on the bed again, weak with relief.

"Hang on, though," he realized. "I said that, and that's the conclusion you jumped to?"

"Men do those things. I've read about it. They *do* do that. Show them around. Put them online, even. And I need to tell you, that would kill me. I'm a private person. I couldn't handle that."

"And you think I'm the kind of bastard who'd do something like that," he said, his face settling into its hardest lines. "That I'd show your photo to my mates. Put it on the bloody Internet."

"Just forget it, OK?" she sighed. "I'm sorry. It was a stupid misunderstanding."

"Yeh, it was. I have a *daughter,* for God's sake. And a bit of common decency too, I hope. Good to know what you really think of me. How much you trust me." He got up himself, pulled on underwear and a T-shirt, his anger clear in his jerky movements.

"I can't just assume you'll do the right thing, though!" she protested.

"Why the hell not?"

"I did that, remember? I found out the hard way. And I'm not doing it again."

"Because I'm a man?" he demanded. "That automatically makes me a dickhead? Or because I'm a football player, maybe? I'm not your bloody ex-husband. How hard is it to see that?"

"But that's not something I can forget," she tried to explain. "He *lied* to me. He cheated on me!"

"Which happened to me too! And I can still judge you for who you are. Not for who Nicole was."

"It's different, though," she pleaded. "You don't understand. I was married to someone who said he loved me, but who didn't even care enough to tell me he was having sex with men, so I could have protected myself! He didn't care if he *killed* me. The first thing I did, the first *day*, was to get myself tested, see if I had HIV. How do you imagine that felt? I don't, by the way," she said bitterly, interpreting his startled look. "I got tested twice to make sure. You've got nothing to worry about. And I'm sorry." She busied herself retying the sash of her dressing gown, tried to hide the tears she couldn't hold back anymore. "I'm sorry that I insulted you. And that I'm..." she gestured helplessly. "Damaged. Whatever. Sorry."

She headed for the door. "Forget it. I'm going to bed now."

"Jenna," he said wearily. "Hang on."

"No. I can't." She lifted a lapel to wipe her face. Remembered her discarded underwear, went to pick it up. "I need to go to bed."

on top of mt. eden

♡

He was gone to the gym by the time she got up the next morning, Jenna found with relief. She couldn't imagine how she was going to face him again. It had taken her hours to get to sleep the night before, replaying the scene in her mind. How had one of the most exciting nights of her life gone so sour? And why *had* she jumped to that conclusion? She'd really insulted him, she realized. But she wasn't sure how to make it better.

She focused on the kids, glad to have something to take her mind off her confused, circling thoughts. She was leaving the showers with them after their swim lesson when she heard her phone ding with a text. Pulled it out of her bag and glanced at it. Finn.

Can you get kids a playdate.

She swallowed her dread, rang Siobhan.

"I can take them now," her friend decided. "Not later this afternoon, unfortunately. Dentist. What a way to spend the last Friday of their holidays, eh. But drop them by on your way home, and I can keep them till two or so. That suit you?"

"Thanks," Jenna told her with relief. Whatever it was Finn had to say, at least it'd be over with quickly.

"Finn?" she called as she stepped into the villa half an hour later. "I'm home."

He came out of the lounge to meet her. "Where are the kids?"

"Siobhan's. Till two."

"Want to go for a walk with me, then? We could have lunch."

"Finn." She was still holding the heavy bag with the kids' swimming gear, she realized, and set it down on the tile floor. "If you're going to fire me, just do it, OK? I can't handle waiting for it."

"What?" He stared at her. "Why would I fire you?"

"Because I was unreasonable last night. I know I was. That I insulted you in the worst possible way."

"Jenna." He came to her, put his hands on her shoulders. "I was planning to apologize for losing my temper. I'm not too good at that, apologizing. Took me a while to work up to it. But I thought, once I did, we could talk about it."

"Oh." She swayed towards him in relief, leaned into him as he pulled her close.

He kissed the top of her head. "Oi," he said softly. "Are you crying again?"

She nodded against his chest, sniffed. Hugged him to her. "I was wrong. I'm so sorry."

"Reckon we were both wrong," he sighed. "And that we should take that walk."

♡

"Let me start," she told him as they set out on the track that led to the top of the Mt. Eden Domain. "I thought about it a lot last night. I don't know why I jumped to the conclusion that you'd do something like that. My mind just...yeah, it jumped. Just like that. It was in my head, all of a sudden, and I was terrified. I did realize, afterwards, that it wasn't the kind of thing you'd do."

"I thought about it too," he said. "I'd like you to trust me, but I can see that your marriage may have shaken your faith. I'd like to think I'm not much like your ex-husband, though."

"Nothing like him. In any sense."

He glanced down at her. "Well, in one sense, anyway, let's hope. But...why would you assume all men are like that? Liars. Users. Why would you assume that about me?"

"Because I've never known any men," she tried to explain. "Look at me. I've been a Year One teacher my whole career. Not exactly a male-dominated profession. How many male primary teachers do you know?"

"None," he admitted.

"That's right. My friends are all women, have always been women. We didn't even have many couple friends. Guess why."

"Your dad, though?" he asked. "What about him?"

"No dad. Well, of course I must have had one," she corrected herself. "But I didn't know him."

"Buggered off, eh."

"Never there to begin with, actually. I don't even know who he was," she confessed.

"Your mum never told you?"

"My mum never knew. She said she was 'partying' at the time, when I asked her. So, yeah. She had boyfriends, while I was growing up. Plenty of those. But they never took much interest. Which is just as well, probably. She didn't have great taste in men. I doubt they'd have enhanced my view of the gender any. So," she sighed. "I'm doing my best here. But I don't have much to work with."

They'd reached the top of Mt. Eden now, stood quietly for a minute looking out at the Harbour, the dotted green volcanoes and neighborhoods that made up Auckland, the Waitakeres rising to the west.

"Don't know quite what to say to all that," he said finally. "I could say, trust me. But I'm not sure that's going to help much."

"But I do!" she protested. "I do trust you. As much as I can. If I didn't, I'd never have slept with you in the first place."

"Thought it was because I was so irresistible." He smiled down at her at last.

"That too," she smiled back. "But also because you're…who you are. A good man."

"OK," he said. "And for the record. I've never made a sex tape. Never taken naked photos of a woman, either. Always more interested in what was happening at the time."

"You shouldn't even have to tell me that," she said, ashamed.

"But can I just say," he went on, pulling her close, "that if I *were* the kind of bloke who took photos, I can think of a few I'd like to have? Starting with last night."

"It didn't ruin it, then? What happened?" She rested against him, snuggling close to fend off the chill of the wind, always strongest here on the peak.

"Nah." She could feel the rumble in his chest as he chuckled. "It didn't ruin it. I don't think a nuclear blast could've ruined that for me."

"It worked pretty well for me too," she admitted. "It's an adventure, being with you."

"Is that the only set you bought, yesterday?" he asked. "Or is there anything else you have to show me?"

"Maybe," she teased, light with relief now that the crisis was over. "Want to see?"

"You know I do." He looked at his watch. "Noon. When do we have to get the kids?"

"Two."

"Mind if I don't take you out to lunch, then, after all? Would you settle for a sandwich, later?"

"Yeah." She smiled up at him. "Are you telling me you want me to model the other outfit? No photos, no tapes? Just you and me?"

"Yeh." He bent to kiss her. "You and me. You missed your run today, eh. Race you home."

♡

"Can I ask you a question?" Jenna asked Natalie on Monday. They were sitting on the floor in front of Nat's coffee table, eating a dinner that Natalie had been especially grateful for, this first day back after the holidays. Finn had taken the kids to school that morning, Sophie complaining vociferously before-hand as always about the end of the break. Fortunately, the Year One students Jenna had worked with today had been more excited about being back at school again, if a bit boisterous after two weeks off.

"Sure." Natalie took another bite of quinoa salad and waved her fork in Jenna's direction. "Shoot."

"Well. As you know, Jeremy was gay," Jenna began.

"Not likely to forget that, am I. Made a bit of an impact, at the time. Is that the question?"

"No. I'm not exactly sure how to ask this. But OK. If you're with someone who *isn't* gay. Someone straight. What's…what's normal? I mean, do you have sex all the time, think about it all the time? Or…or what?" Jenna ended lamely, seeing the sur-prised look on Natalie's face.

"I can't ask anyone else," she said apologetically. "I'm not asking you for a report or anything. I mean, on your relationship now. Just…in general. It would be helpful."

"Doing a bit of research, are you?" Natalie asked, eyes gleam-ing with amusement. "Or do I take it you've entered the land of the living?"

"Just tell me, OK?" Jenna asked desperately. "In general. What's normal?"

"Well," Natalie said judiciously. "If you read the research, they'll tell you, two, three times a week. For Kiwis, anyway. But that's an average. At the beginning, yeh, you tend to do it more."

"More than twice a week," Jenna said. "Every day? Or even more? Do people do it that much? And do you mind saying, do you think about it more? More than you do it?"

"Well, yeh. More than I do it. Not like I walk around in a fog or anything, or even do it all the time, when I've got a partner, like now. That's more when you're a teenager. You remember, when it's all you can think about. All you want to do."

"I don't, actually. Remember, that is," Jenna said gloomily. "I met Jeremy when I was nineteen. And didn't date all that much before then. Nobody I really fancied."

"So what is it you're worried about now?" Natalie asked. "That you think about it too much? Or not enough?"

She sat upright suddenly, pointed her fork at Jenna. "Oi! Finn! *That's* what this is about! I *thought* there was something different about you tonight. What did you get up to, while I was on holiday? Are you telling me that's gone somewhere at last?"

"Well, yeah," Jenna admitted, feeling her color rise. "Yeah, it did. It has."

"And how is it?" Natalie asked eagerly. "Good? Worth all the agonizing I know you did first?"

"Yeah." Jenna smiled across at her ruefully. "Worth it. Really good. I know, I don't have a basis for comparison. But I can't imagine anything better."

"Ah." Nat stood up to gather their plates. "And how's your heart?"

"Involved," Jenna sighed. "But I think his might be too. He's really great. *Really* great."

"What're you still doing here, then?" Natalie demanded. "It's gone eight already. Go on. Go home and get some more of that."

But Natalie hadn't answered her question, Jenna realized on the bus home. Or, rather, she had. And it had been the answer she'd feared.

Finn was there to meet her in the entryway when she stepped inside.

"Kids OK?" she pulled back from his embrace to ask.

"In bed, and asleep," he confirmed. "I checked. So go put on some of that new gear, and come upstairs."

"I'm not sure it's a good idea," she hesitated. "Tonight."

"Why? Are you on your period? Don't care."

"No!" she laughed, blushing. "No. But…Never mind," she capitulated. "I'll ask you later."

"Later would be better," he confirmed. "As in later, in bed. After I've looked at you in those thong panties enough, and taken them off. I have such good ideas."

"OK," she smiled. "But I need a shower first."

"Brilliant," he told her. "We'll take it together, get started in there. And then maybe you'll put on those black things for me, the ones you wore the first night. With the stockings. And we can try something I have in mind. And then I'll take some of it off, and we'll try something else. Because I just remembered. It's your Unbirthday, tonight."

"Finn," she said quietly as they lay together later, still breathing a bit hard. "Am I a nymphomaniac?"

"*What?*" He laughed, propped himself on an elbow to look at her. "You?"

"Because I asked Natalie tonight. How much was…you know. Normal. And she didn't say, exactly. But it seems like I think about it too much." She felt herself blushing, went on determinedly. "All the time. And I want to do it every day. I think that's too much. From what she said. That most women don't feel like that. What does that make me?"

"Hot," he told her firmly. Lay back down next to her and pulled her against him.

"Besides," he went on more thoughtfully, his hand stroking over her back, "seems to me you went through a fair few of your prime years shut down in that department. Could be you're just catching up. And we only have a few weeks here. Got to pay it forward as well."

"That's true," she said more cheerfully. "What about you? You seem to think about it a lot too."

He laughed again. "I'm a bloke. It's what we do. Haven't you heard? Yeh, I think about it a fair bit. And I'm doing some catching up too, remember?"

"What? A few months, maybe? It hardly compares, does it?"

"Oi. For me, it does," he protested. "And remember, I spent those months living with you. And *I* knew what the possibilities were. What I was missing. So I've been saving all this up. Just like you."

"I'm not a nymphomaniac, then." She wriggled closer to the warmth of his big body.

"Dunno. Are you eyeing the postie, these days? Wondering how he looks under that sexy uniform?"

"No!" she giggled.

"My mate Ian looking good to you today?" he asked in mock alarm. "Got you fancying a shag in the supply cupboard after all?"

She hit him in the chest. "You know I'm not. Don't be silly. You know it's just you."

He leaned across her to turn out the bedside light. "Reckon you're not a nymphomaniac, then," he said, rolling her over and settling himself around her spoon fashion, one big arm resting across her chest. "And that I'm a lucky fella. Now go to sleep, please."

"I should go back to my own bed," she protested, nestling into him.

"I'll wake you in time," he promised. "And I love to fall asleep with you. Stay with me."

laundry room

♡

"What the... *Jenna*!"

She winced at the slammed door and the volume of the shout, then took a deep breath and continued sorting laundry, listened to Finn striding through the house, still shouting for her, until he appeared in the doorway of the laundry room, a paper in his hand and a scowl on his face.

"I've been calling you," he told her in frustration. "Why haven't you answered?"

"I can't hear you when you shout that loudly," she told him calmly as she finished loading the machine. "I don't like to be yelled at," she clarified as he stared at her in bafflement. "Now that you're not shouting, though, what can I help you with?"

"This." He held up the paper, shook it for good measure. "Did you see this?"

She nodded, added detergent and fabric softener to the machine. "I found it in Sophie's backpack this morning and put it out for you."

"She's been reading under the desk in class, not paying any attention? So much that the teacher has to write to me about it? I'm going to have a few words for her when she gets home."

"Maybe you should find out more about it first," she suggested.

"What is there to find out about? It's unacceptable." His voice was rising again.

"Please don't yell at me. If you want to discuss this, we'll talk. Otherwise, take your anger somewhere else," she told him.

"What is there to talk about?" he asked again. But he did lower his voice.

"Well, for one thing, is she doing it in every subject, or just in some?"

"What does that matter?"

"I'm thinking if it's during math or science, it's an issue. But if it's just during reading…" Jenna shrugged. "It could be that she's bored. She's reading and writing a couple grade levels above her age, you know. Have you looked at the work she brings home?"

"Not much," he admitted.

"Maybe you ought to do that. It's too easy for her, Finn. She should be doing something that will push her. Maybe she could even join a Year Four or Five classroom every day for reading and writing, or read and write about some of her own books. I don't know for sure, of course, but I'm guessing that could be the issue. You might want to have a talk with the teacher before you discuss it with Sophie."

"Right. I'll do that," he said grudgingly. "But in any case, she needs to pay attention during school. That's her job. She needs to work at it."

"Granted. But it's also the school's job to challenge her."

"Why do you have to be so bloody reasonable?" he grumbled. "You have an answer for everything. You won't even let me yell."

She smiled. "Guess you'll have to save all that explosive power of yours for the rugby field. You're probably too bottled up right now, three whole weeks with no practice or anything." She turned on the washer, leaned over to pull the towels from the dryer, then jumped at the feeling of his big hand closing over her backside.

"You could be right," he told her, his other hand reaching out now to pull her back against him. "Reckon I need another outlet for my...explosive power."

"Finn," she laughed as he pulled her close with one hand and reached around to unbutton her blouse with the other. "I'm doing the laundry here." The laugh turned to a moan as he bent to kiss the side of her neck, one hand pulling off her blouse, under her bra now, the other hand moving beneath her skirt.

"Mmm. So sexy doing it, too," he said. "Barefoot. Very cooperative of you to wear this little skirt. Almost like you were expecting me."

She felt him hard against her and couldn't help pressing back into him as he used both hands now to pull off her underwear, then unhooked her bra and tossed it aside. "It's the middle of the day," she protested weakly.

"Kids in school, hot woman getting her gear off," he agreed. "Works for me." He looked around, walked her over to the big laundry table, the folded clothes stacked neatly on top.

His breath was coming faster now. "Bend over and hold onto the edge," he instructed, undoing his belt and unzipping his jeans.

Her eyes opened wide even as a rush of heat flooded through her. "What?"

"Do it. Please," he amended. She heard the sound of the condom packet ripping. He really did mean to do it right here. Feeling both embarrassed and excited, she bent over and reached out both hands to grasp the table's edge, felt him hard behind her as his big hands came around to cover her breasts. Feeling him like this, not being able to see him, her vulnerable position, his hands on her, pinching the nipples now, all combined in a rush of sensation. She moaned as he let go of her breasts, flipped up her skirt, and positioned her to push himself inside.

It should have been too soon, but she was more than ready for him. She backed up against him as he held her, pushed into her again and again. Heard his breath coming hard now, matching her own. When he reached his hand around to rub her, she pressed back against him, moaning with it now.

"Please. Yes. Harder," she gasped as he thrust into her, his hand never stopping. She was past caring how she looked, bent over the table like this, how hard he was holding her, the force of it. He took her higher and higher, more and more, until she released with a wailing cry.

He needed to see the rest of her, right now. He pulled her upright, lifted her up onto the table, pushed her down and pulled her hips level with its edge, open to him. Stepped up to her, one hand on each white thigh, and slowly, so slowly, entered her again. Watched her head go back, then move from side to side as he thrust.

"Tell me," he got out as he moved. "You need to tell me... aah...which way you like it. When I get the right spot, the right way for you." He shifted position a bit, moved her legs wider apart, reached his hands underneath her to pull her even closer, lift her into him. "Better?"

"Ah..." Her hips rose in his hands to meet him. "Yes. Yes. Do it like that. More." Her own hands went to her breasts, caressing them as he moved in her, and his excitement ratcheted up another notch. She was moaning again now, calling out to him. He felt the moment when she began to go up again, and this time, when she went over the top, he was there with her, in an orgasm so powerful it was almost painful, shouting out his release with her.

Afterwards, he grabbed a dirty T-shirt from the laundry basket at his feet, wiped both of them off with it, zipped himself up again and helped her off the table, steadied her against him when her legs wobbled.

"All right?" he asked her.

She laughed shakily and let him hold her against him, rested her cheek against his broad chest. "Not sure. I'm going to have to fold all these clothes again, too."

He smiled. "Tell you what, I'll help you, since I'm the one who jumped you. Sorry. Not too romantic. Your fault, though. You're too sexy. I needed to throw you down this time. But come on. We'll take a shower and start over again in bed. I'll make it up to you."

"I wasn't exactly complaining."

"You were screaming, though," he grinned. "But you're right, it didn't sound like complaining."

"Very gentlemanly of you to mention that. But I can't. If I don't go to the grocery store before I go meet the kids, you aren't going to have any dinner. You wouldn't want me to get in trouble. I have a very mean boss. You should see what he does to me."

"Bet if you made him happy enough, he'd take you and the kids out to the pub instead," he suggested, his hands moving to pull off her skirt at last. "And I know how you can do that. Starting by walking up those stairs in front of me."

"You already got pretty happy," she pointed out. "And I got *very* happy."

"Come on," he urged. "Come make me even happier. I'll tell you exactly how. And then you can tell me."

♡

"I can't finish, Daddy," Sophie said with a sigh.

"No worries," Finn said, pulling her plate towards him. "I have room."

"I was wondering why you didn't insist that she get the kids' version," Jenna remarked. "Now I get it."

He grinned at her. "They do a pretty fair steak here. But their bangers and mash are choice. And you know how I feel about getting everything I like." He speared a chunk of sausage and smiled at the kick she sent him under the table. "What?" he asked innocently, wiping his mouth with his napkin.

"Well. Fancy meeting you here." He turned around to see Ben Thompson arriving at their table. "Giving Jenna a bit of a holiday from the kitchen, eh."

"That's right." Finn looked Ben over. "You've packed on a kilo or two since the end of the season, haven't you? Bit too much beer, maybe." He nodded to the glass in Ben's hand. "Want to watch that."

"Finn, for heaven's sake," Jenna protested. "Would you like to join us, Ben? We're finishing up, but sit down for a minute and have a chat."

"Dunno." Ben looked at Finn challengingly. "Not sure how welcome I am."

"Nah. Sit down." Finn shoved a chair out with his foot and watched as Ben levered himself into it, taking a sip from his brimming glass. "Jenna thinks I'm rude, so I'll try again. How're you going? Thought you'd be in the Coromandel for the fishing."

"Another couple weeks," Ben said. "Planning a trip to Tonga too, next month."

"Wow. That sounds great." Jenna said. "It's nice, I hear."

"You've never been? How about the other islands?"

"Fiji once, years ago," Jenna said. "But that's it. Do you go a lot?"

"Every year, at least once. Go with a few mates, do a bit of diving, some fishing. I went to Samoa after the semifinal this year, drowned my sorrows."

"Yeh. I heard," Finn said. "And I was serious. You don't want to come back out of condition in January. It may seem like you have heaps of time now, almost three months out. But you'd be surprised how hard it is to climb back if you let yourself go. Want to make sure you're getting the running and the gym time in, too. You're looking a bit soft around the midsection."

Harry reached out with a small finger and poked Ben in his middle. "You're right, Daddy. Ben's squishy. Not all hard like you."

"Harry!" Jenna said. "Don't you remember my telling you that it isn't polite to talk about how people look?"

"You said ladies," Harry protested. "You and Daddy said not to talk about ladies' bottoms. When I said about the wombats. But Ben isn't a lady. And I wasn't talking about his bottom. Anyway, Daddy was talking about it first."

Ben grinned and looked from Finn to Jenna. "Ladies' bottoms? Yeh, Harry. I'd listen to your dad. Leave that one to him."

Jenna looked helplessly at Finn. "That's my cue to excuse myself. This one's yours. Talk to your son. Come on, Sophie. We're going to the toilet."

Ben watched them go. "Bit cozy," he remarked. "Do I take it that you've overcome your scruples?"

"Remember when I told you that what Jenna did was none of your business?" Finn asked, his voice carrying a distinct note of warning. "Leave it."

"Ah." Ben's cheeky good humor appeared unruffled. "No point in my trying again, then. Pity, but there you are." He got up to leave. "No point in my hanging about, either. Because the scenery just got a lot less interesting."

Finn held out up a restraining hand. "Half a mo. I meant what I said, earlier. You need to step up your workouts. I'm at Les Mills most mornings around nine. Come join me."

"Don't have a membership."

"Get one," Finn ordered. "That's your new assignment. And meet me there tomorrow morning."

"Aw, geez," Ben complained. "I stop by to say a friendly hello, and not only do I get warned off, I get dragged into extra workouts during my holiday."

"Right on both counts," Finn said. "And I know why you stopped by. So don't start with that. See you tomorrow at nine."

"Right," Ben sighed. "See you then."

taniwha

♡

"Oh, yeah," Jenna breathed. "That's it. Oh, please, Finn."

"*Daddy!*" The voice registered dimly. She heard the knocking then, came back to herself with a start.

"Finn," she hissed, grabbed him by the hair when she didn't get a response. *"Finn.* Stop."

"*DADDY!*" He heard it now, too, and froze.

"Shit," he groaned as he rolled off her and began to put himself hastily to rights. He pulled his T-shirt and underwear from the floor, tossed Jenna her nightgown. She yanked it on and dashed for the bathroom, shut the door and locked it behind her.

Harry's voice, now, coming clearly to her from inside the bedroom. *"Daddy."* She heard the sobs, the panic in his voice. "I'm scared. And I can't find Jenna. She's gone, Dad."

"Nah." Finn's deep rumble, now. "Just went for a walk, I reckon. Come on. Let's get you a drink of water, get you back in your bed."

She waited, her feet cold on the tiled floor, until she judged that five minutes or so had passed. She opened the bathroom door, crept across to the stairway, looked down cautiously, got down the stairs as noiselessly as she could, peered into the hallway. Harry's door stood a bit ajar, but all was dark and quiet. She made it to her own bedroom, climbed, shivering, back into bed and pulled the duvet over herself, trapped her hands between her knees to warm them. That had been too close.

♡

"Where did you go last night, Jenna?" Harry asked as she poured his orange juice at breakfast. "I went to find you, and you weren't there. I was scared."

"Ah…" Jenna looked across at Finn, who raised his eyebrows at her. "Sometimes I have trouble sleeping. I have to get up and do something before I can go back to bed and fall asleep again."

Well, it was the truth, she thought as she saw Finn hiding a smile behind one big hand. Except that last night, between the near-discovery by Harry and her body's unsatisfied state, it had taken her a long, long time to fall asleep. Maybe she *should* have gone for a walk.

"Why did you come to find me?" she asked Harry now. "What happened?"

"I had a really scary dream," Harry told her. "*Really* scary. Bad."

"A nightmare? What was it about?"

"It was a taniwha," he said with a shudder. "That bad taniwha by Nana's house. He was coming to eat me, like in the story."

Finn saw Jenna's bafflement and explained. "It's in the mountains above Motueka. There's a place with loads of strange-looking volcanic boulders. All grooved and twisted. And there's a legend about them. That there was a taniwha—"

"A monster," Sophie put in helpfully.

"Reckon Jenna knows what a taniwha is," Finn said with a smile. "Anyway, the taniwha was terrorizing the village, stealing people away and eating them. One day, it captured the chief's daughter. The villagers decided they'd had enough of that. They tricked it, fed it meat packed with explosives, and blew it up.

Those strange boulders, they're meant to be what's left, the tani-wha's scales. To be fair, they do look a bit like that."

"And you went on that walk when you visited your Nana and Grandad this time, Harry?" Jenna guessed.

He nodded. "The scales were really, really big. And I imag-ined how big the taniwha must have been. He would've been *enormous*. Last night I dreamt he was chasing me. He was about to get me. His teeth were big and sharp, and he was talking to me." He shuddered. "He was saying he was going to eat me. Then I woke up. And I looked for you, but you weren't there."

"That does sound very scary," Jenna said. "But taniwha aren't real. You do know that, don't you?"

"The Maori think they're real, though," Sophie said.

"A few people do," Jenna said. "You know about myths and legends, both of you. They're stories. Stories people made up a long time ago to explain strange things. But even something that isn't real can be scary in a bad dream," she assured Harry. "It's lucky we can wake up and remind ourselves that it was just a dream."

"Daddy stayed with me," Harry said. "Till I fell asleep again. I knew the taniwha couldn't get me if Daddy was there. Even if he was real."

♡

"I came back to bed last night," Finn said conversationally as he and Jenna walked back home after dropping the kids at school. "After doing my fatherly duty. Imagine my disappointment."

"What?" Jenna asked. "Did you think I'd still be there?"

"I was hoping. We weren't done, if I remember right."

"I wasn't going to hang around there," she protested. "What if Harry'd had another bad dream?"

"I had a bad dream, too," he said. "I dreamt I was making love to a beautiful woman, and she disappeared just when we were getting to my favorite bit."

"I'm just glad I locked the door," she sighed. "I can't imagine, otherwise. But, Finn. It's made me realize, we've become really careless. We can't do this anymore."

"What?" he asked, looking down at her in surprise. "Why the hell not?"

"Not when the kids are in the house," she clarified. "How many nighttime walks am I going to be able to take? And I can't relax and enjoy myself, if you know what I mean, expecting the kids to come knocking at the door any minute."

"Maybe we should tell them, then, stop all this secrecy," he said in frustration. "Because I want to be able to sleep with you."

"We still have the days," she reminded him.

"Until training starts up again," he grumbled.

"And a week after that, you're off on the Tour," she said. "When you come back, I'll be moving out. It's better for them if, while I'm here, I'm their nanny. If it's clear. And after that, even if we're dating, I won't be their nanny anymore, and they'll have Nyree back. They'll have that security. Though I'll still be their friend, I hope."

"Course you will. But meanwhile, what about us? Surely you can still come to bed with me. *With* the door locked. In the middle of the night."

"No," she said. "I'm not hiding in the bathroom again. Or thinking that I'll have to. Nothing else at night. Not unless the kids have a sleepover."

His eyes lit. "Friday night."

"All right," she laughed. "I'll see what I can do."

"And if I'm not allowed to have you at night," he continued, "you'd better be prepared to let some of that housework go, this week. Better be planning on some takeaways too. Because I've just decided how we're going to be spending our days." He opened the gate for her and watched her walking up the steps of the villa ahead of him. "Starting right now."

"I haven't done the washing-up yet," she teased as she used her key to open the front door.

He kicked the door shut with one big foot, his arms going around her. "Sod the washing-up. Upstairs. Now."

"Think you can give me orders, huh?" She smiled up at him as she toed off her jandals.

"I know I can. And I'm doing it. Upstairs."

"That shouldn't work so well on me," she complained. "It's not right."

"Oi. You've just restricted me, laid down the law," he pointed out, his hands clasping her waist as she climbed the stairs ahead of him. "Have to give me some way to assert myself. Wouldn't want me to feel powerless, would you."

"Oh, I don't think that's happening." She smiled up at him, felt the thrill as he pushed her down on the big bed, his hand behind her head to break her fall. "I don't think you're going to be feeling powerless here anytime soon."

♡

"Need to talk to you," Finn said on Wednesday morning.

"I think you've been talking to me," she sighed, settling her head more comfortably against his bare chest. "Or do you mean you actually want to have a conversation, not just tell me what to do?"

"Seem to recall you giving me a few instructions there, too. It wasn't me saying…"

"OK. Moving on," she said hastily. "What do we need to talk about?"

"Labour Day weekend coming up," he reminded her. "A few of the senior players are traveling to the Coromandel together, with their families. Bit of fishing, get the partners and kids together before the Tour."

"And you're going," she guessed. "You and the kids."

"I've been going back and forth in my mind about it, trying to decide. We've gone for years now. It would look odd if I didn't. If you want to come too, say the word," he went on quickly. "Keeping this quiet was your idea, not mine. Maybe it's time to end the secrecy."

"No. It'll be your last chance to spend time with the kids before you leave. Especially if you've been doing that together every year. I'll bet Sophie's already looking forward to it."

"Right," he sighed. "I'm sure you're right. But I don't want to leave you when I'm about to go away for so long."

"It's only three days," she said. "You'll be back after that."

"And doing some serious training, which means I'll be gone most of the day."

"And you leave Monday, right? The second." She thought for a minute. "Playdate, on the weekend," she decided. "That's what we'll do."

"I thought we could have some playdates those nights, too."

"Not *us.*" She saw him grinning at her and laughed reluctantly. "A playdate for the kids, so we'll have some time together before you go. And maybe a couple late afternoons as well. I'll make sure I get Siobhan's kids over here too, so I can ask the favor. OK?"

"If that's all I get," he sighed,"OK. I'll take a playdate."

"And we still have this week," she reminded him.

"That's right." He rolled over, trapped her beneath him. "We do. So we'd better be making the most of it."

♡

Jenna woke knowing this was the day. Labour Day. That was appropriate, she hoped. Anyway, she couldn't put this off anymore. Finn and the kids would be back tonight, and her period was almost two weeks late. She'd been irregular before, but never by this much. And she'd begun feeling queasy, having a difficult time cooking. She was pretty sure, but she needed to know.

She reached under the bed, pulled out the white chemist's bag she'd hidden there, got up and went into the bathroom, pulled the package out of the bag and opened it, spreading the instructions carefully out on the counter. It was the same type she'd used before. She remembered everything about that day. How she'd held her breath, how thrilled she'd been as she'd watched the line form on the test strip.

Today, she followed the instructions, then sat and watched the strip in mingled hope and fear. The two minutes stretched out, second by second. She could feel her heart beating faster as she waited. Was that a faint line forming, though? She held her breath again this time as it darkened, became clearer.

There was no doubt, then. She was pregnant.

She took a deep breath, then stood up, bundled the entire kit and its packaging back into the white bag, dropped it into the plastic bag lining the bathroom wastebasket, then pulled the entire thing out. She wasn't going to risk anybody finding out about this, one of the kids getting curious when they got home tonight, however unlikely that was. Not until she had a plan.

She went through the motions of brushing her teeth, washing her face, moved mechanically back to her room and set the rubbish bag down carefully to be thrown into the bin outside. Then she dressed in her running clothes. She'd think it through during her run, when her mind was at its clearest.

All she could think of as she ran, though, was the first time. The last time. When she'd gone through those first weeks full of joy and hope, even though Jeremy hadn't seemed to share either emotion. And then, the morning when she'd seen the blood. Had called the midwife in a panic, her heart thudding as she arranged a lift with her friend Caroline, so grateful to have the emotional support. Not to have to go alone.

She'd lain on the examining table, dread filling her as she looked at the monitor with the midwife, searching for the pulsing white blip that wasn't there, no matter how hard she willed it to appear.

"I'm sorry," the woman said gently. "There's no heartbeat."

"The baby died?" Jenna asked in a small voice.

"I'm sorry," the midwife repeated. "This one just didn't work, for whatever reason. I know it's hard. But there's no reason to think that you won't be able to have a baby."

There was every reason, though, Jenna thought bleakly. This had been her one chance, and it was gone. Her baby was gone.

"What happens now?" she asked.

"We'll do a D&C," the midwife told her. "Do you want to ring your husband?"

Jenna shook her head. "He's on holiday. I can't reach him." She saw the midwife looking at her oddly, and knew what she was thinking. On holiday, without her? But Jeremy and Alan were on their annual weeklong camping trip, and Jenna had most definitely not been invited.

"Anybody else, then?" the woman asked her. "You're going to need somebody to drive you home, afterwards."

The tears threatened again. "My friend drove me here. She's waiting. She'll take me home." Home to her empty flat. No husband. No baby. There wasn't going to be any baby. She lost the battle, felt the ticklish tears crawling across her cheeks, falling into her hair as she lay on the table.

"You can try again," the midwife assured her. "In a few months, your body will have recovered. You're young and healthy. These things do happen, and most women go on to carry babies successfully to term."

Jenna nodded. She wouldn't explain. She couldn't. That she'd got lucky, literally, on their third anniversary. This had been her one chance. And she hadn't been able to make it count.

♡

She forced herself to breathe more deeply now as she continued to run, pushing herself up the hill to the Domain. That was then, and this was now. She'd done the research, since it had happened. The midwife had been right, she knew. Miscarriages were all too common, and generally had no effect on the chance of a successful future pregnancy. And she couldn't help thinking, irrational as she knew it was, that this was Finn. If anybody could father a healthy baby, surely it was Finn.

Because she wanted this baby. She knew it down to her core. Even more than she'd wanted the first one, if that were possible. Never mind that it hadn't been in her plans, that she might have to do this on her own, that she'd be the single mother her own mother had been.

No, not that. She might be a single mother, but she was going to love this baby. She was going to take such good care of it. And Finn would, too, she thought desperately. Surely he would. He'd implied that he hadn't wanted Sophie at first, and what had happened there? No daughter had ever had a more devoted father. Surely he'd want this baby just as much. Eventually, once he'd got used to the idea.

But she couldn't tell him. Not now. Not yet. Not until she was sure. Until she knew this baby was going to live. Until she saw its heart beat, and knew she'd be keeping it. He'd be leaving in a week anyway. She wasn't going to tell him before then. It was too soon.

steak and lobster

♡

"Going to miss this," Finn said, sliding a hand down her body as she lay next to him on Saturday afternoon. "I'm thinking we'd better do it some more before the kids get home, since it's going to have to last us for a while."

He rolled to his side and pushed himself up on one elbow to stroke a breast as he looked down at her. "I've decided what you remind me of, by the way," he told her. "You're like a gorgeous dish of ice cream. Vanilla, with a few bits of strawberry. And I love ice cream, could eat it every day. Wish I weren't leaving so soon."

"Monday." Her breath hitched at the feeling of his hand on her. "It's coming up so fast. And five weeks is a long time."

"Not so long." He leaned in for a long kiss. "I'll call you every night that I can. Morning, my time. Before training, I reckon. Talk to the kids, talk to you."

"That'd be nice. What will you be doing at night?"

He shrugged. "They come up with some kind of activity for us. Sometimes it's a film, other times something silly. Just to keep the boys busy, stop them getting too restless, embarrassing themselves and the team while we're over there representing En Zed. It can get a bit boring, still, in the evenings, specially round about Week Four. I may have to make a second call," he mused.

"Before bed my time, once the kids have gone to school for you. So I can say everything I'll want to."

"I know we haven't talked about this," she said hesitantly, "and I have no idea what goes on. But I suspect that you get more than restless, and I'm not interested in sharing you. If you can't manage that, tell me now."

"Ah. Wondered when this would come up. Nah. Wasn't there some fella who said, why go out for hamburgers when you have steak at home?" He grinned down at her. "Reckon you're steak. Eye fillet, I'd say. I don't cheat anyway. But knowing I've got this steak dinner to come back to..." He kissed her again. "I won't mind waiting for that."

She smiled into his eyes. "Paul Newman."

"Pardon?"

"The actor. Paul Newman. About his wife, Joanne Woodward. They were married about fifty years, until he died. And I'm betting that's one big reason."

"I know how you feel about it," he assured her. "And for the record, I feel the same way. In case you were wondering whether I'd care. We've both been through that. You're not the only one who doesn't want to go through it again."

"Well, if I'm steak, you're...what's better than steak? Lobster, I guess. That's what you are. Lobster."

"Because you've made such a wide comparison," he smiled.

"Because I'm smart enough to know a good thing when I find it. And I'm guessing all this food talk means you're hungry. I'll go make you a sandwich." She rolled out from under him toward the side of the bed.

He grabbed an ankle, pulled her back across the sheet to him. "Oh, no. Not letting you out of bed yet. I can wait a bit. What I really want now is something else."

She smiled up at him. "Oh, yeah? You know I'm always happy to give you what you want. All you have to do is ask me."

He groaned. "Definitely steak. I'm thinking, though, they may feed us lobster when we're in France, and I'm out of practice. Reckon you are too."

"What?"

"Have you ever eaten lobster?"

"No. Never. Not in my budget."

"Then I'll explain it to you," he said, leaning in for another kiss, his hand moving down her body, caressing the soft skin. "You crack the claws. Then you have to suck the meat out of the shell. Using your lips and your tongue, but carefully. Delicately. You don't want to miss any, either. Because lobster's choice, and you want to savor it. So you go slowly. And you make sure you get every last bit of that meat. All the way to the end. I'm thinking we could both use some practice, just in case."

He moved down her body, kissing and biting his way. "I'm going to be selfish here," he told her, his hand finding her breast again. He smiled against her at the sound of her moan. "Going to do my own practicing first. Then I'll give you a lesson."

♡

She woke on Monday morning to the feeling of him sliding into bed with her, pulling the duvet back over them both.

"What time is it?" she asked sleepily.

"Early. Six."

"Violating our rules," she pointed out.

"Nah. I'll only stay a minute. But I need a bit of privacy to say goodbye to you."

She reached out to stroke his unshaven cheek. "I hate this. I know you have to go. But I still hate it."

He kissed her gently. "Me too. Always. Now more than ever. But I'll call you, and it's not forever. Only five weeks."

But would he want her, after those five weeks were up? She pushed the thought aside, focused on the here and now. On his big body, solid and comforting next to her.

"I'm going to miss you," she told him, feeling the prick of the tears that came so easily these days. She looked into his blue eyes, warm now as he gazed back at her. "But we'll be watching you. Just don't go getting yourself hurt, all right? We don't want to see that. That's not allowed."

"Understood." He ran a hand over her hair. "I'm pretty tough. Pretty hard to knock down for long."

"That's what I'm going to be reminding Sophie," she said. "And what I'm going to be holding on to myself."

"I'll tell you, too. Don't work too hard," he warned her. "It's a long time alone, even with Miriam's help."

"I won't. And now you need to get out of here, before Harry wakes up and comes barreling in."

He gave her one last kiss, his hand moving down her body. "Should've come in here last night," he grumbled. "Whatever we said. That was a stupid rule. I hate leaving without making love to you again."

She sighed against him. "Me too. But we can't. I'm going to get up and fix you breakfast, and we're going to drive you to the airport. And the rest of it, we'll just have to save for later."

"I don't want you to go, Daddy." Sophie was sobbing in the Departures lobby, her arms around his waist.

Finn crouched down, distinctive in his black Adidas warmup suit, the silver fern blazing over his heart. "Here, now. You know that this is my job. And that I need your help, and Harry's, to do it. I need you to talk to me every day so none of us gets too lonesome. And to do well at school, help Jenna at home."

"And to watch you play," Harry reminded him, his own tears falling now too. "I'll watch this time, Daddy. I promise."

"That's my boy." Finn reached out to gather him into his arms. "But if you need to read the dinosaur book sometimes, that's OK too. I'll understand."

He turned next to his daughter, gave her a final cuddle. "Sophie Bee. You'll be watching too, I know that." He held a gentle finger to her forehead, watched her reciprocate, trying her best to check her sobs.

"Bzzz," they said together.

He stood up reluctantly. "Take care of them," he told Jenna. "And yourself, till I get back. I'll ring when we get in." He ached to hold her again, but contented himself with reaching for her hand, giving it a squeeze. He felt the moisture in his own eyes. Geez, he hated this. It got worse every time.

"Bye," Jenna said, her voice sounding pinched, her eyes huge. "Be safe. I mean it, Finn. Be safe. And we'll be here to meet you in five weeks."

He nodded, then turned to join his teammates before this got any harder. Before he got back into the car and drove all of them home again.

♡

"Jenna!" She drifted out of an uneasy sleep to the sound of the wailing cry. "Jenna!"

Harry, she realized. She sat up, immediately regretted it as the tide of nausea rose. She reached for a water cracker from the plate next to her bed and nibbled it as she pulled on her dressing gown. Feeling a little steadier, she got up and made her way through the dark hallway to Harry's room.

He was sitting up in bed and sobbing in terror as she turned on his bedside lamp and sat beside him, pulled him into her arms. "What is it? Was it the dream?"

"It was the taniwha," Harry sobbed. "He said he was going to eat me. I want Daddy."

Jenna stroked a hand over his hair. "It was a dream, buddy. Just a bad dream. There's no taniwha."

"I want Daddy," Harry insisted through his tears. "He won't come when Daddy's here."

"Shhh, now. Your dad's in Ireland, remember?"

This was the third night Harry had woken her. It was time to do something about this. "We're going to beat this thing. I'll tell you what. Tomorrow, after school, you're going to draw a picture of that mean old taniwha. And you're going to tell me your dream, and I'll write it down. We're going to post it to your dad. He can be thinking about making it go away, too. Telling it not to come after his boy any more."

He began to quiet against her. "The taniwha will be scared, if Daddy talks to him."

"He'll be very scared," she agreed.

"D'you promise?" he begged.

"I promise." She reached for a tissue and wiped his face. "Now, lie back down. I'm going to sing you a song to bring you sweet dreams."

"*Hine e Hine?*" he asked, allowing her to tuck him in again.

"That's right." She switched off the light, kept his hand in hers as she began the Maori lullaby, its sweet melody and the poetic language soothing her, too, as she sang.

"E tangi ana koe, hine e hine.
E ngenge ana koe, hine e hine.
Kati to pouri ra,
Noho I te aroha.
Te ngakau o te Matua,
Hine e hine."

"Good night," she whispered to Harry as she finished singing the last verse and bent down to kiss his cheek. "Sweet dreams."

"How are you, buddy?" Jenna asked as Harry came bouncing into the kitchen the following morning, no trace of the night's terrors visible on his beaming face.

"Hungry."

She laughed. "Weet-Bix, coming up. Where's Sophie?"

"Here," Sophie announced, coming in and climbing into her chair.

"Morning." Jenna smiled at her. "Wow. Let's do a ponytail after brekkie, OK? Looks like your hair had a party last night."

She poured milk on their cereal and went to the refrigerator for the juice. "Do you remember having a bad dream in the night, Harry?" she asked him.

He nodded, breaking the biscuit apart with his spoon. "I remember you coming into my room and singing me a song."

"Do you remember what we talked about, too? About drawing a picture and writing the story, and sending it to your dad?"

"I kind of remember," he said doubtfully.

Jenna sat down with them, began to nibble a dry piece of toast, took a sip from her cup of ginger tea to settle her ever-queasy stomach. "Sometimes, when we have bad dreams, that can help. It makes their power go away. I think it might make that taniwha go away too."

"I remember now," Harry said. "Daddy's going to tell the taniwha not to come any more."

"That's right. We'll do that after school," she promised. "Sophie, would you like to send your Dad something too? A story, or a picture?"

"Both," Sophie said immediately. "Can we get some new stickers?"

"Of course we can," Jenna assured her. "We'll stop at the shop after school, and then you can draw him something really special. He'd love that."

"Cheers for the parcel," Finn told her a few days later. "I was never happier to open an envelope."

"Hang on a minute. I'm going to put you on speakerphone." Jenna pressed the button, then hung up the receiver.

"Is everybody there?" Finn's gravelly voice came through the speaker.

"Yeh, Daddy. We're here," Sophie answered.

"Sophie Bee. Thanks for your picture. It's on the wall above my bed right now. It's very, very pretty. Prettiest thing in my room. Heaps prettier than my roomie, I'll tell you that."

"What about my picture?" Harry demanded. "It's a taniwha, did you know that?"

"I did," Finn told him. "It looks very scary."

"He'll be scared of you, though, Dad. Jenna said."

"She said you'd been dreaming about that taniwha again," he agreed.

"Not since I made the picture," Harry informed him. "Jenna said that would make him go away, and she was right. But can you tell him too? Just in case?"

"I'll tell him," Finn promised.

"Where are you, Dad?" Sophie chimed in.

"About to get on the bus to go to training. We've got some work to do before the game on Saturday. We were looking a bit rusty after the layoff. But no worries, we'll get that sorted."

"Too right, Dad," Sophie told him stoutly. "The Irish aren't going to be able to beat you."

"Not if we can help it. We don't mean to be the first ABs squad to lose to them. Not after a hundred and eight years. You'll have to tell me what you think, Sophie. Give me a critique of my performance. I need to go, though. Just wanted to wish you good night."

"Goodnight, Dad," Harry said.

"No taniwha tonight," Finn told him seriously.

"Nah. You've scared it away. I can tell."

"Goodnight, Sophie Bee."

"Night, Dad."

"Loading up. Bye."

He hung up, and Jenna wished she could have said goodnight too. She hoped she'd get her own call soon.

It came as she was finishing the washing-up the following morning. "Wanted to thank you again for sending that envelope," he told her. "I really do have the pictures above my bed. The boys are giving me stick about my artwork, especially Sophie's. It's all those flowers and stickers, maybe. Not to mention the pink paper."

She laughed. "A little girly for an All Black bedroom?"

"This is one All Black who likes his bedroom as girly as possible," he assured her. "In fact, it could use a girl in it about now."

"My bedroom's a bit short on testosterone too," she admitted. "I miss you."

"Miss you too. But the note helped. Seeing your handwriting, somehow."

"It did?" she asked, pleased. "I don't want to tell you how much it cost to send that envelope to Ireland."

"Worth every penny."

"Then I'll have them do more," she decided. "It helps them, too, makes them feel closer to you. Not to mention scaring away the taniwha."

♡

She wished she had someone to scare off her own taniwha as she lay on the table the next day while the doctor did her exam. Her lost pregnancy hung over her like a shadow, making her breath come short as she awaited the verdict.

"We'll do a blood test," the doctor said, straightening up and snapping off her gloves, rolling her stool closer to Jenna's head. "But there's no doubt about it. You're pregnant."

"Does everything look…all right?" Jenna asked.

"Just the way it should," the doctor assured her. "Now, do you have a midwife you're planning on using? Or do you want a recommendation?"

"I need a recommendation." She didn't know whom to ask anyway. She couldn't tell Natalie, or Siobhan. Not when Finn didn't know yet.

The doctor wrote a name and phone number on a prescription pad as Jenna sat up and draped the sheet over herself.

"You should begin taking prenatal vitamins as well, if you haven't already," the woman said. "No alcohol, no caffeine. And what about the dad? Is he in the picture?"

"I don't know." Jenna forced herself to answer honestly. "He doesn't know yet."

"Sooner rather than later would be good," the doctor advised. "In my experience."

crying over spilt milk

♡

*T*hud.

Jenna whirled just in time to watch the three-liter container of milk begin to spill out over the kitchen floor. A lake of white swiftly covered the tiles, to the accompaniment of Harry's wailing cry. She stepped across, unable to avoid the mess, and grabbed the jug before it could spill any more. Not enough left, she saw with dismay, to avoid a trip to the dairy this afternoon. And she'd just bought groceries that morning. Setting the depleted jug down on the kitchen bench, she grabbed three tea towels from the drawer, tossed one each to Harry and Sophie.

"OK, guys. Not a disaster. Help me wipe this up. Harry, please stop crying. It was an accident."

"Why do I have to help?" Sophie complained from her spot at the kitchen table. "I didn't spill it. And I'm reading."

"Because we're all cleaning up," Jenna snapped. "Get up and help."

She regretted her tone as she saw Sophie's face grow mutinous, Harry continuing to sob quietly. She crouched down to begin wiping up the mess, glad to see Sophie rising reluctantly to obey. The movement, and the smell of the milk, brought nausea in its wake. She'd never thought of milk as having a smell, she thought irrelevantly, trying to push the sickness away. Harry was wiping willingly, if inexpertly, Sophie was helping now too, and the lake was becoming a puddle.

"OK." She got up, had to steady herself against the fridge door, give herself a moment. "Go sit at the table, both of you, out of the way. I'll mop the rest of it."

"My feet are all milky," Harry sniffed.

"I'll clean them in a minute. Go sit down."

Sophie protested again at the trip to the dairy. "I have home-work. Can't I stay home?"

"You aren't old enough," Jenna told her. "Come on. We'll call it a walk."

"Why can't we drive?" Sophie complained. "We've walked enough today. Courtney's mum drives her to school. Why do we always have to walk?"

"Because it's six blocks. And only four blocks to the dairy," Jenna said. "I am not driving four blocks. Get your shoes on."

She could hear Sophie muttering as she stomped off. She was clearly having a bad day, and Jenna would need to get to the bottom of that later, she thought wearily. They were well into their third week without Finn, and the strain was showing on both children, especially Sophie. And on herself, she admitted.

The smell of roasting chicken in the dairy's tiny rotisserie assaulted her before they stepped through the door. She took a deep breath of outside air, tried to hold it as she walked past the prepared food area and made her way to the chiller case. No queue, she saw with relief. She'd pay fast, and get out of here before she was sick.

"Can we get Tim Tams?" Sophie was in front of her, holding out the package of chocolate biscuits.

"No. Put them back, please." Jenna held onto her patience with an effort, set the milk on the counter. "We have biscuits at home."

"Only digestives," Sophie complained. "I hate digestives. I want Tim Tams."

Jenna swiped her card to pay for the milk, took the plastic bag with a word of thanks. "Put it back, Sophie. We're going." She had to get out of here, she thought desperately.

Sophie stomped over, threw the packet back on the shelf. Jenna grabbed Harry's hand and headed for the door, Sophie following thunderously behind.

"Why are you so *mean?*" Sophie burst out from behind her before they'd even gone a block. "You never let me have anything I want! *Daddy* would let me have Tim Tams! *Nyree* would let me!"

"Nyree isn't here, though." She was snapping again, Jenna knew, but she couldn't seem to help herself. She'd been sicker than ever, today, had spent thirty minutes in the bathroom after walking the kids to school. She'd thought that was the low point. Unless she got home and sat down, though, she was going to be sick again. She reached for a digestive from her purse, bit off a piece and chewed it slowly.

"*You're* eating biscuits," Sophie accused. "Why do you get what you want, and I don't? You're not our mum! You *work* for us! You're just a nanny!"

Jenna stopped dead, turned to glare down at Sophie. The little girl looked up at her defiantly, but Jenna could see the trepidation in her eyes. It didn't matter, though. Because it was all too much.

"Nobody talks to me like that," she told Sophie furiously. "I'm a *person*. I deserve to be treated with respect." She couldn't help the tears that began to spill over. "I know you've had a bad day, and you know what? I'm sorry, but I've had a bad day too!" She could feel her voice rising, found herself unable to control it. "I'm sick, and I'm tired, and I've had just about enough of you! You're acting like a spoilt brat, and I am *sick* of it!"

She was sobbing now as she held the bag of milk with one hand, Harry's hand with the other. "And I don't want to hear *anything* else. We're going home, and I don't want to hear another word out of you till we get there, do you understand?"

Both children were crying now as well. Somehow, they made it the final three blocks home, Jenna grabbing Sophie's hand at the corners, ignoring her attempts to pull away. When they reached the house again, Jenna kicked her shoes off, shoved the milk into the fridge, grabbed three paper towels and handed one each to Sophie and Harry, wiped her own face with the third.

She took a deep breath. "We are all going to our rooms now," she said, keeping her voice calm with an effort. "We're going to have some quiet time. And then we're going to have a talk."

"I didn't *do* anything, though," Harry sobbed. "Why're you angry at me?"

"I'm not angry at anyone now," Jenna promised. "And you didn't do anything, Harry. But I'm tired, and I feel sick, and we all need to be quiet for a few minutes. Can you go play with your animals, please?"

To her relief, Harry nodded and made his subdued way to his bedroom. Sophie gave her a scared look and followed suit.

She should talk to her now, Jenna knew. But she couldn't. She'd lost it, and she couldn't even care. She went to her own room, shut the door, and lay face-down on the bed, finally giving in to the sobs that overcame her.

It wasn't fair. She was doing her best, she was sick, she was alone, and nobody cared. She knew in one part of her brain that she was overreacting, that she was worn out, hormonal, and overemotional, but she was past being rational. She sobbed until she'd cried herself out, then sat on the bed, wiping her face and blowing her nose, trying to get herself back under control.

She left her bedroom at last, spent another five minutes in the bathroom with a cold cloth on her face, then finally went next door to Harry's room. He was sitting on the floor, surrounded by dinosaurs, softly narrating a scene as he moved Tyrannosaurus closer to a herd of plant-eaters.

"Hey, buddy." She dropped to the floor and put a hand on the back of his neck. "How're you doing?"

Harry looked up at her cautiously. "Are you done being angry?"

"I'm done," she promised. "I'm sorry if I scared you." She reached out to hug him, and he came gratefully into her arms.

"I don't like yelling," he told her. "It hurts my ears, and it makes me sad."

"I don't like it either," she agreed. "I hate losing my temper, in fact. But I guess Sophie had a bad day, and I did too. I lost my patience, and then I lost my temper. I'm sorry about that, and I'll bet Sophie's sorry, too. We're going to have a nice quiet evening. We'll have dinner, and if you both get yourselves ready for bed, we'll watch a DVD together."

"*The Lion King?*" he asked eagerly.

Jenna smiled. "I think maybe not *The Lion King.*" That would be all Sophie needed. Watching Mufasa being killed was guaranteed to set her off again. Too bad they'd watched *Finding Nemo* so recently. That would have been perfect. "We'll choose something good. I'm going to go talk to Sophie now. And then I'll start fixing tea."

He nodded and went back to his dinosaurs. One down. And the tricky one still to go.

She tapped on the closed door of Sophie's room. "Come in," came the muffled voice.

Jenna stepped inside cautiously, saw Sophie stretched out on her bed, face buried in the pillow. Exactly as she herself had looked, fifteen minutes earlier. She sat down on the bed next to the still form. "Hey," she said softly, reached out a hand and stroked Sophie's hair. "How're you doing?"

Sophie rolled over, lifted a swollen, tear-stained face. "Do you hate me?"

"Oh, sweetie. Of course I don't hate you."

Sophie's tears started again. "I didn't mean to be spoilt and... and mean. I'm sorry. I'm sorry," she sobbed.

"Hey, now." Jenna lifted Sophie to sit next to her, reached for a tissue to clean her up. "I'm sorry too. I lost my temper. We both had a bad day, and we said some things that came out of those bad feelings."

"Mrs. Ferguson yelled at me for not listening. And Caitlin played with somebody else, at recess, and I didn't have anybody. And I *miss Daddy.*"

The sobs intensified as Jenna held her closer, her hand going again to smooth Sophie's hair. "Shhh. I know you do, sweetheart. I know." She pulled Sophie into her lap, rocked her as if she were a baby. "It feels like he's been gone a long time, and you miss him so much."

Sophie nodded vigorously against her, burrowing closer.

"He misses you too," Jenna told her. "He loves you, and he's missing his girl. But he's doing what he has to do. He'll be home, just as soon as he can. And we'll watch him on Sunday morning, right?"

"Right," Sophie said, her sobs easing a bit. "I'm his good luck charm. I have to watch."

"That's right," Jenna encouraged her. "Your dad loves you so much. And I have an idea. Why don't you write him a letter, right now? Tell him how you're feeling. Tell him about your day. Because your dad's always with you, you know," she said gently, pulling away a bit so she could look into Sophie's woebegone face. "He's always in your heart. You hold him there. And he holds you in his."

"Really?" Sophie asked, her eyes searching Jenna's.

"Really," Jenna promised. "And there's nothing in this world that can ever take him out of your heart, or take you out of his."

Sophie sniffed, then got up and went to her desk. "I'm going to write to him, then. And tell him about my bad day."

Jenna got up too. "You do that, and we'll put it into the parcel we send him tomorrow."

She let herself out of the room, seeing Sophie already engrossed in her task, and headed to the kitchen. She still felt shaky, but less like an abject failure. Baked potatoes and fish fingers tonight, she decided. She might be able to eat a baked potato.

♡

Jenna reached for the remote to pause the DVD as the phone rang. Seven-thirty. Finn, then, almost certainly.

Harry got to the phone first. "Daddy!" He listened a moment, then said, "No, we had a very, very bad day. Sophie yelled, and Jenna yelled. They hurt my ears. And everybody cried. Jenna cried and cried, Dad. It was really scary. And then we all had time out."

He held out the phone. "Daddy wants to talk to you, Jenna."

She'd just bet he did. "Hi," she said to Finn. "Let me start out by saying we've all calmed down considerably since then."

"What happened?" he asked with concern. "Something with Sophie, eh."

"Yeah. Rough day," she sighed, moving into the kitchen where she could talk more freely. "And I'm afraid I didn't handle it as well as I could have. I let her push my buttons. Harry was right. I yelled. But we've had a good talk, and she's written you a letter to go in your next parcel. She's missing you, that's all."

"It must have been quite the scene, to make you yell," he commented. "I've never heard that before."

"Not my best moment," she agreed. "I apologized, and so did she. I think we're all good. I'm going to turn the phone over to her now, though, let her tell you. She may still have things to get off her chest."

She walked back into the lounge, held out the phone. "Sophie, why don't you go into the other room to talk to your dad? That way you can tell him everything that's on your mind."

♡

"Dad?" Sophie's voice was tentative.

"Sophie Bee," Finn said. "Sounds like you've had quite a day."

"Did Jenna tell you what I said?"

"Nah. Do you want to tell me?"

"Do I have to?"

"Not if you don't want to. Jenna said you two had worked it out, and that you were both feeling better now. Anything you do want to say to me, though?"

"I miss you, Daddy," she burst out. "I want you to be here, with us. I wish you were here. It's not fair."

"I wish I were there too, tonight," he said truthfully. "Would you want me not to be on the squad, though?"

"No!" she said with shock. "You're an All Black, Dad."

"Too right I am. And you know what that means. It means I have to go where they tell me, do my best for the team wherever I am. And it means that I need my family to help me do that. You can be sad that I'm not there. And when you are, you can talk to Jenna about it. You can write and tell me, too, or tell me on the phone the way you're doing now. But you aren't allowed to say mean things to Jenna." His voice was firm now. "She's doing her best to take care of you. You need to do your best to help her. Because that's how you help me. Will you promise to do that?"

"I promise, Dad. I didn't mean to make her cry. D'you think she still likes me?" He could hear the tears again now, and his heart melted.

"You're a good girl. Jenna knows you're trying hard, and I know too. She still likes you, I promise. Jenna said you wrote me a letter, eh. Will you draw me another picture, too, put that in my next parcel? You may want to draw Jenna one as well. That would make her feel better, I'll bet. Can you do that?"

"Yeh," Sophie promised. "I'll draw both of you a picture tonight. I love you, Daddy."

"I love you too, Sophie Bee. Now put Jenna back on, OK?"

"You must feel like a referee," Jenna commiserated. "Don't you need to get on the bus?"

"In a minute. You sure you're all right? I keep hearing about all this crying, and it's got me worried."

"Just a bit off color today," she admitted. "It's made me weepy. We're watching *Beauty and the Beast* now, and we've all cheered up. Tomorrow's another day."

"After we ring off," he ordered, "I want you to ring Miriam, arrange for her to come tomorrow."

"I don't need to do that. The kids will be in school."

"You need an evening off," he said. "And tomorrow's only... Thursday there. Days to go till Monday, and the weekend coming up. Have Miriam get the kids their tea. Go spend the evening with your friend, or go to the pub, or something. And, Jenna. Go to the spa tomorrow, get a massage, or a...a facial, or whatever it is you do. Put it on my bill. It's time for a mental health day, I reckon."

"Miriam may not be available, though."

He sighed. "Then arrange one of those playdates. You've had other kids over enough, you must be due some time of your own. Promise me you'll arrange it, one way or another. I'm going to ring you tonight and ask," he threatened. "You'd better say you have."

"Or what?" she asked with a smile.

"Hmm. Wish I had something better to offer than I do, on that score," he admitted. "But we're only halfway through this thing. I need you fit for the rest of it. Do you promise to arrange all that?"

"I promise. I will. And thanks."

She hung up, wiped away the tears that had surfaced at his kindness. She'd worried, on some level, that he'd blame her for what had happened. She hadn't been any too pleased with herself. But he'd seemed to understand how far her patience had been stretched today. She wondered for the hundredth time if she should tell him. And for the hundredth time, quailed at the prospect of breaking the news on the phone. It was only a couple weeks. And it would be so much better when they could talk face to face, when she could read his expression, see what he was really feeling.

She picked up the phone again and punched the speed dial for Miriam. A massage, and an evening off. She felt her spirits lift at the prospect, her doubts and fears receding.

Finn stuffed the phone back into his pocket, picked up his bag and headed out of the hotel room toward the lift. He needed to get his skates on, or he really would be late getting on the bus.

Everyone on the squad with a partner or kids was feeling the same way just now, he reminded himself. Nothing on earth came without a price attached. Not even the All Blacks.

long distance

♡

"Where are you calling from?" Jenna asked with pleasure, ten days later.

"Hotel lobby. Trying for a bit of privacy to talk to you."

"In the lobby? Doesn't sound too private."

"Standing in the passage, next to the loos," he admitted. "Not too scenic, but quiet. Anyway. Sophie said you were feeling a bit crook again yesterday. Are you better now?"

"It's just something I've been fighting." Well, actually, a baby that had been fighting *her*. She welcomed every bout of morning sickness as proof that her hormones were still doing their job, responding to her continuing pregnancy. She'd feel even more reassured, she hoped, after her first appointment with the midwife on Thursday.

"I'm glad," Finn was saying. "Get Miriam in to help you as much as you need her, though."

"I'm fine," she assured him. Time to move the conversation away from her queasy stomach. "I don't know why we're talking about me anyway. How are *you* feeling? That game looked brutal, when we finally saw it on tape delay last night. Sophie was pretty worried. She kept calling them 'the filthy French.'"

He laughed. "Yeh, they have a bit of a reputation. They've been known to cross the line into dirty play. Eye-gouging, going after the wedding tackle. We kept them in line this time, though."

"Those boots," she guessed.

"Maybe a bit," he acknowledged with a smile in his voice. "Got the win, anyway. That's the main thing."

"So are you hurt? Take a picture in the mirror and send it to me. I want to see."

"A few stitches," he admitted. "No worries. It looks worse than it is."

"A picture," she demanded. "As soon as we hang up and you go back to the room."

"Right," he sighed. "I should ask you for one too. That'd be more worth looking at."

"I look the same, though."

"And I haven't seen how you look for four weeks. You may recall that I wasn't allowed to bring any photos of you with me. At least you've seen me on the telly. A photo isn't the same as having you here, but I'll take what I can get."

His words warmed her. "So what did you do today to recover? Besides eat. I have that one figured out."

"Pool day. We went to a big place in the suburbs. They roped off a couple lanes and the diving pool for us. A lot of clowning around, pretty ridiculous. But it was fun. The boys let off a bit of steam after last night, loosened up in the water. It was good."

"Did you dive?"

"Only off the low board. You still have the record there. But I'll have to tell the kids, I jumped off the highest platform. It was a fair way up there, too."

"Is there a picture of *that?* I'd love to see it."

"The film crew was taping, yeh. Because the clips of the squad with their shirts off are always the most viewed, for some reason. I'll see if I can get an advance copy for you."

"Can't imagine why people would want to see that," she agreed. "Do send the clip to me, if you can. The kids would love it. And *I'd* love to see you in your togs. It's been a long time for me, too."

"I'll do my best. Only seven days to go till we see each other in the flesh. And I can't tell you how much I'm looking forward to your flesh."

"You sound like a cannibal," she laughed.

"Feel like one, too. I miss you every way a man can. That way most of all. But also—not sure how much longer I can take rooming with Lackie."

"Driving you crazy?" she asked sympathetically. "What's he doing?"

Finn groaned. "He's a bloody pig, that's what. Not a bad kid, but you should see his side of the room. Dirty clothes in heaps, dirty dishes, stuff everywhere. Nightmare. You'd think a man with two kids would be used to a bit of mess, but you've got me too spoilt. Turns out his mum still comes over and cleans up after him, can you believe it? The bloke's twenty-two."

"Remember when I interviewed?" she reminded him. "And I told you I believed in kids helping with chores and keeping their rooms clean? Behold the rationale."

"And you were so right. Because I hate to think of my kids living that way."

"Weren't you messier, though, when you were that age?"

"Hope I wasn't that bad. But probably not as good as I think I was."

"Too bad they didn't match you up with another seasoned citizen," she commiserated.

"Nah. They never put the oldies together. That mentoring thing again. Babysitting, more like. Want to make sure the young boys aren't slipping out and getting on the piss. Or bringing girls back to the room."

"You aren't allowed to do that?" she asked in surprise. "Well, *you* aren't, obviously. We had that conversation too. But, nobody is?"

"Nah. Too much opportunity for things to go wrong. There was a horror story a couple years ago with one of the Baby Blacks. The Under-20s," he explained. "In Safa for the world championships. They lost in the final, got pissed in a club afterwards, drowning their sorrows. One of them had a girl in his room that night, and it ended in a rape inquiry. He wasn't charged, and who knows what the true story was, but I reckon it ended his chances in Super Rugby. That's the extreme result, but heaps of things can go wrong. No girls in the rooms, no going out on the razzle without the team. And that's me, the chaperone. The Morality Police."

"The dad."

He laughed. "Can't escape it, I reckon. Anyway, I'm used to it. It's not too bad. Except the mess. That's getting to me, a bit."

"You have a day off again tomorrow, right?" she asked. "No training? Hopefully you won't be spending too much time in the room. What's on the agenda?"

"Versailles in the morning. Then we get on the plane for Edinburgh. Back to practice again the next day, prepare for that final match."

"Versailles? That sounds great."

"My tenth Northern Tour, remember? And probably my fifth trip to Versailles. I'm looking forward to Scotland, though. We didn't go last year. Good tucker. You'd be surprised."

"Well, obviously that's the most important thing. You do sound jaded, though."

"Listen to me, whingeing about having to sightsee. Revolting, isn't it? The truth is, though, this gets harder every year. I miss the kids. And this time, I miss you too, so it's even worse."

"Maybe you should arrange to have the kids get out of school a week early next year," she suggested. "They could see your last game, and you could all spend some time together afterwards, wherever that is. They're old enough to make that long trip, and to get something out of the travel. It'd give you something outside the rugby to look forward to."

"World Cup next year, in England," he reminded her. "No Northern Tour. But it's an idea. I could have them join me for the last bit. The final, and then we could do a bit of traveling."

"You're pretty confident. That you'll be in the final."

"Semifinal, anyway. Every World Cup but one, we've got at least that far. I'm tempting fate by assuming I'll be on the squad. May as well go all the way and plan to play in the final."

They talked a bit more, Finn promising to call the next morning to tell the kids about his high-dive prowess. After he rang off, though, a niggle of anxiety surfaced as he thought back on their conversation. She'd talked about the kids joining him next year. But only the kids. She'd encouraged him to tell her about what he was doing, but had volunteered almost nothing about herself, beyond the kids' activities.

He went into the men's toilet to snap a photo with his iPhone in the mirror and text it to her. He wasn't sure his bruised, stitched face was anything to make her heart sing. But at least it would remind her that he was thinking of her.

Seven more days, he told himself. One more week. That wasn't long. Then they could pick up where they'd left off.

♡

"This is the big day, eh." The midwife, Rose Albertson, pulled the sheet down and Jenna's gown up, squirted the cold jelly on her abdomen. "We'll have a look at what's going on here. Always an exciting moment."

Jenna tried to be excited, but felt only a sick dread. She began to get lightheaded, forced herself to breathe as the wand moved over her belly. The seconds stretched on, her fear mounting with each moment that passed.

"And there we are," Rose said triumphantly at last. "There's your baby."

Jenna stared at the screen, at that pulsing white spot. Her baby's heart, beating strongly inside her. Her eyes filled with tears that spilled over, blurring her view.

Rose smiled and handed her a handful of tissues. "A beautiful sight, isn't it?"

Jenna nodded, sobbed with the relief of it. "I can't tell, though. Can you show me what you're seeing?"

"Head," Rose pointed out. "Forehead, nose, see? And here are the torso and legs."

"You can't tell the sex yet?"

"Another six weeks or so. And then only if the baby cooperates. Sometimes they're shy, keep you guessing."

"But everything looks all right?" Jenna asked anxiously.

"Everything looks perfect," Rose assured her. "And from this, I'd say our dates are spot on. Coming up on twelve weeks. You should be through the worst of that morning sickness any time now, feeling a bit better in general."

"I don't care about that. I'm just…" Jenna fought back the tears that threatened to overwhelm her again. "I'm just so happy to see it."

"I'll make you a disk, shall I?" Rose asked. "So you can take it home, look at it. Email a photo to your mum."

That wasn't happening, but Jenna wasn't going to explain. She'd be looking at those images every day, she knew.

"And," Rose said, helping Jenna sit and seating herself as well, "this would be a good time for me to ask about the baby's dad. He isn't here today, I notice."

"No. He's traveling."

"And?" Rose prompted. "Does he know about your pregnancy?"

"Not yet. I'm planning on telling him once he's back."

"And when will that be? It's hard to do this without support, you know. And I'm guessing you don't have any family close by."

"No. No family." Jenna swallowed the lump that rose in her throat. "He'll be back in a few days. The baby's dad, I mean. And I'll tell him then."

"Meanwhile, what other support systems do you have?" Rose asked.

"I have a couple friends." That sounded pathetic. "I mean, in Auckland," Jenna went on hastily. "I do have more than two friends. I haven't mentioned it to them yet, either. But I will, soon."

"Do that," Rose told her firmly. "This isn't the time to be independent. You need to ask for help. And if the baby's father doesn't come through the way you're hoping," she added gently, "there are services for that as well. I can help get you started with it."

Jenna nodded, not trusting herself to speak.

Rose handed her the disk she had made. "That's it, then. Keep taking the vitamins, and take care that everything you do eat is nutritious. You've lost a few kilos, but that's all right at this stage. Get your rest, get any help you can. And I'll see you next month."

"And, Jenna," she said as Jenna prepared to leave. "Good luck."

homecoming

♡

"Do you think you could take the kids next Tuesday, sometime?" Jenna asked Siobhan. They were sitting in the café celebrating the last day of school before the summer holidays. Her last day of freedom, Siobhan had joked.

"Course," Siobhan said. "When does Finn get back?"

"Monday evening at six." Jenna took a sip of her mint tea and nibbled at a digestive biscuit from the packet she carried in her purse all the time now. "But it's such a long flight, Edinburgh to London, then home. More than twenty-four hours. He'll be pretty jetlagged. I thought he could use a rest, that next day."

"Overexplaining," Siobhan told her with a knowing smile. "Never mind. Declan and I like to take those 'rests' ourselves, when we can get them."

She smiled again at Jenna's startled look. "What? Did you think I didn't know?"

"I..." Jenna couldn't think of an answer. "How?"

"Dunno. Could've been the shag rays coming off the pair of you every time you walked the kids to school together. Or the fact that you *did* walk the kids to school together. Or maybe the way you asked me to take them three times that last week he was here. Or..."

"OK. Stop." Jenna was laughing in spite of herself. "I get it. I just hope everyone else isn't as sharp as you are."

"There may have been a bit of guessing. Gossiping," Siobhan admitted. "But I didn't say anything, no worries. Denied knowing anything about it. Which was the truth. You've been discreet, I'll give you that. Why, though? What's the secret?"

"The kids. And, you know, the jokes. Shagging the nanny." Jenna shuddered. "We decided to keep it quiet, till he gets back. Till I move out."

"Which is when?"

"A week after he gets home."

"Which is all good, right?" Siobhan asked. "So why're you looking like that?"

"Like what?"

"Like you're about to be sick. Oh." Siobhan's eyes suddenly went wide, her mouth opening in shock. "Oh. That's it. The penny's dropped. Whoa."

"What?" Jenna faltered.

"The mint tea. The bikkies. How green around the gills you've been." Siobhan assessed her, eyes calculating. "Are you telling me he doesn't know?"

"Know what?" Jenna asked desperately.

"Come on," Siobhan said impatiently. "This is me you're talking to. I've had two kids, and had my head in the toilet both times. Candied ginger, by the way. That's the best. Think I lived on that, with Eth."

"All right," Jenna capitulated as Siobhan continued to stare at her expectantly. "You're right. I would've told you. It would have been a relief. But I didn't think it was right for anyone else to know before Finn did."

"You're worried about how he'll react," Siobhan guessed. "That's why you've kept it to yourself."

"Yeah." Jenna finished her tea, reached for her bag. "I figure we might need some time, when I do tell him. Pretty hard to have that conversation with the kids around. Or in the middle of the night." She flushed. Too much information. "So, Tuesday?"

"Tuesday," Siobhan promised, clearly restraining herself with an effort from probing further. "Two o'clock do you? I'll take them to the beach."

"Perfect," Jenna said in relief. "Thank you so much. And I'll be expecting the kids tomorrow night."

She followed Siobhan as the other woman made her way to the door.

"If you still want them," Siobhan said dubiously once they were outside again.

"I need the distraction. Then we'll watch that last ABs game on Sunday morning, and the next day he'll be home. And I'm so nervous about the whole thing," Jenna burst out. "Terrified." It was a relief to say it at last. She rubbed her hands over her arms to calm the shakes that had come over her at the admission.

Siobhan turned in the middle of the pavement to give her a comforting hug. "If he doesn't want you, my love, he's a bloody fool. And I don't think Finn's got where he is by being a fool."

♡

Jenna repeated Siobhan's words desperately to herself on Monday evening. The kids had been impossible all day, alternately wildly excited, squabbling, and bursting into tears. She'd felt like bursting into tears herself, more than once. Now they were fidgeting beside her, their eyes on the monitor above the big sliding doors in International Arrivals, waiting for the first sight of a black-clad figure.

She smoothed a hand over her hair. She'd stood in front of the mirror for a full forty-five minutes earlier that afternoon, trying on and discarding outfits, looking for the perfect combination. Something that would conceal the little belly she was having a harder time disguising now, but that would still look good.

And appeal to Finn, she admitted. She'd settled on a yellow tank with a floaty blouse over it, with skinny low-rise jeans whose waistband rode under her bump. The jeans fit better than ever, thanks to her persistent morning sickness. And her pregnancy had emphasized her centerfold proportions, forcing her into the shops to buy new bras a few weeks ago. She knew that, at least, would have plenty of appeal for Finn.

He wouldn't be getting too close today, and after tomorrow, for better or worse, the truth would be out there. After that, she could wear whatever she wanted, could show off her belly instead of working so hard to hide it.

"Sophie," she said sharply now, pulling the little girl back to her again. "Stay with me. He'll be here in a minute." She took a deep breath, looked up at the monitor again, took another sip of water to quell the nausea that rose in response to her tension.

Come on, Finn, she begged silently. *Come home.*

Finn stepped through the doors, his eyes searching the crowd. He registered the gathered supporters, ecstatic over yet another victorious Tour. As they surrounded the squad, eager hands thrusting out paper and pen, he shifted his duffel on his shoulder, shook hands, signed autographs, focusing as always on the kids, the rugby-mad boys who were his most fervent admirers.

His eyes swept the crowd from the advantage of his height until he spotted Jenna at the back, restraining the kids while he did his duty. He watched her face light up as their gazes met, and a wave of emotion swept over him. He'd thought he'd realized how much he was missing her, but he hadn't known the half of it. His kids, too, jumping up and down now, waving. He couldn't stand here any longer. He scribbled his name a couple more times, smiled his thanks, and pushed through the crowd to them.

"Geez." He dropped his duffel, lifted his son and daughter into his arms to kiss them. "You've both got bigger. What have you been feeding them?" he asked Jenna, smiling into her eyes. "Magic beans, I reckon."

"Nah, Dad," Harry protested. "We don't eat *beans*. We eat *meat*. And I had to get new shoes! My feet got bigger!"

"Did they, now." Finn set his children down, reached for his duffel again, then took a hand in each of his own. "Must be the meat, then."

"Good trip?" Jenna turned around to ask as she led the way out the doors. "We're parked close by. In case you're worn out, especially after that exhibition you guys put on the other night."

"It's a long flight," he admitted. "No matter how well they look after us. Wish I could run home, and that's the truth. Don't fancy sitting again for a day or so, at least."

"We watched your game!" Harry exclaimed. "I watched almost all of it, Dad! I would have watched it all, but Ethan was there. And he's little, you know. He can't concentrate."

"*I* watched it all," Sophie assured him. "Jenna too. She woke us up early to watch. You did great, Dad. Were you the tackle leader? They didn't say."

"Nah." He smiled down at her. "Second. Behind Drew, as usual. Made sixteen, though."

Jenna was quiet on the drive home, he noticed, seeming content to listen as the kids overflowed with questions and information.

"You look good," he said quietly as they stopped at a traffic light. "Buy some new clothes while I was gone?"

"A few things."

"They suit you." She looked beautiful, in fact. A bit thinner, maybe, but just as curvy as he remembered. The dull fatigue had lifted when he'd seen the three of them, and his heart felt light to be back again, the Range Rover traveling through the familiar streets, the tidy neighborhoods, green gardens filled with all the rioting blossom of a Southern Hemisphere December.

"Who wants to take a walk to the top of Mt. Eden with me?" he asked as Jenna pulled the car to a stop outside the villa. "Soon as I drop this bag in my room and pop into the shower?"

"Me! Me!" Harry and Sophie chimed in chorus.

"Jenna?" he asked.

"You go on," she told him. "It's almost seven-thirty already. I want to get dinner fixed. I know you must be hungry. I'm sure they didn't feed you guys nearly enough on the plane."

"You're right. Forty-five minutes, OK?"

"Perfect."

♡

It was after nine by the time they had eaten, and ten before the overexcited Harry and Sophie had finally settled in bed, Sophie succumbing to one final tearful outburst beforehand.

"Geez," Finn sighed as he came out of her room at last and sank onto the couch. "Has she been like that?"

"All day," Jenna said with a sigh of her own. "Both of them, actually. But especially Sophie."

"You must be worn thin."

"A bit. It's been a long day. Not as long as yours, though. Want a beer?"

"You know I do. Don't get up. I'll go."

He came back in a minute with bottle in hand. "The Poms think they make good beer, but to my mind, it doesn't compare to Mac's."

"It's all in what you're used to, I suppose," she said.

He looked across the couch at her, sitting as usual with her feet tucked under her. "Still not drinking, eh."

"Nope. New leaf continues."

"Wouldn't have said you needed reforming. Except in certain areas." He grinned across at her. "I missed you."

"Me too." She smiled back at him.

He was just scooting across to join her when Harry appeared in the doorway, glasses askew, PJs rumpled.

"I need a drink of water," the boy complained. "I woke up and I was thirsty."

Jenna got to her feet on a long breath. "OK. Let's go."

She came back into the lounge five minutes later. "Guess that was our cue to say goodnight, because that might not be the last journey out of bed for them. Not going to work. The kids have a playdate tomorrow, though."

"A playdate, eh." His smile grew. I'll have to look forward to that, I reckon. And meanwhile." He hauled himself up off the coach, where he felt like he'd taken root, and pulled her into his arms. "I'm not going to bed without kissing you. No matter who needs a drink of water."

He felt her wrap her arms around him to draw him closer, and deepened the kiss. It felt so good. And it had been so long. "Sure?" he murmured.

"He's going to be popping up again in five minutes," she sighed against him. "Or Sophie will have a bad dream. Tomorrow. Two o'clock."

"Two o'clock," he said reluctantly, letting her go and watching as she went to the door. "Too long."

not too flash

♡

Jenna looked up from her book at the knock at the door. "Come in."

She set the paperback down with surprise as Finn came through the door and closed it softly behind him, his thumb flicking the lock shut. "What are you doing here? We just agreed about this."

He came to sit on the bed next to her. "I got to thinking about it. Only a week left till the end of our contract. We can end this tomorrow, if we want to. I don't mean end it," he said hastily, seeing her frown. "I mean, end the nanny thing. You can move out now. I'll help you, if you need someplace to stay. We can go from living together to dating, out in the open."

He leaned over to kiss her, lingered there. "I've missed you so much. Couldn't wait to be with you again, that's the strength of it. I'm bloody tired, but I couldn't sleep, thinking of you down here in bed without me, after I spent all these weeks alone."

"You had a roommate," Jenna pointed out weakly, feeling her resolve evaporating.

He laughed, pulled the duvet back to climb into bed with her. "Lackie's not a bad young fella, but he isn't quite in your class."

She sighed with pleasure at the feel of his hand stroking her hair back from her face, of his mouth on hers. Once would be all right. Just once, before she told him. She deserved that, didn't she?

Tell him now, the voice of reason said sternly. *He needs to know.* But her body was saying something else, drowning out that sensible voice.

Finn wasn't rushing tonight, despite the long separation and the need she sensed in him, a need she felt just as strongly, pulling her toward him, into him. She pulled his T-shirt over his head, wanting to feel his skin against her hands, to memorize the look and feel of him.

She'd forgotten so much. This curve, where the muscle rose from his neck along the top of his shoulders. The swell of his bicep under her palm as he propped himself on an elbow, the silky skin of his inner arm. His mouth, moving over hers, kissing her as if he'd missed this as much as she had.

His hand moved down to stroke a breast, and she flinched involuntarily at the touch. He felt it, pulled back. "What's wrong?"

"They're a little tender right now, that's all. Can you be really careful? And can we turn out the light? I'm feeling a little shy," she tried to joke. "It's been a long time."

He frowned, but moved to comply. "I'd rather see you. Course I will, though, if that's what you want." He came back to her, felt for the hem of her nightgown, pulled it over her head. "Where were we?"

"You were kissing me," she told him in the dark. "And it was feeling really good."

"I was, wasn't I. And I was touching you. Gently." He went back to kissing her again, moved his hand carefully over her breast, keeping it soft. Then stroked down her side, over her abdomen. And froze.

"What the hell." His voice was strained now. He sat up, fumbled for the light again, turned it on. And stared down at her beneath him. At the fine lines of blue veins, always visible through the pale skin of her breasts, so much more prominent now. The nipples darker, breasts fuller than they had been. And that firm swelling below her navel.

"How far gone are you?" he asked. "And why didn't you tell me about this?"

"You can tell?" she faltered.

"Course I can tell," he said impatiently. "I have two kids. How far gone?"

"Twelve weeks," she admitted. "Ten weeks since conception. That's what the midwife says."

"And?" he prompted when she fell silent. "Why didn't you tell me, sometime in those ten weeks?" He reached for his T-shirt, pulled it back on with jerky motions.

Jenna leaned over to pick her nightgown up from the floor where he'd dropped it, wanting to be dressed for this conversation. It wasn't going anything like the way she had envisioned. The way she had hoped it would be.

"Before you left," she began, "I wasn't sure, at first. And then I was, pretty sure. But I had a...I had a miscarriage before, when I was married. I couldn't believe it would work, that the baby would live. And I wanted it to, so much. I thought I would wait and see first. I didn't want to tell you, and then," she swallowed, "then have it die again. If that was going to happen, I needed it to just be me who knew."

"I don't understand that. It's mine too. Isn't it?" he asked sharply. "Is that what you're saying?"

"No!" She stared at him, horrified. "You know it is. You know I hadn't been with anybody else. How can you ask that?" Her breath was coming shorter now. She felt the nausea rising, swallowed it back.

"How, then?" he challenged. "We used protection, every time. I was bloody careful. How could that happen?"

"Because it isn't perfect! You aren't a kid. You know it isn't perfect."

"Weren't you using anything else, for God's sake?"

She looked at him, stricken. "Of course I wasn't. How could I have been? I'd probably had sex twenty times in my life. I hadn't had it at all for years. Then you came along. You know what happened. You were there too. You know how it was, how fast it was. You have to remember."

"But after the first time," he said with frustration. "Didn't you think about it?"

"Did *you*?" she challenged, getting angry now. "You're the one with the experience. Anyway, it probably *happened* that first time. Ten weeks, Finn. Count back."

"Aw, shit." He put his head in his hands. "Bloody vending machine condom. How could I have been so stupid? Twice. I can't believe it."

She looked down at him, the cold seeping through her. She hadn't expected him to be thrilled, of course. Well, she'd hoped, in some part of herself, that he would be. That he'd want this baby, would want her, as much as she wanted both of them. She was the one who'd been stupid. That was obvious now.

He lifted his head, eyes narrowing again, hard now. "Right," he rapped out. "You didn't tell me before I left. I've been gone five weeks, Jenna. You had to know all those five weeks. Everything's obviously going on according to plan, based on how you look. Baby's growing, heart's beating, all that. So why the hell didn't you tell me?"

"On the phone? How was the game, and by the way, I'm pregnant?"

"Yeh," he snapped. "Exactly. I had a right to know. Why didn't you tell me?"

"Because I was scared, all right?" she burst out. "I was scared you'd react exactly the way you're doing right now. And I wouldn't even be able to see you, talk to you. I thought it wouldn't matter, that I could wait till you came home. I even hoped you might be happy about it." Her eyes were welling with tears now, and she dashed them away impatiently with one hand. "Stupid. But you're such a good dad. I thought, I hoped, maybe you'd want it as much as I did."

"Right," he shot back. "You thought I'd be rapt that I'd got the nanny up the duff."

She reared back as if he'd hit her, her eyes going wide with shock and pain. Her hand went to her mouth as she stumbled out of bed.

"Don't run away from me." He was in front of her now, glaring at her. "We're talking about this."

"Sick," she got out from behind her hand, pushed past him and ran for the door.

"Shit." He watched her go, sank down on the bed again, his hands gripping the edge of the mattress, head bent. Took a few deep breaths and pulled himself back under control with an effort. Shook himself like a dog and stood up to go find her.

He waited in the hallway until he heard the toilet flush, then walked cautiously through the bathroom door to find her still huddled on her knees over the toilet, gripping the bowl.

"Aw, geez." He pulled a hand towel from the rack and wet it at the sink, squatted down next to her to wipe her face. She was crying in earnest now, and the guilt twisted inside him. "Hang on. I'll get you a glass of water."

When he came back with it, she was standing again, holding onto the sink with one hand and slowly brushing her teeth with the other. Her face still looked paper-white, and she didn't appear any too steady on her feet.

"Come on," he urged as she spat the toothpaste into the sink and rinsed her mouth with the water he offered. "I'll help you back to bed. Have you been crook all this time? This bad?"

She nodded, still not looking at him.

He exhaled. "Let's go, then. We can talk more tomorrow, figure out what to do. You need to lie down now."

"No." She lowered the toilet seat and sank down onto it. "I'm going to stay here for a minute." She swallowed. "Still sick."

"Right." He leaned back against the wall to wait.

She pulled her hair back from her face with one trembling hand and looked up at him with weary eyes. "Please go away. Go to bed. I don't want you here with me right now."

He looked down at her helplessly. "Are you sure? Can I help?"

She shook her head tiredly. "Just go. Please."

"We'll talk tomorrow, then," he said again. "Sorry. Wasn't expecting it, that's all. Bit of a shock."

Her mouth twisted. "Yeah. Shock to me too. Go to bed. You've said enough. I get it. And I need to be alone now."

He hesitated, then pushed himself off the wall and left the bathroom, closing the door quietly after him. He couldn't have made more of a hash of that if he'd tried. He winced inwardly at the memory of her stricken face, the pain in her eyes. He'd apologize again tomorrow. They'd make a plan. He pushed a hand through his hair and made his way down the long hallway, up the stairs to his own room, all the weariness of the journey back in full force.

Pregnant. Bloody hell.

♡

"Daddy!" Finn woke from the doze he'd finally fallen into as Harry, always the early riser, jumped onto the bed next to him.

"What time is it?" he asked, pulling the alarm clock towards him.

288

"Morning," Harry pointed out unnecessarily. "And Jenna isn't up. Jenna's *always* up when I get up, Dad."

"We'll let Jenna sleep a bit this morning," Finn told his son. "Where's Sophie?"

Harry sighed. "Reading in bed. Of *course.*"

"I have an idea. We'll get dressed and walk to the café for breakfast. A treat. How would that be?"

"Jenna too?" Harry scrambled for the edge of the bed.

"Nah, Jenna needs some rest. She wasn't feeling too flash last night." Because of him, Finn thought guiltily.

Harry nodded. "Jenna feels crook a lot. She has a funny tummy. That's what she says. 'Just my funny tummy.' One time she had to stop the car. And then she spewed on the verge. All over the *grass,* Dad. It was *disgusting.*" Harry shuddered at the memory. "Sophie and I were really scared. But then she got better."

Finn winced. "Well, we'll let her give her tummy a rest today, now that I'm home. Go get your gear on. And tell your sister."

"OK." Harry ran off, and Finn moved into the bathroom to get himself ready. He'd take the kids out, then put on a DVD for them and have a quiet talk with Jenna. It wasn't ideal, but after the disaster last night, he couldn't afford to wait.

♡

"Jenna!" Harry and Sophie ran ahead of Finn into the house, Sophie clutching the white bakery bag. "We brought you a scone! Jenna!"

Finn went into the kitchen, looked around with surprise. Was she still asleep, then?

"Dad!" he heard from the other end of the house. Then both his kids were running back to find him. "She isn't here!"

"She probably went for a run," he told them. "Took advantage of you monsters being out of the house for once."

"No, Dad," Sophie said soberly. "Her room's empty."

"What do you mean, empty?" A chill ran through him at the look on their faces, and he followed them down the hall. Paused outside the open door to Jenna's room and looked inside.

They were right, it was empty. Cleaned out. The bed was neatly made, but the few personal items that usually sat atop the bedside table were gone, and her cardigan was missing from its usual spot across the chair back. He moved across to the closet, pulled the door open. Nothing but hangers, looking forlorn in the empty space.

Sophie came to join him, her eyes too old in her small face. "She went away," she told him. "Why didn't she say goodbye to us, Dad?"

"No!" Harry shouted. "Jenna wouldn't go away. She *loves* us. She *loves* us, Dad. And I love Jenna. I want Jenna." He started to cry, and Finn looked at him helplessly, reached an arm out to pull him close.

Sophie was there again, handing him a folded sheet of paper. "I think she left you a letter, Dad. It has your name on it. It was on the bed."

He took it, not trusting himself to open it in front of them, sat on the bed and pulled them down to sit beside him. "I think Jenna had to go away for a while," he told them. "But she'll be back. She had something to do, that was all. She waited until I was home again to take care of you, then she went."

"But why didn't she tell us?" Harry asked, eyes streaming. Sophie was sobbing now too, more quietly, and Finn looked at the pair of them, not knowing what to do.

"I don't know," he finally answered. "But I'll talk to her soon, and find out. She loves you both. She'll be back to see you, I'm sure of it." Even if she didn't want to see him, he knew, she'd never leave Sophie and Harry like this. Not for good.

Finally, he had the kids settled. He parked them in front of a DVD, moved into his bedroom and sank down on the bed, pulled Jenna's note out of his pocket and unfolded it.

Finn,

I'm sorry for leaving without saying goodbye to Sophie and Harry. Please tell them I had an emergency, and that I love them and will see them soon, if that's OK with you. And that I'll post their Christmas presents to them. This isn't their fault, and they need to know that. Please tell them so, for now. That's what they'll be worried about, especially Sophie.

I'll contact you later to make plans. If you'd rather I talk to your lawyer instead, let me know. I will of course make the baby available for any paternity testing you or your lawyer think is necessary. I wish I didn't have to ask you for maintenance, but I will, after the baby's born. I have some money saved, but a teacher's salary only goes so far.

I hope you'll want to be part of this baby's life, and I'll do everything I can to make that possible. I know you wouldn't have given Sophie up, even though she wasn't what you'd planned. You're a great dad, and I hope you can find it in your heart to be that dad to this baby too.

You don't have to worry that I'll talk about this to anyone. It doesn't reflect well on me, I know. It was the wrong thing to do, but I can't be sorry about the baby. I hope, eventually, you won't be sorry either.

Jenna

He read it through once, twice. Folded it in half and set it down next to him, picked it up again and read it a third time. Every sentence seemed to slice at him, and he squeezed his eyes shut to stop the tears of pain and guilt. Had he really asked her if the baby was his?

Where was she now? Where had she gone? She was sick, and alone. He pushed back the fear, picked up his mobile to ring her. It went straight to voicemail.

"Jenna. This is Finn. I'm sorry for what I said, and I'm worried about you. Ring me. Please."

He hesitated, then rang off. He had a feeling she wasn't going to be ringing. Where would she have gone? He couldn't think. The holidays were coming up. Even if she had a job for the next term, it wouldn't be starting until late January. Some kind of temporary post? She'd been working in a café before she'd come to him, and this was summer, the busiest season. She could be anywhere.

a bull's roar

♡

Jenna reached into the huge laundry basket for another sheet, pegged it onto the line. Her back was aching again. She liked the idea of hanging out the washing, but found herself wishing, just this once, for a dryer.

The wind whipped one end of the heavy, wet fabric out of her hand, and she exclaimed in frustration and grabbed for it as Sarah approached.

"Jenna. I wanted to ask…" Sarah stopped, staring at Jenna's midsection, the blouse pulled against her body by the wind as she stretched to re-peg the errant sheet.

"What?" Jenna looked over, then faltered at the expression on Sarah's face.

"Suddenly, everything's becoming very clear to me," Sarah said slowly. "Finn's, I assume."

Jenna flushed, bent to the basket for another sheet to hide her confusion. "Yes."

"Does he know?"

Jenna laughed humorlessly, pegged the sheet to the line. "Oh, yeah. He knows."

Sarah frowned. "And he turfed you out? That doesn't sound like Finn. Besides, seemed to me he was fair gone on you."

"No." Jenna forced herself to answer honestly. "He didn't actually throw me out. But I didn't have much choice, either. Because you're wrong about that. Sure, he wanted me to take care of his kids. He liked me as a nanny just fine. And he wanted to have sex with me. He sure wanted that. That's what you were seeing. But that was it. He doesn't want either one of us now. He made his feelings pretty clear, trust me." She brushed the sudden tears away. "Stupid hormones," she muttered. "I know he's your brother. Sorry. I'm sure you don't want to hear this."

"He let you go, just like that? Without any help? Sarah asked, outraged.

"I didn't ask. I left. Don't worry," Jenna hastened to assure her. "I'm sure he'll do his duty, pay the maintenance. And meanwhile, I'm fine. I can take care of both of us, thanks to you. Just don't tell him I'm with you, OK? You promised, remember."

"I didn't know then, though," Sarah answered slowly. "Just thought you'd parted on bad terms, and needed to start the job a bit earlier. This is different. I won't go out of my way to tell him, but if he asks me, I'm not going to lie."

Jenna nodded. "That's fair. I can't see why he'd ask anyway. And it's not for that long. It's almost Christmas already. Another few weeks, and I'll head back up to Auckland for the start of the term and the new post. I'll be getting in touch with him then— or his lawyer, I guess. Seeing the kids too, if he's OK with that. That'll take you out of the middle. Sorry to put you there in the first place, but I didn't know what else to do. I had to leave. I couldn't stay there, not once I knew how he felt about me."

"I'm not too comfortable with this," Sarah said. "But since that's my niece or nephew in there, and my dill of a brother hasn't stepped up, I'm glad I have you here where I can keep an eye on you. I'm shifting you, though," she decided, coming over and taking the other end of the heavy sheet. "I don't want you cleaning the cabins anymore. You're working in the office with me."

"I'm feeling much better now," Jenna protested. "Everyone's right when they say the second trimester's easier. The sickness is finally going away. I've even gained a kilo."

"After losing, what?" Sarah looked her over critically. "I've noticed."

"Four. But I'm much better now," Jenna added hastily. "Not as tired, either. I can clean. I don't mind."

"The office," Sarah told her firmly. "Starting tomorrow."

♡

"So how're you coping, on your own with the kids?" Sarah asked three days later, standing in the kitchen of her comfortable home and arranging leftover ham from Christmas Eve tea in a plastic container.

Finn shrugged heavily. "Not too bad. Nyree's cousin Miriam's been helping a bit. And Nyree'll be back after the New Year."

"I didn't realize Jenna was leaving so soon," Sarah ventured. "I'd thought she was staying on another week."

"Yeh. Well." Finn finished scraping the plates, pulled the rubbish bag out of the bin and tied it shut with a few quick movements, shook out a new bag and lined the bin again. "Something happened."

"Oh? Must have been something pretty big, to make her leave the kids. They're still teary about it. I thought she was attached to them. Yet they don't seem to have talked to her since she left."

"It was," he admitted. "Pretty big, I mean. My fault. I said some things."

"What kind of things?" Sarah probed.

"D'you have to be such a bloody stickybeak?" he flashed. "Bad things, all right? The wrong things. Wish I could take them back, but I can't find her to do it."

Sarah turned, wiped her hands on a tea towel, and leaned against the bench to face him. "What happened, baby brother? I just watched your kids crying over their Christmas tea, and you look awful. So tell me. What did you do? I thought you fancied her. Is that it?"

"Fancied her? Yeh, you could put it like that. Or you could say that I fancied her so much she fell pregnant, and I didn't find out till I got back from the Tour. And that I was a bloody fool when I did find out, made her think I didn't want her or the baby, drove her away. And that I've been trying to get her back ever since, and I haven't come within a bull's roar of it. And that I don't bloody well know what else to do, or I'd be doing it," he finished defiantly, his voice rising until he was almost shouting.

He wrenched the kitchen door open, and Sarah heard the clatter as he threw the rubbish bag into the wheelie bin with unnecessary violence, then watched him come back into the kitchen and sink down on a chair, his head in his hands.

"Shit, Sarah," he went on, his voice quieter now. "I don't know what to do. I've tried ringing her, emailing her, but she's changed her accounts. I rang her friends and asked them. But if they know where she is, they aren't telling me. I even paid someone to look for her. Nothing. She's disappeared, and I don't know how to find her. And I'm so worried about her by now, I'm useless. Wandering round like a stunned mullet."

"Do you think she won't let you see the baby?" she asked cautiously. "That she'll leave, go back to the States, maybe? Is that what you're worried about?"

"Nah. She wouldn't do that. Nothing to go back to, from what I know. Anyway, she'll do the right thing. She always does. But she was feeling so crook. And now she's out there somewhere, working too hard, thinking I didn't care, thinking she has to do this alone."

"But did you care?" Sarah pressed. "That's what I don't understand. Did you care then? Do you now? I know you care about the baby," she hurried on. "And I can see how guilty you feel. But what about Jenna? Do you care about her? Do you want her, setting the baby aside, setting your kids aside? And if you do, why on earth wouldn't she know that?"

"Because I never told her so," he admitted wretchedly. "I was just going along, enjoying things. Didn't occur to me to say anything. And then, when I did, I said…I pretty much said the opposite, I reckon. But I can't make it right if I can't find her."

"Well, if she's going to let you see the baby, if she's going to ask you for maintenance, she's going to have to contact you sometime," Sarah pointed out reasonably. "Why don't you wait till she does, then tell her what's on your mind?"

"What about in the meantime?" he demanded. "She's alone, nobody to take care of her, nothing to fall back on. I can't let her keep on like that, when it's my job to look after her."

"Why?" Sarah asked bluntly. "Besides the baby. Why?"

He stared at her. "Because I love her, of course."

She exhaled with relief. "How long have we been talking here? How long did it take you to say it? A word of advice, baby brother. When you do see her again, when she does talk to you, lead with that."

over the counter

♡

"Why are we going to the holiday park?" Sophie asked, looking out the car window as they neared Motueka. "I thought we were going to the beach. And that's the other way."

"Auntie Sarah asked us to pop by, said she had another Chrissie pressie for you," Finn told her. "She wanted to give it to you today, on Christmas. And she can't leave the park, she says. Hardly anyone working today."

"What kind of pressie?" Sophie wondered. "She already gave us our pressies yesterday."

"Dunno." He shrugged. "But you want it, don't you?"

"I want Jenna," Harry said stubbornly from behind him. "That's what I want for Christmas, Dad. I want Jenna back. I told you, and I told Santa. And I didn't get it. But I still want it. Please, Dad."

"She *told* us." Sophie looked across at her brother in exasperation. "She's on a trip. She wrote to us and sent us our pressies, and she said she'd see us soon."

"I don't want to see her *soon*," Harry said, the tears starting again. "I want to see her *now*."

"You love Nyree, though," Finn protested. "And she's coming back in the New Year. I know your old Dad isn't much chop," he tried to joke, "but I've been doing my best. And soon you'll have Nyree cooking for you again."

"Nyree doesn't *understand* like Jenna. She doesn't *discuss* like Jenna."

"You'll hurt her feelings, if you tell her that," Finn warned. "You don't want to do that."

Harry sniffed, ran his arm under his nose to wipe it. "OK. I won't say."

"Here we are," Finn said, trying to be cheerful as he pulled into the holiday park's big carpark, nearly full now. "Let's see what that pressie's all about, and then we'll be off to the beach."

He grabbed Harry's hand and kept Sophie close to him for the walk across the carpark, leaving the summer heat as they stepped into the air-conditioned office. Sarah looked up and smiled briefly at them, then turned back to the French couple she was checking in at the long counter.

"Can you fix my strap, Dad?" Sophie asked, trying to reach the twisted neck tie of her sundress. "It's gone wonky."

Finn crouched down, began to work at the knot, feeling clumsy and awkward.

"Jenna!" Harry shrieked. Finn looked up fast to see Jenna coming out of the back office. His eyes met hers in mutual shock. He registered Harry rushing forward toward the counter separating them even as he watched Jenna sway, her face going white, a hand reaching out and finding only air.

"Shit." In the next instant, he was vaulting the wooden counter, grabbing her as she fell, looking around for a chair and pushing her into it, a hand at the back of her head.

"Put your head between your knees," he ordered. "Breathe."

He dropped to a knee in front of her, his hand still on the back of her head, and glared up at his sister. She and the French couple were staring at him, mouths open, while his children jumped up and down in front of the high counter, trying to see across it.

"What were you thinking, giving her a shock like that?" he demanded angrily. "You know she's pregnant!"

"Sorry," Sarah told him with a satisfied smile. "Reckon she needs someone to look after her better than I have been."

"Are you all right?" he asked belatedly, realizing his hand was still on the back of Jenna's head. He removed it hastily. "Jenna. Talk to me. Are you all right?"

She sat up, swayed again. "Oh. Maybe…"

His hand went back to her head again, pushed it gently down. "Another minute," he told her. "Hang on. Glass of water." He looked around at Sarah again. She obligingly pulled a water bottle out of a small fridge under the counter, handed it to him.

"Dad! Dad!" Harry called. "We want to see Jenna!"

"Dad," Sophie chimed in. "Let us come back there. Auntie Sarah, please. We want to see Jenna."

"Excuse me," one of the French tourists said with exasperation. "May we check in now?"

"Hang on a tick," Sarah told them absently. "Half a mo, kids. I think your dad has a few things to say to Jenna first." She made an urgent motion with her head at Finn.

"Jenna," he said, still kneeling, handing her the water bottle and watching her lift her head to take a careful sip. "You've been here, all this time?"

She nodded, and he exhaled in relief. "I've been miserable as a shag, worrying about you," he told her. "How're you feeling? Has that been happening? The fainting?"

"Lightheaded sometimes, that's all. I'm all right, really. It was just…the shock. I didn't know you were here. Sarah didn't say."

"Sarah didn't say a fair few things," he said grimly, shooting his sister a glare. "Might have saved us both some misery if she had."

"Oi," Sarah objected. "Got you here today, didn't I?" She jerked her head at him again. "Go," she mouthed.

He took a deep breath, took Jenna's hand. "Now that I've found you, I need to tell you. I need to ask you to come back to me. Please. I know I did everything wrong when you told me. I didn't mean what I said. Please come back. Please give me the chance to make it up to you."

She was already shaking her head. "No, Finn. I startled the truth out of you, that's all. I needed to know how you really felt about me. Now I do."

"But that isn't how I feel! I need you, Jenna. You have to believe me."

"Too right," Sarah pointed out helpfully. "I've never seen a man look more pathetic. Please, put him out of his misery. It's more than a sister can bear."

"D'you mind?" Finn scowled at her. "Trying to propose here."

"And you're making dog tucker of it," Sarah said. "What did I tell you to say?"

"Maybe if I could get a bit of privacy, I could do better," he said in exasperation.

"All this is very affecting," the Frenchman complained. "But we'd like to check in. We've been waiting long enough."

"Here." Sarah thrust the key at them, together with a map of the park. "Cabin 18. Sorry. I'll come see you in a bit, make sure you're sorted. But we have a…family emergency here, as you can see."

She ushered them to the door, flipped the sign to *Closed.* "Come on, kids. Let's go get an ice cream."

"Then can we see Jenna?" Harry pleaded.

"First ice cream, then Jenna," Sarah promised. "Let's go." She turned back to Finn, gave him a thumbs-up, closed the door firmly behind her and turned the key in the lock.

"Jenna," Finn said as he heard the door shut at last behind the others. "I'm trying to ask you to marry me here. Trying to tell you I love you, and I need you with me."

"No," she told him sadly. "I can't. I married somebody once who didn't really love me. Not in the right way, the way it should be. I'm not going to make that mistake again. If I ever get married again, it'll be to somebody who wants me and needs me for myself. You don't have to marry me to see your baby. I won't keep that from you. I'll stay in Auckland, and we'll work it out. I promise."

"Damn it, I'm not asking you for the baby!" he exploded. "I want the baby," he went on hastily. "But I need you. I'm so selfish, I don't want you for the baby, or my kids, or anything else, even though all those things matter too. I want you because you make my life so much better. Because I can't imagine living the rest of it without you. And because ever since you left, I've been wandering round thinking about you, worrying about you. Because even when I was on tour, I wanted you with me. Why d'you think I rang you every night? Because I missed you so much. I don't know what else to say," he ran down at last. "That's everything I have. I love you, and I'm asking you to marry me. If I had a ring, I'd be pulling it out now. I don't even have that. All I have is my heart, but that's yours."

She looked at him, her doubts showing clearly on her face. "Do you mean this? Please, Finn, please don't say it if you don't mean it. I can handle the truth. But I can't handle a lie."

"I mean it. I don't know how to convince you. But I'll spend the rest of my life proving it." He took a deep breath, decided to try again. "Jenna." He took both her hands in his. "Will you marry me? Because I love you more than I can say."

"Maybe," she said cautiously. "I have a few things to tell you, though. And some things I need to know."

"Tell me," he begged, relief beginning to take hold now.

"I'm not going to change. I don't want a big career. I don't want to run any companies or anything. Or any schools, even. I'm good at teaching little kids. And I'm good at taking care of people. That's what I want to do. What I plan to do."

"Then I'd be the luckiest man in the world if you were taking care of me and our kids, wouldn't I?"

"And I don't even want to teach while the kids are little," she went on, eyes searching his face. "I want to stay home and be a mum and a wife, if I can. Are you going to be OK with that?"

He laughed in relief. "Is that your condition? Yes, Jenna. I promise. I'll make the living. But I need you to make the home."

"It means you're going to have to find a new job for Nyree," she said. "I'm not sharing my kitchen."

"Done. So many of the boys are having babies now, that'll be easy as. We're keeping the housecleaners, though. You're not doing everything."

She nodded. "And if you go someplace else to play in the future. Japan, Europe, all those places you guys end up. It's not all right with me for you to go alone. We're coming, too. All of us."

"All of you," he promised.

"And one more thing," she told him. "This might not be the last baby. Are you OK with four?"

"I'm OK with six," he assured her. "Whatever you want."

She smiled. "I think four will do it. But we'll see."

"Is that it?" he asked. "All the conditions?"

She nodded. "I think that's it. Do you have any for me?"

"Just one. I need to know that you'll love me. Even when I say the wrong thing and hurt your feelings. That you'll put me right when I cross the line, trust me enough to stay with me and work it out. Because I'm going to need you forever. Will you be able to put up with me that long?"

She laid a gentle hand on either side of his face, held him there a moment, then kissed him with all the love she had in her beautiful heart.

"I promise." She pulled back again, her tears spilling over, running down her cheeks unheeded. "I'm sorry I gave up on you. I didn't know. I didn't believe. But if you'll really need me forever, I promise I'll be there for you just that long. Because I love you, too. And I always will."

epilogue

♡

"Ready for bed?" Finn got up from the couch as Sophie and Harry approached, dressed in nightgown and pajamas.

"In a minute." Sophie reached for the remote and clicked off the cricket match that was playing on the big screen. "We have something very important to say first."

"Do you want to talk to your dad alone?" Jenna asked. She lifted a sleepy Lily from her breast, putting her against her shoulder and beginning to pat her tiny back.

"Nah. We want to talk to both of you," Sophie assured her.

"Go on, then," Finn urged with a smile, settling back onto the couch as he saw Sophie flip open her notebook. "I can see you have a list. Better read it to us."

"We want to call you Mum," Sophie told Jenna. "For these reasons. Reason One: We don't have a mum anymore." She looked at Finn. "I know we *did*," she clarified. "But we don't now. And the other kids do, Dad."

"I know," he told her soberly. "I know you don't. And I know that's been hard."

"Your mum must have loved you both so much, though," Jenna put in. "She must have been so sad to leave you. And she'll always be your mum, even though she's not here anymore."

"We don't *remember*, though," Harry said. "We want a mum we *remember*."

"*Harry*. I'm still *saying*," Sophie told him impatiently. "Reason Two," she went on. "You're Lily's mum. And we want you to be ours, too."

"Oh, Sophie." Jenna's eyes were filling with tears now. "I'd be so proud to be your mum. Your *other* mum. If it's OK with your dad." She looked at Finn, eyes questioning.

"Course it is," he said. He reached for Sophie and Harry, drew them close. "Is that the list, then? Because I reckon we're done here."

"But Sophie didn't say the most important thing!" Harry objected. "We want Jenna to be our mum because we *love* her. Don't we, Sophie?" He looked at his sister, got a firm nod in reply.

"D'you want us to be your kids?" he demanded of Jenna. "Your *real* kids, I mean? Like Lily?"

Jenna's tears were falling in earnest now. She looked at Finn, saw the moisture in his own eyes as he lifted Sophie and Harry onto the couch to join them.

"You already are my real kids," she promised as she settled Lily in one arm, reached out with the other to hug them both. "And I want to be your mum more than anything in the world. You're my family, and I love you so much."

Finn looked down at her, holding their children so close. The day she'd walked into this room, wet and bedraggled, had been the luckiest of his life. He didn't know what he'd done to deserve her, but his heart filled with gratitude for his beautiful wife, and all the love and happiness she'd brought him.

He stood up and took Lily from her, settled the sleepy baby in one big arm.

"Well, now that Sophie's read us her list and we've got that sorted, I reckon it's bedtime at last," he announced.

"And I'm thinking," he decided, smiling down at Sophie and Harry, "that we may need a bit of a change from the normal routine. So I'm going to go on and get Lily settled in her cot. Because I have a feeling your Mum wants to put you both to bed tonight."

The End

Sign up for my New Release mailing list at www.rosalindjames.com/mail-list to be notified of special pricing on new books, sales, and more.

Turn the page for Jenna's recipes, a Kiwi glossary, and a preview of the next book in the series.

the recipes

MULLIGATAWNY SOUP
4-6 servings

1 cup diced onion
2 cloves garlic, minced
2 tsp. fresh ginger, minced
2 carrots, diced
4 ribs celery, diced
3-4 Tbsp. butter
3 Tbsp. flour
4 tsp. curry powder
8 cups chicken broth
2 bay leaves
½ cup diced tart apple (Granny Smith is good)
1 cup cooked rice
1 cup diced cooked chicken
2 tsp. salt or to taste
½ tsp. pepper or to taste
¼ tsp. thyme
1 tsp. grated lemon zest (yellow part only)
1 cup half & half or milk (can use everything down to 1% milk, depending how rich a soup you prefer)

Saute onion, carrot, celery, garlic, ginger in butter in large soup pot. Add flour and curry powder; stir and cook about 3 minutes.

Pour in chicken broth and bay leaf and simmer 15 minutes. Add other ingredients except cream/milk and simmer 15 minutes more. Immediately before serving, stir in cream or milk.

If you are making a quantity that you won't use up that day, keep the rice separate and add it to each bowl of soup, so it doesn't get mushy.

QUINOA SALAD
6-8 servings (recipe can be doubled. Makes a great workday lunch over arugula and/or spinach—protein, vegetables, vitamins, fiber, AND low-calorie!)

1 c. uncooked quinoa, rinsed very well and drained (the soapy substance tastes bitter if you don't rinse it off)
Vegetable or chicken broth, if desired
1/2 c. chopped green onions, white and pale green parts only (about 2 bunches)
¾ c. chopped fresh parsley
3-4 Tbsp. chopped fresh mint, to taste (optional)
1 clove minced garlic
1 c. grape or cherry tomatoes, cut in halves or quarters
½ cucumber, chopped
½ cup diced red or yellow pepper
1 can black beans, rinsed and drained (optional)
½ tsp. salt, or to taste (less if you are cooking quinoa in a salted broth)
¼ tsp. pepper, or to taste
3-4 Tbsp. extra virgin olive oil
3-4 Tbsp. fresh lemon juice (1-2 lemons)

Cook the quinoa as directed on package—normally about 15 minutes. If it is well rinsed, use about 1-3/4 cups water, or vegetable or chicken broth, for 1 cup of quinoa. It is done when the quinoa sprouts little curly "tails." If all liquid is not absorbed, strain it to remove the liquid.

Chill the cooked quinoa if possible; add vegetables and herbs (and beans, if using).

Whisk olive oil, lemon juice, salt & pepper in a bowl with a fork until well blended. Add to salad and mix thoroughly. Taste & correct salt & pepper. Chill salad if possible; the flavors will blend as it sits.

Other vegetable/herb choices: carrots, zucchini, cilantro (instead of mint).

SAUSAGE & PEPPER SPAGHETTI SAUCE

6 servings. Almost as easy as using a canned sauce, and so much tastier!

3-4 Italian sausages (can use chicken or turkey sausage), hot or mild or a combination
1-2 onions, chopped, depending on size
2 cloves garlic, minced
3 red peppers, chopped
2 16-oz cans chopped tomatoes (Italian recipe, or in juice, or in puree)
2 8-oz cans tomato sauce
1 tsp. dried oregano
1-1/2 tsp. dried basil

Take sausages out of casings (cut along the casing and squeeze out the meat), break into pieces. Cook with onions, garlic, and red pepper until meat is cooked and vegetables are soft. Drain fat. Stir in tomatoes and sauce, and herbs. Cook 1 hour, partially covered.

GLAZED SALMON

4 servings (just cut everything else in half if cooking for two). Basic idea for this comes from Cook's Country. Quick and easy; makes a delicious company dinner with roasted potatoes and a green salad.)

4 salmon fillets, rinsed, patted dry, sprinkled with salt and pepper. 1" thick (if thinner, cook shorter time)
¼ cup balsamic vinegar
¼ cup orange juice
2 Tbsp. honey
2 tsp. olive oil (not extra-virgin as it smokes too easily)
2 Tbsp. butter

Whisk vinegar, juice, and honey together in small bowl. Heat oil in nonstick skillet over medium to medium-high heat until very hot. Cook salmon fillets without moving for 4-5 minutes (shorter time if the fillets are less than 1" thick). If the fillets are skin-on, start with the skin side facing up. Flip fish and cook 2-3 minutes more, until cooked through but not dry. Transfer to warm plate and cover with foil to keep warm.

If you cooked salmon with skin on, wipe pan out with paper towels. Lower heat to medium. Pour balsamic mixture into pan and simmer about 5 minutes, until thick and syrupy. Stir in butter and pour sauce over salmon.

BUTTERMILK PANCAKES
3 servings for hungry people (or men). Recipe can be doubled.

3 Tbsp. butter
2 cups buttermilk
2 eggs, beaten
1-1/2 cups flour (try substituting 2 Tbsp. cornmeal, ½ cup oatmeal, and 2 Tbsp. almond meal, if you can find it, for ½ cup of the flour—delicious!)
2 tsp. baking soda
¾ tsp. salt
2 Tbsp. white sugar

Melt butter in large bowl in microwave. Whisk in buttermilk, then beaten eggs. Sift or stir together dry ingredients separately, then stir in with a few quick strokes. Cook on a 375-degree griddle or over medium heat until bubbles form and edges look dry; turn and cook about a minute more.

Add any of the following to make your pancakes extra-special: blueberries; peaches; nectarines; bananas and chopped pecans; bananas and mini chocolate chips; bananas and chopped macadamia nuts.

PEAR/DRIED CHERRY COFFEE CAKE
Coffee Cake
3/4 cup sugar
¼ cup butter
1 egg
½ cup milk (higher-fat is tastier, but 1% is OK too)
2 cups flour
2 tsp. baking powder

½ tsp. salt
1 can pears in juice, drained and chopped
¼ cup dried cherries (optional)

Filling/Topping
½ cup brown sugar
¼ cups flour
2 tsp. cinnamon
3 Tbsp. butter, melted

Preheat oven to 375 degrees. Spray a 9" square glass baking pan with nonstick cooking spray.

Mix together butter and sugar with an electric mixer; add egg. Stir in milk. Sift together dry ingredients, or mix in a separate bowl; stir in. Carefully stir in fruit. Spread half the batter in pan. Sprinkle half of filling/topping mixture over batter. Spoon remainder of batter over filling and smooth over. Sprinkle rest of filling/topping mixture over top of batter. Bake until toothpick comes out clean, 25-30 minutes.

Other ideas: peaches (fresh or canned), nectarines, blueberries (omit dried cherries if using other fruits).

GINGERBREAD WITH CUSTARD SAUCE
Gingerbread
1/2 cup butter (1 stick)
2 Tbsp. sugar
1 egg
1 cup dark molasses (or can use light molasses if you prefer a less intense flavor)
1 cup boiling water

2-1/4 cup flour
1 tsp. baking soda
½ tsp. salt
1 tsp. ginger
1 tsp. cinnamon

Preheat oven to 325 degrees. Spray a 9" square glass baking pan with cooking spray.

Cream together butter and sugar with electric mixer; add egg. Measure boiling water in a 2-cup glass measure and add the molasses (this will make the molasses come out of the measuring cup more easily). Blend molasses/water mixture into creamed mixture. Sift together dry ingredients, or mix in separate bowl; stir in.

Bake for 45 to 50 minutes or until a toothpick comes out clean. Cut into squares.

Custard Sauce (a bit like vanilla pudding, but more liquid)
2 Tbsp. sugar
2 tsp. cornstarch
1/8 tsp. salt
¾ cup milk (full fat works best, but can use 2%)
1 egg yolk
1 tsp. vanilla

Put the egg yolk into a glass measuring cup and beat lightly with a fork.

Whisk the sugar, cornstarch, and salt together in a small saucepan. Whisk in the milk and cook over low heat until it just boils. Remove from heat. Slowly pour about half the custard mixture into the beaten egg while whisking with a fork to mix well. Then pour the egg/custard mixture back into the rest of the custard in the pan. Cook over low heat until the mixture begins to thicken (don't boil it). It will be quite runny, as it's a sauce. Add the vanilla. Use warm, or refrigerate until ready to use. Can be served warm or cold.

Other toppings for your gingerbread: whipped cream, ice cream (coffee ice cream is surprisingly good, but vanilla and chocolate are tasty too), applesauce.

CHOCOLATE CAKE WITH EASY CHOCOLATE GLAZE
Cake

½ cup butter (1 cube)
¾ cup white sugar
¾ cup brown sugar
2 eggs
1 tsp. vanilla
2 cups cake flour, or 1-3/4 cup regular flour (cake flour gives your cake a more tender crumb)
2/3 cup unsweetened cocoa powder
1-1/2 tsp. baking soda
1 tsp. salt
1-1/2 cups buttermilk

Heat oven to 350 degrees. Grease and flour 13x9x2" pan, or two 8" cake pans.

Cream butter and sugar with electric mixer. Add eggs and vanilla and mix. Sift together dry ingredients or mix in separate bowl; add to mixture alternately, in about 3 installments, with the buttermilk, beating after each addition. Beat the whole thing on high speed 3 minutes. Pour into pan(s).

Bake until wooden pick inserted in center of cake JUST comes out clean, with a few moist crumbs; oblong 33-38 minutes; layers 28-33 minutes. (check carefully!)

Frost with your favorite icing, or for a simple solution (or if you are in a country where unsweetened chocolate and powdered sugar are not available), use the easy glaze below.

Easy Chocolate Glaze
1 best-quality chocolate bar (Lindt, etc.): 70-85% cocoa solids
About ¼ cup half & half or cream
About ¼ cup white sugar, or to taste, depending on how bittersweet your chocolate bar is

Break up the chocolate bar and add it to a saucepan with the half & half and sugar. Cook over low heat, stirring constantly. Add more sugar and/or half & half if it seems necessary. Spoon the glaze over warm cake. Add sliced almonds if desired.

BREAD PUDDING
4 slices bread (higher-quality is the best. Avoid thick, chewy crusts or sourdough. Challah or brioche is extra-special!)
2 Tbsp. butter
1/3 cup packed brown sugar
½ tsp. cinnamon
1/3 cup mini chocolate chips
3 eggs, beaten with a fork
1/3 cup white sugar

1 tsp. vanilla

1/8 tsp. salt

2-1/2 cups milk, scalded (very hot). Whole milk is richest; can use every-thing down to 1%, but don't use skim.

Preheat oven to 350 degrees. Spray a casserole dish (about 1-1/2 quarts; can also use a 9" baking dish, but it'll make a flatter pudding) with cooking spray.

Scald the milk in the microwave (best is with a glass measuring cup; heat the milk for about 2 minutes, until it's not quite boiling).

Toast bread slices lightly. Mix the brown sugar and cinnamon in a small bowl. Spread slices with butter and sprinkle with the brown sugar/cinnamon mixture. Cut each slice in 6 pieces. Arrange pieces sugared side up in your casserole or baking dish, sprinkle with chocolate chips (in layers).

Mix the eggs, white sugar, vanilla, and salt; slowly stir in the hot milk. Pour the mixture over the bread.

Put your casserole dish into a larger pan (I use a roasting pan) on the oven rack. Pour very hot water 1" deep into the larger pan to make a water bath for your casserole dish. This makes your pudding come out moist. Bake until a knife comes out clean, about 65 to 70 minutes. (less time if you bake the pudding in a 9" square pan.) Remove casserole from the hot water. Can be served warm or cold.

Optional toppings: ice cream, whipped cream.

a kiwi glossary

A few notes about Maori pronunciation:
- The accent is normally on the first syllable.
- All vowels are pronounced separately.
- All vowels except u have a short vowel sound.
- "wh" is pronounced "f."
- "ng" is pronounced as in "singer," not as in "anger."

ABs: All Blacks

across the Ditch: in Australia (across the Tasman Sea). Or, if you're in Australia, in New Zealand!

advert: commercial

agro: aggravation

air con: air conditioning

All Blacks: National rugby team. Members are selected for every series from amongst the five NZ Super 15 teams. The All Blacks play similarly selected teams from other nations.

ambo: paramedic

Aotearoa: New Zealand (the other official name, meaning "The Land of the Long White Cloud" in Maori)

arvo, this arvo: afternoon

Aussie, Oz: Australia. (An Australian is also an Aussie. Pronounced "Ozzie.")

bach: holiday home (pronounced like "bachelor")

backs: rugby players who aren't in the scrum and do more running, kicking, and ball-carrying—though all players do all jobs and play both offense and defense. Backs tend to be faster and leaner than forwards.

bangers and mash: sausages and potatoes

barrack for: cheer for

bench: counter (kitchen bench)

berko: berserk

Big Smoke: the big city (usually Auckland)

bikkies: cookies

billy-o, like billy-o: like crazy. "I paddled like billy-o and just barely made it through that rapid."

bin, rubbish bin: trash can

bit of a dag: a comedian, a funny guy

bits and bobs: stuff ("be sure you get all your bits and bobs")

blood bin: players leaving field for injury

Blues: Auckland's Super 15 team

bollocks: rubbish, nonsense

boofhead: fool, jerk

booking: reservation

boots and all: full tilt, no holding back

bot, the bot: flu, a bug

Boxing Day: December 26—a holiday

brekkie: breakfast

brilliant: fantastic

bub: baby, small child

buggered: messed up, exhausted

bull's roar: close. "They never came within a bull's roar of winning."

bunk off: duck out, skip (bunk off school)

bust a gut: do your utmost, make a supreme effort

Cake Tin: Wellington's rugby stadium (not the official name, but it looks exactly like a springform pan)

caravan: travel trailer

cardie: a cardigan sweater

chat up: flirt with

chilly bin: ice chest

chips: French fries. (potato chips are "crisps")

chocolate bits: chocolate chips

chocolate fish: pink or white marshmallow coated with milk chocolate, in the shape of a fish. A common treat/reward for kids (and for adults. You often get a chocolate fish on the saucer when you order a mochaccino—a mocha).

choice: fantastic

chokka: full

chooks: chickens

Chrissy: Christmas

chuck out: throw away

chuffed: pleased

collywobbles: nervous tummy, upset stomach

come a greaser: take a bad fall

costume, cossie: swimsuit (female only)

cot: crib (for a baby)

crook: ill

cuddle: hug (give a cuddle)

cuppa: a cup of tea (the universal remedy)

CV: resumé

cyclone: hurricane (Southern Hemisphere)

dairy: corner shop (not just for milk!)

dead: very; e.g., "dead sexy."

dill: fool

do your block: lose your temper

dob in: turn in; report to authorities. Frowned upon.

doco: documentary

doddle: easy. "That'll be a doddle."

dodgy: suspect, low-quality

dogbox: The doghouse—in trouble

dole: unemployment.

dole bludger: somebody who doesn't try to get work and lives off unemployment (which doesn't have a time limit in NZ)

Domain: a good-sized park; often the "official" park of the town.

dressing gown: bathrobe

drongo: fool (Australian, but used sometimes in NZ as well)

drop your gear: take off your clothes

duvet: comforter

earbashing: talking-to, one-sided chat

electric jug: electric teakettle to heat water. Every Kiwi kitchen has one.

En Zed: Pronunciation of NZ. ("Z" is pronounced "Zed.")

ensuite: master bath (a bath in the bedroom).

eye fillet: premium steak (filet mignon)

fair go: a fair chance. Kiwi ideology: everyone deserves a fair go.

fair wound me up: Got me very upset

fantail: small, friendly native bird

farewelled, he'll be farewelled: funeral; he'll have his funeral.

feed, have a feed: meal

first five, first five-eighth: rugby back—does most of the big kicking jobs and is the main director of the backs. Also called the No. 10.

fixtures: playing schedule

fizz, fizzie: soft drink

fizzing: fired up

flaked out: tired

flash: fancy

flat to the boards: at top speed

flat white: most popular NZ coffee. An espresso with milk but no foam.

flattie: roommate

flicks: movies

flying fox: zipline

footpath: sidewalk

footy, football: rugby

forwards: rugby players who make up the scrum and do the most physical battling for position. Tend to be bigger and more heavily muscled than backs.

fossick about: hunt around for something

front up: face the music, show your mettle

garden: yard

get on the piss: get drunk

get stuck in: commit to something

give way: yield

giving him stick, give him some stick about it: teasing, needling

glowworms: larvae of a fly found only in NZ. They shine a light to attract insects. Found in caves or other dark, moist places.

go crook, be crook: go wrong, be ill

go on the turps: get drunk

gobsmacked: astounded

good hiding: beating ("They gave us a good hiding in Dunedin.")

grotty: grungy, badly done up

ground floor: what we call the first floor. The "first floor" is one floor up.

gumboots, gummies: knee-high rubber boots. It rains a lot in New Zealand.

gutted: thoroughly upset

Haast's Eagle: (extinct). Huge native NZ eagle. Ate moa.

haere mai: Maori greeting

haka: ceremonial Maori challenge—done before every All Blacks game

hang on a tick: wait a minute

hard man: the tough guy, the enforcer

hard yakka: hard work (from Australian)

harden up: toughen up. Standard NZ (male) response to (male) complaints: "Harden the f*** up!"

have a bit on: I have placed a bet on [whatever]. Sports gambling and prostitution are both legal in New Zealand.

have a go: try

Have a nosy for…: look around for

head: principal (headmaster)

head down: or head down, bum up. Put your head down. Work hard.

heaps: lots. "Give it heaps."

hei toki: pendant (Maori)

holiday: vacation

honesty box: a small stand put up just off the road with bags of fruit and vegetables and a cash box. Very common in New Zealand.

hooker: rugby position (forward)

hooning around: driving fast, wannabe tough-guy behavior (typically young men)

hoovering: vacuuming (after the brand of vacuum cleaner)

ice block: popsicle

I'll see you right: I'll help you out

in form: performing well (athletically)

it's not on: It's not all right

iwi: tribe (Maori)

jabs: immunizations, shots

jandals: flip-flops. (This word is only used in New Zealand. Jandals and gumboots are the iconic Kiwi footwear.)

jersey: a rugby shirt, or a pullover sweater

joker: a guy. "A good Kiwi joker": a regular guy; a good guy.

journo: journalist

jumper: a heavy pullover sweater

ka pai: going smoothly (Maori).

kapa haka: school singing group (Maori songs/performances. Any student can join, not just Maori.)

karanga: Maori song of welcome (done by a woman)

keeping his/your head down: working hard

kia ora: welcome (Maori, but used commonly)

kilojoules: like calories—measure of food energy

kindy: kindergarten (this is 3- and 4-year-olds)

kit, get your kit off: clothes, take off your clothes

Kiwi: New Zealander OR the bird. If the person, it's capitalized. Not the fruit.

kiwifruit: the fruit. (Never called simply a "kiwi.")

knackered: exhausted

knockout rounds: playoff rounds (quarterfinals, semifinals, final)

koru: ubiquitous spiral Maori symbol of new beginnings, hope

kumara: Maori sweet potato.

ladder: standings (rugby)

littlies: young kids

lock: rugby position (forward)

lollies: candy

lolly: candy or money

lounge: living room

mad as a meat axe: crazy

maintenance: child support

major: "a major." A big deal, a big event

mana: prestige, earned respect, spiritual power

Maori: native people of NZ—though even they arrived relatively recently from elsewhere in Polynesia

marae: Maori meeting house

Marmite: Savory Kiwi yeast-based spread for toast. An acquired taste. (Kiwis swear it tastes different from Vegemite, the Aussie version.)

mate: friend. And yes, fathers call their sons "mate."

metal road: gravel road

Milo: cocoa substitute; hot drink mix

mind: take care of, babysit

moa: (extinct) Any of several species of huge flightless NZ birds. All eaten by the Maori before Europeans arrived.

moko: Maori tattoo

mokopuna: grandchildren

motorway: freeway

mozzie: mosquito; OR a Maori Australian (Maori + Aussie = Mozzie)

muesli: like granola, but unbaked

munted: broken

naff: stupid, unsuitable. "Did you get any naff Chrissy pressies this year?"

nappy: diaper

narked, narky: annoyed

netball: Down-Under version of basketball for women. Played like basketball, but the hoop is a bit narrower, the players wear skirts, and they don't dribble and can't contact each other. It can look fairly tame to an American eye. There are professional netball teams, and it's televised and taken quite seriously.

new caps: new All Blacks—those named to the side for the first time

New World: One of the two major NZ supermarket chains

nibbles: snacks

nick, in good nick: doing well

niggle, niggly: small injury, ache or soreness

no worries: no problem. The Kiwi mantra.

No. 8: rugby position. A forward

not very flash: not feeling well

Nurofen: brand of ibuprofen

nutted out: worked out

OE: Overseas Experience—young people taking a year or two overseas, before or after University.

offload: pass (rugby)

oldies: older people. (or for the elderly, "wrinklies!")

on the front foot: Having the advantage. Vs. on the back foot—
at a disadvantage. From rugby.

Op Shop: charity shop, secondhand shop

out on the razzle: out drinking too much, getting crazy

paddock: field (often used for rugby—"out on the paddock")

Pakeha: European-ancestry people (as opposed to Polynesians)

Panadol: over-the-counter painkiller

partner: romantic partner, married or not

patu: Maori club

paua, paua shell: NZ abalone

pavlova (pav): Classic Kiwi Christmas (summer) dessert.
Meringue, fresh fruit (often kiwifruit and strawberries) and
whipped cream.

pavement: sidewalk (generally on wider city streets)

pear-shaped, going pear-shaped: messed up, when it all goes
to Hell

penny dropped: light dawned (figured it out)

people mover: minivan

perve: stare sexually

phone's engaged: phone's busy

piece of piss: easy

pike out: give up, wimp out

piss awful: very bad

piss up: drinking (noun) a piss-up

pissed: drunk

pissed as a fart: very drunk. And yes, this is an actual expression.

play up: act up

playing out of his skin: playing very well

plunger: French Press coffeemaker

PMT: PMS

pohutukawa: native tree; called the "New Zealand Christmas Tree"
for its beautiful red blossoms at Christmastime (high summer)

poi: balls of flax on strings that are swung around the head, often to the accompaniment of singing and/or dancing by women. They make rhythmic patterns in the air, and it's very beautiful.

Pom, Pommie: English person

pop: pop over, pop back, pop into the oven, pop out, pop in

possie: position (rugby)

postie: mail carrier

pot plants: potted plants (not what you thought, huh?)

poumanu: greenstone (jade)

prang: accident (with the car)

pressie: present

puckaroo: broken (from Maori)

pudding: dessert

pull your head in: calm down, quit being rowdy

Pumas: Argentina's national rugby team

pushchair: baby stroller

put your hand up: volunteer

put your head down: work hard

rapt: thrilled

rattle your dags: hurry up. From the sound that dried excrement on a sheep's backside makes, when the sheep is running!

red card: penalty for highly dangerous play. The player is sent off for the rest of the game, and the team plays with 14 men.

rellies: relatives

riding the pine: sitting on the bench (as a substitute in a match)

rimu: a New Zealand tree. The wood used to be used for building and flooring, but like all native NZ trees, it was over-logged. Older houses, though, often have rimu floors, and they're beautiful.

Rippa: junior rugby

root: have sex (you DON'T root for a team!)

ropeable: very angry

ropey: off, damaged ("a bit ropey")

rort: ripoff

rough as guts: uncouth

rubbish bin: garbage can

rugby boots: rugby shoes with spikes (sprigs)

Rugby Championship: Contest played each year in the Southern Hemisphere by the national teams of NZ, Australia, South Africa, and Argentina

Rugby World Cup, RWC: World championship, played every four years amongst the top 20 teams in the world

rugged up: dressed warmly

ruru: native owl

Safa: South Africa. Abbreviation only used in NZ.

sammie: sandwich

scoff, scoffing: eating, like "snarfing"

second-five, second five-eighth: rugby back (No. 9). With the first-five, directs the game. Also feeds the scrum and generally collects the ball from the ball carrier at the breakdown and distributes it.

selectors: team of 3 (the head coach is one) who choose players for the All Blacks squad, for every series

serviette: napkin

shag: have sex with. A little rude, but not too bad.

shattered: exhausted

sheds: locker room (rugby)

she'll be right: See "no worries." Everything will work out. The other Kiwi mantra.

shift house: move (house)

shonky: shady (person). "a bit shonky"

shout, your shout, my shout, shout somebody a coffee: buy a round, treat somebody

sickie, throw a sickie: call in sick

sin bin: players sitting out 10-minute penalty in rugby (or, in the case of a red card, the rest of the game)

sink the boot in: kick you when you're down

skint: broke (poor)

skipper: (team) captain. Also called "the Skip."

slag off: speak disparagingly of; disrespect

smack: spank. Smacking kids is illegal in NZ.

smoko: coffee break

snog: kiss; make out with

sorted: taken care of

spa, spa pool: hot tub

sparrow fart: the crack of dawn

speedo: Not the swimsuit! Speedometer. (the swimsuit is called a budgie smuggler—a budgie is a parakeet, LOL.)

spew: vomit

spit the dummy: have a tantrum. (A dummy is a pacifier)

sportsman: athlete

sporty: liking sports

spot on: absolutely correct. "That's spot on. You're spot on."

Springboks, Boks: South African national rugby team

squiz: look. "I was just having a squiz round." "Giz a squiz": Give me a look at that.

stickybeak: nosy person, busybody

stonkered: drunk—a bit stonkered—or exhausted

stoush: bar fight, fight

straight away: right away

strength of it: the truth, the facts. "What's the strength of that?" = "What's the true story on that?"

stroppy: prickly, taking offense easily

stuffed up: messed up

Super 15: Top rugby competition: five teams each from NZ, Australia, South Africa. The New Zealand Super 15 teams are, from north to south: Blues (Auckland), Chiefs (Waikato/

Hamilton), Hurricanes (Wellington), Crusaders (Canterbury/Christchurch), Highlanders (Otago/Dunedin).

supporter: fan (Do NOT say "root for." "To root" is to have (rude) sex!)

suss out: figure out

sweet: dessert

sweet as: great. (also: choice as, angry as, lame as…Meaning "very" whatever. "Mum was angry as that we ate up all the pudding before tea with Nana.")

takahe: ground-dwelling native bird. Like a giant parrot.

takeaway: takeout (food)

tall poppy: arrogant person who puts himself forward or sets himself above others. It is every Kiwi's duty to cut down tall poppies, a job they undertake enthusiastically.

Tangata Whenua: Maori (people of the land)

tapu: sacred (Maori)

Te Papa: the National Museum, in Wellington

tea: dinner (casual meal at home)

tea towel: dishtowel

test match: international rugby match (e.g., an All Blacks game)

throw a wobbly: have a tantrum

tick off: cross off (tick off a list)

ticker: heart. "The boys showed a lot of ticker out there today."

togs: swimsuit (male or female)

torch: flashlight

touch wood: knock on wood (for luck)

track: trail

trainers: athletic shoes

tramping: hiking

transtasman: Australia/New Zealand (the Bledisloe Cup is a transtasman rivalry)

trolley: shopping cart

tucker: food

tui: Native bird

turn to custard: go south, deteriorate

turps, go on the turps: get drunk

Uni: University—or school uniform

up the duff: pregnant. A bit vulgar (like "knocked up")

ute: pickup or SUV

vet: check out

waiata: Maori song

wairua: spirit, soul (Maori). Very important concept.

waka: canoe (Maori)

Wallabies: Australian national rugby team

Warrant of Fitness: certificate of a car's fitness to drive

wedding tackle: the family jewels; a man's genitals

Weet-Bix: ubiquitous breakfast cereal

whaddarya?: I am dubious about your masculinity (meaning "Whaddarya…pussy?")

whakapapa: genealogy (Maori). A critical concept.

whanau: family (Maori). Big whanau: extended family. Small whanau: nuclear family.

wheelie bin: rubbish bin (garbage can) with wheels.

whinge: whine. Contemptuous! Kiwis dislike whingeing. Harden up!

White Ribbon: campaign against domestic violence

wind up: upset (perhaps purposefully). "Their comments were bound to wind him up."

wing: rugby position (back)

Yank: American. Not pejorative.

yellow card: A penalty for dangerous play that sends a player off for 10 minutes to the sin bin. The team plays with 14 men during that time—or even 13, if two are sinbinned.

yonks: ages. "It's been going on for yonks."

Find out what's new at the **ROSALIND JAMES WEBSITE.**
http://www.rosalindjames.com/

"Like" my <u>Facebook</u> page at facebook.com/rosalindjamesbooks
or follow me on <u>Twitter</u> at twitter.com/RosalindJames5
to learn about giveaways, events, and more.
Want to tell me what you liked, or what I got wrong? I'd love
to hear! You can email me at **Rosalind@rosalindjames.com**

by rosalind james

Cover design by Robin Ludwig Design Inc.,
http://www.gobookcoverdesign.com/

Read on for an excerpt from
Just for Fun
(Escape to New Zealand, Book Four)

just for fun—chapter one

♡

Nic Wilkinson wasn't looking to change his life. He just wanted to go home. Instead, he quit watching where he was going, stepped in a puddle, and swore. It had rained the night before, and this part of the field was still muddy. The hundred or so boys gathered for the last day of Rob Euliss's rugby camp weren't helping a bit. They'd churned up the grass good and proper this week, Nic saw with disgust as he felt the water squelch inside his shoe. This wasn't his idea of a fun way to spend a Sunday morning during a rare bye week. The kids were OK. He wasn't always too keen on the parents, though.

But Rob was a neighbor, and a mate. Anyway, when a legendary former All Black asked a favor, you didn't say no. So here he was, trying to avoid the rest of the muck around the edge of the huge field that made up the North Harbour Rugby Club, and preparing to do his duty.

Nic squinted around the clusters of boys, playing their final matches of the Easter-week camp under the watchful eyes of volunteer coaches and a sprinkling of dads who'd been pressed into service. He finally spotted the still-imposing figure of Rob, issuing impatient instructions to a hapless dad, and made his way toward the pair.

"Get them to stay onside," Rob was barking at the harassed-looking volunteer, intimidating the poor bloke with his trademark volcanic frown. "They know better."

Nic waited until the chastened dad took himself off, then offered, "Morning, Rob."

"Nico. You took your time," Rob grumbled. "I said ten."

"Sorry. Claudia wasn't rapt about my plan for the day. Where do you want me?" Nic could see a few of his Blues and All Black teammates, each surrounded by a little knot of starstruck boys, their parents hovering close. "I'll help out here, if you like."

"Don't want to meet the mums, eh. Don't blame you. Stay with me a minute, then. I'll find a spot to pop you into."

They fell silent, watching the boys in front of them play. "Second year?" Nic asked, watching as a pass fell uncaught at a small pair of feet.

"Yeh. Six," Rob answered briefly.

"That one's good," Nic remarked as a boy from the opposing team picked up the ball, made two defenders miss with his abrupt changes of direction, then passed the ball accurately behind him to a teammate who ran in for the score.

"Yeh. Got a boot on him, too. Can't use that in Rippa, of course. But he'll be making his mark in a few years," Rob said. "Hell of a kick."

"Some talent there," Nic agreed as the boy darted in, on defense now, and ripped an opposing player's flag from his belt. "Fast-twitch fibers, I reckon. Reminds me of someone. Somebody's kid?"

Rob looked at him oddly. "You. Who he reminds you of, I mean. Good pair of hands, reflexes. And a boot as well. They usually aren't much chop at this age, but he's different. Been watching you, I'd say. Got your moves. Even has a bit of a look of you. They're about done here. Stay here and you can see for yourself, when you do your meet and greet."

It was on them soon enough. The boys crowded around, offering up mud- and grass-stained backs for autographs. Nic signed jerseys with the Sharpie Rob wordlessly handed him, offered a bit of chat to the kids. The boy with the skills, he saw, hung back a bit, waiting for the crowd to thin, his eyes on Nic. A good-looking kid, straight dark blond hair getting a bit long over the forehead and at the back.

The boy came forward at last, turned his back. "Can you sign huge?" he asked. "I want yours to be the biggest."

"Can't turn that down, can I," Nic answered good-humoredly. "There. Straight across. Nobody'll miss that."

"Thanks," the boy said. He stood aside as Nic signed the jersey of a boy with a comical, mobile face and a mop of wild red curls.

"I saw you hurt your leg last week," the blond boy offered as Nic finished. "Has it got any better? Will you be able to play in South Africa?"

"Not too bad," Nic assured him. "Bit of a crocked thigh, that's all. Be right as rain by Saturday." Which wasn't strictly true, but it was the kind of niggle you expected, midway through the season.

"Would you run, though, normally?" the boy asked hesitatingly. "When you have a bye like this, I mean? If you weren't injured? On your days off?"

"Yeh, I would," Nic answered.

"See, Graham. Told you," the blond boy said triumphantly to his redheaded friend. "Graham said you just rested. But I said you have to keep training, if you really want to be good."

"You're right," Nic said. "Plenty of blokes with talent. You have to have more than that, if you want to make it to Super level. Takes a fair bit of discipline. Do you do some training yourself, then? You're pretty good."

The boy flushed with embarrassed pride. "Yeh. I run before school, lots of days. With my mum. She likes to go too," he hurried on to explain. "Not because she has to take me."

"Good on ya," Nic said. "You've got a pretty fair boot, too, Dan tells me. What's your name?"

"Zack. Zack Martens," the boy said.

"Good to meet you." Nic shook the offered hand. Manners, he saw. "And who's this?"

"Graham MacNeil," the redhead said, offering his own hand and turning a violent shade that clashed with his hair.

"Well, Graham, your mate's right. Do all the running you can. You boys better get off and get some more signatures on those jerseys, though. Ben over there looks like he's about to pack it in."

"C'mon, Zack," Graham urged.

"Thank you for signing," Zack said politely. Dark brown eyes fringed with long, thick lashes looked shyly up at Nic's own before the boy turned to run off with his friend.

"Nice kid, that Zack," Nic told Rob a bit later from the middle of another group of kids.

"Got a nice mum, too," Rob said, nodding toward a group of parents on the sideline. "Quite pretty. Think she's single, too. Most of them don't show up without a dad, the last day."

"You old goat," Nic chided him. "Lucky I don't tell Rebecca."

"Still got a pair of eyes, haven't I," Rob countered. "That one there, see? Kind of blonde. The small one. Tell me I'm wrong."

Nic looked where Rob was gesturing. Suddenly his sodden feet seemed to be sending a chill straight through his entire body. He saw Zack again, excitedly showing off his newly collected autographs to the slim, graceful figure bending towards him. The honey-blonde hair was shorter now, but her curls still fell around her face in the way he remembered. She straightened, turned. And stood stock-still at the sight of him.

He wasn't more than twenty meters away, but she moved fast. With a quick word to Zack, she'd melted behind the group of parents and was lost in the taller crowd within moments.

Nic stood, poleaxed. He recovered his wits as another group of boys crowded around him, signed jerseys and rugby balls mechanically, offered encouraging words. But kept an eye out for that slight figure. He didn't see her again, though. And to his frustration, by the time he could look for her properly amidst the thinning crowd, she was gone.

♡

Rob was issuing more instructions to the volunteers who were helping to round up equipment. He turned, though, at a hand on his elbow. "Still here, mate?" he asked in surprise. "Thought you'd left with the rest of them."

"Need to ask you a question," Nic said. "I need to know something about that kid. Zack."

"Rightyo, then." Rob was surprised, but agreeable. "Hang on a tick whilst I finish up here. Or better yet, give us a hand."

"Now," he said fifteen minutes later, packing file folders into a carrier bag inside the Rugby Club's office. "What did you need? Are the Blues scouting them that young now?"

"Zack Martens." Nic brushed the joke aside. "You said he was six. When's his birthday?"

"Why? You planning on sending him a present? Too late, I reckon. He's one of the young ones. Just turned six, I think. That's what surprised me about the skills. They usually can't even offload worth a damn that young, let alone kick like that."

"His birthday," Nic insisted. "When is it?"

Rob sighed. "Hang on, then." He pulled a ring binder from the bag he'd been loading, found the sheet. "February 15th. Barely made it under the cutoff. Happy now?"

Nic felt his mouth go dry as he subtracted in his head. Saw those dark eyes again, raised to his own. The way they turned down at the outer corners to give him a sleepy look, fringed by lashes his mum had always said were wasted on a boy.

"I need his mum's address," he told Rob.

"Mate. You know I can't give you that." Rob was puzzled now, and a bit alarmed as well. "What's this all about? Better not be something about you I don't know."

"Don't be bloody stupid," Nic said impatiently. "I need his mum's address. Emma's address. Because that's my son."

Printed in Great Britain
by Amazon

49339841R00213